C000076144

SHE CASTS A LONG SHADOW

Also by Madalyn Morgan

Foxden Acres
Applause
China Blue
The 9:45 To Bletchley
Foxden Hotel
Chasing Ghosts
There Is No Going Home

Madalyn Morgan

SHE CASTS A LONG SHADOW

Madalyn Morgan

She Casts A Long Shadow © 2020 by Madalyn Morgan
Published Worldwide 2020 © Madalyn Morgan

All rights reserved in all media. No part of this book may be
reproduced or transmitted in any form by any means, electronic
or mechanical (including but not limited to: the Internet,
photocopying, recording or by any information storage and
retrieval system), without prior permission in writing from the
author.

The moral right of Madalyn Morgan as the author of the work
has been asserted by her in accordance with the Copyright,
Designs and Patents Act 1988.

All characters in this publication are fictitious and any
resemblance to real persons, living or dead, is purely
coincidental.

ISBN: 9798664325997

British Library Cataloguing in Publication Data.
A catalogue record for this book is available from the British
Library.

Acknowledgments

Formatted by Rebecca Emin
www.gingersnapbooks.co.uk

Book Jacket Designed by Cathy Helms
www.avalongraphics.org

I would like to thank editor Nancy Callegari and proofreader Maureen Vincent-Northam.

Thanks also to Nick Miller who was the highest bidder for a copy of There Is No Going Home in the 2019 auction for Children In Read. As promised I have named a character after him. Thank you, Children In Need and The Authors' and Illustrators' for giving me the opportunity to contribute to such a worthy cause. She Casts A Long Shadow will be auctioned for Children in Need this year.

Thanks to Liz Hurst for donating a raffle prize to proofread the first 10,000 words of a manuscript, which I won at Swanwick Writer's Summer School in 2019.

Thank you to my cousin Margaret White for the loan of the original 1950s passports.

Thank you Alan Richardson who also bid for There Is No Going Home and who also has a character named after him. And thank you to all my wonderful readers. Without them there would be no reason for me to write.

She Casts a Long Shadow is dedicated to my mother and father

Ena and Jack Smith

CHAPTER ONE

'Do you still love Henry, Ena?'

'What?'

'Do you still love your husband?' Ena's sister, Bess, asked.

Ena blinked back her tears. 'Of course, I do.'

'Then what's the matter? I can see you're not happy.'

Before Ena could reply, the door swung open and Henry appeared. He reached for the light switch, flicked it up and the lights went out. Behind him the stout figure of Foxden Hotel's chef - his moonlike face eerily lit by a dozen flickering candles on a birthday cake - sashayed into the room to a round of applause.

Ena, grateful that the chef's arrival had given her time to control her emotions, nudged Bess. 'If he doesn't put that cake down soon the candles will burn out and the icing will be covered in wax.'

Bess laughed. 'It will. Chef can be an awkward old so-and-so and his ego expands with his girth, but so does his popularity. He's worth his weight in candles.'

Ena wrinkled her nose at the thought. 'That would be a lot of candles,' she said, forcing herself to laugh with her sister.

The chef eventually arrived at the table of the middle-aged woman celebrating her birthday. He put down the cake, the woman blew out the few candles that were still alight and everyone sang 'Happy Birthday.' When the chef turned to leave, Henry switched the lights back on.

Having played the part of lighting assistant, Ena expected her husband to return to his seat next to her. She looked across the room. He was standing in the corridor with his back to the door, but she could tell by the way he lifted and dropped his shoulders that he was talking to someone. She waited for the person to come into view. They didn't. Henry turned and looked at her. She smiled and beckoned him, but he looked away.

Ena drank what was left of her wine and banged the glass down with a thump. 'We've grown apart,' she said, bitterness overtaking the sadness she felt. She looked back at Henry. He had gone.

'Do you want to talk about it?'

'I do, but it…'

'It's his job?'

'And mine. Damn it! I do want to talk about it. I need to talk about it. If I don't, I'll go mad.'

Bess poured them each another glass of wine and Ena looked around the room. The people on the table to her left were being helped into their coats by hotel staff. Those on her right, already wearing their outdoor clothes, were shaking hands and kissing each other goodbye. When both tables had been vacated, Ena brought her focus back to Bess. 'Habit,' she said.

'Do you remember when I came up to see my old boss, Herbert Silcott, in the autumn?' Bess nodded. 'I was investigating Frieda Voight. You knew her as Freda King. She worked with me at Silcott's Engineering in the war.'

'Yes, I remember Freda. Why were you investigating her?'

'I saw her in London in the summer. There would have been nothing remarkable in that, except she was supposed to be dead. I told Henry I'd seen her and he said I was mistaken. He said it couldn't have been Frieda because we had been to her funeral ten years earlier.'

'Reason enough for him to think you were mistaken.'

'How could I mistake seeing Frieda Voight? Not only had we worked together for four years, but I…'

'You…?'

'Discovered she was a spy.'

'What?'

'It's a long story that I can't talk about.' Ena wanted to tell Bess everything, but the work she did in the war for Bletchley Park, a cypher and codebreaking facility, was top secret. Exposing Frieda and her brother Walter as spies, was also top secret - as were the cold cases she currently investigated for the Home Office. She took a breath and began to explain how she knew it was Frieda Voight she had seen.

'Frieda was ten years older and she had bleached her hair blonde, but I'd have known her anywhere. Henry was adamant it wasn't her and asked me…, no, he told me to forget about her.'

'But you didn't.'

'How could I? I saw someone who I knew to be dangerous, who I'd exposed as a spy and who was supposed to be dead. And, even though every document that would have proved her existence in the war had been removed from Silcott's by MI5 - and they refused to let me see them - I opened a cold case file on her.'

'And that's when you and Henry started to grow apart?'

'Yes, I think it was. I went up to…' Ena stopped speaking. The fact she had been to Bletchley Park was irrelevant. It was what had happened afterwards that was important.

'Ena?'

'Sorry. I went to see the director of a facility that Silcott's had done work for in the war. Although he was retired, he remembered Frieda and me. He told me

3

I needed to speak to an old friend of his, McKenzie Robinson, the Director of MI5 - and Henry's boss. He said he would write to him and ask him to help me. At the time Director Robinson was in hospital recovering from a mild stroke. I made an appointment to see him the following week, but he died unexpectedly on the day I was due to see him. I found out later that he had been murdered.

'When my colleague, Sid Parfitt, who worked with me on the Voight case was close to discovering who Frieda was working for, he was also murdered and his body thrown over Waterloo Bridge. Then Henry again asked me to stop the investigation.'

'And did you?'

'No! It was obvious to me that whoever had killed Sid, had also killed Director Robinson. I stepped up the investigation.'

'And was Henry alright with that?'

'No, but there was nothing he could do about it. He had no authority to stop me, so he had me followed. He set up round-the-clock surveillance and bugged the flat. For my safety, he said.'

'What happened to Frieda?'

'Frieda turned up at our flat just before Christmas. She was angry and very depressed. She told me she had been sent to kill me, but said she was no longer going to be anyone's puppet. All she wanted was to be with her brother, Walter, who *was* buried on the day of her fictitious funeral. She said she and Walter had been lovers.'

Bess took a sharp breath. 'Lovers?'

'Yes. They weren't actually related. When they were teenagers they found out that they had both been adopted.' Tears blurred Ena's vision. She wiped them away with the back of her hand and whispered, 'Frieda committed suicide that night.'

'Oh, Ena.' Bess laid her hand on top of Ena's. 'I am sorry.'

'I believe that was her last act of kindness, if you can call it that.' Ena brought to mind everything Frieda had told her on the night she had sat with her in the rain on the wet leads of the bell tower of St. Leonard's Church in Brixton and shook her head. 'She had planned to kill Henry before killing herself.'

'Why kill Henry?'

'Henry was Frieda's handler at MI5. He recruited her after the war to spy for British intelligence. Frieda told me that Henry had promised to get Walter out of prison and back to Berlin, if she worked for the Russians, as a double agent.'

'And did he?'

'No. Walter died in prison. Frieda hated Henry for making her work for the Russians, and she blamed him for Walter's death. That night, on the roof of the church, Frieda told me there was a mole at MI5. She was about to tell me who it was when Henry arrived. When she saw him, Frieda pulled a gun and threatened to shoot him. Henry stood in front of me with his arms outstretched to shield me and I took his gun from the pocket of his overcoat. I told her if she shot Henry, I would shoot her. She said she didn't want me to shoot her, that she didn't want me to have her death on my conscience and put her gun down. I laid Henry's gun next to it and she smiled at me. For the briefest moment she was the old Freda who I had worked with in the war. I smiled back at her and she leaned sideways. A second later she threw herself off the roof.'

'Now you'll never know if she killed your colleague, Sid.'

'Frieda told me she hadn't killed Sid.'

'And you believed her?'

'Yes.' Ena picked up her glass and sipped her wine thoughtfully. 'I had reason to stay in Brighton with McKenzie Robinson's personal assistant of thirty-plus years. When I returned to London, I found newspaper cuttings of Sid's when he was a reporter for The Times. He was in Berlin in nineteen thirty-six covering Hitler's Olympics. One of the photographs was a Hitler Youth rally and on it was Robinson's PA who I had stayed with in Brighton. She was twenty years younger, but there was no mistaking her. I believe she's the mole at MI5 and I shall be gathering evidence to prove it as soon as I go back to work in the New Year.'

'Have you told Henry?'

'No. I told him there was a mole at MI5 and I told him I knew who it was. I expect he's joined the dots by now. Henry likes to play a sweet old-fashioned guy, but he's as sharp as a blade. He learned from the master, McKenzie Robinson.'

'Who *was* murdered by Frieda,' Bess said.

'No. I don't think Frieda murdered him, either. I don't think Frieda killed McKenzie Robinson, nor do I think she killed Sid Parfitt.'

'Then who did?'

'I don't know. I confronted Frieda about both murders and she swore to me that she had nothing to do with either of them. I can't remember her exact words, but she said something like, look closer to home.'

'You don't think Henry had anything to do with the murders, do you?'

'Of course not.' The words her boss at the Home Office had said to her before Christmas came into her mind, '*The things we have to do to keep our country safe, Ena. Not always morally right, but always necessary.*'

CHAPTER TWO

'Have you seen Henry?' Ena asked Frank, her brother-in-law.

'I saw him just before he left.'

'Left?'

'Yes.' Frank looked from Bess to Ena. 'I thought you knew.'

'No, I didn't.' Ena leapt out of her chair and grabbed her handbag from under the table. 'How long ago did he leave?'

'I'm not sure, five or ten minutes ago, perhaps a little longer. He came into reception from the direction of the dining room, so I assumed he'd been in here and told you he was leaving.'

'He didn't tell me he was leaving because he didn't come in here. The last I saw of him he was talking to someone in the corridor.'

'Probably the men he left with.'

'Men? What men?'

'Colleagues. He said they needed his help with something back in London.'

Spooks from Leconfield House, Ena thought. Don't they ever have a bloody day off? 'Henry's colleagues coming all the way from London on Boxing Night can only mean something important has happened.'

'I assumed they were his colleagues. They were big blokes.'

'Could they have been military men?' Ena asked.

'It's possible. As I said, because he came from that direction, I thought he'd been in there with you and you'd know who they were.' Frank dropped onto the chair next to Bess. 'I'm sorry, Ena.'

'Don't be. Henry wouldn't have told you who they were, anyway.' Ena lifted her bag onto her shoulder and looked at her wristwatch. 'Five minutes ago, you said?'

'Ten, or longer,' Frank said, as Ena made for the door. 'They'll be long gone now, love.'

'Ena, wait for me!' Bess jumped up and followed Ena out of the restaurant.

'If Chef hadn't spent so long pontificating before bringing that damned birthday cake in, Henry would have been with us when his so-called colleagues turned up.' Ena turned to cross the marble hall and was met by the receptionist. She kept walking.

'Henry asked me to tell you he's been called back to London.'

'I know.'

The receptionist, trying to keep up with Ena as she strode towards the entrance foyer of the hotel, looked at Bess and pulled a 'don't shoot the messenger' face.

'Did he say why, or tell you who the men were?' Ena asked, without slowing her pace.

'He didn't say why, only that the men were from a branch of the company he worked for.'

'A branch?' Ena's stomach lurched, but she didn't stop. What was so important that Special Branch needed to send two men up to Foxden during the Christmas holiday to take Henry back to London? What the hell did they want with him? Ena pulled open the main door of the hotel and stepped out into the freezing night. From the top of the circular steps, she looked down the drive. Not a car in sight. Only the indents from their tyres were visible. Ena looked up at the sky. It was snowing heavily. Soon the drive would be blanketed in snow and there would be no trace of cars having come to Foxden Hotel, or gone from it.

Bess put her arm around Ena's shoulder. 'Come on, let's go inside. There's nothing you can do tonight,

Ena.'

'No, you're right,' Ena said, defeated. 'By the time I had packed and got the car...' She turned to the receptionist. 'I presume Henry wasn't driving.'

The receptionist shook her head. 'I don't think so, but I can't be sure.'

'The car keys are in our room. Did you see him go upstairs after the men from London arrived?'

'No. He didn't even...'

'Didn't even, what?'

'Have time to get his overcoat from the office.'

'Something is wrong. Something is very wrong.'

After a restless night and an early breakfast of tea and toast with Bess and Frank, Ena left the hotel.

Bess, her arm linked in Ena's, and Frank carrying Ena's suitcase and Henry's holdall, went outside with her to wave her off.

'Give me the keys, Ena,' Frank said, 'I'll bring the car round.'

'Take your time driving back to London,' Bess said, her arms wrapped around Ena.

'I will.'

Frank pulled up in Ena's Sunbeam, left the engine ticking over and jumped out. While he put the luggage in the boot, Ena settled herself into the driver's seat.

'Drive carefully, darling, and let us know what's happening with Henry as soon as you can,' Bess shouted as Ena drove off.

The roads were treacherous. The Boxing Day sun had started to melt the snow, but as night fell so had the temperature making long stretches of the road as slippery as an ice rink. Cars were bumper to bumper going through some of the small towns from the sheer weight of traffic. It seemed everyone who had been north for Christmas was now going south at the same time. To make matters worse, an accident on the Edgware Road in Kilburn brought the traffic to a standstill, adding half an hour to Ena's journey.

Exhausted from having hardly slept, Ena arrived home at midday. She hauled her suitcase and Henry's holdall from the boot of the car, locked it, and lugged them up the steps to the flat.

She unlocked the door and nudged it open with her knee. 'Henry?' There was no reply. She dragged the cases into the bedroom, unlocked her suitcase and flung it open. Leaving it on the floor, she returned to the hall and took off her coat. After hanging it up she looked in the sitting room. There was no sign of Henry.

In the kitchen, she touched the kettle. It was cold, but then it would be. Henry would have left for work hours ago. She turned on the cold tap, added enough water to make a pot of tea and switched the kettle on. There was half a bottle of milk in the refrigerator. Ena took it out and sniffed. It had been in there four days but it smelt fine.

While the kettle boiled Ena spooned tea into the teapot and rummaged through the cupboards for something to eat. She had intended to buy food on the way home, but had been distracted and forgot. The cupboard of the kitchen cabinet gave up its meagre fare: a packet of Jacobs Cream Crackers and a jar of fish paste. From the refrigerator, she took a block of butter and a quarter of a pound of cheese. When the kettle had boiled she made the tea, put the cup and the food on a tray and went into the sitting room. The room was cold. Henry had laid a fire before they went up to Foxden for Christmas. He obviously hadn't felt the need to light it when he got home, if indeed he had been home. She took a box of Swan Vesta from beside the wood basket, struck a match, and held it against the tapered ends of the plaited newspaper under the kindling. It caught straight away. After adding a couple of small logs, she sat in the chair at the side of the fire and ate her lunch.

Feeling more satisfied after a cup of strong tea than she did after the makeshift meal, Ena leaned back in the chair and looked around the room. The door of the small drinks cupboard in the sideboard was open. Henry never closed it properly. She swept up the tray and took it to the kitchen. Annoyed with him for failing to leave her a note, she banged the small cupboard door shut with the side of her foot as she passed.

When she had washed up and put away the dishes, Ena went to the bedroom, unpacked and hung up her and Henry's clothes. She took off the clothes she'd travelled in, dropped them into the laundry basket and went to the bathroom. After she had washed and cleaned her teeth, she put on a clean skirt and jumper and returned to the sitting room. She placed a hefty log on the back of the fire and put the guard in front of it. If nothing else, the flat would be warm when she returned.

She thought about closing the curtains to keep out the draught, but it was still light. Closed curtains in the day told burglars that no one was home. Since the break-in the year before, Ena had been more careful. She looked out of the window and squinted through what looked like sleet. Dark clouds, low in the sky, moved gloomily towards the city. It would probably snow before nightfall. Snow on the streets of London usually turned into slush. Only in the parks, and then only occasionally, did it stay crisp and white like the snow that fell at Foxden.

In the hall, Ena put on her boots and her thick winter coat. She wrapped a scarf around her neck and pulled on her hat. The wind gusted into the hall when she opened the door. She left the flat quickly and, holding onto the handrail, made her way down the icy steps to the car.

Ena drove to Leconfield House, parked, and without stopping to lock the car, ran into the building. 'I'd like to see Henry Green. Would you buzz him and tell him Ena is here?' she said, smiling, in an attempt to mask her panic.

The receptionist consulted a notepad attached to a clipboard with 'Christmas Holidays' written at the top of the page. She ran her finger down a list of names. 'He hasn't returned from Christmas yet, Mrs Green.'

'Would you check again, please?'

The receptionist looked down the list of names again, this time more slowly. 'No, he isn't here. I'm sorry.'

'We travelled back from the country separately. When he comes in, would you ask him to telephone me at the Home Office?'

The receptionist wrote Ena's message on a separate piece of paper and, with the pen poised to write more, looked up at her.

'Ah... It's my first day in a new office. I don't know my extension number, but the switchboard operator will find me.' She thanked the receptionist and left.

Ena yawned. The journey back to London had been long and frustrating and she still didn't know where her husband was. She jumped into the Sunbeam, gunned the engine, and put her foot down hard on the accelerator. She had a dozen questions to ask Henry when she caught up with him. The first was, where the hell did he go last night? More importantly, why hadn't he told her he was leaving? How long would it have delayed him to pop into the restaurant and tell her he had to leave? She cuffed a tear. 'Damn him!' She'd had enough of her husband going AWOL without telling her. Two weeks the last time and when she confronted him on his return, he'd been to Berlin. Frieda had then been the reason for that, but this time he wouldn't be in Berlin.

Ena drove into King Charles Street, parked, and approached her new place of work. Still annoyed with Henry she pulled open the door of the Home Office, marched across the reception area and was met by a woman she had never seen before.

'Good afternoon, Mrs Green. Did you have a nice Christmas?'

'Yes, thank you.' Before she was able to ask where her new office was, the woman gave her a buff envelope. Ena turned it over in her hands. It was sealed but not addressed. She opened it and pulled out a handwritten note. '*Come to the old Mercer Street office as soon as you get this. Artie.*'

Rope, tied to saw-horses on either side of the road, stretched across the top of Mercer Street. A policeman stood in front of it waving the traffic along Long Acre to Leicester Square. Ena took the first right to Slingsby Place and parked the Sunbeam. She showed the policeman her Home Office ID and said she had been ordered to come to No 8 Mercer Street, 'as soon as possible,' she added. She omitted to say who had ordered her - and thankfully, the PC didn't ask, he just untied the rope and let her through.

While she was repeating the story to the constable outside the door of No 8, Artie came out.

He flung his arms around her. 'Thank the Lord you're here, Ena. They won't tell me anything.'

Before Ena could ask Artie who he was talking about, he had taken her by the hand and was dragging her through the indoor courtyard of the building. The door to her old office had been wrenched from its hinges and was propped up against the wall. She stood in the doorway and gazed inside.

'Ena?'

'Inspector Powell? What on earth has happened?'

'I was hoping you could tell me that.'

'Me? I haven't been here since the day the office was boxed up and sent to the Home Office in King Charles Street.'

In the middle of the room, there was a round table and two chairs. One chair was upright, the seat tucked under the table, the other had been knocked over and was lying on its side. Taking care to not get too close to what was obviously a crime scene, with Detective Inspector Powell in attendance, Ena walked around the room. On the table there was a bottle of Teachers

Whisky and two glasses. The whisky was in the centre of the table with a glass on either side. One glass was upright, one, nearest to where the chair had fallen, had been knocked over. Whisky, she assumed, had spilt onto the table, settling in a balloon shape before soaking into the wood of the tabletop. Taking care not to touch anything, Ena stepped closer and crouched down until her eyes were level with the stain. Her heart was thumping. She took a sharp involuntary breath. The caramel coloured balloon-shaped spillage was peppered with white specks that looked like powder. She moved closer still and the faint odour of bitter almonds filled her nostrils. Cyanide.

Ena sensed DI Powell behind her, watching her.

'Do you recognise the bottle of whisky, Ena?'

'*Recognise* it? It's a bottle of Teachers Whisky.'

'Is it the brand of whisky that you and your husband drink at home?'

'Yes.' Ena was about to say, 'You know it is, you've drunk the stuff with us.' Instead, she said, 'And it's a brand thousands of people drink.'

'And the glasses?'

'Whisky tumblers! Mass-produced! Sold in most high street stores.' She looked again at the tumblers. They were exactly the same size and shape as the glasses she and Henry drank from at home.

Ena turned and looked squarely at DI Powell. 'Inspector, I've had a long drive, I'm tired, hungry, and I would like to see my husband. Would you please tell me what's going on?'

'Helen Crowther is dead. Murdered. Her body was found next to the upturned chair.'

'Good God! Do you have a suspect?' As soon as she asked the question the image of Henry leaving Foxden Hotel with two men the night before angered her. She rounded on the DI. 'You can't think Henry had anything to do with Helen Crowther's death?'

The inspector didn't answer.

'If you suspect Henry, why not me, or Dick Bentley?' It was me who discovered Helen Crowther was the mole at MI5. It was me who told Director Bentley at the Home Office. And it was me who was going to investigate her to prove she was a traitor and get her hanged. She could have got wind of it, lured me here to kill me, but instead, I killed her? Or, someone knew I'd found out she was the mole, leaked it, and whoever she worked for killed her. Once a spy's cover is blown, they're as good as dead. So why Henry? He didn't even know Crowther was the mole at Five.'

'I'm afraid the evidence…'

'What evidence? A bottle of whisky and a couple of glasses? Circumstantial at best. Wouldn't hold up in court and you know it. Come on, Inspector! If it was leaked that she was the mole at MI5 she might as well have worn a sign saying 'target' on her back.'

Ena slowly and purposely cast her eyes over the scene. She made a mental note of the position of the chairs and where each item on the top of the table was in reference to the other. This time she committed the smallest of details to memory.

'Who found her?'

'Three lads playing on the waste ground across the road yesterday afternoon. They said the door was open and they came in to get out of the cold.'

'Did they touch anything?'

'They said they didn't. They scarpered pretty quickly from what they said. Seeing a dead body frightened them.'

'It would have,' Ena said, absentmindedly. 'Can I process the scene?'

'No. I'm waiting for the fingerprint boys to get here. Even with the naked eye, you can see prints on the bottle. And there's at least one print on the knocked over glass.'

Ena crouched down again and leaned towards the glass. The DI was right. There was a print. 'The sooner the print boys get their job done the better.'

'Ena, come to the station, and I'll explain everything.'

Ena had forgotten Artie was standing by the door. She went over to him. 'The Sunbeam is in Slingsby Place. Would you drive it over to Bow Street Police Station and park it in a side street?' She gave Artie the car keys.

'Do you want me to wait for you?'

'No. Go back to the Home Office. Dig out every file relating to the Frieda Voight case.'

'Director Bentley hasn't returned Sid's file.'

'Then go and see his secretary, make an appointment for me to see Dick tomorrow, and while you're there ask her if the director has finished with the file. It's a long shot, but it could be in a pile somewhere waiting to be sent over to us.'

'Will do.'

'Leave the Sunbeam's keys with the desk sergeant at Bow Street, tell him where the car's parked, and get a taxi to King Charles Street.' She looked from Artie to Inspector Powell. 'I assume Dick Bentley knows Helen Crowther is dead?' He nodded. 'Good,' Ena said under her breath. 'Right! You'd better go Artie. And get hold of Henry, will you? Have the telephones been installed in the new office yet?'

'Yes.'

'That's something, I suppose. Did you find my diary and telephone book when you unpacked?'

'Both on your desk next to your telephone.'

'Thanks, Artie. By now Special Branch should have realised their mistake and let Henry go. Telephone the flat first. If he isn't at home, try his office at Leconfield House, or ring the branch - the number is in my telephone book under T for thugs! You could ring Dick Bentley. Damn it! Ring Uncle Tom Cobley if you have to, but find my husband, please!'

Artie put his arms around Ena. 'I'll find him. He has to be somewhere.'

Ena stepped back and eased herself from Artie's embrace. She put the back of her hand up to her nose. 'Don't start me off. I'm wavering between tears and screaming. I'd rather scream.'

Artie turned to leave, but Ena called him back. 'Inspector Powell's number is also in my phone book. I shall be with him at Bow Street for the next hour or so. If you find out *anything*, ring the station. Ask to speak to Inspector Powell,' she called after Artie. He lifted his hand, a gesture that meant both yes and goodbye.

Ena turned her attention to the inspector. 'This setup,' she said, nodding in the direction of the table, 'is exactly that - *a set-up!* The stage is set like a badly staged Victorian melodrama with props that have been placed for maximum effect.

'The fact that two Special Branch heavyweights came up to Foxden on Boxing Night and took Henry away, tells me that the branch also suspect my husband of killing Crowther. Am I right?'

DI Powell didn't answer. He beckoned to two men who had been standing in the doorway into the room and told them to check everything for prints.

'Well?'

'We'll talk at the station.'

CHAPTER FOUR

Inspector Powell opened the door of his office for Ena to enter. She had been in the inspector's office many times before. Because Sid was murdered on Waterloo Bridge, the DI was in charge of the case. He was also involved in the investigation into McKenzie Robinson's death and knew that Ena had investigated Frieda Voight. She couldn't prove it, but her gut feeling was that Frieda Voight was involved with Helen Crowther. Two spies from Berlin killed within weeks of each other. There had to be a connection.

'I'm sorry your Christmas holiday was cut short,' the inspector said, as he entered the office. He pulled out the chair from under his desk for Ena, before going around the desk and making himself comfortable in his own chair.

'I had planned to come back today, I just hadn't planned on going to a murder scene at my old office, or to be told my husband was the chief suspect. That was why Special Branch brought Henry back to London last night, wasn't it?'

'Yes.'

'Hence the questions about the whisky bottle and tumblers.'

'You were right when you said the whisky could have been bought from any off licence, and the glasses from any store, but Henry's MI5 ID couldn't have been bought anywhere.'

'What?'

'Henry's ID card was found in Mercer Street.'

'It couldn't have been Henry's ID. He'd have known if it was missing. He'd have said something.'

'I'm sorry, Ena, but it was Henry's ID. I saw it myself.'

Ena got up, went over to the window and looked out. It was snowing. 'When exactly did the two boys find Crowther's body?'

'Yesterday afternoon.'

'Then Henry couldn't have killed her. We were both a hundred miles away having tea with his parents.'

There was a tap on the door. DI Powell called, 'Come,' and WPC Jarvis brought in a tray of tea and biscuits. She smiled at Ena and asked if the DI needed anything else. He said no and she left.

'So,' Ena said again, 'it wasn't Henry.'

'Helen Crowther had been dead for at least four days. The pathologist thinks she was killed late afternoon, or early evening, on December the twenty-third'.

'Then it definitely wasn't Henry who killed her.' Ena exhaled with relief. 'Henry was at home in Stockwell at six o'clock. I telephoned him just after six and asked him to bring something I had forgotten to pack. I phoned again around eight-thirty, to remind him the Christmas presents were in the spare room, and not to forget to bring them. The bag was too heavy for me to take on the train.'

'So, *you* went up to the Midlands by train?'

'Yes, I can show you my train ticket.'

'That won't be necessary. And you went up on...?'

'The twenty-third. I broke up for Christmas before Henry, so I went to Foxden early. Henry had to work and came up on Christmas Eve.' If it had been anyone other than DI Powell asking questions she had already answered, Ena would have lost her temper and walked out. However, the inspector had been a good friend to her in the past, he had been her confidant and she had trusted him when there was no one else she could trust, not even Henry.

21

'Why is it important that I went up to Foxden by train and Henry drove up in the car?'

'A Sunbeam Rapier, the same year and colours as yours was seen parked on the waste ground in Mercer Street in the late afternoon of December the twenty-third. The day you went to the Midlands by train was the day the pathologist said Helen Crowther was killed.'

Ena put her elbows on the inspector's desk, put her hands up to her face and closed her eyes. She knew DI Powell had no agenda other than to find Helen Crowther's killer. She also knew the DI liked Henry. If not liked him, he'd got on with him on the occasions they had been in each other's company.

'My God!'

'What is it?'

'Henry has been framed.'

DI Powell shook his head. 'Ena, who...'

'Hear me out, Inspector. All the evidence: the whisky bottle, the glasses, the body found in my old workplace, points to Henry having murdered Helen Crowther. Even our car was seen on the day Crowther was killed. The Sunbeam Rapier is not a common car. Someone went to a lot of trouble to hire, steal or borrow an identical car and park it outside the building where Crowther was found. And why? To frame Henry. It's obvious. Our whisky, our glasses, our car - Henry's ID!

'Henry's an experienced MI5 agent. If he had killed Crowther, there wouldn't be any evidence. There'd be nothing to link Henry to her death; not a fingerprint or a hair, never mind half a second-hand furniture shop, which no doubt you'll find the purchase receipts for in Henry's name hidden somewhere *obvious* in our flat.' Ena flicked her hand at the idea of Henry being

Crowther's killer as if she were flicking away a fly. 'And, he would have an alibi. Henry killing Helen Crowther is ludicrous.'

'Is it?'

'Yes, it is! What possible reason would he have for killing her? He didn't know she was the mole at MI5. Only you, Director Bentley and I knew that. And, you know what is worse?'

'No, but I'm sure you're going to tell me, Ena.'

The real killer is out there laughing at us because he's got away with murder.'

'No one has got away with murder. If Henry didn't kill Helen Crowther, we will find out who did,' a familiar voice boomed from the doorway of the inspector's office.

Ena turned to see her boss from the Home Office, Director Bentley. She leapt out of her seat to greet him. 'Am I pleased to see you, Sir,' she said, shaking the director's hand. 'You don't believe Henry is capable of killing someone in cold blood, do you, Sir?'

Director Bentley didn't answer.

'Well? Do you?'

'I don't know, Ena.'

'What? But you know Henry. You know he isn't a murderer.'

Director Bentley looked blankly at her.

'This is madness and you know it! Why would Henry kill Helen Crowther? He worked with the woman, he liked her. He had no idea she was the mole at Five, so his motive couldn't have been for Queen and country,' she spat.

'I'm sorry, Ena, but I can't ignore the facts. The evidence.'

'Argh!' Ena threw her hands in the air. 'So much for telling me you respected my husband. You even had me believe you liked him. Now you're telling me you can't ignore *the facts, the evidence*. What are the facts? Where is the evidence that will stand up in court?'

While she waited for her boss to reply, the last words he had said to her in reference to Henry and his job at MI5 before she left the Home Office for the Christmas holiday pushed their way into her mind for the second time. *'The things we have to do to keep our country safe, Ena. Not always morally right, but always necessary.'*

'... and, because I am not certain, I would like you to stand down.'

'Stand down? What do you mean?'

'Leave the investigation into the murder of Helen Crowther to Special Branch and the Met.'

'When my husband is being wrongly accused of killing her? Not likely. The only way you'll get me off this case is to sack me!'

'That won't be necessary.'

Ena sighed with relief. She needed to be at the Home Office. She needed access to the files. 'Thank you, Director.'

'Don't thank me, Ena. You have left me no choice but to suspend you. Until the murder of Helen Crowther has been solved you are relieved of your duty at the Home Office.' Director Bentley stood up, leaned across the DI's desk and shook his hand. 'Goodbye, Inspector,' and, after a brief nod to Ena, he turned on his heels and walked briskly out of the DI's office.

The DI raised his eyebrows at Ena, said, 'I won't be a minute,' and followed Director Bentley out of the room and closed the door.

Ena jumped up and crossed to the door. She put her

ear against it. She could hear them talking, but couldn't make out what they were saying. The odd word here and there soon became muffled until the conversation was a long stream of indistinguishable mumbling.

Suddenly aware of footsteps in the corridor, she returned to her chair and looked around the room. Nothing had changed since the last time she was there, before Christmas. The inspector's desk stood in the same place, as did the small table under the window. She took the chair Director Bentley had been sitting on, stood it against the wall next to the table, and looked out of the window at Covent Garden. There was hardly anyone in the market. The stall holders in thick coats, woollen scarves and fingerless gloves, were packing up.

On her way back to her chair Ena stopped at the DI's safe.

'The envelope you gave me to keep for you is still in there,' the inspector said, coming into the room. 'Do you want it?'

Ena, still seething after being suspended, said, 'Yes. I might not have access to my cold case files, but I'll be able to look at some of Sid's photographs and newspaper cuttings. Oh my God!'

'What is it?'

'Not what, but who?'

'Go on.'

'You remember when we found a newspaper cutting of Helen Crowther on a Hitler Youth march?' The DI nodded. 'She was looking up at a young boy. It was hard to tell his age, but he looked about fifteen. That boy is in his mid-thirties now, his name is Shaun O'Shaughnessy, and I met him in Brighton at Helen Crowther's house.'

'I don't understand how this helps Henry.'

25

'O'Shaughnessy works for MI6, or he did. He knew details about Sid's death that hadn't been released to Five or Six, and he almost killed Artie. He followed him to The Salisbury, Micky Finned his drink and pumped him for information.'

'That still doesn't prove he had anything to do with Helen Crowther's murder.'

'It doesn't prove it, no. But,' Ena said, becoming exasperated, 'if he knew Crowther's cover had been blown - and there was no time to get her out of the country - he would have had no choice but to kill her.'

'To save his own skin.'

'And people higher up the chain. He's a nasty piece of work. You need to find O'Shaughnessy. I wish I could get my hands on the newspaper cuttings of them in Berlin that I gave Dick Bentley before Christmas.'

'What about the envelope in my safe? Is it of any use?'

'It could be. But Dick Bentley has the photographs of Crowther and O'Shaughnessy, Sid's journal and the lion's share of the letter.'

'Which, at some point, I shall have to read.'

Ena grinned. 'And when you do, you could let me see it again.'

'I could, but until then you need to keep a low profile. You're suspended, relieved of your duty if you remember. You can't interfere with the investigation, Ena. Director Bentley isn't stupid. If he thinks I'm going to show you the contents of the file he won't send it here, he'll tell me to go to the Home Office to look at it.'

'I'll roll over and play the little housewife if that's what it takes.'

The inspector laughed. 'I can't see you doing that,' he said, taking a ring with a dozen keys on it from his desk drawer. He went to the safe, unlocked it and took out a large brown envelope with 'Sid Parfitt, Berlin 1936' written on the front and handed it to Ena.

She held it in both hands as if weighing it, but didn't open it. 'There might be something, someone in the photographs, that I missed when I went through them before.' She pushed back her chair and stood up. 'Thank you for looking after this,' she said, putting the envelope in her bag.

The inspector nodded. 'I'll see you out. I need to arrange a car to take me to St. Thomas' first thing tomorrow.'

'To the morgue?'

'Yes.'

'Can I come?'

'No! What happened to keeping a low profile and playing the little housewife until Dick Bentley is satisfied you're keeping your nose out of the Crowther investigation?'

Ena put her hands up in a gesture of surrender. 'Okay, it's your case.'

'And don't forget it.'

'But it's my husband who's been framed for murder,' Ena said. 'Damn Dick Bentley! Damn O'Shaughnessy! And damn the bully-boys at bloody Special Branch!'

'I'm glad you still tell it how it is, Ena,' the inspector said.

At the front desk, Ena shook Inspector Powell's hand and thanked him again.

'I have an appointment with a DI at Special Branch tomorrow afternoon, which is why I'm going to see Sandy Berman in the morning.'

'Oh! And you are telling me this because...?'

'Because I thought you'd like me to give Sandy

your regards.'

'What?'

The inspector laughed. 'I have your home telephone number. I'll be in touch.'

CHAPTER FIVE

Loud rapid banging put an end to Ena's concentration. In case it was Henry, she ran into the hall and pulled open the front door. 'Mr Grimes?' she said, unable to hide the disappointment in her voice that the man standing at her door was the landlord of the block of flats and not her husband. 'What on earth's the matter?'

'I'd like to speak to Mr Green. Alright if I come in?'

Ena put out her arm and barred his way. 'My husband is away on business. Can I help?'

'I would rather speak to your husband, Mrs Green. When will he be back?'

'Next week,' Ena said, off the top of her head.

'Oh.'

'Mr Grimes, don't think me rude, but it's late and I'm busy. If you could tell me what the problem is…?'

Grimes cleared his throat. 'There have been some strange comings and goings from your flat.'

Ena was suddenly interested. Grimes might shed some light on the date the whisky and glasses were taken. 'Come in,' she said, 'out of the cold.' The landlord stepped into the hall and Ena closed the door. 'Strange comings and goings? Can you tell me when this was?'

'While you were away at Christmas.' He gave Ena an accusing look from beneath coarse grey eyebrows. 'Have you got a lodger, Mrs Green?'

'No, Mr Grimes. It was…' Who the hell could she say it was? 'It was my sister. She's a doctor. A surgeon, actually. She stayed here a couple of nights when she assisted in an operation to save a very important person's life at St. Thomas' Hospital.'

Grimes didn't look convinced. 'On December the twenty-fourth?'

'Yes. Ruined her Christmas, but it was a life or death situation. And,' Ena blew out her cheeks, 'thank goodness the operation to save this particular VIP was a success.'

'VIP you say?'

Ena winked. 'A very important person. I can't tell you who exactly, but he was the politician who took the country to…'

'Its finest hour?'

Ena put her hand up to her mouth. 'I shouldn't have said anything. I promised my sister I'd keep her confidence. Please don't repeat our conversation to anyone. And, although he's elderly now, I'm sure you'll agree that the country wouldn't want to lose him.'

'Definitely not. Thank you for clearing that up, Mrs Green.'

'My pleasure, Mr Grimes. I couldn't tell you before I went away at Christmas because I didn't know myself. But I should have told you when I got back. It isn't likely, but should it happen again, you'll be the first to know.'

Ena shook the landlord's hand and opened the door. He winked and put his forefinger up to the side of his nose. 'Mum's the word.'

'Thank you, Mr Grimes,' Ena said, sweetly. 'I know I can rely on your discretion.' Ena closed the door on the landlord who was not only a tight-wad, he was a nosy old blighter.

No sooner had she locked the door and returned to the sitting room than there was another knock. Ena groaned. 'Coming,' she called, closing the sitting room door before crossing the hall. She put on a smile and opened the door.

'Margot?'

'Hello, Ena.'

'And Claire,' Ena said, as the sister nearest to Ena in age popped up behind Margot. 'What are you two doing here?'

'Three!' Bess called, mounting the steps after locking the car, a shopping bag in one hand and Margot's walking stick in the other.

'Come in,' Ena said, as her sisters clattered into the hall. She pushed open the door to the sitting room and they filed in while she hung up their coats and hats.

'I can hardly believe my eyes. Driving all this way in this weather.' She added coal to the fire. 'I'll make a pot of tea. You must be parched,' Ena said, heading for the kitchen.

Bess took hold of Ena by the shoulders and propelled her round. 'Sit down. Claire and Margot will make the tea.' Claire jumped up and gave Margot a sideways nod. Claire picked up the bag and Margot picked up her stick and followed Claire out of the room.

'You must be hungry. I haven't got much in.'

'We've brought food with us. You know what Margot's like. She's always thinking of her stomach. She told Chef we were coming to visit you and he put together enough food to feed an army.'

Ena had so far not allowed herself to be upset. Seeing her sisters was a threat to her reserve. 'It's lovely to see you, but with Henry accused of murder it isn't the best time.'

'Au contraire,' Bess said, 'it is the perfect time.'

'Tea up!' Claire shouted, coming in from the kitchen carrying a tray with teapot, cups and saucers.

'And cake!' Margot called, following her.

Keeping her emotions in check, Ena joined in with her sisters' chatter. When they had finished drinking tea and eating cake - and had caught up with each other's news - Ena again asked what her sisters were doing there.

They looked at each other. Then Bess said, 'We've come to help you.'

'We'll stay for as long as you need us,' Claire said.

'For as long as it takes to find the bugger who killed the woman and framed Henry,' Margot added.

'I think we should make a toast.' Claire went to the sideboard and opened the cupboard. 'I see you still like a drop of whisky.' She took an unopened bottle of Teachers and put it on the dining table.

'And, glasses,' Margot said, reaching into the cupboard and producing four tumblers.

While Bess poured whisky into three of the glasses, Margot went to the kitchen and returned with a bottle of lemonade.

'A toast,' she said. 'The Dudley sisters!'

'The Dudley sisters!' Bess, Margot and Claire raised their glasses and laughed - and Ena burst into tears.

'Hey, come on, love. You're not on your own now. We're here. And, we'll find whoever framed Henry, won't we, girls?'

'Yes!' they shouted in unison.

Ena shook her head. 'God knows how.'

'Between the four of us, we have all the skills needed to find him, or her.'

'And clear Henry's name!' Margot waved her stick in the air and despite feeling deeply unhappy, Ena laughed.

'I know what you're thinking, our Ena. You're thinking, what possible help would an ex-hoofer with

32

arthritis and a stick be? Well, for a start, someone of my age having to use a stick gets the sympathy vote every time.'

Ena laughed. It was a bittersweet comment. Margot was too young to have arthritis.

'And another thing, anyone old enough to go to the theatre, or to some of the *better* nightclubs in the West End,' Margot batted her eyelashes, 'during the war, will remember Margot Dudley, leading lady of The Prince Albert Theatre, and the Talk of London who sang and danced her way through the Blitz. You'd be surprised what people tell you when you are, or were, famous.'

'And while Margot is distracting them with her show business anecdotes,' Claire said, 'I shall be quietly nosing around. You're not the only Dudley sister with a photographic memory, Ena. It can be very useful. And, I still know a few important people in London.'

'Your languages will help too,' added Bess.

Claire laughed. 'I may not be required to eavesdrop on conversations between SS Officers, but Bess tells me some of the less salubrious people you know are from Germany. In which case, understanding German will be helpful. But,' she continued, 'better still would be a French woman in London who is lost, or finds herself in a place she shouldn't be and, "parlez vous français" will come in handy.'

'And, if all else fails,' Ena said, 'you can bat your big blue eyes.'

'Batting my eyes worked once or twice when I was with the French Resistance.'

'It worked with Mitch,' Bess said, laughing.

'More than once.' Claire opened her eyes wide and lifted her right shoulder. 'But seriously, girls, it will be the skills I learned with the SOE that will help find this creep.'

Everyone agreed that together they stood a good chance of finding Helen Crowther's murderer and proving Henry innocent.

'So, what's the plan for tomorrow?'

'First, the scene of the crime.'

'Okay, we'll start early. Oh, but they'll have changed the locks. I don't have any keys.'

'We won't need keys,' Claire said, 'and I doubt there'll be police there now.'

'If there is, the lady with the stick will distract him.'

'Okay, I'll take you to Mercer Street first thing tomorrow morning, and then I'm going to Frieda Voight's funeral.'

'Is that wise, Ena?' Claire asked.

'Probably not, but I want to see who turns up. I might recognise someone.'

'Then I'll come with you.'

CHAPTER SIX

The afternoon of Frieda Voight's funeral was bitterly cold. Dark clouds threatened snow and the squally wind, in sudden gusts, blew dried leaves and sweet wrappers into the churchyard from the High Street, leaving a drift of debris against the porch of St. Leonard's Church. Unable to stop herself from looking up, Ena gazed at the parapet where Frieda had deliberately fallen to her death. An icy shiver ran down her spine and warm tears fell onto her cold cheeks.

The clear, well spoken, voice of the vicar brought her out of her reverie. Frieda's coffin was being lowered into the frozen earth next to that of Walter. The undertaker offered Ena soil to throw into the grave. She shook her head.

As each mourner took soil from the silver dish the funeral director was passing round, Ena studied their faces. Were their eyes red from crying, or were they emotionless? She noted their appearance, their demeanour; were they standing upright, there out of duty, or were they unable to hold their heads up because they weren't able to cope with their loss?

Ena's eyes settled on a man who stood head and shoulders above the other mourners. She estimated his age to be around fifty. He wore a black coat, a light grey scarf and a dark grey trilby. He also refused the soil.

Taking a handkerchief from her coat pocket, Ena lifted her hand to wipe her tears. At the same time, her elbow brushed against Claire's arm and she tilted her head discretely in the direction of the man.

When the vicar began the final prayer, the tall man took several steps back.

'He's leaving,' Claire whispered.

'So are we,' Ena replied.

Keeping their distance, stopping to look in a shop window when the man stopped to light a cigarette, and again when he looked to his right before crossing the road, Ena and Claire followed him to The Angel, a pub on Coldharbour Lane. Relieved to finally be inside, Claire found a table near the fire and Ena went to the bar.

'Two whiskies, please. Teacher's if you have it.'

'Put them on my tab,' an educated and slightly effeminate voice said.

Ena looked round. The man she and Bess had been following was standing behind her. 'Thank you, but there is no need to buy our drinks.'

'Oh, but there is, Mrs Green. You and your friend have passed three very good public houses to drink in my local. It's the least I can do.'

Ena felt the heat of embarrassment creep up her neck.

'Highsmith,' the man said, offering Ena his hand. 'Friend of the late Sid Parfitt. We covered the Berlin Olympics together in thirty-six, for The Times.'

'Berlin?' Ena said, feigning surprise. She took Highsmith's hand. 'How do you do, Mr Highsmith?'

'I'm doing well, Mrs Green. Better than your husband, I'd wager.'

Ena shot him a questioning look. What did Highsmith know about Henry? Before she could ask him, the barman arrived with their drinks.

'Shall we join your friend?' Highsmith grabbed his glass of scotch from the bar. Doing her best to control her shaking hands, Ena picked up her and Claire's drinks and followed.

'Are you alright, Ena?'

'I'm fine,' she lied. She looked at Highsmith. Her

heart was pounding. She wasn't fine at all, far from it. 'Claire, this is Mr Highsmith. He was a friend of my late colleague, Sid Parfitt, and he's about to tell us where Special Branch is holding Henry.'

Now it was Highsmith's turn to be embarrassed. Ena sat down next to Claire. 'So, Mr Highsmith, what did you mean when you said you were doing better than my husband?'

'That was not what I said, Mrs Green.'

'Semantics, Mr Highsmith. It was what you meant.'

Ena recalled what she had read about *Rupert* Highsmith in Sid's journal. Highsmith was in Berlin, in 1936, and he was a foreign correspondent for The Times, reporting on the Eleventh Olympiad, Adolf Hitler's Olympic Games, which had been paid for with Nazi Reichsmarks. Ena suspected that working for The Times was a cover for Highsmith.

Sid was already a court reporter for The Times, but because he had lived in Berlin and gone to boarding school there, he was given the role of sports correspondent. He was at school with Walter Voight, which was probably the principal reason why he was sent to Berlin. Someone had leaked the date of Sid's arrival to Walter Voight who was 'by chance' at the airport when Sid arrived. Ena now suspected it was Helen Crowther who had leaked that information.

As Sid was fluent in German, Highsmith ordered him to spend as much time as he could with Walter Voight. Sid had joked that it wouldn't be difficult if Walter's sister Frieda was there. Sid had been smitten with Frieda since the day he met her. He was in his early teens; Frieda a little older. And, according to what he wrote in his journal in 1936, his feelings for her hadn't changed. Meeting Frieda again in Berlin was to be his undoing. Frieda used the love he felt for her to discredit him, and in 1958 she used it to blackmail him.

Although Sid was in Berlin to report on the Olympic Games, he was also working for military intelligence. He had worried that if he were to spend too much time with Frieda and Walter Voight, he wouldn't be able to do his job as a sports correspondent properly. Highsmith told him that because he spoke German, he was more useful socialising with the Voights and keeping his ears and eyes open.

Sid had to give his reports on the Games - and what he had learned about Hitler from the people he spoke to - to Highsmith, who then amended them for Prime Minister Baldwin. Baldwin was keen to appease Hitler. Highsmith said Hitler was a ticking timebomb and Baldwin was doing his best to accede to his demands. Anything Sid wrote that Highsmith thought would provoke Hitler he amended before wiring the report to London. Sid wasn't happy with the arrangement, but Highsmith told him that was how it had to be because, unlike Sid, he wasn't only answerable to military intelligence, he was also answerable to the Prime Minister.

When Ena recalled how Sid had been set up by Highsmith, military intelligence and even The Times, she felt overwhelmed by sadness.

Ena hadn't liked what she'd read about Rupert Highsmith in Sid's journal. She thought he was pompous and arrogant. Typical of so many public schoolboys born into money. She liked him even less now she had met him.

'When I asked Mr Highsmith how he was, he said he was doing well, and then,' Ena looked into the mid-distance and squinted as if she could see the words but they were just beyond her reach. 'Ah! "Better than your husband, I'd wager." Wasn't that what you said, Mr Highsmith?'

'I said that because I'd heard Green was being questioned by Special Branch who are looking into Helen Crowther's murder. I assumed that because your husband worked with her…'

'There you go again, making assumptions.' Highsmith's nostrils flared. Ena was getting under his skin. 'Did you hear it from military intelligence or the Prime Minister's office? Are you Harold Macmillan's eyes and ears, as you were once Stanley Baldwin's?'

Highsmith's face flushed crimson. 'No! Sometimes we have to do things that aren't…'

Ena put her hand up palm first, 'Spare me the old school tie mantra, please! If I hear that *pathetic excuse* for the intelligence services not taking responsibility for their actions once more, I swear I'll hit the person who says it.' Ena picked up her scotch and drank it down. 'Now! Would you please tell me what you have heard about my husband?'

'Yes. But first, would you like another drink?'

Ena wanted to scream she was so exasperated. 'For God's sake get on with it, man!'

Claire got up and collected their glasses. 'Three whiskies?' Neither Ena nor Rupert Highsmith answered.

'That was a stupid remark I made about your husband, Ena, for which I apologise.'

Ena gave a curt nod. It was the first thing he'd said that she believed. 'Do you know where Henry is?'

'Not the exact location, but I know he's safe.'

'In one of Special Branch's *safe* houses?'

'I can't say. Even if I knew I couldn't tell you.'

'Then let me tell you something. Henry did not

murder Helen Crowther.'

'If he didn't, he has been framed by an expert.'

'Expert or not, I'm not going to stop looking for the person or people who framed him.'

'Nor should you. If Henry didn't kill Crowther and you stop looking, whoever did kill her will go to ground. Worse still they could leave the country, then it would be impossible to find them. No, carry on as you are.'

'Helen Crowther had me in her sights for some time. I don't suppose that will change because she's dead. Whoever she was working for, or whoever was working for her, will be watching me now.'

'Which is why you have to be careful. Don't take any unnecessary risks. Don't go out on your own after dark.'

'You've been watching too many Alfred Hitchcock films.'

'I'm serious.'

Ena shivered. Was Highsmith warning her, or threatening her?

Claire returned with the drinks.

Highsmith took his scotch, drank it down and stood up. 'Keep doing what you're doing, but if you have a breakthrough don't tell anyone, especially not the spooks at MI5 or Six. I work at GCHQ. This is my number.' He took a small white card from the inside pocket of his coat. 'Call me, anytime. I'll give you my home number too, in case you need to speak to me out of office hours.' He scribbled the number down on the back of the card and gave it to Ena. 'Day or night,' he said and left.

'When I see the friend I told you about from my days with the SOE, I'll ask him who Rupert Highsmith really is.'

'And your friend will know?'

'Yes,' Claire said, in a way that told Ena not to ask her how.

Ena knew better than to question Claire about the people she knew or had worked with in the SOE. Like Bletchley Park, work done by the Special Operations Executive was top secret.

Ena and Claire watched Highsmith as he said goodbye to the barman. After joking with a couple of elderly men at the bar, he strolled jauntily out of the pub.

Ena reread Highsmith's card, before putting it in her coat pocket. 'Would you trust him?' she asked Claire.

'Not as far as I could throw him.'

'I thought not. Nor would I.'

CHAPTER SEVEN

'How was your day?'

'Productive.' Margot took Ena's telephone book and diary from her bag with an extravagant a gesture as her arthritis allowed. 'Are these any use?'

'You bet they are. How did you get them?'

'Your young colleague, Artie, gave them to me.' Margot began to giggle. 'Who could resist taking their theatrical, slightly dotty, long-lost aunt out to lunch?'

'Oh my God! You two went to the Home Office?'

'Only me,' Margot said. 'The charming young woman on reception looked so much like a friend that I had worked with in the theatre that I just had to ask her if her aunt or mother had been in the shows at The Prince Albert Theatre in the war. They hadn't of course, but asking her prompted her to ask me if I had been in the theatre. We had a lovely chat about the shows and the music during the war. She was most impressed when I told her the theatres never closed, not even during the Blitz.' Margot giggled. 'She phoned through to my *nephew* Artie and told him his famous aunt, Miss Margot Dudley, was in reception hoping to see him.'

Ena's sisters laughed and applauded.

'Artie came to the reception and immediately suggested that as he hadn't seen me for such a long time, he took me out to lunch.'

'And the diary and telephone book?'

'He had them secreted about his person,' Margot said, theatrically, 'and gave them to me in the little café down the road.'

A thought suddenly struck Ena. 'Who paid for lunch?'

'I did, of course. The poor boy was in such a rush to

see me that he came out without his wallet.'

Ena laughed. 'That's Artie. I'll reimburse you, Margot.'

'You will not. I haven't had as much fun in years. I put Margot Dudley in a box along with her costumes when I left London in forty-five. It was about time I took her out and gave her an airing. And,' Margot said, tears in the corner of her eyes, 'I enjoyed being her again. Made me feel young.'

Ena put her arms around her older sister and hugged her. 'Margot Dudley was the talk of London; a star, and don't you forget it.'

'She still is, if that performance today is anything to go by,' Bess said.

Claire agreed, and when the sisters had finished assuring Margot and she had wiped her tears, Ena looked at Bess. 'Where did you go, Bess?'

'I went to see our old friend, Natalie Goldman, at The Prince Albert to ask her if we could use one of the rooms at the theatre as a meeting room to coordinate our findings. There used to be several.' Bess looked at Margot for confirmation. She nodded.

Ena's eyes widened. 'Why?'

'With all due respect, love, while your flat is… cosy, it's too small for the four of us. What we need is a room where we can get together at the beginning of each day, agree on a plan of action, and meet again at the end of the day. Somewhere that the people who bugged your flat, who it appears come and go as they please, don't know about.'

'That isn't fair, Bess.'

'Ena, they came into your home at Christmas while you weren't here and took a bottle of whisky and two glasses that they knew would have yours and Henry's fingerprints on them. Goodness knows what else they

43

took that you don't yet know about. Or what they may have planted,' Bess said, pointedly, looking up at the light in the ceiling.

Ena followed her gaze. 'I'll check for listening devices. They're easy to find and, if there are any, we'll get rid of them. It's easy to do that too.'

'Ena, whoever framed Henry came into your home and you didn't know until your landlord told you.'

'I'll get the lock changed.'

Claire put her hand on Ena's arm. 'It won't make any difference, Ena. Spooks, spies, whoever, don't need keys.'

'Lockpicks,' Ena said, 'I know! Alright, so what do you suggest?'

'I suggest we have a cuppa, have a rest, then get washed and changed and go out for dinner. But first, did you see anyone you knew at the funeral?'

'Not knew, but we saw someone I knew of.'

Ena and Claire told Bess and Margot everything that had happened at the funeral and afterwards in The Angel pub in Brixton, where they had met Rupert Highsmith. Ena flicked Highsmith's card across the dining table.

'Mmm... He works for GCHQ.' Bess sounded impressed.

'He does now. He might even have done in thirty-six when he was in Berlin with Sid. Sid worked for The Times, Highsmith said he did. They were both recruited by British intelligence. Sid reported to Highsmith, Highsmith reported to the intelligence services - and to Stanley Baldwin.'

'He was difficult to read,' Claire said.

'He's a snide little toff,' Ena added.

Bess got up from the table. 'I need to write up everything that has happened today. I'll go to the bedroom.'

Ena got up too. She looked at her watch. 'It's far too early to go out for dinner, so I'll make some tea and sandwiches to keep us going.'

Claire followed Ena out of the room. 'I'll help.'

'Use the dining table, Bess. I'm going to give Bill a quick ring, let him know we're alright,' Margot said, 'and then I'll have a lie down.'

Bess dropped her notebook and pen on the table and sat down again. She took her reading glasses from her handbag and put them on. After listing the day's salient points from each of her sisters, she picked up Ena's work diary and began to read. She noticed that at the side of some of the dates there was a small red cross. It was these pages she concentrated on.

'Last year was heavy going,' Bess said when Ena returned to the sitting room. 'God knows how you coped with everything that happened.'

'For some of the time, I had my colleagues Sid and Artie. After Sid was killed I was on my own for a while. Artie struggled. He got himself into a bit of bother.' Ena didn't elaborate. That Artie had been drunk and told Helen Crowther's friend Shaun O'Shaughnessy a name, which at the time should have been kept secret, was irrelevant now. 'Artie did his best, but it was the detective in charge of Sid's murder, Detective Inspector Powell, who was the most helpful to me. He believed me when no one else did. There was a time when DI Powell was the only person I could trust.'

Ena took the buff envelope the inspector had given her, on the day she got back to London, from the sideboard drawer. 'DI Powell kept this for me over Christmas. Apart from you, Claire and Margot, he's still the only person I can trust.'

'Good Lord!' Bess said, taking photographs from the envelope and turning them sideways and then upside down.

Ena laughed. 'That's what the inspector did when he first saw them.'

Bess was looking at a photograph of Sid surrounded by naked bodies. 'Who are these women?'

'Street girls, drug addicts, alcoholics, anyone who needed money. Walter Voight paid them to perform lewd acts.'

'I'm guessing your colleague didn't agree to any of this.'

'No, he didn't. What you see there never happened. It's clever photography. One photograph overlaid on top of another photograph somehow. Sid was at the cabaret.' Ena pointed to the photograph of the cabaret singer straddling Sid. 'The photograph of the nude women has been added to one of Sid watching the show. The cabaret singer is real, and she did straddle Sid, but Voight had got him so drunk he didn't know what he was doing.'

Bess picked up another photograph. 'Was Sid homosexual?'

'Not as far as I know. If he was, he was discreet about it.' Ena shook her head. 'As I said, the Voights got Sid drunk the night of the cabaret. From what he said in a letter he wrote to me, they took him somewhere - a cheap hotel probably - carried on celebrating and drugged his drink.'

'And the naked men sprawled across his bed were also paid to do it?'

'Yes. Sid couldn't remember anything that happened after he left the cabaret club.'

'The Voights used the photographs to blackmail Sid into working for them?' Bess said.

'Yes. The photographs and newspaper cuttings of Sid were doctored. But not the newspaper cuttings of Walter and Frieda Voight, or Helen Crowther and...'

'Ena, what is it?'

'Helen Crowther had a much younger male friend. A nasty character by the name of Shaun O'Shaughnessy. He could often be found propping up the bar of The Salisbury, or the Lamb and Flag. Fancy going on a West End pub crawl after dinner?' Ena asked, scouring the newspaper cuttings trying to find another photograph of Crowther and O'Shaughnessy on a Nazi rally. There wasn't one.

'Who's going on a pub crawl?' Claire asked, bringing in a plate of sandwiches.

'We could. Might be fun,' Ena said, clearing the photographs and newspaper cuttings from the table and replacing them with a tablecloth.

'I'll get Margot,' Bess said, heading for the door.

'If you lay the table, Ena, I'll bring in the tea.'

'This is lovely,' Margot said, 'the Dudley sisters sitting down together and having tea.'

Everyone agreed.

'Ena suggested going for a drink in the West End, tonight.'

Margot's eyes lit up. 'We could go to some of the old clubs where I used to sing.'

'I was thinking more along the lines of an early dinner at Restaurant Fleur on St. Martin's Lane and afterwards go across to The Salisbury for a drink. Or we could nip to the Lamb and Flag in Rose Street.'

'Why those pubs in particular?' Claire squinted at Ena. 'What are you up to?'

'Nothing. I just thought...'

'She thought she might see a character by the name of O'Shaughnessy in one or other of the pubs,' Bess

47

said. 'He was a Nazi supporter when he was a boy and knew the woman who Henry is accused of murdering.'

'Have you got a photograph of him, Ena?'

'No. I had newspaper cuttings of him and Crowther in the thirties, but I gave them to my boss at the Home Office.'

'What does he look like?'

'He's six feet tall, short blond hair,' Ena thought for a second. 'His hair is parted on the left and he has pale blue-grey eyes. He looks Germanic now I think about it. Oh, and he has a phoney Irish accent. I say phoney because it changes when he becomes theatrical. He professes to be an actor. He's full of anecdotes and bull.'

'And, what do we do if we see him? Do we talk to him?'

'I don't know.' Tears filled Ena's eyes. 'I'm sorry.'

'You have nothing to be sorry for,' Margot said. 'Come on. Leave O'what's-his-name for now and let's get ready and go out. I bags the bathroom first,' she said, putting up her hand.

They took it in turn to wash up, tidy up, and use the bathroom. The hustle and bustle of all four sisters getting ready at the same time reminded Ena of when they lived at home before the war, and the arguments they had about whose turn it was to get ready first. The Dudley house didn't have a bathroom in those days, they washed in the scullery and the kitchen sink with water heated on the stove. Ena laughed to herself. How did they ever manage?

Today being together, all wanting to get ready at the same time was fun, but Ena could see why, if they were going to take finding Helen Crowther's killer seriously, they needed more space and a proper plan of action. Bess was right. When they were dressed in suitable clothes for dining out in London's West End, make up on and their hair styled, courtesy of Ena, the sisters put on their coats and set off for London's West End in Bess' car.

CHAPTER EIGHT

Instead of crossing the Strand and turning into Covent Garden, or heading for Long Acre and Leicester Square, Bess drove along Kingsway to Holborn and Russell Square, past Euston Station, north towards Hampstead Heath.

Ena looked out of the car window. The area was unfamiliar. 'Where are we going? I thought we were going to the West End.'

'We are,' Margot said, 'after we've eaten.'

'Are we eating in Camden?' Ena asked as they passed the old railway roundhouse. 'I've never eaten out in Camden. Is there anywhere decent to eat in Camden? I suppose there must be,' she mumbled, peering out of the window again.

Bess sighed loudly. 'I have no idea, Ena. Just sit back and enjoy the ride. We'll soon be there.'

Ena nudged Claire and rolled her eyes. The next time she looked out of the window she saw the quaint shops and cafés of Hampstead. Bess swung the car into Heath Street and turned almost immediately into a narrow lane on the south side of the Heath.

Bess brought the car to a halt outside a large detached house. As Ena got out of the car she saw Bess and Margot's friend, Natalie Goldman, running from the front door to greet them.

Natalie threw her arms around Bess and welcomed her. She then turned to Margot. 'It's been too long,' she said, hugging Margot. Without letting go of her, Natalie held Margot at arm's length. 'What's this?' she asked with concern in her voice seeing Margot with a walking stick.

'It's my teacher's cane,' Margot said. 'It's the only way I can keep my sisters in check,' she laughed.

Natalie hugged Margot again. 'Please go into the house. It's freezing out here.'

Natalie turned to Ena and took hold of her hands. 'It has been a very long time, Ena.' Natalie kissed Ena on both cheeks. 'And, Claire?' she said, smiling, 'I'm so pleased to meet you at last.'

Claire smiled and put out her hand. 'I'm pleased to meet you too, Natalie.'

With Ena on one side and Claire on the other, Natalie led them into the house. Bess and Margot had already taken off their coats and hung them up in the downstairs cloakroom. 'Go through to the sitting room,' she said to them, 'while I take Ena and Claire's coats.'

A coal fire roared in the fireplace of the spacious sitting room. A double bay window looked out onto the front garden. The room was warm and comfortable with a big over-stuffed sofa and two equally comfortable armchairs in a floral fabric with large soft matching cushions edged in the dusky pink colour of the curtains.

Natalie's home was familiar to all the Dudley sisters, except Claire. Claire had not been to the house before, nor had she met Natalie Goldman or her late husband, Anton. She had never seen a show at The Prince Albert Theatre either, although she had been to the theatre twice during the war. The first time with Mitch. He wasn't *Mitch* to her then, he was Captain Alain Mitchell, an RCAF pilot and SOE operative, who had trained her and who would be her partner in German-occupied France working undercover with the French Resistance. They had been walking up the Strand from Lyons Corner House and she had pointed out the theatre where her sister Margot worked. The doors and windows were boarded up after a stray bomb had fallen in Maiden Lane, bringing down the building opposite the stage door of the theatre.

Mitch had promised to take her to see Margot in a show after the war. At the time she hadn't long been recruited by the Special Operations Executive and Britain's cities were being bombed to smithereens by the Luftwaffe. The end of the war seemed a very long way away.

The second time Claire visited the theatre was four years later. She was on her own and out of her mind with worry. Mitch had been captured by the SS. She didn't know whether he was still in France, been taken to Germany or Poland, or even whether he was dead or alive. She went into the foyer of the theatre and sat down beneath a full-length photograph of Margot in a gilt frame. She sat for so long she lost track of the time. She also lost her nerve and left.

Walking away from the theatre, Claire knew Margot wouldn't have come through the public entrance. She would have entered by the stage door and would by now be in her dressing room. It was better she didn't see her. What would she say? What could she say to her? She couldn't tell her she was an agent with the SOE, that she worked in occupied France, had fallen in love, or that she had a child.

The memory of that worrying time took Claire's breath and she inhaled sharply.

'Are you alright, Claire?'

'I'm fine.' She looked at Ena and Margot. Natalie was showing them photographs of Margot and her fellow dancers. 'I'm sorry I didn't get to meet Natalie and her husband during the war. I know how good they were to you when you lived in London, and later how they helped Margot.' Tears fell onto Claire's cheeks.

52

'And I'm sorry I didn't see Margot perform on stage.' Claire looked at Margot's stick leaning against the arm of her chair. 'Now it's too late.'

Bess picked up an album of photographs from the table at the side of the settee. 'Dry your eyes, darling,' she said, moving closer to Claire. 'You weren't in the country; you weren't able to see her.'

'I came to London when Mitch was missing. And I went to the theatre. I didn't trust myself not to break down and tell Margot everything that had happened in France, so I left. I wish I'd stayed now.'

'We all regret things we did or didn't do in the war.'

Claire opened the album. The first photograph was of Anton Goldman. 'I'm so lucky to have Mitch,' she said, tears filling her eyes again.

'I feel the same about Frank. He could have been killed when he was shot in Africa. It was a miracle that he only lost an eye and not his life.'

Bess turned the page. 'Anton was a very special man, a kind and generous man not only to Margot and me, but to hundreds of young people in the war. It doesn't seem right that after all the good he had done, he should die suddenly of a heart attack. It was so unfair.'

'How does Natalie manage without him?' Claire asked.

'She immerses herself in work. The theatre was Anton's dream and she carries it on for him. And she has children and grandchildren. I should like to see them again, but they work and the children are at school, so…' Bess looked at her friend again. 'Natalie's a strong woman. Running the theatre keeps her busy.

'It was in nineteen thirty-nine that I first met Natalie and Anton, I was at teacher training college. When the war started Margot and Bill were newly married and rented rooms from them. Bill worked as a document courier for the MoD and Margot an usherette at The Prince Albert Theatre.

'After the war, Bill returned to the Midlands to find a home for him and Margot, as they had agreed he would do. But by then, the theatre, being the leading lady and singing in nightclubs was Margot's life. The public loved her and she loved them. She started drinking. Socially at first, but she was working long hours and began to drink more heavily. She was taking pills to help her sleep and pills to get her up in the mornings - and she became addicted. She hid her addiction for some time, but one day Natalie found her on the floor of her dressing room. She was incoherent, belligerent, and unable to stand. She begged Natalie not to send for Bill, so Natalie took her home and looked after her until she was clean of sleeping tablets, pain killers, prescription and social drugs, and of alcohol.'

CHAPTER NINE

When they had finished eating, Ena and her sisters sat round Natalie's dining table drinking coffee and chatting. Bess brought up the subject of needing somewhere to work from.

'Don't be offended, Ena, but your flat is too small for four of us to live and work in. As I said earlier, we need a base and Natalie has been kind enough to offer us one.'

'I want to help, if you'll let me,' Natalie said to Ena, 'so I wondered if you would like to use a room at the theatre. There are several that are unused.'

'Not dressing rooms seven and eight then?' Margot said. The colour drained from her face and her eyes became moist.

'No, dear, I was thinking of a room on the ground floor. I have one in mind that I'm sure will suit the purpose. It's a fairly big room, unfurnished at present, but we could go to the theatre's warehouse and get anything you need. There's everything imaginable in the furniture and props department. What do you think?'

'The theatre is central,' Ena said, 'and it's easy to get to from Stockwell.'

'And,' Bess added, 'it won't be under surveillance.'

'There is that.' Ena looked at Claire and Margot. They both nodded. 'Thank you, Natalie, basing the operation at the theatre is a great idea.'

'Now for the sleeping arrangements,' Bess said. 'Margot and I will stay here with Natalie at night and drive into the West End each day, and you and Ena,' she said to Claire, 'stay at Ena's in Stockwell. I thought that was best, as Ena and I have cars. What do you think, girls?'

'Good idea,' Claire said. She looked at Ena.

'I agree.'

'That's settled then. Tomorrow we'll take a look at the room and get it cleaned. No offence, Natalie. I didn't mean…'

Natalie laughed. 'None taken. It was the room we called the *visitors'* room during the war. We used it when Jewish students were smuggled out of Germany. The father of one of the dancers in the company…'

'George,' Margot said.

Natalie smiled. 'Yes, George's father had a network of people who brought students out of Germany to France, and then across the Channel to England. From Dover, George's friends brought them up to London. They stayed here at the house first.'

'Didn't anyone notice young people coming and going?'

'No. They arrived at night. We aren't overlooked by our neighbours and at that time there were no street lights. There was usually only one, sometimes two, at the same time and they were never here long. As each young person's papers and tickets came, we took them to the theatre to await their travelling date.'

'They sometimes sang with the chorus - costumes allowing, or held poses as Egyptian or Greek maidens,' Margot laughed. 'Hidden in plain sight.'

Claire's eyes widened. 'It must have been a huge operation.'

'It was. Anton and I didn't only run a theatre, we ran escape routes from London to Ireland, Ireland to America, and one from London to Liverpool to America.'

'People who would otherwise have been sent to concentration camps.'

'Or worse,' Margot said.

'And what relevance did dressing-rooms seven and eight have?' Claire asked, looking from Margot to Natalie.

'As far as everyone who worked at the theatre was concerned, dressing room seven was my private sitting room. A place where I went to relax, where I wasn't to be disturbed. Dressing room eight was similar but it was Anton's room. He often worked at night, so, if it was very late, or if the roads were closed after a bombing raid, he slept at the theatre. At least that is what we told the company and the staff. The real purpose of dressing rooms seven and eight was to sleep our young Jewish people. Claire was right. If they had stayed at the house for too long someone would have noticed. Because of the blackout, any chink of light showing through the curtains when the children and their nanny had been evacuated and Anton and I were working, would invite questions. We couldn't risk it. But at the theatre, no sooner had a new stagehand, cleaner, dresser or seamstress got the hang of the job they would be called up. People, young people especially, coming and going was an everyday occurrence and didn't cause comment.'

Bess looked at her wristwatch. 'Goodness, it's gone ten. I'm sorry to break up the party, but it's getting late. We won't get back to south London until eleven. We'd better give the West End a miss tonight so we can make an early start in the morning.' She stood up. 'When we've set up the visitors' room at the theatre, Margot and I will bring our stuff here, if that's alright with you, Natalie.'

'Of course.'

'And you and Claire can look for the O'Shaughnessy character in The Salisbury.'

'Sounds like a plan.'

After thanking Natalie for the lovely meal, they said goodnight and set off for Stockwell.

CHAPTER TEN

When they got back to Ena's flat, Margot went to the bathroom and Ena, Bess and Claire went into the sitting room. Ena took the bottle of scotch from the cupboard and poured a double measure into three glasses.

'While Margot isn't here, I'll explain why I paired us up the way I did. Apart from the obvious, you and I have cars, Ena, I don't want Margot tramping around the pubs and clubs. She's been sober for thirteen years and while I'm positive she will never drink again, it isn't fair to put temptation in her way.'

Ena and Claire agreed.

'There's something else.' Bess took a drink of her whisky, put the glass down, and inhaled deeply. 'She doesn't want you to know. She doesn't want anyone to know, but she isn't well.'

'Is her arthritis worse?'

'The arthritis is worse, yes, but it isn't that. Margot has a heart condition. Bill told me she has a hospital appointment coming up at the Walsgrave in Coventry. They want to do tests, so when the time comes, I'll take her back to the Midlands and you two stick to the plan down here, whatever the plan is, which we must decide tomorrow.' Bess drained her glass. 'So, treat Margot as normal. For goodness sake don't let her know I've told you about the tests.'

When Ena and Claire had finished their drinks, Bess took the glasses to the kitchen.

On her way back she stopped outside the bathroom door. 'Shake a leg, Margot.'

'Finished,' Margot called. As she left the bathroom Bess went in.

Opening the sitting room door, Margot said, 'You

don't get to stay this lovely without looking after yourself. I call it the cream regime,' she chuckled.

Ena forced herself to laugh with her sister. 'And you are still lovely, Margot. You were on the front row when they gave out the looks.'

Margot, still laughing, said, 'You weren't far behind me, our Ena. Don't wake me when you come to bed, Claire. I need my beauty sleep. Night, night,' she said, turning and leaving the room with the back of her hand up to her forehead, imitating Greta Garbo in the 1932 film, Grand Hotel.

Claire shook her head and laughed good-heartedly. 'Hey,' she said to Ena, 'stop that.' She put her arm around Ena's shoulder. 'She's only going for tests. If they do find something… they'll treat it.'

'Will they?'

'Yes! Now stop crying.'

'Next!' Bess called from the hall.

'You go,' Claire said, 'I'll hang on here, give Margot more time to get off to sleep.'

Ena got up. At the door, she looked back at Claire and whispered, 'Goodnight.'

'Something smells good,' Claire said, following Margot into the sitting room.

Ena put a serving dish of fried eggs, one of bacon, and a rack of toast in the middle of the table. 'Sit down, you two, and help yourselves. There's tea in the pot.'

'Where's Bess?'

'Washing up. I'll get her.'

When she returned with Bess, Claire was tucking into eggs and bacon and Margot was buttering a slice of toast. Ena opened her mouth to tell Margot she needed to eat something to keep her strength up, but closed it when Bess poked her in the ribs.

Bess gave Ena a sharp look, as if to say don't make a fuss, and sat down next to her. 'I only want toast,' Bess said, 'I'm still full from last night's dinner.' She smiled across the table at Claire and Margot and helped herself to a slice of toast. Reaching for the butter, she said, 'Come on, our Ena. You said you were hungry when you woke up.'

'Give me a second to pour the tea, Bess, unless you want it stewed.' When everyone had a cup of tea in front of them, Ena put an egg and a rasher of bacon on her plate. Bess added a slice of toast.

Ena blew out her cheeks and crossed her eyes. 'Enough!' she shouted, as Bess forked another rasher of bacon.

Bess opened the threadbare curtains of the nearest window in the visitors' room. The pale winter sun shone through the small pane of glass in a dagger shape shaft, cutting through millions of tiny specks of dust. She opened the second pair and more light came in. Beneath each window was a long maroon velvet seat. Ena stepped up and looked out of the window. It needed a clean, but then the entire room needed a clean. She jumped down, clapped the dust off the palms of her hands and looked around the room.

'It's a good space,' Ena said, arriving with Claire.

'It is,' Bess agreed, 'it's just right for what we need.'

'Where's Margot?' Ena asked, waving dust particles away.

'With Natalie. They've gone to the theatre warehouse to sort out some furniture. We need to get rid of this dust before Margot gets back.'

Ena took a long-handled brush from against the wall

and pushed it a few inches along the floor. A cloud of dust flew up and almost choked her. 'As I thought. We need a wet cloth on the bristles of the brush to stop the dust from flying all over the place.'

'We also need clean wet cloths to wipe the window sills and walls.'

'The cupboard where the cleaning equipment is kept is along the corridor next door to the staff room. I'll see what I can find.'

'I'll get some water,' Claire said, following Ena out of the room.

When Ena returned it was with an Electrolux vacuum cleaner. 'Look what I've found. Be perfect for the seats of the chairs and the curtains,' she said. 'This is one of the new cleaners. It's supposed to do hard floors too, but I think we need to wash the floor.' She unwound the lead, pushed the plug into the electric socket, and turned it on. 'All yours, Bess.'

Claire came in carrying a bucket and two mops. 'I'll wash the floor and you follow behind me and dry it off, Ena.' Claire put the bucket down and handed Ena a mop. 'Let's get started.'

Ena and Claire mopped the floor to the rattle and rumble of Bess vacuuming the window seats. By the time Margot and Natalie arrived, there was no dust in sight. Not a speck had escaped the enthusiastic thrashing of Ena and Claire's mops.

'It's gone eleven,' Natalie announced, 'time for a break.'

'Let's go to the café next to the stage door. I'd love to see it again.'

'It's changed since you were last there, Margot. It's what's called a coffee bar now. Lots of young men and women sitting around drinking coffee and smoking cigarettes, talking about politics and the last record

62

they bought.'

'When Natalie first took me there it was a French restaurant called The Fleur Jardin Café. It had a really bohemian clientele. Young writers, poets and artists sat outside on wooden tables drinking coffee and talking animatedly about literature, art and music. I envied them their lifestyle and wondered, if there was a war, how long it would be before their carefree lives changed.'

'The Fleur Jardin,' Natalie said, wistfully.

'It had blue and white checked tablecloths and a striped awning above the window.'

'We sat in the window and we ate onion soup.'

'And the waiter was sweet on you.'

'Eric,' Natalie said, laughing.

Bess squealed. 'I can't believe you remember his name.'

'Every time I spoke to him, the poor boy blushed scarlet.'

Everyone laughed except Ena. 'The coffee bar might just be the kind of place Shaun O'Shaughnessy would frequent. He's a regular at The Salisbury, which isn't a million miles from here. He calls himself an actor, so he more than likely hangs around West End theatres and cafés. He likes young men and he's nothing if he isn't political.'

Everyone was suddenly serious. Ena had doused the flames of fun with a dose of reality.

'Right!' Bess said, 'let's go to the coffee bar; see if this character is in there.'

The Fleur Jardin Café, where Bess and Natalie had lunched in 1939, and Margot and her dancer friends had frequented in the 1940s was unrecognisable. Gone were the blue and white checked tablecloths, the quaint table decorations, pretty curtains and Alpine-style wooden shutters. Now there were easy to wipe clean tables and a Formica counter like those in Lyons Corner Houses. But, instead of queuing at the counter to order your refreshment, choosing your drink and food, and taking it to a table, teenagers sat at the counter on stainless steel high stools tapping their feet, clicking their fingers, and swaying to music that thumped out of speakers on either side of a jukebox.

Natalie led the way to a table for four on the far side of the coffee bar and asked a young woman clearing mugs from a nearby table if it was alright to take a chair from it. The young woman nodded, piled up her tray with used coffee mugs and sauntered off with them to the counter.

A couple of minutes later she returned to the table, pushed a bowl with cubes of sugar into the middle. 'Five espressos?'

'Yes, please,' Natalie replied.

The young woman looked across the room to the man behind the counter and called out the order. A young man with dark hair curling over the collar of his open shirt took her by the hand and holding her close, swayed in time to the music. He then pushed her away and straightaway pulled her back to him. He pushed her away again and this time let go of her hand and she twirled round on her own. The boy flicked a shilling at her, she caught it and he told her to put on some decent sounds. Shaking out her long blonde hair she half walked, half danced, to the beat of Move It by Cliff Richard and The Drifters and dropped the coin into the slot on the front of the jukebox.

A second later Jailhouse Rock by the American singer, Elvis Presley, boomed out of the machine, turning the tapping of feet and clicking of fingers to frenzied jerking of heads and slapping of hands on tabletops. The song that followed was a ballad. To Know Him Is To Love Him by The Teddy Bears didn't assault the ears as much as the first record she had chosen. The girl sashayed back to the counter, picked up a tray with five small cups of coffee and a jug of milk on it and took it across to Natalie's table. Smiling dreamily, she placed a small cup and saucer in front of each of the women and slowly danced her way around the small round tables collecting empty cups and glasses until she was again back at the counter.

'No sign of O'Shaughnessy.'

'I don't think a coffee bar is his scene, as they say.'

'The clientele too young for him?'

'No. Too innocent.'

'Mrs Green?' Stan, the stage doorman called, as Ena and her sisters entered the theatre through the stage door. 'There have been a couple of telephone calls for you.'

'Did they give their names or leave a message?'

Stan lifted up the piece of paper he'd written the message on and read, 'It was a Mr Powell. He said you'd left something in his office and he would hold on to it for you.'

Ena turned to her sisters. 'I think Inspector Powell has the envelope I gave my boss at the Home Office before Christmas. I'm going to Bow Street.'

'If you can make it back for lunch. Where shall we meet?'

'There's a café called Dooley's on the Strand. It's almost opposite the theatre,' Margot said. 'How about we meet there at one?'

Ena left the theatre to a chorus of good luck and see you later.

65

CHAPTER ELEVEN

Ena's mood had changed from pessimistic to optimistic. 'Do you have good news for me?'

DI Powell took the brown envelope that Ena had given Director Bentley before Christmas from his desk drawer.

'Can I take it with me?'

'What?' The DI blew out his cheeks. He raised his eyebrows in disbelief.

'Well?'

'Ena, you know you can't.'

'But I need to show the contents of this envelope to my sisters.'

'Your sisters?' DI Powell repeated. With his elbow on his desk, he closed his eyes and pinched the bridge of his nose with this thumb and forefinger.

'Yes, they've come down from the Midlands to help me find Crowther's killer.'

'Ena, I've given Director Bentley my word that this envelope will not leave my office.'

'I won't tell him if you don't.'

'Not funny. No. I'm sorry, Ena…'

'Hang on a minute,' Ena said, putting up her hands. 'Technically this envelope belongs to me. Sid left me the clues to find it, not Dick Bentley. Neither of you has the right to stop me taking it.'

'It's evidence in a murder case.'

'Evidence that I gave you in the first place.' Ena slammed the palms of her hands down hard on the DI's desk. 'Fine! Will you let one of my sisters come here to read the newspaper cuttings.' The DI didn't answer. 'Come on, Inspector, surely…'

'Alright! Tomorrow.'

'Today.'

The DI threw his arms in the air. 'This afternoon, then.'

Ena stood up and pushed back her chair. 'Thank you. I'll go and get her.'

'Aren't you interested in what else I have here?'

Ena wrinkled her nose. 'You haven't got the pathologist's report, have you?'

'No, but the fingerprint boys have sent in their report.' The inspector pushed a manilla folder across his desk. 'And, before you ask, no! You can't take it out of the office either.'

Ena tutted and rolled her eyes in fun, before opening the folder and peering at pages covered in patchy fingerprints. 'I have no idea what Henry's prints look like, but I'm guessing these initialled 'HG' are his.'

'They are. We matched them against the prints on his file at MI5.'

'Then why are you showing them to me? We've established that it was our whisky bottle and our glasses on the table at the murder scene, so the prints on them are bound to be Henry's or mine.'

'Because the prints on the whisky bottle are full prints.' The inspector handed Ena a magnifying glass.

'So? They're still Henry's prints, aren't they?'

'Yes!' Ena could hear the frustration in the inspector's voice. 'But the prints on the glasses are not full prints, they're partials.'

Ena looked again at the photographs of the glasses. 'I don't understand. If they are Henry's prints, what difference does it make.'

'Ignore the fingerprints.' The inspector moved the images of the glasses and fingerprints out of the way and passed Ena the written report. 'Read this.' He pointed to a hand-written note at the bottom, titled

'Inconsistency'.

The fingerprints on both glasses belong to Henry Green, whose prints are also on the whisky bottle. However, there are inconsistencies in depth and clarity on one of the glasses. The fingerprints on the glass taken from the left of the whisky bottle are clear - no smears, no smudges, just the well-defined prints of four fingers and a thumb from Henry Green's right hand. The prints on the glass taken from the right of the bottle, although the same hand, are different in density and texture. The three lower prints are clear, but the prints on top of the glass - the forefinger on the far side and the thumbprint on the nearside - are unclear partials.

It is my opinion that sometime after Henry Green held the glass, it was held by someone wearing gloves. Thus, the top of the print from the glass on the right of the whisky bottle - the glass containing traces of cyanide - has been rubbed off and the lower part has been smudged.

Ena flopped back in her chair. 'As I thought. Someone killed Helen Crowther and placed our glasses with Henry's fingerprints on the table to make it look like Henry murdered her.'

'It looks that way.'

'Now do you believe Henry didn't kill her?'

'I didn't believe Henry killed her in the first place. But,' the inspector picked up the fingerprint report and read the note again, 'the fingerprints on the bottle and those that aren't smudged are still a problem.'

'But what about the inconsistencies?'

'Not enough to prove Henry didn't murder Crowther. He could have killed her and set the scene to make it look as if he was set up.'

'I know. But, it's the first fly in the ointment of

whoever did kill Crowther. I need to know if the German newspaper cuttings say anything about Crowther. My sister Claire understands German, she could translate them.'

'How long will it take her to get here?'

'Ten minutes. If I could use your telephone…'

The inspector lifted the telephone receiver from its base.

'Damn! I don't know the number. Do you have a telephone directory?'

'Where is she?'

Ena didn't want anyone to know where she and her sisters were based, not even the inspector, but she had no choice. 'The Prince Albert Theatre on the Strand.'

The inspector put the phone to his ear and dialled nought and eight. 'WPC Jarvis, would you find me the telephone number of the…?' He looked at Ena, 'Stage door?' She nodded. 'The stage door of The Prince Albert Theatre?' He smiled at Ena and wrote the number in his telephone book. 'Thank you.'

The DI turned the book around so it was facing Ena and handed her the telephone. 'I'll be back in five minutes,' he said, getting up and going to the door.

When he had gone, Ena dialled the number. 'Hello, Stan, this is Ena. Could you tell me if Natalie and my sisters are still in the theatre...?

'Thank you. I need to speak to Claire. She's probably in the visitor's room, but I'm not sure if a telephone has been installed yet. Would you try Natalie's office? Thank you.' Ena held the receiver for some time before Natalie answered. 'Hello, Natalie. Is Claire with you?'

'No, the girls are in the visitor's room. Shall I get her for you?'

'There's no time. Would you ask her to come to

Bow Street Police Station as soon as possible? I want her to look at the newspaper cuttings of Crowther and O'Shaughnessy on the Nazi rally in Berlin. I need her to translate them for me.'

'I'll tell her straight away. See you for lunch if you can make it.'

Ena put down the telephone, left the inspector's office, and went to the reception area to wait for Claire. She hadn't thought to ask Natalie to give Claire directions to the police station. though she was sure Natalie would.

Looking through the glass in the upper part of the door, Ena saw Claire turn into Bow Street and ran out to meet her. 'Claire,' she called, waving to her sister as she crossed the road. She put her arm through Claire's and looked up at the window in the inspector's office. He was looking down at them. He hadn't gone far when he left her on the telephone. She waved.

'Thanks for coming so quickly.'

'It wasn't far. I remembered the way. Mitch and I spent a lot of time in this part of London.'

'Come and meet the wonderful copper who helped me with the Frieda Voight investigation. He's a really decent man. And, more to the point, I trust him.'

'Was he the Investigating Officer in the Voight case too? That's a coincidence isn't it?'

Ena heard suspicion in her sister's voice. 'No. It wasn't until after Sid had been killed on Waterloo Bridge, which is on his patch, that I got to know him. And, because Helen Crowther was murdered in Mercer Street, which is also on his patch, it's his case too. Well, his and Special Branch.'

Ena pushed open the door into the police station. She waved at the desk sergeant and as she and Claire approached the door marked private, he opened it for them.

Outside the DI's door, she said, 'Some of the photographs are sexually explicit. The newspaper cuttings aren't, but you're bound to see the photos.'

Claire shrugged, 'I've probably seen worse things in the war. Besides, I'm here to translate words, not to look at pictures.'

Ena knocked on the inspector's door and waited, expecting him to shout, 'Enter.' Instead, he opened the door. 'Come in,' he said, leading the way across the room to his desk.

'Detective Inspector Powell, may I introduce my sister, Claire Mitchell?'

The inspector offered Claire his hand. 'How do you do, Claire?'

'How do you do, Inspector? I've heard a lot about you.'

'Don't believe what your sister tells you.'

'Oh, but it was all good,' Claire said, laughing.

'And this,' Ena said, 'is WPC Jarvis.' The WPC smiled and put down a tray of coffee and biscuits on the DI's desk.

'Is there anything else, Sir?'

'No, thank you, Jarvis.' When the WPC had left, Ena poured three cups of coffee and the inspector gave Claire the envelope that Ena's murdered colleague, Sid Parfitt had left for her in the left luggage department at Waterloo Station.

While they drank their coffee, Claire looked through the photographs and newspaper cuttings.

'These are what Frieda Voight used to blackmail Sid into stealing information for her; first for the Germans and then the Russians.'

'No wonder he agreed to work for her,' Claire said. 'If these cuttings had found their way into the hands of

Special Branch, he'd still be in prison today.' Claire took a notebook and pen from her bag and began to write.

And he'd still be alive, Ena thought. 'He was more worried about his mother and sister seeing the photographs than he was going to jail.'

Claire picked up the magnifier and looked along the edges of several photographs. 'These have been expertly doctored. One photograph has been laid over another.' Claire put the photographs down and picked up the newspaper cuttings.

Looking quickly through them she made two piles. 'These,' she said, her hand on top of the first pile, 'appear to be more general. I'll read them properly when I've translated these.' She peered closely at the smaller of the two piles. 'Interesting. The reporting in these is more detailed, more specific. There are names of meeting places, towns and streets.' Claire flicked through several pages of the Berliner Tageblatt. 'Nothing much in this. I expect it's because the Tageblatt was a liberal paper. The Nazis closed it down in thirty-nine. Ah! This is more like it. Der Angriff or The Attack - a socialist propaganda paper. The Nazis were very proud of this paper and its sister rag...' Claire looked into the mid-distance thoughtfully. 'Its name escapes me but between the two papers the Nazis spread lies and hatred over the whole of Germany.' She looked up from the newspaper and said, 'Could I work on the table by the window, Inspector? Some of this print is difficult to read.'

'Of course.' The DI got up when Claire did and took her chair over to the table.

'I'll read Sid's letter again,' Ena said.

When he came back to his desk the inspector picked

up Sid's journal. 'Would you like me to read through this?'

'There's a lot of it.'

The DI looked at the clock on the wall opposite. 'I'll be called into a meeting in half an hour, but I can make a start. From what I remember reading last year, Berlin in thirty-six was interesting. So, if it's alright with you?'

'Be my guest. If you see anything you think is relevant, or you think I ought to read, make a note of the page number, would you?'

The inspector took a large notebook from the drawer in his desk. 'What are you looking for, specifically?'

'Names. Christian, surname, or both. Hang on, are the pages numbered? I can't remember.'

'No, should I number them as I go?'

'Good God no, Dick Bentley would have a heart attack.'

'He won't know. He'll have finished with it by now. He wouldn't have sent it over here if he hadn't.'

Ena screwed up her face. 'If you say so.'

'I'll use a fine pencil. The numbers will be so faint the old boy won't notice.'

Ena rummaged in her shoulder bag, took out a notepad and pen and began to read Sid's letter.

Half an hour later, immersed in Berlin 1936, Ena jumped when there was a knock at the door.

'Come.'

WPC Jarvis poked her head into the room. 'The meeting is about to start, Sir.'

'On my way, Jarvis,' the inspector called after her as she shut the door. He closed the journal, got up, and rotated his shoulders.

'Good timing. I've just finished Sid's letter. Did

you find anything interesting?' Ena asked, opening the journal.

'Some names. A few places. I've listed them on sheets of paper and put them in the journal as bookmarks.' DI Powell made no attempt to leave his office.

Ena looked up at him and groaned. 'We can't stay in here if you're not here, can we?'

'I'm afraid not.'

Claire put down her pen. 'I'm starving.' She jumped up and grabbed her coat from the back of the chair. 'We're meeting our sisters and our friend, Natalie Goldman, in a restaurant called Dooley's.'

'It's on the Strand, opposite the main entrance of The Prince Albert Theatre. If you finish your meeting in the next hour or so, come and join us. Meet the rest of the clan,' Ena said laughing.

'I might just do that.' The inspector opened his office door.

Ena put on her coat and threw her scarf around her neck. 'See you after lunch, if not before.'

'Unfortunately, I have another meeting and it's in here.'

Claire slipped the newspaper cuttings that she had read into the envelope leaving a couple of cuttings that she hadn't had time to read on the window sill. 'We could take these to the theatre.'

'And the journal,' Ena added, pulling it towards her. 'They'd be safe in Mrs Goldman's office. And we'd bring them back when we'd finished with them.'

The inspector reached across his desk, snapped the journal shut, and dropped it in his drawer. He gave Ena a look of disbelief and shook his head.

'We'd bring them back at the end of today,' Claire said.

The inspector raised his eyebrows. 'Your sister knows full well that I have given my word to the Director of the Home Office that the contents of the late Sid Parfitt's case will *not* leave this station,' he said pointedly. He looked again at the time. 'I really do have to go, but…' He sighed heavily. 'Come back this afternoon after two o'clock. Interview Room 1 is being used to store boxes awaiting transportation to The Met's archive facility. I can't vouch for the cleanliness of the room, but you won't be disturbed. The light isn't good, I'm afraid,' he said to Claire.

'I don't care. I'll bring a torch. As long as I can carry on translating.'

'I'll get PC Jarvis to take everything to Interview Room 1.' The inspector stepped briskly into the corridor. 'Now, I really must go.' Ushering Ena and Claire out of the room, he closed and locked the door.

'DI Powell is a good copper to have in your corner,' Claire said, as she and Ena left the station and crossed the road to Floral Street.

'He is. He's nice too.'

'Oh yes?'

Ena tutted. 'My husband is being held by Special Branch accused of murdering a spy who he worked with and you're suggesting I have romantic aspirations for a policeman? And not any old policeman, but the inspector in charge of the case.' Ena laughed, turned up the collar of her coat and batting her eyelids, looked coquettishly at her sister.

'A regular Mata Hari, eh?'

Ena laughed again. She took Claire by the arm and together they walked down Southampton Street and crossed the Strand. 'We're here,' she said, mounting the steps to Dooley's restaurant.

Ena caught sight of Bess, Margot and Natalie sitting at an oblong table at the back of the room and waved.

'We've only just ordered,' Bess said, beckoning the waiter, as Ena and Claire sat down.

The waiter gave Ena a menu. She looked at it and passed it to Claire. 'Tomato soup, and lamb chops with mash and carrots for me, please.'

'Make that two. Thanks,' Claire said, handing the

menu back to the waiter.

While they waited for their food, Bess brought Ena and Claire up to date with what they had done in the visitor's room at the theatre. 'We've cleaned and polished it to within an inch of its life. And we found some lovely pieces of furniture in the theatre's furniture store.' She marked each piece off on her fingers. 'There's an oval table that's big enough for all of us to sit around, two smaller tables, two padded benches, half a dozen chairs and a tall chest of drawers that locks, for paperwork we don't want anyone other than the five of us to see.'

'It will arrive sometime after four this afternoon,' Natalie said.

'And,' Margot added, 'courtesy of Natalie, we'll have a telephone.'

'That's amazing. You've done so much in such a short space of time.'

'We've not done badly,' Bess admitted. 'What about you two?'

'Well, I'm going through Sid's letter and journal again, writing down names and places. And Claire's translating the newspaper cuttings. We've made a decent start but we need to go back after we've eaten.'

'We'll have tables and chairs later. You could bring the stuff to the theatre and work from there.'

'Not possible, I'm afraid. Inspector Powell won't let us take the documents out of the station. Dick Bentley, my boss at the Home Office, only agreed to let the DI see the contents of Sid's case on the condition it didn't leave the police station.'

'God knows what he'd say if he knew I was translating the newspaper cuttings.'

'We don't have clearance to see it, let alone translate it. The inspector is putting his head on the line for us.' Ena shuddered. 'I dread to think what Dick Bentley would do if he knew I'd been at Bow Street today reading Sid's journal and letter.'

'But it was you who took the information to your boss at the Home Office in the first place, so he knows you've read it.'

'Yes, but he's stood me down. He gave me specific orders to stay away from the investigations. If he got wind that the inspector had allowed me to see the contents of the case again, he'd take the documents back and he'd report the inspector to the Chief Constable.' Ena shook her head. 'It isn't worth the risk. Anyway, I still have Sid's letter to me and quite a few photographs that I didn't give Bentley. We'll put what I have with what Claire's translating now and hopefully it will be enough for us to work with.'

'Ena's policeman is sticking his neck out letting us go back this afternoon.'

'He is not my policeman!'

The waiter arrived with Natalie, Bess and Margot's food and the women changed the conversation.

'Look who's here!' Ena waved at Inspector Powell as he entered the restaurant. She leapt out of her seat to greet him. 'Glad you could make it. Let me introduce you to my sisters. This is Margot. Margot, this is Detective Inspector Powell.'

The inspector took Margot's hand. 'It's a pleasure to meet. I saw you in several shows at The Prince Albert when I was home on leave during the war.'

'You must have been very young.'

The DI laughed. 'So must you.'

'This is our friend, Natalie Goldman.'

The inspector nodded. 'Hello, Mrs Goldman.'

'Good to see you again, Inspector.'

'And, last but by no means least, my sister Bess.'

'Pleased to meet you, Bess.'

'How do you do, Inspector?' Bess slid along the seat to make room for the DI to sit down. 'You'll join us, won't you?'

'Thank you, but I'm afraid I can't stay. Another time perhaps?'

The inspector looked flushed. Ena thought it was because he had come into the warm restaurant out of the cold afternoon air. She looked closer. He was perspiring. 'Is something wrong, Inspector?'

'Nothing to worry about,' he said to the assembled group of women, 'but if I could have a word in private, Ena?'

'Of course.'

Ena followed the inspector to a table on the far side of the room, away from the window. Neither sat down. 'Special Branch came to the station just after you and Claire left. They went to my office while I was in the meeting and put the photographs and newspaper cuttings in Sid Parfitt's bag, taped it up and left.'

'But you locked your office. I saw you.'

'WPC Jarvis was in there. She was putting the photographs and cuttings into the Gladstone bag before taking it to Interview Room 1. Special Branch relieved her of it.'

'Why would they do that? You're working the case with them for goodness sake. You have clearance from the Director of the Home Office.' Ena caught her breath. 'Do you think they knew Claire and I had been at the station? We might have been followed when we left the flat this morning. I was careful. I didn't see a tail, but it has happened before.'

'I don't think they knew you'd been there, but it was my fault.' The inspector frowned. 'I told Alan

Richardson; the Special Branch DI I'm working with, that I didn't think Henry had killed Helen Crowther. He banged on about the evidence and I told him that in my opinion it was planted and that I believed Henry had been framed. Before I left his office, Richardson asked me if I knew you. I told him I did and I assured him that knowing you had no bearing on my findings, nor would it have on the investigation.'

'You're not off the investigation, are you?'

'No, but DI Richardson is a stickler for protocol. He'll have reported back to his bosses at the Branch and they probably don't trust me now.'

'They know they can't manipulate you, more like.'

'Maybe. Richardson is a good policeman, but I now know not to voice my opinion if it differs from his.' The inspector gave Ena a serious but sympathetic look. 'I'm sorry, but you're going to have to stay away from the station. I need to toe the line for a while and win back the Branch's trust.'

'I understand.' Ena scrunched up her shoulders. 'Well, that's that then. Bloody Special Branch has the most important newspaper cuttings with Crowther and O'Shaughnessy on the Hitler march.'

The DI smiled. 'Actually, they don't. WPC Jarvis said she was so shocked when the men from Special Branch barged into my office that she dropped the newspaper cuttings that Claire had left on the window sill. They became stuck between the leg of the table and the wall. She didn't want to make a fuss and left them there until the men had gone.' The inspector took a brown leather handbag out of his briefcase. 'I think this belongs to you. Jarvis said you left it in her office?'

Ena smiled at the inspector. 'If I wasn't a married woman, I would kiss you right here,' she said. She cleared her throat and put on a serious face. 'Thank you, Inspector, I wondered where I had left my handbag.' Ena clutched the bag to her. 'Be sure to thank WPC Jarvis for me, won't you? Tell her it was kind of her to look after it. And,' Ena said, biting her bottom lip to stop herself from laughing out loud, '*thank you* for bringing it to me.'

Ena saw a flicker of a smile in the DI's hazel eyes. 'Make sure you take better care of your belongings in the future, Mrs Green,' the inspector said. He then whispered, 'It not only contains the cuttings of Crowther on the rally, it also contains the journal.'

'Oh my… You took the journal off me and put it in the drawer of your desk.'

The inspector threw his head back and laughed. 'That's why Special Branch didn't see it. Bit of luck, eh?'

'I should say. So,' Ena said, 'how long have we got?'

'Until six o'clock tonight.'

'That doesn't give us much time. Claire and I had better get back to the theatre. There's still a lot to do.'

'I'm sorry I can't give you more time. I'll tell Richardson I was in a meeting till five-thirty. I shall also tell him I'm not happy that his agents barged into my office unannounced, and if he'd had the courtesy to inform me they were coming, I'd have been there to give them *all* the Home Office's documents. I'll telephone Special Branch before I leave and, because the documents are classified top secret, I'll tell Richardson I'll take them to Whitehall personally.' The inspector looked at his watch. 'I'll be at the stage door at six.'

'I'll be waiting for you.' Ena laughed. 'Taking what the Branch's goons forgot will go some way to getting them to trust you again, won't it?'

'We'll see.'

The inspector left the restaurant and Ena returned to her sisters.

'What was that all about,' Margot asked when Ena sat down.

'The newspaper cuttings are in this bag,' she whispered.

'What?'

'It's a long story.' Ena took a drink of her coffee and grimaced. It had gone cold.

'Do you want another cup?' Bess asked.

'No, there isn't time. We have these until six o'clock tonight,' she said, turning to Claire. 'We need to go. Will you pay our share of the bill, Bess? We'll square up with you later.'

'Of course, you go.'

'Is the visitor's room open, Natalie?'

'It is, but there'll be a lot of coming and going this afternoon. Use my office. I don't need it until this evening.' Natalie took a keyring from her handbag and took a key from it. 'You won't be disturbed.'

'Right, Claire,' Ena said, 'Let's go, we have work to do.'

CHAPTER THIRTEEN

Ena and Claire had been working in Natalie Goldman's office for two hours - Ena, reading her late colleague Sid's journal from Berlin 1936, listing names and making notes, Claire, translating German press cuttings into English - when there was a knock at the door. Ena got up and unlocked it.

'I thought you might like some refreshment.' Natalie said, handing her a tray.

'Tea? You must be psychic, Natalie. I'm parched. And biscuits too. That'll keep us going for a while.'

Natalie looked at her watch. 'It's five o'clock. You have an hour,' she said and left. Ena put the tray on the table, returned to the door and turned the key in the lock.

'Ena, look at this.'

'Crowther and O'Shaughnessy on a Nazi rally. What does it say?'

'Ignore the people to the right of Crowther and O'Shaughnessy. If we assume the names beneath the photograph are listed from left to right - Crowther is Frau Krueger and O'Shaughnessy is Herr Krueger.'

'So her real name is Krueger?'

'And she was married in thirty-six when this photograph was taken.'

'O'Shaughnessy has the same name. He must be her brother. She isn't old enough to have a son of his age, is she?'

There was another knock at the door. Ena jumped up and unlocked it.

'Sorry to disturb you again, but the theatre photographer has been here taking photographs of the cast for the display cases out front and I thought, as time is running out, this might be of help.' Natalie gave Ena a camera. 'He's having a cuppa in the green room. You've got it for as long as you need it. Or, for the next thirty-five minutes. Oh, and you'll need these.' Natalie took four flashbulbs from her pocket.

'Natalie, you're a star.' Ena gave the camera and bulbs to Claire. When she turned back to the door, Natalie had gone.

'I haven't got much more to translate,' Claire said, 'ten minutes should do it, so let's take a photograph of the cutting with Crowther's face on it.' Claire looked around the room. 'The writing blotter will do as backing.' She took the blotter from Natalie's desk and stood it up on the table. 'Hold it at an angle, Ena. Good.' Claire leant the newspaper cutting with the photograph against it. 'That's good.' Looking through the lens of the camera, she pushed down the button on top and the bulb flashed taking both women by surprise.

'I'll photograph the other cutting too. I don't think there's anyone important on it, but you never know.' She took out the hot melting bulb and replaced it with a new one. Ena held the second cutting in the way she'd held the first and Claire snapped it.

'The photographer coming to the theatre today was a bit of luck. I wonder if he develops photographs too.'

'It won't be easy explaining why we need photos of German newspaper cuttings.'

'It won't, but better him than a nosy manager of a photographic shop on the high street.'

'How are you getting on with the journal?'

'Well. I didn't read the Olympic stuff again. It isn't as important as far as Crowther is concerned. And I have the letter Sid wrote to me at home. As it's personal, I didn't give it to Dick Bentley. So,' Ena blew out her cheeks, 'I'll look through the last half dozen pages again in case I've missed anything.' She flicked through to the end of the journal. 'No. I've made a note of everything that I believe to be important.'

Ena closed Sid's journal and returned it to the leather handbag that Inspector Powell had given it to her in.

'That's me done!' Claire put down her pen and placed the newspaper cuttings on top of the journal.

Ena snapped the bag shut and took a deep breath. 'So, if that's all?' Claire nodded. 'I'll take this to the stage door.'

'I'll straighten Natalie's office and take the camera back to the visitor's room. See you in there.'

Ena followed the green fluorescent dots on the floor along a labyrinth of backstage passages that the artists referred to as the 'rabbit warren' to the stage door. She arrived with a couple of minutes to spare. The nerves on the top of her stomach fluttered with excitement. She couldn't wait to read Claire's translations of the Berlin newspaper cuttings. Waiting at the stage door, she watched the second hand on the wall clock in Stan's office circle the moonlike face twice.

'Is there something I can help you with, Mrs Green?' Stan asked, looking through the open hatch of his small office.

'No thank you, Stan. I'm waiting for the inspector. He said he'd be here at six.' She looked at the clock again. It was dead on six.

A steady stream of young people came through the door chatting, some in winter coats, boots and hats, with scarves wrapped around the lower part of their faces. Singers, Ena thought, scarves over their mouths to stop the cold air from getting to their throats and chests. Some, young men mostly, dressed more flamboyantly, skipped in. Dancers Ena mused. She was watching a young man demonstrate dance steps to one of the girls when she felt someone tap her on her shoulder.

'Inspector? You startled me.'

The DI laughed. 'You were miles away.'

'I was.' Ena sighed. 'Oh, to be young and free with songs and dances to look forward to instead of...'

'A date with Special Branch.'

Ena pulled an unhappy face. 'Rather you than me.'

'I'd better get going. I hope this was helpful, Ena.'

'I couldn't begin to tell you how helpful.'

'Good.' The inspector glanced at the stage doorman and saluted. Stan saluted back. 'I'll let you know if we have a breakthrough in the investigation.'

'And I'll let you know,' Ena said. 'Claire has found Helen Crowther's real name. We think O'Shaughnessy must be her brother. If not her brother, he's related to her in some way. They have the same surname - Krueger.'

'Could he be her son?'

'That's what I wondered. I don't know how old O'Shaughnessy is, but he must be in his mid-to-late-thirties and she's only fifty-something. She'd have been very young when she had him.' Ena gave the inspector the handbag. 'Where's your briefcase?'

'In the car.' He put the handle of the bag over his wrist and swung his arm from side to side.

Ena shook her head and laughed. 'I hope the meeting with Special Branch goes well and you regain the confidence of the agent you're working with.'

The inspector took the bag from his wrist and tucked it under his arm. 'I'm sure it will. Goodbye, Ena.'

Ena watched the DI leave. She liked him. He was

on her side in the Crowther investigation as he had been when she had investigated Frieda Voight.

Waving her thanks to Stan, Ena followed the fluorescent dobs of paint back along the corridors to the visitor's room. She hardly recognised it from the dusty empty space she had left that morning. A large round table dominated the room. There were a couple more desks on the far wall, new curtains at the windows and rugs scattered on the wood floor.

'Did you tell Bess what we discovered?' Ena asked, Claire.

'Yes. And she agrees with me that Frau Krueger, Helen Crowther as you know her, looks older than she says she is.'

'I wonder what her age is on her MI5 ID?'

'Do we have any way of finding out?'

'I don't. But...' Ena said thoughtfully, 'Inspector Powell will have. Damn it! I told him Crowther's real name was Krueger. I should have asked him how old she was. He'll have seen her ID when she was killed.'

'We can't do anything about Frau what's-her-name tonight,' Margot said, 'so who's up for a winter warmer, a quick snifter, at The Salisbury?'

The room was suddenly silent. Ena looked at Bess and raised her eyebrows.

'I'm not talking about me drinking, but I'd like to see what the old place looks like these days.'

'Alright,' Bess said, 'I could do with a drink. It's been a dusty day.'

'Then let's go.' Ena looked round. 'Where's Natalie?'

'Gone up to wardrobe,' Margot said, 'a problem with one of the costumes. I'll go up and tell her where we're going. Won't be a tick.'

'I don't want to take these to The Salisbury,' Claire announced, taking half a dozen large sheets of writing paper that she had folded in half from her handbag. She opened the top drawer of the wooden cabinet and dropped them in.

'Put this in too,' Ena said, handing Claire her notebook. 'Better be safe than risk having them stolen.'

Claire turned the key in the lock. Once she was satisfied the drawer was secure, she pushed the small brass key deep into the sugar bowl. 'There.' She gave the dish a shake and the white granules found their own level.

Bess pulled a disapproving face.

'What? It's as good a place as any to hide the key,' Claire said.

'I'm not saying it isn't, but it's not very hygienic.'

'It doesn't have to be, does it? None of us takes sugar.'

As the sisters began to laugh, Margot returned. 'What's going on?'

'Just Claire being right as usual,' Ena said, in fun.

'Glad someone is,' Margot took her coat from the coat stand. 'Natalie isn't coming to The Salisbury, she has work to do. She said she'll be here until about nine. If we're not back by then, she'll see us at home, Bess.'

'Are you alright to walk there, Margot?'

'Of course.' She leant on her stick in the way Charlie Chaplin did. 'We're only going to St. Martin's Lane. It's a stone's throw away.'

'If you're sure.'

Margot gave her sister a bored look and sighed. 'Alright, I'll leave the car here.'

'I'll leave mine here too.'

Coats buttoned up and belted, scarves and gloves

on, hats pulled down to keep out the cold wind and the damp city air, the sisters walked the short distance to St. Martin's Lane.

'Margot, you and Bess go in first. Claire and I will follow in a while.'

'We shouldn't sit together either.'

'Best if we don't know each other.'

'Don't drink too much and keep your ears open.'

'And, Margot, when you've had enough, love, let me know and we'll leave,' Bess said. 'Claire and Ena will stay.'

Margot rolled her eyes at Bess. 'Yes, mum.'

'Right. Are we ready?'

Bess nodded. 'Let's go.'

'See you tomorrow morning for a debrief,' Claire said, as Bess and Margot crossed St. Martin's Lane. A few seconds later they disappeared into The Salisbury. Ena and Claire continued down St. Martin's Lane as far as Trafalgar Square. By the time they had walked back, ten minutes or more had passed, and they entered the warm, dark, smoky saloon bar of The Salisbury.

CHAPTER FOURTEEN

Chatting about their day, the office, or whether to buy this hat or that, Ena and Claire entered The Salisbury without a care in the world. Looking just as if they were out for a drink after work, or before going to a show in one of the nearby theatres, they strolled into the pub and crossed the room to the bar.

'Two whisky macs, please.' When the barman returned with the drinks, Ena took a pound note from her purse and gave it to him. She handed one glass of whisky and ginger wine to Claire and when the barman gave her the change, she asked where the ladies toilets were.

'On your left, madam,' he said, pointing to the end of the horseshoe-shaped bar.

'Thanks. Shan't be minute,' she said to Claire.

On her way to the toilet, Ena scanned the room, observing as many people as she could. Sudden raucous laughter stopped her in her tracks. She spun round. She could have sworn the exaggerated guffaw was O'Shaughnessy's theatrical roar. She looked in the direction of the merriment. Three men, already the worse for wear, were toasting each other. O'Shaughnessy wasn't one of them.

Ena slipped into the 'Ladies', held the door slightly ajar and searched the faces of the men at the bar. She saw no one she knew. After using the toilet and washing her hands, she powdered her nose and added a layer of lipstick. A strand of hair fell onto her forehead. She quickly wound it around her finger and pushed it into place, securing it with a Kirby grip.

Leaving the toilet, she crossed the saloon bar making a note of everyone on her left. She didn't recognise anyone. She looked to her right, no one she knew there either. On the far side of the room, sitting with their backs to the wall, she spotted Bess and Margot. They were talking to a couple of city types in pinstriped suits. Bess looked over the shoulder of the man sitting opposite her and Ena caught her eye. She looked away.

'Recognise anyone?' Claire asked, when she returned to the bar.

'No.' She drank her whisky and ginger wine. It slid down her throat effortlessly, warming her as it went.

'Another?'

Claire nodded to the barman. 'Two whisky macs please.' She half-turned as if she was miles away, or maybe impatient, and glanced across the room. Margot and Bess were leaving.

'The girls have just left,' Claire said.

'Do you want to go home, or shall we have a drink at The Lamb and Flag?'

'We might as well have one at The Lamb as it's nearby.'

'Okay. I'll grab Bess and Margot's seats. You bring the drinks over.' It wasn't as easy to see the faces of The Salisbury's customers from a sitting position, but Ena's feet ached. She'd been standing in high heels for too long.

'It feels good to take the weight off,' Claire said, putting the drinks on the small table and sitting down. 'See anyone you know?'

Ena sipped her replenished whisky mac and looked over the rim of the glass. 'No one I know, or have even seen before.'

Ten minutes later, having finished their drinks, Ena and Claire left The Salisbury and walked the short distance to The Lamb and Flag in Rose Street.

'It's my round,' Ena said.

Before she had time to ask Claire what she wanted to drink, a familiar voice said, 'Mine's a gin.'

'Artie!' Ena threw her arms around her colleague. 'What a happy coincidence.'

'Happy, but not a coincidence. I went to see Director Bentley's secretary, *again,* to ask her when she was going to send the files over to our office. She said they'd been sent to the police inspector in charge of the Crowther murder investigation and promised to let me know as soon as she got them back.'

'Which she won't because they've gone to Special Branch.'

Artie blew out his cheeks. 'That means we'll never see them, then.'

'You still haven't said how you knew we were here.'

'I went to see the lovely Inspector Powell, but he wasn't there. So, I decided to go for a drink at The Salisbury. I cut through Maiden Lane and saw your car by the stage door of The Prince Albert. Then, to my delight, I saw your sister, Margot, getting into a car next to yours. She told me you'd all been to The Salisbury, and by now you'd probably be here. So,' Artie put his hands up, 'here I am.'

Ena hugged Artie again. 'Artie, this is my sister Claire. Claire, this is my dear, dear, work colleague, Artie Mallory.'

They exchanged greetings and when they had their drinks found a corner table with a good view of the room, but where they wouldn't be overheard.

Artie told Ena and Claire everything that had happened since he had moved into the new office, which was nowhere near as much as Ena had planned before Christmas.

Ena was more guarded with her information. It

wasn't that she didn't trust Artie, it was that she couldn't tell him that DI Powell was helping her. Artie knew about Sid's journal, the photographs used to blackmail him, and the newspaper cuttings of Helen Crowther and Shaun O'Shaughnessy on Nazi rallies. Except for Helen Crowther's real name, he knew as much as she did - until she was able to read the newspaper translations.

'A name connected to Helen Crowther has cropped up, Artie. I can't remember seeing it in our files, but you may have. Frau Krueger? Do you recognise it.'

Artie's eyes narrowed in thought. 'It sounds familiar.' He repeated the name several times. 'I've seen it somewhere, but I don't think it was Frau. I think it was Herr Krueger.'

'A man? Could it be the real name of O'Shaughnessy?'

'No. At least I don't think so. He'd have been too young when Hitler was Chancellor. Old enough to be on Hitler youth marches and rallies, but... No, I've got a feeling the man with that name was in the military. I'll go through the Nazi files tomorrow. If we have Herr Krueger on file, I'll find him.'

'Krueger is quite a common name in north-eastern Germany,' Claire said.

'But worth checking.' Ena lifted her glass. 'Cheers, Artie!' She turned to Claire and again said, 'Cheers!'

They sat and chatted and every now and then one of them glanced round to see if they recognised anyone. They didn't. Ena told Artie about Frieda's funeral, about Highsmith who covered the 1936 Olympics in Berlin with Sid being there, and told him what Highsmith had said about Henry.

'I didn't like him much after reading Sid's journal, I thought he was arrogant. After meeting him I know he is arrogant.'

'He said he worked at GCHQ,' Claire said. 'It won't be too difficult to find out about him.'

'It won't be difficult at all. I have a good friend at Cheltenham,' Artie replied. 'Hugh Middleton, an old pal I was at school with, has been at GCHQ for a couple of years now. We used to get together every so often. I'll give him a call, meet him for lunch and find out what he knows about Rupert Highsmith.'

Aware that she and Claire had a great deal of work to do the following day, Ena said it was time she and her sister went home.

'I think I'll go on to the Blue Beau in Mayfair for a nightcap. It's *the* place for gossip. If the conversations you overhear in there are to be believed, half the customers work for British intelligence, the other half are Russian spies. And,' Artie said with a twinkle in his eye, 'you never know, I might bump into Mr High-and-mighty Smith.'

Ena wondered about Highsmith's preferences in sexual partners and hoped that, if he was homosexual, he didn't take advantage of Artie. Highsmith was not a nice character. She didn't want to put Artie in danger. 'Promise me you'll be careful.'

Artie saluted and grinned.

Leaving The Lamb and Flag, Ena and Claire walked the short distance to Garrick Street where Artie hailed a cab to take him to Mayfair and Ena and Claire walked on to Maiden Lane, where they picked up the car.

Ena kicked off her shoes. They were soaking. 'Not the footwear for this weather.'

Claire stuffed her gloves into the pockets of her coat, took it off and hung it up. She bent down and took off her boots. 'These have sheepskin linings. You should get a pair.' She yawned. 'I'm going to the bathroom and then to bed. Night, night,' she said, standing her boots in the corner of the hall.

Ena took off her coat, hung it up and pushed open the sitting-room door. The room was cold. It was bound to be. There hadn't been a fire since the night before. She was tired, but too cold to sleep. She took a box of matches from the side of the fire, knelt down and took out a match. She struck it and held it against the plaited newspaper. The draft from the chimney pulled on the flames and soon the dry kindling on top of the paper caught. Pleased, now that she had gone to the trouble to lay a fire before she left for The Prince Albert that morning, Ena leaned against the seat of the armchair. Warming her feet by the fire, she watched as the flames flickered up the back of the chimney creating sparks like stars in the soot. Her eyes felt heavy and she closed them.

A loud knock on the front door woke her. 'Who the dickens is calling at this hour?' She heard Claire's bedroom door open. Stockwell wasn't the safest place, especially after dark. She looked at the clock on the mantelshelf. It was a quarter to midnight. She didn't want Claire answering the door at this hour. 'I'll get it, Claire.' She pulled open the sitting-room door. 'Henry!'

Ena flew into her husband's arms. She was shaking with emotion. 'Thank God the Branch has let you go. Do they know who killed Helen Crowther?'

Henry's jaw dropped. 'Helen Crowther is dead?'

Ena saw the shock in Henry's eyes. 'Yes. The Met and Special Branch think you killed her.'

CHAPTER FIFTEEN

Henry took a step backwards. 'Me, kill Helen Crowther? Why would I kill her?'

'Wasn't it because of Helen Crowther that Special Branch came up to Foxden on Boxing Night and took you back to London?'

'Yes, but not because she was dead. They told me it was because of my relationship with her and Mac Robinson. I assumed it was because Mac had been murdered and you'd discovered Crowther was the mole at MI5.'

'They said that?'

'Not in so many words. They led me to believe that because I had worked for Mac - and in doing so, for Helen - I was able to help them to nail her.'

'But you knew I was investigating the mole at MI5.'

'Which is why I knew they were lying. It crossed my mind that they thought I was part of Crowther's spy ring, but I dismissed it.'

'You? That's as preposterous as thinking McKenzie Robinson was a spy.'

'Good God!' Henry hung his head. His eyes glistened. He was near to tears.

'What is it, darling?'

'They were on a fishing expedition. As I didn't know Crowther was dead, I told them everything I knew about her; answered all their questions in the hopes something would come to mind to help them with their investigation.' Henry's face hardened. The muscles in his jaw tensed. 'And all the time the bastards were trying to frame me for her murder.'

Ena shivered. 'Let's go into the sitting room.' She took Henry by the hand. 'Do you want a drink?'

'Yes, a large one.'

The room had warmed up. Ena took a bottle of whisky and two glasses from the sideboard cupboard and poured them each a double. She gave Henry a glass, put the bottle on the coffee table in front of the fire and sat down on the settee.

They drank in silence. Henry stood in front of the fire for a couple of minutes before joining her. 'Do you know when Helen Crowther was killed?'

Ena reached for the bottle of scotch and topped up their glasses. 'December the twenty-third.'

'That's why they think I killed her. I was in London on the twenty-third, I didn't drive up to Foxden until Christmas Eve.'

'She was killed in my old cold case office on Mercer Street, but her body wasn't found until Boxing Day, which is why Special Branch came to Foxden that night and took you away.'

'Crowther, killed in your old office?' Henry's question didn't require an answer. He ran his hand through his hair. 'How do you know all this?'

'I came home the next day and you weren't here, so I went to Leconfield House. You weren't there either. I didn't know what to do, so I went to the Home Office to see Dick Bentley. I didn't get to see him because Artie had left a message for me at reception telling me to go to Mercer Street. When I arrived, the office had been broken into and the police were there. DI Powell walked me through what he and Special Branch thought had happened.'

'Go on.'

'There was a table and two chairs in the middle of the room. One chair was lying on its side next to the chalk outline of a body.'

'Crowther's body?'

'Yes. On the table was a bottle of Teacher's whisky

and two glasses.'

'And the bottle and glasses had my fingerprints on them?'

'Yes.'

Henry knocked back his scotch. 'Someone went to a great deal of trouble to make it look like I killed her.'

'She died from cyanide poisoning.'

'Which had no doubt been put in our whisky.'

'In a glass.'

'I had a couple of drinks the night before I came up to Foxden. I washed the glass and put it in the cupboard. So,' Henry exhaled a cynical laugh, 'only my fingerprints were on one of the glasses.'

'Which someone walked in and took late on Christmas Eve, according to Mr Grimes.'

'And that's why Claire is here?'

'Bess and Margot are here too. They're staying with Natalie Goldman.'

Henry laughed. 'If the Dudley sisters are on the case, I can't see Crowther's killer getting away with her murder.'

'They won't if I have anything to do with it.'

Henry leaned forward and kissed Ena. 'Be careful, darling. Whoever killed Crowther knows what they're doing.'

'So do I! And, so does Inspector Powell, who, by the way, doesn't believe you killed Crowther. Like me, he thinks you were framed.'

Henry stroked Ena's hair. 'What does Dick Bentley think?'

'He banged on about evidence and took me off the case. That's why the girls came down; to help me investigate. And,' she said, taking Henry's hand, '*we* have discovered things about Helen Crowther that neither the Home Office nor Special Branch know.'

'Ena, you don't know who you're dealing with. Let Powell and the Branch investigate. These people are dangerous.'

'Don't start, Henry! I won't stop, so you might as well save your breath.' Ena put her glass on the table, moved closer to Henry and kissed him. 'I don't want to spend our first night together after such a long time arguing. I suppose you'll be going to Leconfield House tomorrow.'

'I won't be going into work tomorrow.' Henry drained his glass, got up and put the guard in front of the fire. 'Let's go to bed.'

Ena snuggled up to her husband. His arms tightened around her, she felt his warm breath on her cheek and wriggled down the bed until her head was resting on his chest. He kissed the top of her head. One of his hands was in the small of her back, the other caressing her. Was she dreaming? It felt so real. She raised her head, lifted her face to his and opened her eyes. 'Henry?'

'Shush.'

'Henry, I…'

Henry put his forefinger to Ena's lips, replacing it almost immediately with his mouth. As he kissed her, Ena felt an urgency in the pit of her stomach; a need to have the man she loved take her - and she arched her back. Henry lifted her to him and without speaking they made love as passionately as they had when they were first married; when they were hungry for each other.

'I can't believe you're here,' Ena whispered, spent and out of breath. 'I thought it would be weeks until I saw you again.'

Henry reached out and took his cigarettes and

lighter from the bedside cabinet. He offered the packet to Ena. She shook her head and stroked his chest. He took one for himself, lit it, and inhaled. When he returned the cigarettes and lighter to the cabinet, he exhaled a long stream of smoke before turning and facing her. 'It might be weeks, or even months before you see me again, darling.'

Ena's eyes filled with tears. 'But you said…'

'I said I wasn't going into work tomorrow. And I'm not. I don't know how long Special Branch will keep me in custody.'

'Custody? What do you mean?' Ena said, blinking back her tears.

'I've been detained, for want of a better word. I was in one of our London safe houses. They're moving me to the country tonight.' A short cynical laugh escaped Henry's lips. 'Now I know why Frieda Voight hated me so much.'

'Is it awful?'

'Yes, it is. It's in what Frieda called, the middle of nowhere. The nearest village is two miles away. It's a stone cottage surrounded by several acres of woodland. The kind of place you'd imagine Little Red Riding Hood's granny to live in. It's old with a thatched roof and dog roses growing over the front door.'

'It sounds pretty.'

'It's far from that. The only access to it is along a rutted dirt track off a country lane. Low ceilings and narrow windows keep the interior permanently dark. The furniture's old. It's comfortable enough, but it would look better in the Lord of the manor's house, the rooms in the cottage are far too small, and it's damp. Condensation runs down the kitchen and bathroom walls.' Henry took a drag of his cigarette. 'A requisite of all the Special Branch's safe houses, except the safe house in Holland Park, which is where they kept me until tonight.'

'You've been staying at the house in Dean's Crescent?'

'Yes.'

'Wasn't that where Frieda lived with the Russian diplomat I saw her with in Oxford Street, the one who died?'

'Yes. She hated it there too.'

'How could she have hated living in such a gorgeous big townhouse in a lovely part of London?'

'Because she was wasn't allowed to go out, not even to the park opposite. She'd escaped the day you saw her in Oxford Street. She went down to the kitchen, told the housemaid she felt faint and needed air. The girl opened the back door and put a chair by it for Frieda to sit on. After a while Frieda said she felt a little better but she was cold. The silly girl went upstairs to get her coat and when she got back, Frieda had scarpered leaving a note saying, *Gone clothes shopping. Don't wait up*. Clothes shopping?' Henry laughed. 'The woman had more clothes in that Holland Park safe house than Grace Kelly, Audrey Hepburn and Coco Chanel put together.'

'I can't imagine being locked in anywhere. It must be awful, knowing you can't leave the place.' Ena shuddered.

'That's why they're called safe houses. While you're there, locked in, you're safe. Once you leave, you're not. Nor are the people looking after you.'

'Was it because of Frieda that the diplomat died?'

'Yes. He was working for us.'

'The papers said he'd had a heart attack.'

'That's what the police report said. Thanks to Frieda going AWOL the Russians found out about the house,

101

as you did. They were after Frieda, but we'd moved her by then. She wasn't at Dean's Crescent, but Sergi Romanovski was and they killed him.'

'Did they know he was working for the British?'

'Not until they saw him at the safe house.'

Henry eased himself up onto his elbow and stubbed out his cigarette. 'I have to go.'

'Can't you stay a little bit longer?'

'I shouldn't be here at all. I persuaded the bloke driving me to make a detour.'

'Will he report back that you came home.'

'He wouldn't dare. He owes me a favour. He was caught with his pants around his ankles in the back of a club when he first joined the Branch. He made a stupid mistake. He was drunk. He said it was the first time; the only time he'd compromised himself. It would have cost him his job so I ditched the file for him.' Henry kissed Ena on her forehead. 'I'd better grab some clean clothes and go. I don't want him coming to get me, which he will if I'm not out of here soon. I'll take enough clothes for a few weeks.'

Ena pushed herself up into a sitting position. She looked into her husband's eyes. 'Be careful?'

'You know me. I'm always careful.' Henry swung his legs over the side of the bed, picked up his underpants from the floor and pulled them on.

'Leave your dirty clothes here. You've clean ones in the drawer.' Ena jumped out of bed and put on her dressing gown. While Henry took a case from the bottom of the wardrobe, she took clean socks, underpants, and shirts from the tallboy and placed them on top of the trousers and jumpers that Henry had already placed in the case. She went to the bathroom, returning with shaving soap and brush, razor and an assortment of Henry's toiletries.

He took them from her, dropped them into the case and closed it. 'I must go.'

'I'll see you out.'

'No. I want you to stay here.'

Ena's heart was drumming. She felt anxious and sick with worry. 'I don't want you to go.'

'You know I have to.'

'Then at least let me come with you to the door. I want to spend as many seconds with you as I can, before…'

Henry took Ena by the hand and led her back to the bed. 'And I want to think of you in our bed, waiting for me until the next time I persuade Bozo to bring me home.'

Ena dropped onto the bed. She looked at him through her tears. 'He won't bring you home again, will he?'

Henry didn't answer. He picked up his case and opened the bedroom door. Before leaving he looked back. He looked sad, but he smiled. Ena wanted to run to him and beg him not to leave, but that would make their parting even harder. Instead, she sat up and forced herself to smile back. Neither spoke. There was nothing more to say.

Ena heard the front door close and ran from the bedroom to the sitting room. Without putting on the light she made her way to the window. Aware there was light in the room from the fire, she opened one curtain an inch and peered out. A man, taller than Henry and twice as wide, got out of a dark saloon car. He took Henry's case and stood it on the ground. What he did next shook Ena. Henry held out his arms, made loose fists of his hands and put them together, then the man clasped handcuffs around his wrists, opened the back door of the car and waited for Henry to lower himself onto the back seat. He slammed the door shut and took Henry's case to the back of the car, threw it into the boot, and returned to the front of the car. Opening the driver's door the man's bulk disappeared inside. A second later the car's headlights came on, the car pulled out into the road and motored south along St. Michael's Square. A second later it was gone.

Ena's head began to spin. She felt dizzy and lightheaded as if she was going to faint. She let go of the curtain, turned her back on the window, and gripped the backrest of the settee. The pain she felt was intense. She wanted to scream. She stood for some minutes breathing deeply. She told herself the feeling would pass. 'Breathe,' she said, 'breathe.'

When she had calmed down, she crossed to the fireplace, put a log on the dying embers and sat in the armchair. When the first flickers of flame wrapped themselves around the log, she replaced the fireguard and tiptoed back to her bedroom. She crawled into Henry's side of the bed and buried her face in his pillow. She inhaled his scent. A combination of sandalwood shaving soap and perspiration from their lovemaking filled her nostrils. She pulled down his pillow until it nestled between her head and her shoulders and pulled up the bedclothes. Wrapped in what remained of her husband, Ena closed her eyes.

Unable to sleep, Ena rolled over and lay on her back. She had no idea what time it was. The dull grey light of another winter dawn crept into the room above the curtain rail and Ena sighed. It would soon be morning. She stared at the shadows on the ceiling and reminded herself of everything that she and Henry had talked about in the sitting room. Then, the memory of their love making filled her heart and her mind, and tears filled her eyes.

Aware that her bedroom door had opened and was now closing, Ena called, 'Come in, Claire.'

'I hope I didn't wake you?'

'I couldn't sleep after Henry left.'

Claire put a tray with two cups of tea and a plate of buttered toast on the bed. 'I thought you might like a cuppa. Tea and toast are what I call comfort food,' Claire said. She passed Ena a cup of tea and a plate.

'Thanks.'

When they had finished eating, Ena told Claire everything that Henry had told her. 'I can't believe Special Branch would think Henry was a spy. He's what Five calls, a 'straight arrow'. He always has been. And, to suggest his late boss, McKenzie Robinson was a spy too.' Ena shook her head. 'The Branch is so far off the mark with Henry and with Mac…'

Claire was deep in thought. 'What is it?'

'You told me if it was leaked in the security services that Helen Crowther was the mole at MI5 - and there wasn't time to get her out of the country - whoever she worked for would have to kill her.'

'I don't know if that happened in Crowther's case, but it's what usually happens. When a spy's cover is blown, they're a liability to themselves and to the rest of the cell. Whoever she worked for wouldn't take the risk she'd keep her mouth shut.' Ena scoffed. 'Knowing Crowther, she would rather die than betray her fellow spies.'

Claire shook her head in disbelief. 'How was it possible for a German spy to get a job with the boss of a military intelligence agency like MI5?'

'It wouldn't have been difficult before the war. Not if she had the right qualifications and references. Henry said Five and Six were hard pushed to get good people to work in the intelligence services in the thirties and forties.

'There were rumblings that Hitler was itching for a war ten years before it actually started. The security agencies were up to their eyes trying to recruit good people. Being an intelligent woman - and she was highly intelligent - they'd have thought they were lucky to get her.

'Crowther would have started working in McKenzie Robinson's office as a clerk or a secretary and worked her way up to being his personal assistant. She was always at Mac's side. She knew as much about military security as he did. I can see why Special Branch questioned Henry about the likelihood of Mac being a spy.

'When I stayed at her house, Crowther hinted that she'd had an affair with Mac. I knew by the way she looked when she was telling me, the way she smiled and her eyes softened, that for her it was more than an affair. She was in love with him.'

'That would have conflicted with her work as a spy.'

'It would, but she loved him, alright.'

'And Mac?'

'Even if he had been in love with Crowther, he wouldn't have left Eve. He'd have lived with the heartbreak rather than put her through the shame of a divorce.'

'Is she Catholic?'

'I've no idea. But Mac was a good man, a decent man. He would have thrown himself into work.' Ena brushed away her tears with the back of her hand. 'It's so unfair. He trusted that bloody woman and it cost him his life.'

'Hey, come on, love. We don't know that.'

'I'm bloody sure of it.'

'Okay, but for now, let's concentrate on what we know. We know Henry didn't kill Crowther.'

'Special Branch don't know that. Or do they? DI Powell's counterpart at the Branch shot him down when he told them he thought Henry had been framed.'

Claire shook her head. 'Does the Branch think Henry killed Crowther, and they're trying to catch him out? Are the agents interrogating him hoping he'll say something to incriminate himself?'

Ena gasped. 'Or, did someone in the security services kill her and they're trying to fit Henry up?'

'At least now he knows why he's being held.'

'Yes, and Special Branch doesn't know he knows?'

Claire looked at Ena questioningly.

'What is it?'

'The guy who brought him here must know you'd tell Henry.'

'He won't say anything. He was caught in a compromising position some years ago and Henry *lost* his file.'

Claire's mouth fell open. 'And you said Henry was a straight arrow?'

Ena laughed. 'He is compared to most of them.'

CHAPTER SIXTEEN

'Inspector Powell?'

Ena hung up her coat, dropped her handbag on her desk and joined the inspector and her sisters at the large conference table where they gathered every morning to discuss what each of them had planned for the day, and again at night to share their findings.

'Do you have news about the case?'

'I'm afraid not.'

Ena physically slumped.

'But I do have something I'd like you to see. Can you come to the station today?'

'I'll come now.' Ena looked at her sisters. Margot nodded. Bess shrugged her shoulders as if to say why not. 'Ah! But what if I'm being followed? I don't think we should be seen together.'

'We'll leave separately.'

Natalie got up. 'I'll take you through the front of the house to the box office. You can leave by the main doors on the Strand and Ena by the stage door.'

'I'll go now. See you later.'

'See you in twenty minutes,' Ena said. 'As soon as I know what everyone's plans are for the day, I'll be with you.'

When the inspector had left, Ena told Bess and Margot that Henry had been to the flat the night before - and that Special Branch hadn't told him Crowther had been murdered. 'Claire will fill you in when Natalie gets back.'

Ena took her handbag from her desk, grabbed her coat from the stand and opened the door. A casually dressed, bordering on a scruffy, young man with a goatee beard and long black hair stood with his fist poised to knock. He stumbled backwards in shock.

'Did you want something?'

'Yes, to see Natalie. I'm the theatre photographer,' he said, holding an envelope in his other hand.

Ena looked over her shoulder at Claire. She was already on her feet. 'She'll only be a minute if you'd like to wait for her?'

'Or I can give the photographs to her,' Claire said.

'Natalie said I was only to give them to her, so if it's okay, I'll wait.'

As she left, Claire was leading the young man across the room to the table. Ena prayed that the photographs would be of use in the investigation. She would have to wait to find out.

Greeting Ena with a broad smile, the jovial desk sergeant at Bow Street unlocked the door marked private, ushered Ena through and locked it behind her.

The inspector's door stood ajar. 'That was quick,' he said, when Ena entered, 'Take a seat.'

Ena sat in the chair opposite the inspector. 'Because you came down to the theatre this morning, I thought what you had to tell me must be important.'

'It's that alright. Our friendly pathologist, Sandy Berman, sent over the autopsy report on Helen Crowther first thing.'

'Is there anything in it we didn't know?'

'Oh yes.' The inspector gave Ena a wry smile. 'Miss Crowther was considerably older than her MI5 ID, employment records, passport and birth certificate stated. Her passport is real. Her first, probably a forgery to get her to England like her birth certificate, was replaced after she reported a small house fire when she first started working for MI5. But that's by the by. It's this that I think you'll find interesting.' The inspector pushed a cream folder across his desk.

Ena read the report. As she neared the end, she gasped, 'Good God!' and read the last paragraph aloud. "The toxicology report confirms that the deceased died of cyanide poisoning. There is bruising on the right side of the forehead and right cheek, consistent with falling from a sitting position onto a hard surface. From the condition of the organs, I deduce that the age of the deceased is between *fifty-eight and sixty*." Ena looked at the inspector. He nodded. She carried on reading. "It is not possible to tell if the deceased has given birth more than once, but based on the condition of the uterus and the amount of perianal scarring - both of which are normal in a healthy woman - she has had at least one pregnancy."

Ena closed the report. She didn't speak, and neither did the inspector. A heavy silence filled the room. Only the sound of the clock, as the minute hand ticked past the hour, was audible. The inspector reached across the desk and drew the pathologist's report to him. He said nothing. He didn't have to. Ena could see by the look on his face that he knew how important this revelation was to her and, more importantly, Henry.

'That Crowther had had a child could be the reason why she was killed. It's flimsy, I know. But it throws doubt on the theory that Henry, or someone from MI5, killed her.'

The inspector nodded. 'Maybe.'

'It happens. What if the child was illegitimate and Crowther left him in Germany, had him adopted, or put him in an orphanage? When he grew up he would resent being abandoned.'

The inspector raised an eyebrow.

'Alright, it's a bit of a stretch, but what if Crowther left the baby with her mother to bring up. It happens all the time. A young girl has a baby, her mother brings him up as her own, and the girl goes away to start a new life. It isn't until the child needs a birth certificate to get a passport or get married, or the woman he thinks is his mother dies, that he discovers his mother is his grandmother and the woman he believes is his sister is his mother. It isn't beyond the realms of possibility that the child, now an adult, came looking for his real mother and when he found her she, Crowther, sent him away.'

'A revenge killing, you mean?'

'It isn't uncommon. She may even have sent him away for his own safety. If Crowther's child came here asking questions that threatened to blow her cover, it would be reason enough for her spymasters to get rid of her.'

'Whatever the reason, this new information is helpful to Henry because it adds to the list of suspects.'

'Have you told Dick Bentley and Alan Richardson?'

'I don't have to. Sandy Berman will have sent the Home Office and Special Branch copies of the report.' A cynical smile crossed the inspector's lips. 'It will be interesting to see if they agree that Crowther's child is a suspect.'

Ena was deep in thought and didn't reply.

The inspector leant forward. 'Are you alright, Ena?'

'Sorry? Yes. I was thinking.'

'About what?'

'That we've been blind. We haven't seen what was staring us in the face. What if Crowther didn't abandon the baby? What if the baby is Shaun O'Shaughnessy?'

'Good God. Now we know Crowther was older than she said, it's a distinct possibility.'

The cold hand of fear gripped Ena's heart. 'If O'Shaughnessy is Crowther's son - and he believes

Henry killed her - Henry is in trouble. O'Shaughnessy has worked for MI5 and MI6. He'll know where the safe houses are.'

'He may know where military intelligence safe houses are, but he won't know where Special Branch's ones are.'

'Henry was moved last night to an MI5 safe house?'

The inspector shot Ena a look of surprise. 'How do you know?'

'He came to see me on the way there.'

'What? How...?'

'The Special Branch driver owed Henry a favour.'

'It must have been a big favour. Can I ask?'

'Best not.' Ena blushed and pressed her lips together.

'I'll telephone DI Richardson at Special Branch and tell him to get a message to the safe house where Five are keeping Henry; warn them about O'Shaughnessy.'

'And I'd better get back to the theatre, update the girls.' Ena got up and walked round the inspector's desk. 'I appreciate what you're doing to help me, to help Henry.'

'I'm an old-fashioned copper, Ena. I don't like people being used as scapegoats even if it is for the good of National Security. I shall find Helen Crowther's killer and I shall arrest him. And,' the inspector said with a twinkle in his eye, 'if I embarrass the brass at the Home Office, British intelligence or military security, it's hard luck.'

Ena put her arms around the inspector and whispered, 'Thank you.' By the time she had put on her coat, gathered her scarf and handbag, the inspector was speaking to his colleague at Special Branch.

'Meeting, sisters.'

112

Everyone stopped what they were doing and took their seats around the conference table except Bess. She dialled Natalie's extension and said, 'Ena's back.'

Within two minutes Natalie arrived and she and Bess joined the others at the table. 'What's happened? What did the DI want you for?' Bess asked.

'He wanted to show me the pathologist's report on Helen Crowther. She is six, maybe, eight years older than her ID states.'

'And how does that help us?'

'It doesn't, not on its own, but she has also been pregnant, which means there could be an abandoned child somewhere who had a grudge.'

'Or the child could be Shaun O'Shaughnessy,' Claire said.

'That was my first thought.' Bess looked from Ena to Claire. 'Whoever it is, Henry isn't the only suspect.'

'No. But, if the child didn't kill her, he may think Henry did and go after him.'

'We need to find Shaun O'Shaughnessy,' Claire said.

'That's exactly what I've been thinking.'

'How are we going to do that? You're the only one who knows what he looks like now, Ena,' Bess said.

Claire left her seat and crossed the room to the filing cabinet. She returned with the envelope containing four photographs that the theatre photographer had brought that morning. She took out two of Crowther and O'Shaughnessy and put one in front of Bess and one in front of Margot. The newspaper cutting, she gave to Natalie. 'That's him with Crowther. He'd be in his teens in that picture, he'll be in his late thirties now.'

'He'll have changed a lot in twenty-two years,' Bess said, 'aged.' She picked up the photograph. 'It's a

113

good reproduction. It's clear, but…' She shook her head. 'All we know about him is, he's tall and blond with blue eyes.'

'Blue-grey eyes, and he has an Irish accent.'

'Other than that—'

'Artie!' Ena said. 'Artie knows him. I'll give him a call and ask him if he'll accompany you and Margot to some of the clubs and pubs O'Shaughnessy frequents and we'll go to the others.'

'We didn't have any success looking around the pubs last time,' Bess reminded her.

Ena looked at her sister angrily. 'Do you have a better idea?'

'Yes.'

'Then tell us.'

'You said O'Shaughnessy lives in Brighton.' Ena nodded. 'So while we're looking up here, why don't you and Claire look round some of the pubs in Brighton?'

'That's not a bad idea. We could ask questions. See what we can find out about him.'

'He may be known to the police.'

'He is known to the police. So am I for that matter, which,' Ena said, 'could be very helpful.'

'We could go to Helen Crowther's house,' Claire said.

'Not a good idea,' Bess warned.

'You're right. It isn't a good idea.' Ena glanced at Claire. She winked.

Bess looked at her notes. 'I forgot to tell you. Rupert Highsmith telephoned while you were at Bow Street. He didn't leave a message. He said he'd ring back.'

'I really should return his call.' Ena thought for a moment. 'I'll telephone Artie first, see if he's able to accompany you and Margot tonight.'

'You and Claire get off to Brighton. I'll telephone Artie.'

'He has a friend who works at GCHQ. He was meeting him today to ask him about Rupert Highsmith. Find out what his friend said, will you?'

'Yes. Now go.'

Ena took her coat from the back of the chair and picked up her handbag. 'Sorry I was short with you earlier, Bess.'

Her oldest sister smiled. 'Were you? I didn't notice.'

CHAPTER SEVENTEEN

'This'll be him now, in the black Humber.'

'Who?'

'Nick Miller, the owner of The Minchin Club. When I stayed down here last year, with Helen Crowther, O'Shaughnessy told me Miller was a South London gangster. He said The Minchin Club was both the most famous and infamous club outside South London. According to him it isn't only frequented by gangsters, but by West End actors and actresses - of which Miller always had his pick - producers and directors. He said they come down from London to enjoy themselves because they know their photographs won't be plastered all over the front pages of the newspapers the next day. O'Shaughnessy would be in his element around people like that.'

Ena and Claire watched the Humber glide to a halt in front of The Minchin Club. A tall man in an expensive tailored suit and wearing a fedora stepped out onto the wet pavement. The door on the other side of the car opened and a fair-haired man in his mid-thirties, slighter in build but as tall as Miller, jumped out. He reached back into the car and brought out an overcoat which he took to Miller and draped around his shoulders.

With a swagger, his hat worn at a tilt and a cigar in his hand, Miller mounted the steps. His companion ran ahead of him and put out his hand to open the door to the club. It opened before he reached it and two men came out. Built like proverbial brick out-houses they stood on either side of the entrance, bowing and scraping as Miller approached.

'Doormen?' Claire whispered.

'Bouncers,' Ena said, watching Nick Miller talking

to one and then the other of the men. They responded with laughter.

When Miller went inside, the two bruisers looked along the road to the left and right before following their boss into the club and closing the door.

'It looks smart from the outside,' Claire mused.

'It does, but the Regency grandeur is fake.'

Claire exhaled loudly. 'Even so, you'd need a lot of money to buy a club like this one.'

'Miller has a lot of money,' Ena said. 'Artie discovered, while he was looking through the cold case files, that Miller made a killing during the war buying up fabric, dried and tinned food, and all sorts of luxury items from the owners of bombed-out factories and warehouses. He took advantage of rationing, sold the goods on the black market and made a fortune.'

'And that's how he could afford to buy The Minchin Club?'

'Yes! The Inland Revenue has been after him for decades, but Miller is too clever for them. He always has the correct documentation and the right number of purchase receipts, even for goods bought overseas. There were several times he was so close to being caught that he openly joked about it in The Minchin Club.

'His first *legitimate* enterprise was a petrol station in South London where he sold second-hand family cars like Vauxhalls, Fords and Hillmans. Then he had a showroom built and stocked it with Daimlers, Rovers and Jaguars - all bought at knockdown prices from people who needed cash and didn't read the small print on the sales document. For the last six years, he's kept a low profile. He calls himself a legitimate businessman, but Nick Miller is a career criminal and a serial womaniser. He is never far away from the next big deal and the next beautiful woman.'

'Look! The door's opening.'

Dim light spilt onto the top step and the man who had arrived with Miller left. He ran nimbly down the steps and headed towards the seafront.

Ena turned the key in the ignition and pulled away from the kerb. Keeping the man in sight, she took her foot off the accelerator. In neutral the car rolled quietly down the road. At the junction, the man turned right. A few seconds later, Ena drove slowly across the main Brighton to Hove Road. The man was nowhere to be seen.

Ena pulled back the sleeve of her coat and squinted at her watch. 'As the man has done a Houdini and disappeared into thin air, and neither The Minchin Club or The Dome - the other club O'Shaughnessy frequents in Brighton – are open until eight o'clock, how about we look for somewhere to eat?'

A few cafés were still open along Brighton's seafront. 'It looks bitter out there. The sea's lashing against the shingle,' Claire said, her nose pressed against the car's passenger window. 'There's no one about. I expect it's too cold for even the hardiest of prom strollers.'

'I could murder a cup of tea,' Ena said, 'I'll stop at the next café.'

The owner of the café met them at the door. He was about to put the closed sign on the window but welcomed them, insisting that they came in out of the cold.

'There's only tomato soup and sandwiches. What would you like, ladies?'

'Soup and a cheese and pickle sandwich,' Ena said, 'and a pot of tea?'

'No soup for me. A ham and mustard sandwich if you have it, please, and tea for me, too.'

The soup, a regular tin of tomato, Ena thought, warmed her. And, considering the time of day, the sliced bread was fresh, the fillings were tasty and plentiful, and the teapot held four cups of tea, which the women drank eagerly.

As the café owner had remained open for them, they didn't want to outstay their welcome. However, it was still too early to go to The Minchin Club.

'We could kill some time by driving along to Hove and you could show me where Helen Crowther lived.'

Ena shot Claire a look of surprise. 'Why?'

'I'm curious to see the house?'

'You won't see anything, it's too dark.'

'Dark is good. Safer to snoop around when it's dark.'

'You're doing no snooping,' Ena said.

'Don't be such a spoilsport. Look, there's a sign for Hove.'

'Alright, but I don't have a good feeling about this. The suburb of Brighton where Helen Crowther lived is about half-a-mile this side of Hove.'

'The rain's coming down in torrents.' Ena peered through the windscreen. 'Good job we stopped and ate something when we did, the shops and cafés are all closed along here.'

'This is it,' Ena said, 'I recognise the jetty and the boats.' She reversed into a space between two large cars on the opposite side of the road from the crescent-shaped terrace of houses where she had stayed with Helen Crowther.

'Damn, I can't see the house from here.' Claire opened the passenger door and got out. She pulled on a handle at the side of the seat and it clunked forwards.

119

She scrambled into the back of the car, pulled the passenger door too, and then slid across the seat until she was behind Ena. 'That's better. Now I can see the house. Oh my God!' Claire said, 'There's a light in one of the upstairs rooms.'

Ena wound down her window. 'Good Lord, it's the bathroom light. Unless it's Crowther's ghost who the hell— O'Shaughnessy.' She wound up her window as it was too cold to keep it open.

The bathroom light went out and one in the room next to it came on.

'That's Crowther's bedroom.'

'If whoever is using the house, isn't living there, they know it well enough to come and go - and put lights on.'

'We could ask the neighbours,' Ena said.

'That's what I was thinking, but hang on. Let's see what the bod in the bedroom is doing first. He, or she, may go out, in which case we'll go in.'

'What? Break-in?'

Claire laughed. 'I can hardly knock on the door and ask if I can have a snoop around. It won't be difficult,' Claire mused, 'these old houses are easy to access.'

'I don't want to know,' Ena said.

'Then don't ask.'

'The bedroom light went out.' Both women waited for lights elsewhere in the house to come on. Only a pale light could be seen through the narrow window on the first-floor landing. 'The person must have come down. They could have gone into a room at the back of the house.'

'The kitchen's at the back.'

'How many rooms on the ground floor and what are they like?'

'On the left of the front door, as we're looking at

the house, is the main living room. It's a large lounge and dining room in one with bookcases in alcoves on the left as you go in. The bay window is opposite and the fireplace is on the right. There's an assortment of comfy chairs by the fire and a table that Crowther worked on. She told me Mac Robinson's wife wanted her to write his memoirs. I don't think she'd started writing them when I was there. If she had she didn't show me.'

'What's on the right of the entrance.'

'A guest bedroom. It has a small bathroom with a toilet off it. It's where I slept when I stayed with her.' Ena shuddered at the memory.

'And the stairs?'

'Next to the guest bedroom. I'm sorry. I don't have any idea how many bedrooms there are upstairs, I didn't go up there.'

'That's alright. I just need to get an idea of the layout. Presumably, the kitchen is behind the living room?'

'Yes. The back door opens onto a veranda. There are steps from it into a small garden and a path that leads from the back to the side of the house.'

'Is there access to the front of the house from the path at the side?'

'Yes. The path goes all the way round. It joins the path leading from the gate to the front door.'

A light came on illuminating the silhouette of a man standing at the lounge window. Ena wound down her window again and peered through the sleeting rain, hoping to see who the man was. She wasn't disappointed. He turned around, raised his arm and the light went out.

'There are two people in the house,' Ena said. 'Someone switched the living room light on and off and it wasn't the man looking out of the window.'

'Did you recognise the man in the window?'

'Yes.' Ena had only glimpsed the man fleetingly, but there was no mistaking him. 'It was Shaun O'Shaughnessy.'

CHAPTER EIGHTEEN

Ena and Claire waited for half an hour without seeing any further sign of life. They were about to give up and go home when the front door opened. The street light was thirty yards away, but Ena could see it was a woman who left the house first.

The woman walked down the path and at the gate turned to her right and walked slowly along the pavement. O'Shaughnessy locked the door, and then caught her up.

As the woman neared the street light Ena gasped with shock.

'What is it?'

'The woman with O'Shaughnessy… It's Eve Robinson. Henry's late boss, McKenzie Robinson's widow.'

'What's she doing with O'Shaughnessy? If he's walking her home, how long do you think it will take him to get to her house and walk back?' Claire asked.

'They might not be going to her house,' Ena said.

'No, but how long would it take if they were?'

'Eve lives in Hove, Victoria Crescent, which can't be too far away. Why do you ask?'

'I was wondering if he'd be away from the house long enough for us to have a look around.'

'No!' Ena said. 'She doesn't live that far away.' She thought for a moment. 'When I drove down for Mac's funeral it was ten minutes at the most from Brighton - and that was in daytime traffic. Before that, when I came down to see Mac in the hospital on the day he died, I remember passing Victoria Crescent. It isn't far from here. O'Shaughnessy could be back in ten or fifteen minutes.'

'In that case, we don't have time. Come on, we'll

follow them.'

'Wouldn't it be better to go in the car? The streets are virtually empty; O'Shaughnessy might spot us if we walk.'

'A Sunbeam Rapier identical to yours was seen on the waste ground in Mercer Street when Crowther was murdered. If O'Shaughnessy or Eve Robinson had anything to do with her death, they'll recognise your car immediately.' Claire opened the door and jumped out. 'Got a brolly?'

'In the boot.'

She took Ena's umbrella from the boot of the car and put it up. 'Come on, there's nothing more natural than two girls on a night out huddled under one brolly, chatting.'

From a safe distance, Ena and Claire followed Eve Robinson and O'Shaughnessy to Victoria Crescent, the house where Eve had lived with her husband until he was murdered in the autumn of 1958 and where, after Mac's funeral, Ena had met and been befriended by Helen Crowther.

Ena and Claire took shelter in the doorway of an old boathouse. As the streetlights were on the other side of the road they were in shadow. The path leading to Eve Robinson's front door was well lit and they watched Eve unlock the door and step inside out of the rain. She didn't put on the light. O'Shaughnessy shook her hand, said something and turned as if to leave.

'O'Shaughnessy isn't going into the house.'

Ena pushed back the wet sleeve of her coat and peered at her watch. 'I can't see the time, but it's too early for him to go to either of the clubs he hangs out in.'

'He'll be as wet as we are by now. If he's going out tonight, he'll have to go back to Crowther's house and change into dry clothes. Let's go; get back before him.'

Leaving the shelter of the boathouse, Ena lifted the umbrella to open it. Claire took it from her. 'We had the umbrella up when we followed O'Shaughnessy, if we put it up now he's likely to recognise it.' Claire linked her arm through Ena's and together they walked briskly back to the car without speaking. Ena glanced over her shoulder a couple of times. There was no sign of O'Shaughnessy.

'I'm soaked to the skin.' Ena lowered herself into the car behind the steering wheel.

'Here he comes,' Claire said, sliding down in the back seat.

They watched O'Shaughnessy take the steps to the front of the house, unlock the door and go inside.

'What now?'

'We wait.'

They didn't have to wait long. Only ten minutes had passed when a taxi pulled up. Curtains on the first floor, presumably O'Shaughnessy's bedroom, opened briefly and he looked out. A couple of minutes later he left the house and ran to the car. He said something to the driver, before opening the back door and jumping in.

As the taxi pulled away from the kerb, Ena turned the key in the ignition of the Sunbeam.

'What are you doing?'

'I thought we could follow him.'

'What we could do,' Claire said, 'is have a look around the house. We'll give him fifteen minutes, if he isn't back by then, chances are he won't be back until the early hours of the morning when the clubs chuck out.'

'It's stopped raining, thank God,' Ena said. 'The last thing we want to do is drip all over

125

O'Shaughnessy's carpet. It's weird thinking of Helen Crowther's house as O'Shaughnessy's house,' she mused.

'It must be weirder for him living there after she's been murdered. The woman isn't buried yet. Talk about jumping into her grave...' Claire looked at her watch. 'Fifteen minutes. He won't come back now.'

It had stopped raining, but it had made no difference to the temperature, Ena thought, as she opened the car door. She got out, stretched and looked up. The rain clouds had cleared and the sky - deep ink blue - sparkled with a million stars. The moon shone brightly on the sea. Its reflection, an intense golden ball on the horizon, spreading out in the shape of an open fan, highlighted the tumbling waves as they rolled into the shore, crashing noisily onto the shingle.

Claire nudged Ena to get her attention. 'Ready?'

'Yes.'

There was enough light from the moon to show them the way around the side of the house to a narrow veranda and the back door. The old rocking chair with its collection of odd cushions that Ena had sat in on the night she'd stayed with Helen Crowther was no longer there, and only one plant out of the dozen that had decorated the veranda remained. Someone, probably Crowther before she had been murdered, had covered it with newspaper and tied it at the base with string to keep off the frost. It looked like a miniature air balloon.

'Ena?' Claire hissed, holding up the kitchen window, 'The key must be in the lock, I can't get the lockpicks in the keyhole. You'll have to go in through the window.'

Ena took a torch from her pocket. She switched it

on and aimed its pale beam at the draining board. There was nothing on it. Nothing to knock off.

'Quick as you can, Ena. This damn sash cord is loose, the window keeps sliding down.'

Claire held the window open while Ena hauled herself onto the ledge and then clambered into the familiar kitchen. It was pretty much as she remembered. She unlocked the door and Claire lowered the window before joining her.

Claire went over to the kitchen cabinet and picked up a pile of papers. She flicked through them. 'Household bills.'

'He's left something in the oven.' Ena opened the door. 'There's a joint of beef in here. It's about cooked. And,' she lifted the lids from two saucepans on top of the cooker, 'the veg has been prepared. I don't think we have much time, Claire.'

'In which case we'd better get a move on. There's nothing of interest in here.' Claire walked around the scrubbed kitchen table to the door on the far side of the room. Ena followed.

'The hall. So that must be the lounge.' Claire pushed open the door on her right. 'You take this room and I'll check out the rooms on the first floor.'

'But you don't know the layout upstairs.'

'Do you?'

'No, I've never been up there.'

'I want to see O'Shaughnessy's room. I'll start with the one where he changed when he came back from Eve Robinson's.' Claire crossed the hall and ran up the stairs and Ena went into the lounge.

A fire roared up the chimney. If O'Shaughnessy is Crowther's son, his inheritance is literally going up in flames. She shone her torch around the room. Nothing had changed since the last time she was there. The

127

typewriter and a pile of Helen Crowther's papers were at one end of the dining table, at the other end were two place settings, two wine glasses and a bottle of red wine, opened, left to breathe.

Ena picked up what must have been two hundred typewritten pages. *The Man At The Top. A Memoir of McKenzie Robinson.* So, Helen Crowther had agreed to write Mac's memoirs after all. Ena took the last two pages from the bottom of a pile and read them. They described the end of Mac's military career concluding with the work he had done overseas during the war in shining detail. The account stopped halfway down the last page. Ena wondered whether O'Shaughnessy would finish writing Mac's memoirs and if that was why Eve Robinson had been at the house earlier?

'Ena?' Claire flew into the room.

Ena spun round. 'Good God, you made me jump.'

'A car has just pulled up outside.' Claire ran to the window and carefully pulled back the nearest curtain. 'It's O'Shaughnessy. He's getting out of a taxi. We need to go. Now!'

Taking care to leave the pages of manuscript exactly as she had found them, Ena placed the two pages she had taken from the bottom of the pile back, before straightening the rest.

'Ena! Come on!'

Ena ran out of the lounge, leaving the door slightly ajar, and made a bolt for the kitchen. Claire had already unlocked the back door. Once she was safely outside Ena locked it and, leaving the key in the lock she turned it sideways, making sure that too was how she'd found it. A second later Claire pushed up the window and was holding it open for her. Ena climbed onto the draining board, swung her legs over the narrow window ledge and, as she heard the front door open, dropped onto the veranda. Jumping up, she helped Claire to lower the window.

Claire fled down the steps into the back garden as the light in the kitchen came on. Ena, standing between the door and the window, froze.

CHAPTER NINETEEN

Not daring to move, Ena watched O'Shaughnessy and a man enter the kitchen. She clasped her hands over her mouth to stifle a gasp of surprise. The man with O'Shaughnessy was the man she'd seen at The Minchin Club with Nick Miller.

O'Shaughnessy ran across the room, Ena presumed to the cooker, and his guest followed. When she was sure neither man could see her, she crouched down until she was on all fours and crawled under the window.

From the garden, Claire looked through the railings of the veranda. 'What now?'

Ena shook her head. 'Don't know.' Still on her knees, she whispered, 'Am I clear of the window?' Claire nodded.

Using her hands as levers, Ena pushed herself to her feet. She looked back. The kitchen light shone through the window, illuminating the steps and the garden. The only way she was going to leave without being seen was to climb over the railings at the far end of the veranda. Claire shadowed her as she tiptoed along. A drainpipe ran from the guttering under the roof to the ground. She gave it a tug. It felt firm. Whether or not it would take her weight, she would soon find out. Its circumference was wider than the span of Ena's hand. She couldn't do anything about that and reached for the pipe again. Her gloves were wet and she lost her grip, so she took them off and stuffed them into her pocket. She took hold of the pipe again. Without gloves, she had a better grip.

She looked over the side of the railing. It wasn't a steep drop to the ground, but if the pipe came away from the wall the noise would be heard in the kitchen and O'Shaughnessy would be out in a flash. Ena held the pipe with her left hand, the top of the railings with her right, and lifted her right leg. At that moment the back door opened. Light flooded the steps and garden. Slowly Ena lowered her leg and let go of the drainpipe. She stepped back into the shadow beneath the roof of the veranda and held her breath. With her back pressed against the wall, she prayed O'Shaughnessy wouldn't bring his dinner guest out to look at the view. He didn't.

After listening to raucous laughter and jokes about burning the place down, Ena realised the door had been opened to let out smoke from the burnt roast beef. Eventually, the beam of light from the open door of the kitchen narrowed until the veranda was once again in darkness. When she heard the door shut and the key turn in the lock, she looked to the heavens and sighed.

More laughter rang out from the kitchen and she could hear water pouring out of the sink's waste pipe into the drain. She was trembling, but she knew if she was going to get away, it had to be now. She grabbed the drainpipe with one hand and the top of the railing with the other, and for a minute straddled the top of the handrail. She edged forward towards the drainpipe, grabbed it and lifted her left leg over the rail. Now all she had to do was put one foot on the rose fitting that held the drainpipe and kitchen waste pipe in place, and then the other.

She took a deep breath. 'You can do it,' she whispered, and with both feet placed securely on the fitting, she took her left hand off the pipe and placed it beneath her right hand. She did the same with her right hand and again with her left until she was far enough down the pipe to jump - she hoped without breaking her neck.

Ena felt Claire tap her leg. 'Let go. I'll catch you.'

Ena's hands felt as if they'd been welded to the pipe, but she did as Claire said and taking her feet off the rose, she let go of the drainpipe and dropped to the ground.

Claire put up her thumb. 'Are you alright?'

Ena scrambled to her feet and did the same. 'Fine.'

Keeping their heads down, Ena and Claire walked briskly from the side of the house to the front. They had no sooner gone through the gate than they were grabbed from behind.

A leather glove closed around the bottom half of Ena's face and a man hissed, 'Don't make a sound.'

Ena, taken by surprise, was helpless to escape the man's hold on her. Claire, on the other hand, reacted in the way she had been trained to react by the SOE. In a flash she had brought her elbow forward and jabbed it back, driving it into the man's ribcage knocking the breath out of him. He doubled over, she turned, grabbed his left arm, twisted it behind his back and marched the gasping man into the shrubs that ran along the drive of the house next door.

'Who are you?'

The man holding Ena loosened his grip on her. 'Police. East Sussex Constabulary.' He took his warrant card from inside his coat and held it up for Claire to read it. 'Detective Constable Allen.' He nodded at the man Claire had in a half-Nelson, 'Detective Sergeant Morgan.'

Claire released the sergeant with a shove. 'What the hell were you doing creeping up on us like that? You could have got yourself killed.'

The sergeant looked at Claire, his mouth opened in disbelief.

'And it would have been self-defence!'

'Shush!' Ena said, 'voices.'

Edging their way deeper into the small shrubbery, Ena, Claire and the two detectives stood in silence. They listened as O'Shaughnessy and his friend left the house. They heard the front door close, the two men walk down the path and out through the gate. A moment of quiet followed before they began to chat and laugh. From the safety of the neighbour's garden, they watched O'Shaughnessy and the man Ena had seen earlier at The Minchin Club saunter down the road arm in arm.

When they were out of sight DS Morgan asked Ena and Claire to follow him and the DC to John Street Police Station. 'Or, do I have to arrest you?' he asked Claire, massaging his shoulder.

Claire gave him a cold stare and shrugged.

'It would give me the greatest of pleasure to charge you with assaulting a police officer.'

Ena knew her sister had no intention of replying to the detective. 'We'll follow you, Sergeant.' Ena nudged Claire and took her by the arm. Ena crossed the road and Claire followed. Neither woman looked back.

Claire opened the car door and dropped onto the passenger seat. 'That was close.'

'Too close. I'm still shaking. Being grabbed from behind like that, I thought they were O'Shaughnessy's lot.'

'So did I, which is why I almost broke that copper's arm.'

Ena laughed. 'You should have seen his face. He didn't know what had hit him.' She turned the key in the ignition and the Sunbeam fired into life. It was sandwiched between two larger vehicles and took Ena a couple of manoeuvres before she was safely able to pull out of the parking place. She saw the lights of a dark Ford Anglia flash on. It pulled into the road and slowed when it drew level with the Sunbeam. As the unmarked police car passed, Ena turned the steering wheel sharp right, put pressure on the accelerator, and bumped the Sunbeam off the pavement onto the main road and followed the police car into Brighton.

'Find anything of interest in the lounge?' Claire asked.

'The beginning of Mac Robinson's memoirs. But, more importantly, O'Shaughnessy's guest was the man we saw with Nick Miller.'

'Are you sure?'

'Positive. I got a good look at him when he passed the car.'

'Do you think Miller is involved with O'Shaughnessy?'

'Looks like it.'

As John Street Police Station came into view, the police car turned left and swung into a car park. A sign at the entrance said, 'Police Vehicles Only'. Ena followed the Ford Anglia and parked alongside it. 'What about you? Anything interesting upstairs?'

'I'll tell you later. Come on. The sooner we get in there, the sooner the interrogation will be over and we can get home.' Claire reached for the door handle.

'Hang on a minute. Should we tell them we saw Eve Robinson with O'Shaughnessy earlier?'

'I was wondering about that. They may have seen her too. It depends how long they'd been watching Crowther's house.'

'They knew we were there.'

'True. Even so, we'll play it by ear. If they ask specific questions it usually means they already know the answer, or think they do, and they want confirmation. What they don't know, they'll wait for

134

us to tell them. So, no, we won't tell them we saw Eve Robinson with O'Shaughnessy, nor that we saw O'Shaughnessy with the man we'd seen earlier at The Minchin Club. They'll have guessed we were in the house looking for evidence to clear Henry. If they ask if we found anything, we say no.'

'Okay.'

Ena and Claire followed the detectives into John Street Police Station. The detective constable showed them into an interview room on the ground floor and left.

'I hope they don't keep us waiting for hours,' Ena said, stomping across the room. She flopped down on a chair at a table that had two chairs on either side.

Claire joined her. 'The police always stick you in a room and forget about you.'

'It's to make you sweat,' Ena said.

'It's too bloody cold in here to sweat.'

'Do you think they can hear what we're saying?' Ena looked around the room. 'There isn't a mirror on the wall, so they're not watching us.'

Claire laughed. 'We're in Brighton, Ena, not the Port Of New York.' Unable to stop herself, she looked up at each corner of the room. She shook her head. Ena's wasn't the only imagination working overtime.

'At last,' Claire said when the door opened.

A tall, well-built, middle-aged man entered the room and walked around the desk. He sat in the chair opposite Ena. The detective sergeant who had brought them to the station followed and sat in the chair facing Claire.

'Mrs Green?'

'Yes.'

'Detective Inspector Armstrong.' The older man offered Ena his hand and she shook it. 'I'm pleased to meet you, Mrs Green. I understand we have a mutual friend.'

'Inspector Powell at Bow Street.'

'The very same.' He turned to Claire. 'How do you do, Mrs Mitchell?'

'Inspector!' Claire held his proffered hand briefly.

'Now,' he said, 'I would like to explain my involvement in the investigation into the death of Helen Crowther. The case is Detective Inspector Powell's because she was killed in Covent Garden. However, because she was a resident here in Brighton, I am working with Dan Powell.' He opened the folder and looked at Ena. 'I am aware that your husband is being held by Special Branch but I assure you that although the evidence points to him killing Miss Crowther, he is not the only suspect.'

'That's good to know.'

'There are several potential suspects in Brighton and Hove - including the man who is currently living in her house.'

He gave Ena a sympathetic smile. 'Now, to the business that brings you here today. Why did you break into the late Miss Crowther's house?'

'I'd have thought that was obvious,' Claire snapped. 'My brother-in-law has been wrongly accused of murdering the woman.'

'We were looking for anything that might help us to prove Henry's innocence,' Ena said. Damn! The first question they'd been asked and she had said too much.

'And did you find anything?'

'No, but that doesn't mean there isn't anything. I'm sure you've been told that the man living in the house, Shaun O'Shaughnessy, came back before we had time to look very far.'

'And you, Mrs Mitchell?' Out of the corner of her

eye, Ena saw the detective sergeant flinch. 'Did you find anything to prove your brother-in-law is innocent of murder?'

'No. As my sister said, we didn't have time. O'Shaughnessy, as I'm sure you know, is a German spy. If you were to search the house you'd find enough evidence to put him away for a very long time.'

'I'm sure you're right. And, when the time comes, we, the police, will search the house.' He looked at Ena. 'In the meantime…'

The inspector paused long enough to cause Ena's heart to beat faster than it had since O'Shaughnessy had almost caught her on Helen Crowther's veranda.

'In the meantime,' he repeated, 'I suggest you leave the investigation of Mr O'Shaughnessy - and any investigation relevant to him, to us. And that includes the investigation of your husband and the part he played in Helen Crowther's death.'

Ena took a long deep breath. She wanted to scream. Instead, she made fists. She dug her nails into the palms of her hands to stop herself from telling the inspector to take a running jump off Brighton pier.

'Mrs Green?'

Ena said nothing. She looked down at her clenched fists.

The inspector assured her again that there were other suspects, and then said, 'Thank you for coming in.' He straightened the case notes on his desk that he had hardly referred to, returned them to the folder and stood up. 'Detective Sergeant Morgan will see you out.'

Ena and Claire jumped up and followed the detective sergeant out of the room.

'What now?' Claire asked the DS, as they walked along the corridor.

'You can go.'

'What? We're not being charged with breaking and entering?'

'No. O'Shaughnessy would have to be told if we charged you,' the DS said.

'Of course he would. I hadn't thought of that.'

'Which doesn't mean you can go breaking into his house again.'

'Of course not. Whatever makes you think we would do such a silly thing again?' Claire said, making no attempt to hide the sarcasm in her voice.

'Let's find a pub.'

'Not in Hove or Brighton. We can't run the risk of bumping into O'Shaughnessy and his boyfriend.'

'I doubt they'll go to a pub. A braggart like O'Shaughnessy will be showing off his friend in an expensive restaurant, especially if he has Crowther's money.'

'*If* she left him her money.'

'Why wouldn't she? She must have left him the house, or he's squatting.'

'They might even be at The Minchin Club. Come on, Ena, let's find a pub, have a drink, something to eat, and sit by a roaring fire?'

'Okay, you win, but we'll go to a pub on the way back to London.' Ena put the key in the ignition and turned it. While the engine ticked over, she blew hot breath into her cupped hands. 'My hands are stiff from being cold for so long.'

'Where are your gloves?'

'In my pocket. I couldn't grip the drainpipe properly with them on.' She dug her hands into her pockets and then leaned forward and patted the floor of the car by her feet. 'Oh, God.'

'What is it?'

'My gloves. They must have fallen out of my pocket.' She looked out of the window. 'They're probably on the road. Damn!' She hit the steering wheel with the palm of her hand. 'What if they're on the path outside Crowther's house?'

'Or on the veranda?'

Ena exhaled loudly. 'We should go back and get them.'

'No, we shouldn't! We can't risk O'Shaughnessy coming back to the house and seeing us. Last time was too close for comfort. There isn't anything about them that says they're yours, is there?'

'Not exactly.'

'What do you mean, not exactly?'

'Well, there's a zig-zag pattern around the wrist that's quite distinctive, and I might have worn them when I stayed at the house last year, but O'Shaughnessy wouldn't have seen them.'

'In which case, if he comes across them, he'll assume they were Helen Crowther's.'

'He'd have no reason to think otherwise. They're just an ordinary pair of woollen gloves. You can buy them anywhere,' Ena said, trying to convince herself as well as her sister.

CHAPTER TWENTY

To say that The Plough Inn was off the beaten track was an understatement. An arrow beneath a car park sign pointed to a narrow strip of tarmac that ran along the side of a small spinney. Two dark saloon cars and an old pick-up truck were already parked. Ena reversed the Sunbeam between the cars. She was sure that, as distinctive as the car was, it couldn't be seen from the road.

Ena and Claire headed for the entrance to the pub from the car park. The first door on the left bore the sign, 'Ladies'. After using the lavatory, Ena took a handkerchief from her handbag, wet it thoroughly under the hot water tap and rubbed Palmolive soap onto it. She bent forwards and scrubbed at her knees. 'Now my knees are red,' she said, 'and I've turned a snag in my stocking into a ladder.'

'Let me look.' Ena lifted her skirt above her knees. 'I can hardly see the ladder and you're your knees look better red than covered in mud.'

Both sisters combed their hair and reapplied their makeup.

'A dusting of face powder and a dab of lipstick and we look almost respectable,' Ena said, laughing.

Claire stood next to her and looked in the mirror. 'We Dudley girls scrub up well, don't we?'

'We do,' Ena replied. 'We could be two ladies from town having a quiet evening out in the country - as long as no one looks at our clothes.' She pulled on the collar of her coat, straightened the belt and ran her hands down the coat's skirt. 'That's better. No one would guess that a few hours ago we'd been soaked to the skin while we were following a spy.'

'Or, that you'd been crawling along a filthy veranda

on your hands and knees before climbing down a drainpipe after breaking into someone's house.'

Ena put her hand up to her mouth. 'Don't remind me. God knows what O'Shaughnessy would have done if he'd caught us.'

'He didn't. So, come on, forget about him. I need something to eat, I'm starving.'

'I need something to drink,' Ena said, following Claire out of the lavatory.

The saloon bar was empty but for a middle-aged man and a woman, deep in conversation, sitting on the left of a roaring fire and three elderly men with ruddy complexions wearing corduroy trousers, thick sports jackets and heavy duty boots, who were drinking pints of dark beer under the window. A blackboard at the end of the bar boasted the best fish pie in three counties.

Claire nudged Ena. 'Fancy fish pie?'

'Lovely. And a scotch.' Ena opened her handbag and took two pound notes from her purse. 'I'll grab that table near the fire,' she said, leaving the money on the counter.

After ordering and paying for their meal, Claire joined her. She placed two glasses of whisky on the table and sat down. Not long after, the barman brought their food which they ate hungrily. When they had finished, they discussed seeing Eve Robinson with O'Shaughnessy.

'What would Eve Robinson be doing with O'Shaughnessy?' Claire asked.

'I don't know. Crowther was writing Mac Robinson's memoirs. Perhaps Eve wants him to finish writing them.'

'Crowther was writing Eve Robinson's husband's memoirs?'

'Yes. She told me last autumn that she had wanted to write Mac's memoirs for years. After he died, she said she didn't feel she could be truthful about him. She said the man she knew was very different to the man married to Eve. She said it would hurt Eve to read his memoirs from her point of view, but she must have had second thoughts because there were at least two hundred pages of typed manuscript on the dining room table.' Ena took a drink of her scotch. 'I think Mac and Crowther had an affair. How serious it was for Mac I don't know, but the way Crowther talked about him, it was obvious that she'd been in love with him.'

'It happens when people work closely together,' Claire said, with a twinkle in her eye.

Ena laughed. 'It does.' She had been working with Henry when she fell in love with him.

'Do you think Eve Robinson found out about the affair? If she did, it might have been her who killed Crowther?'

'I don't know. When I went to the house after Mac's funeral, Eve spat venom at me. She blamed me for her husband's death. I was horrified by what she said, but I didn't feel threatened. She accused me of all sorts, which at the time I put down to grief.' Ena took a sip of her whisky. 'Then, I wouldn't have thought her capable of killing anyone, but after seeing her coming out of Crowther's house today, and later seeing the half-written manuscript of Mac's memoirs on Crowther's dining table, I'm not sure. If Mac did have an affair with Helen Crowther and Eve found out...' Ena lifted her shoulders. 'Who knows?'

'It isn't that long since her husband's death.'

'Murder!' Ena corrected.

'Death from natural causes, or murdered, Eve Robinson was grieving when she confided in her husband's colleague, her friend and confidant.'

'And if she later found out that the woman she thought was her friend had been having an affair with her husband for her entire married life, it might well have been enough to tip her over the edge.'

The barman collected their plates and asked if they'd enjoyed the fish pie. Both women said they had. He asked if they wanted anything else.

'I couldn't eat another morsel.' Ena looked at Claire.

'Nor me, but perhaps another drink.' Claire gave the barman the money.

'Two whiskies coming up.'

'What about the chap O'Shaughnessy brought back to the house tonight?' Claire said when the barman left.

'He looked pretty cosy with the owner of The Minchin Club earlier.'

'He looked pretty cosy with O'Shaughnessy too.'

'Changing the subject, did you find anything upstairs?'

'Three passports in three different names. One had a photograph of O'Shaughnessy when he was much younger and two had recent photographs.'

'Was one of them in the name of Krueger?'

'Yes. It could have been the passport he used to get into Berlin in nineteen thirty-six.'

'We know he was in Berlin in thirty-six, we've got photographs of him and Crowther on Nazi rallies. Were there any other aliases?'

'Not really. One was in the name of O'Shaughnessy, obviously. The other was in the name of Crowther.'

'Good God! Shaun Crowther! So O'Shaughnessy is Helen Crowther's son?'

'He could be, but there are other reasons why he might have a passport in her name. It could be that they'd travelled abroad together as mother and son since she'd lived in England. It would have been a great cover. Who would suspect a nice English lady and her queer son of being spies?'

'Crowther had an English birth certificate. If O'Shaughnessy does, and Helen Crowther's down as his mother, he won't have to squat in her house, he'll inherit it.'

'And her money. Did she have any?'

'No idea, but she must have earned a fair amount at MI5 over the years.'

'Does she have family?'

Ena shook her head. 'Not that I know of.' A smile played on her lips. 'We know the passports are forgeries and we know Crowther was born in Berlin, but O'Shaughnessy's birthplace isn't known. What if he isn't Crowther's son? What if he's part of the same spy network and having worked closely with her, fears his cover will be blown, so he kills her to save himself.'

'People have killed for less.'

When the barman brought over the drinks, Ena asked him whether there was a public telephone she could use. There was one in the village, but he said if she was telephoning a local number she was welcome to use the pub's telephone.

Ena accepted his offer, but said, 'It isn't a local call, it's long-distance. I'll make it a trunk call and then the operator will telephone you when I've finished and tell you how much the call cost. Is that alright?'

'Bess and Margot won't be at the theatre now.' Claire checked her watch. 'It's gone seven.'

'I don't expect they will, but they might have left a

144

message at the stage door.' Ena took a sip of whisky and got up. 'Won't be long.'

She picked up the receiver. When the operator answered, she asked if she could make a trunk call to the stage door of The Prince Albert Theatre in London, the operator said yes and Ena was soon connected.

'Hello, Stan, it's Ena. Are my sisters still in the building?'

'No, Ena. They left half an hour ago. Bess said you might ring and left a message.' Ena could hear paper being shuffled. 'Got it. Are you there?'

'Yes, I'm still here.'

'Bess said, there's an important meeting tomorrow morning at nine o'clock. And, she said she and Margot were meeting Artie at The Blue Beau in Mayfair. That's a nightclub,' he said.

'Sounds like a rum place to me, Stan,' Ena said, laughing.

'Rum indeed. And, not the sort of place I'd have thought your sister, Bess, would have frequented.'

Ena laughed again. 'But Margot would. Thank you, Stan. See you tomorrow.'

No sooner had Ena replaced the telephone's receiver than it rang. She picked it up and handed it to the barman.

'That's right, a call to London. Three and sixpence, you said? Thank you. Goodnight. Three and six,' he repeated, replacing the receiver on its base.

Ena gave him four shillings and waved away the sixpence change.

'You were right,' she said to Claire when she returned to her seat. 'The girls left an hour ago. They've gone to a club called The Blue Beau to meet Artie.'

Claire laughed. 'If the club is anything like its name

suggests, our Bess will love it, I don't think?'

'It's time she lived a little,' Ena said, laughing. 'And there's a meeting tomorrow morning at nine o'clock. So,' Ena knocked back her drink, 'let's go home, get out of our wet clothes and relax in front of the fire.'

The drive back to London was nowhere near as long as the drive down to Brighton had been. There was less traffic for one thing. It was still a filthy night. It snowed for most of the journey. Only when they reached the suburbs in south London did the snow ease up, eventually turning to rain.

'We're here,' Ena said, tapping her sleeping sister on the arm.

Claire opened her eyes and shivered. 'Thank God for that. I'm freezing.' She slid down in the seat, wrapped her arms around her chest and dropped her head until her face was half-buried in the sleeves of her coat.

Ena got out of the car, walked round to the passenger side and opened the door. 'Are you staying in the car then?'

'Noooo…' Claire yawned, grabbed her handbag from the floor and stumbled out of the car. Ena locked it and helped her sister up the steps to the flat.

Ena picked up several letters and a card from just inside the door. 'Bills' she said, yawning. Leaving Claire in the hall, she went through to the sitting room, dropped the post on the coffee table and went over and lit the fire. Claire wandered in and flopped onto the settee. Once Ena was sure the flames from the kindling had taken hold of the logs, she joined her.

'Want a hot drink?'

'I want a bath and my bed.'

146

'I'll put the kettle on and by the time you've finished in the bathroom there'll be a hot water bottle in your bed.' Ena got up and went to the door. 'I'm going to make myself a mug of cocoa. Are you sure you don't want one?'

Claire raised her eyes pretending she had to think about it and then smiled sleepily.

'I'll bring one to you when you've had a bath. Chop-chop, and don't use all the hot water.'

Ena was making notes; listing bullet points of everything that she and Claire had done that day - and what they had found in the house in Brighton. She smiled to herself. Unless someone had the same cryptic mind, they wouldn't know what they had done. Claire would be able to decipher what she had written, but she was sure no one else she knew would. More importantly, no one she didn't know would be able to decipher what she'd written.

Claire stuck her head around the sitting-room door. 'Your bath's running.'

'Thanks, love.' Ena read through her notes and when she was satisfied that she hadn't left anything out, went to the kitchen and made Claire's cocoa. By the time she took it into Claire, she was asleep, so she switched off the bedside lamp, tiptoed out of the room and closed the door.

In the bathroom she turned off the hot water and while the bath cooled, returned to the sitting room. After putting the guard in front of the fire she sat in the armchair, drank Claire's cocoa and opened the post.

Between the electricity bill and a receipt for the first quarter's rent, hand delivered by her landlord Mr Grimes, was a postcard from Henry. Ena's eyes filled with tears. There was no mistaking Henry's handwriting. She hastily wiped her eyes with the back of her hand and read: *Lincoln is a small city. Though the Cathedral is grand. Nothing compares to St. Paul's for me. Do visit if you are able. Stone Gallery I recommend you see. Nelson's tomb, also. One day I shall take you there. Until then... xx*

Ena read the message again. The first word was Lincoln. She wrote down the first letter - L. The second sentence began with the word, though. She wrote the third letter, O. The third sentence, the word, nothing. She ran her finger along the line to the sixth letter, N. Then back to the beginning for the fourth sentence, D for do. The fifth letter, O again, from the word stone and the sixth, N from Nelson's tomb - spelling, LONDON. Henry is coming to London. She leapt up, held the card against her heart and twirled round. Henry is coming to London. He hadn't specified a time, but the code from Bletchley Park had been three words and then three. Three o'clock on the third.

Ena took the card to the bedroom and put it under Henry's pillow. When she had bathed, she climbed into bed and slept on Henry's side, her head on his pillow and the card beneath it.

CHAPTER TWENTY-ONE

Bess sat at the top of the table. She had called the meeting so was in the chair. When everyone was seated with cups of tea, notepads and pens, she opened the meeting. 'Margot?'

Margot, first to speak, looked around the table and grinned. 'Natalie has asked me if I would put the chorus girls through their paces today,' she said, unable to hide the delight in her voice. 'The choreographer's assistant is off with flu, so, if you girls can manage without me, I'd like to take the rehearsal.'

Margot's sisters, happy for her as her arthritis was often so disabling that she'd had to give up teaching at her dance school in Coventry, agreed that she must help Natalie, and assured her that they would manage without her.

Margot looked up at the clock. Her eyes sparkled with excitement and she pushed herself out of her chair. 'Rehearsals start in fifteen minutes, so,' she said to Bess, 'if Natalie and I leave now before the meeting starts properly, we won't interrupt you telling the girls about last night?'

Bess agreed and, with her sisters, wished Margot luck as she and Natalie left. The room fell silent. Each sister busied herself drinking tea and making notes. What they were really doing was thinking about Margot. Ena worried about her older sister, as she knew her other sisters did. Like them, she was happy that Margot was enjoying being back in the theatre, the environment she loved. But similarly, she worried that Margot's arthritic body would let her down. Ena prayed it wouldn't.

'I'll keep the minutes and the diary until Margot is back,' Bess said, breaking the silence, 'which is one reason why I called this meeting. Other reasons; the meeting with Artie Mallory at the Blue Beau nightclub, and your visit to Brighton,' she said, looking at Ena and then Claire. 'We'll start with Brighton.'

Ena told Bess what had happened the night before, recalling how she and Claire had seen the owner of The Minchin Club with a man who they later saw with Shaun O'Shaughnessy at Helen Crowther's house. And how they had seen Eve Robinson leaving Crowther's house with O'Shaughnessy and that they had broken into the house and found part of McKenzie Robinson's memoirs.

Claire added that she had found three passports belonging to O'Shaughnessy, each in a different name. She also told Bess that she and Ena, unbeknown to them, had been seen by two policemen who all but arrested them when they left the house and took them to John Street Police Station.

Bess shook her head and rolled her eyes. 'And the outcome?'

'Slap on the wrist and told not to do it again.'

'And to leave the investigation into Helen Crowther's death to the police,' Ena said. 'What annoyed me was, the DI in charge of the murder squad said they had several suspects for Crowther's murder including O'Shaughnessy, but they were still investigating Henry's part in her death. If the DI hadn't been a friend of Inspector Powell's I'd have docked him one.'

'Good job you didn't. You wouldn't be much good to Henry if you were locked up too.'

'I'm no bloody good to him now.'

Ignoring Ena's remark, Bess put her hand on her arm. 'You didn't tell them you'd found the memoir and passports?'

150

'No. We only told them what we thought they already knew.'

'Good.'

'What about you and Margot? Did you go to the Blue Beau last night?'

'Yes. We went there to find out about Rupert Highsmith from your colleague, Artie Mallory.'

'And did you?' Ena asked.

'No. He didn't show up.'

'That's not like Artie,' Ena said, worry making her mouth dry. 'It may have been once, but not these days. Do you know why he didn't show up?'

'No idea. We weren't concerned at the beginning of the evening. We just thought he was running late - had to work longer than he'd hoped - or he was stuck in traffic and would eventually arrive. When he hadn't arrived at ten o'clock, we left.'

'Didn't he telephone the stage door and leave a message?'

'No. I asked Stan as soon as I got here this morning.'

'I'll telephone the Home Office when we finish the meeting,' Ena said.

'Claire, what are you doing today?'

'I'm meeting a friend who I worked for in the war. He has contacts in Berlin and I asked him to find out what he could about Crowther because she's from Berlin. Her name was Krueger. We think she was probably married before she came to England.'

'And you trust this friend?'

'With my life.'

Ena and Claire left the table at the same time. Ena went to her desk and picked up the telephone, Claire put on her coat and hat and left. To ensure she documented every detail of the day before, as well as make a record of where her sisters were going today, Bess remained at the table.

Ena put down the telephone. 'We have a problem.'

Bess looked up. 'Artie?'

'He isn't at work. I rang his home number and there was no answer. He could be en route, I suppose.' A dark feeling engulfed her and she shuddered.

'What is it?'

'Something isn't right. Six months ago, I'd have said Artie had had a better offer last night and was having breakfast with the latest love of his life. But not today. Not since the night O'Shaughnessy drugged him.'

'O'Shaughnessy?'

'Forget O'Shaughnessy. He couldn't have had anything to do with Artie not turning up last night, he was in Brighton.'

The last time Ena saw him flashed through her mind. Where did he go when he left the house with a chap she had seen earlier at The Minchin Club? Would he have had time to get to London for eight o'clock? He didn't have a car, so would have had to catch a train...

'Ena?'

'Sorry, I was trying to work out whether O'Shaughnessy had time to get from Brighton to London for eight. He wouldn't. I'll try the Home Office again. If Artie hasn't arrived, I'll go round to his flat. He may just have had too much to drink and be in bed nursing a hangover.' Ena knew that was no longer Artie's style. She couldn't shake off the feeling that something was wrong. As she reached for the telephone, it rang.

'Hello, Stan. Yes it's Ena. Say that again. When? Hang on, let me get a piece of paper and a pen.' She picked up her pen and flicked open the pad. 'Ready.' She wrote down what Stan was saying. 'Hang on. Did you say, Tollson Street? Sorry, Jolson Street, as in Al Jolson? Got it. Good idea, Stan. At least then the roads and streets will be spelt correctly. I'm on my way. What? Shoes? Alright, give me five minutes.' Ena put down the telephone.

'What was all that about?'

'Artie. A man has just telephoned and left a message with Stan for me. He said Artie was in the derelict glass factory on Jolson street, off Brick Lane. Apparently, the man was walking his dog, and the dog ran into the factory and started barking. The man went in after the dog and found Artie. Artie gave him ten bob and asked him to telephone The Prince Albert stage door and tell whoever answered to get a message to Ena Green and tell her to come and get him.'

'Well let's go.'

'Should we tell Natalie and Margot where we're going?'

'We'll leave a note. Brick Lane isn't far. We'll be back before they break for lunch.'

'Oh, and he said, bring him some shoes.'

Bess' mouth fell open. 'Wardrobe?'

'Yes, they'll have loads. Come on.'

Ena picked up her notepad, tore a sheet of paper from it and scribbled a note for Claire. *Hold the fort. We'll be back asap* and Bess took an A to Z of London from her desk drawer. They both put on their coats and ran up to Wardrobe.

The wardrobe mistress, used to odd requests, looked fazed when Ena asked to borrow a pair of men's shoes.

'No time to explain,' Ena said.

'What size?'

'I don't know… ten? No good if they're too small.'

'Size ten,' she said, handing Ena a pair of brown brogues. 'Will they be coming back?'

'Hope so,' Ena shouted, already halfway down the stairs.

Running out of the stage door, Bess shouted, 'We'll go in my car.'

Ena collected the sheet of paper with the address that the man with the dog had given Stan and followed her sister out to the street. With the engine already running Ena jumped into Bess' car. Minutes later the sisters were driving along Victoria Embankment to London Bridge on the way to Brick Lane and Jolson Street.

Ena was navigating the route with the help of the A to Z. 'This is Brick Lane.'

Bess pulled up outside a pub called The Bricklayers Arms and took the A to Z from Ena. 'It's called a lane, but it's a damn long one.' She ran her finger along the orange line of Brick Lane. 'It goes from Swanfield Street in Bethnal Green and crosses Bethnal Green Road in Shoreditch.'

'Which is what we've just done,' Ena said.

'And ends up in Whitechapel.'

'Which is where we are now.' Ena took back the A to Z and peered at the small streets off the High Street. 'And there's Jolson Street,' she said, pointing at a short street tucked around the back of Whitechapel High Street.

Bess put the car into gear, stuck her arm out of the window, and pulled into the traffic.

'It's around here somewhere.' There were so many market stalls and street traders they almost missed the turning to Jolson Street. 'There!' Ena shouted. 'Turn left.'

Bess swung the car into a street that was no wider

than most people's front drives.

'Follow the street round. The factory must be along here.'

'All the buildings look the same. How do we know which one is… I can see it,' Bess exclaimed! Taking her foot off the accelerator, she let the car coast to the end of the street.

Ena grabbed the shoes they'd brought for Artie from the back seat and got out of the car. Bess left the car and locked the doors.

A weather-beaten sign saying 'Bottles and Jars' swung precariously by one nail at the end of the lane. The factory along with all the other buildings in the street had been bombed out in the war and, because they hadn't been repaired or in the case of this building, pulled down when the war ended, they were what the man walking the dog called derelict.

Ena ran across the road. The door had been boarded up with planks of wood. The bottom two planks had been wrenched off and lay in the street. She pulled on another. The nails holding it in place were so rusty the wood split and it came away immediately. Ena stepped aside as it fell to the ground, narrowly missing her feet.

'Be careful,' Bess said, from behind Ena. 'There's no telling how safe this place is.'

'Artie?' Ena called. Her eyes quickly adjusted to the dark interior of the factory's windowless entrance. 'Artie? Are you in here? Can you hear me? I hope this the right place. Artie?' she shouted again.

Claire tapped her on the shoulder. 'Shush! I heard something.'

Ena strained her ears.

'There it is again.'

'*Here…*'

Ena ran towards the muffled sound. 'He's over here,

Claire.'

Artie sat on the stone floor, his back against the wall, beneath a small greasy smoked-stained window, hidden by a half-demolished wall that was being propped up by longer and bigger wooden planks than the ones across the entrance. His handkerchief had been used as a makeshift gag and his scarf bound his hands.

Artie shook his head rapidly from side to side.

Ena stopped in her tracks. 'What is it?'

He looked down and nodded at the floor.

'Glass,' Bess said. 'Be careful, Ena, there's a lot of it.' Together the women picked their way through dozens of broken bottles. When they reached Artie, Ena took off the gag and Bess untied his hands.

'My God am I pleased to see you,' he said, bursting into tears. Ena put her arms around him. 'I thought they'd brought me here to kill me.'

'You must be freezing, love,' Ena said.

'I'm cold, but my feet are freezing. The bastards took my shoes and socks.'

Ena put one shoe on him and Bess the other. 'We'll soon have you out of here.' Ena on one side of Artie, Bess the other, each gripping his elbows while supporting his back, hauled him to his feet.

'Are you okay to stand?'

'Yes, I can stand. Just get out of here.' The three of them carefully stepped through green, brown and clear glass - over millions of shattered shards - doing their best to avoid narrow bottlenecks and the thick round bottoms of bottles.

Once outside, Artie took several deep breaths. He looked up at the sky. 'I didn't think I'd walk out of there.'

'Well, you did and we'll soon have you home.'

Ena opened the back door of Bess' car and Artie flopped onto the seat and leaned his head against the soft leather of the backrest. Bess, already at the wheel, started the engine and when Ena was settled in the passenger seat and had closed the door, pulled out into Jolson Street with a jolt.

Artie opened his eyes and looked out of the window. 'Stop! Stop the car.'

Bess slammed on the brakes.

'That's the man!' Artie twisted round in his seat and looked out of the back window. 'There's a man in that doorway. It's the same man who came into the factory earlier after his dog. Look! He's standing in the doorway of the next building. Back up, please?' he begged. His voice a combination of anger and fear.

Bess reversed the car until it was level with the entrance to the bottle factory.

Ena looked across the road at the buildings on the left and right of the factory. There was no man in either doorway. She gave Bess a sideways glance and raised her eyebrows. 'The man isn't there now, Artie,' she said. 'Let's get you home.'

Ena had seen a man with a dog when they drove into Jolson Street. She had been worried that she wouldn't find Artie and it hadn't registered.

CHAPTER TWENTY-TWO

Bess knew South London. She had been a teacher before the war. She had taught English at Christchurch Secondary School in Clapham and had rented a flat on Clapham Common's east side. She had settled in London, got on well with the other teachers at the school, and loved her job and the children she taught. However, her teaching career was short-lived when a directive came from the Ministry of Education saying war was imminent and London's schoolchildren would be evacuated. The pupils of Christchurch School - and some of the teachers - were sent to Dorset. Bess declined the offer to go to the West Country, returned to Foxden, and with a team of land girls, turned the Foxden Estate into arable land.

She drove back along The Embankment from the East End of London to the West End, down the Strand, along the south side of Trafalgar Square, past the Houses of Parliament and along Millbank to Vauxhall Bridge. Once across the river, she took the South Lambeth Road. Driving through the streets of South London reminded her of the happy - and sad - times she'd had when she lived on Clapham Common. Her flat had been the home of the chauffeur to a wealthy family.

Artie's apartment was on the ground floor of a small block of flats that had been built after the war by Lambeth Council. 'You're home, Artie.' Ena got out of the car and opened the back door. She gave Artie's knee a shake. 'Wakey-wakey.'

He woke, yawned and looked past Ena with tears in his eyes. 'I shall never complain about my little flat again.'

Ena held the car door open. 'Are you alright?'

'I'm fine. That's what I don't get.' He dug his hands into his trouser pockets and took out his house keys. 'My keys!' He opened the flat door. Ena helped him out of his overcoat. 'And,' he said, taking his wallet out of the inside pocket of his coat and looking through it, 'I have no idea exactly how much money I had in here, but look?' He opened the wallet wide. 'A fiver and half a dozen pound notes. Whoever kidnapped me didn't do it for my money.'

Or a ransom, Ena thought. It was a warning. They were trying to scare him.

'Ena?'

'Coming.' She followed Artie into the small sitting room. Bess had switched on the light in the kitchenette, at the far end of the room. By the sound of cups and saucers clinking and the whistle of a kettle, Bess was making Artie a hot drink.

The grate was full of ashes. Ena took a two-bar electric fire from the side of the cream tiled fireplace and switched it on. The two electric bars gradually turned from black to orange and then to bright red. Ena moved the fire round until it was facing Artie, and then sat on the settee next to him.

Bess brought in three cups of coffee on a tray. She put it on the small occasional table in front of Ena and Artie, took her cup from it and sat in the armchair facing them.

'Can you remember what happened last night, Artie?'

Artie bristled. 'Of course I can. I wasn't drunk!'

Ena had been too direct. She'd upset her friend, which she hadn't meant to do. 'I didn't think you were.'

'Sorry, Ena.' He took a sip of his coffee and put it back on the tray. 'I wasn't drunk, but I was stupid.' He exhaled loudly and shook his head. 'I fell for the oldest trick in the book.'

Neither woman spoke. They waited until Artie was ready to tell them.

'At lunchtime I met my friend Hugh Middleton - who I told you works at GCHQ. I came home, washed and changed, and set off to The Blue Beau to meet with Bess and Margot. Well...' Artie shook his head again. 'I arrived at the club and was about to open the door when a bloke asked me for a light. I reached into my coat pocket to get my lighter and that was the last I knew until I woke up. I say woke up, but it was more that I came round. I felt sick and was non compos mentis for goodness knows how long. When my head stopped thumping and I was able to open my eyes and focus properly, I saw I was in a hotel room.'

'Did you recognise the man who asked you for a light?'

'No. I'd never seen him before, but I'd know him again if I saw him. He was my height and build, clean shaven, with dark brown hair. Not easy to tell the exact colour of someone's hair under the blue light outside the club, but his hair was dark brown. It was the bloke who had asked for a light that took the bag off my head in the hotel and again the following morning when they left me in the old bottle factory.'

'Strange that the kidnappers didn't take you straight to the factory. How long were you in the hotel?'

'All night. I got to The Blue Beau at eight and from there I was taken to the hotel.'

'Do you remember anything about the journey to the hotel?'

Artie shook his head.

'Nothing at all?'

'No. I was unconscious. I don't remember anything

until I woke up in the hotel room.'

'Okay.' Ena smiled sympathetically. She didn't want to push Artie, but she needed him to remember as much as possible. 'What was the room like? Can you describe it?'

Artie laughed wryly. 'It was ordinary. An ordinary hotel room like thousands of other hotel rooms, I imagine.'

'Take your time. Think about it for a second.' Ena pushed herself off the settee and stretched. 'I'm going to make more coffee. I expect you two want another cup?'

'Yes please,' they said in unison.

Artie told Bess about The Blue Beau until Ena returned with the drinks. She gave Artie his, left hers and Claire's on the tray and sat down.

'Right!' Artie said. 'The hotel room was clean. The curtains were wide. Yes,' he said, 'I remember thinking how strange it was that a room so small should have such a big window. The curtains covered the entire wall. They looked expensive. They were a deep dusky pink. The bedspread was the same colour and the wallpaper had a floral design with rosebuds in the same colour as the curtains. The wallpaper was good quality too.

'I don't think it was a cheap hotel. The room was small because it was a single. You know the type? Big hotels have cheaper rooms at the back or on the side of the building; rooms that don't have views or look out onto the kitchens or the car park. And, there was a sink in the room.' Artie closed his eyes. 'There was a drinking glass on the shelf above the sink and a mirror. A white towel hung from a rail at the side of the sink and… And it had a crest or an emblem on it.'

'Do you think it was the name of the hotel?'

161

'Could have been. The Savoy has its name on the towels. The Dorchester's name is on everything. Damn!' he opened his eyes. 'I can't remember.'

'Don't worry. I don't expect whoever took you left their calling card anyway. What about sounds? Did you hear any distinctive noises? A church clock chiming the hour?' Artie shook his head. 'What about traffic? Cars, buses? Did you hear any trams or trains?'

'I'm sorry. Nothing when I was in the hotel. I heard plenty of traffic when they were taking me to the bottle factory.'

Now we should get somewhere, Ena thought. She took a gulp of her coffee. 'Did you see the car?'

'No, they put a bag over my head. The room they kept me in was on the sixth floor. I know that because when we left the room they put me in a lift. It slowed down and juddered six times. I'd swear it wasn't the lift the hotel's guests used. It was too noisy and there were ridges on the floor.'

'It would have been the service lift.'

'It was. I put my hand out to steady myself and the side of the lift was rough to the touch. When it stopped and we got out, they bundled me into the back of a car.'

'At a guess, how long did it take to get from the hotel to the derelict factory in Jolson Street?'

'Twenty minutes, half an hour. I heard sounds then. Besides cars, I heard trains. We didn't cross the Thames, but we must have driven alongside if for some time because I heard the beep of a tugboat's horn and the duller longer peep of a cargo barge. I'd only been in the bottle factory a couple of hours when the old man's dog came in and started barking.'

Ena picked up her cup, took a sip of coffee and looked over the rim at her sister. 'What are you

162

thinking, Bess?'

'That whoever abducted Artie had no intention of hurting him.'

'I agree.' Ena directed her next question to Artie. 'The men who took you to the hotel last night obviously didn't want you to speak to Bess and Margot. But why?' she said, as much to herself as to Artie. 'It must have had something to do with what your friend from GCHQ told you.'

'What did your friend say about Rupert Highsmith?' Bess asked.

'Nothing much. At least nothing worth kidnapping me for. He said he didn't trust Highsmith.' Ena looked at Bess. She didn't trust Highsmith either. 'Hugh said he was a show-off, the arrogant sort. He said he was queer and had a lot of friends. Friends in high places was the phrase Hugh used. He didn't like Highsmith. He said Highsmith was only where he was today because he'd been to the right school and university.'

Where *is* Highsmith today, Ena wondered.

'When you told your abductors what Hugh Middleton had said, they must have realised that they had nothing to worry about.'

'That's just it. I didn't tell them. I've learned to keep my mouth shut,' Artie said.

'Even so, they didn't hurt you.'

Artie held up his bruised wrists and grimaced. 'I wouldn't call tying me up, gagging me, taking away my shoes and leaving me barefoot in a bombed-out factory surrounded by broken bottles not hurting me.'

'I would.'

'Ena's right, Artie. They could have killed you and dumped your body in the canal, or disposed of you somewhere where you'd never be found. Instead, they kept you in a hotel room until daylight when, because they knew there'd be a lot of people around Brick Lane market, they took you to Jolson Street. They knew there was a good chance that you'd be found. When you weren't, they sent the chap and his dog into you and you did what your captors knew you'd do, you got the man to telephone Ena at the theatre.'

'I believe the man who said he found you and telephoned the theatre was the man you saw in the doorway of the building next to the factory.'

'So you do believe me?'

'I saw him too, but not when we were leaving the factory. I saw him earlier. When we turned off Brick Lane there was a man with a dog standing on the corner of Jolson Street.' Ena picked up her coffee and finished it. 'I've no idea what your abductors wanted, but it wasn't to hurt you.'

'Maybe not, but I didn't know that. I was bloody frightened in that factory. What they could have done to me doesn't bear thinking about.' Artie shuddered. 'What if they come after me again?'

'They won't.' Ena reached out and laid her hand on his. 'Whoever took you from the club had no intention of hurting you, love. They only wanted to scare you.'

Artie didn't look convinced.

'It's the only explanation,' Bess said. 'If the reason they abducted you in the first place was to stop you talking to Margot or me, something must have happened to make them change their minds because they did in effect let you go.'

'So, why aren't they worried that Artie would tell us what he learned about Highsmith?'

'I don't know. They could be stalling for time. Or maybe something did happen after Artie had spoken to his friend from GCHQ that made the reason for kidnapping him irrelevant.'

'Or they could be using Artie's abduction to send us a message; scare us.'

'It still doesn't make sense.'

'Nothing about what happened last night makes sense. Unless your friend did tell you something incriminating about Rupert Highsmith?'

'He didn't!' Artie snatched his hand away from Ena.

'That's enough for today.' Ena got up and put her cup on the tray next to Bess'. 'You look all in,' she said, taking Artie's empty cup from him. 'Can I get you something to eat?'

He shook his head. 'I'm too tired to eat. I'll make something when I've had a sleep. If I dare close my eyes.'

Ena smiled. Artie didn't. 'Are you going to bed?'

'No, I'll have a siesta here.'

Bess took the tray to the kitchenette and began to wash up, and Ena took off Artie's shoes. 'I'll take these back to the wardrobe department. No point you keeping them, they're like boats on you. Put your feet up,' she said, 'I'll get a blanket.'

'Take one off my bed. The second door along the hall,' Artie called. Ena returned with a pair of socks as well as a blanket. 'I hope you don't mind, but I had a snoop around and found your sock drawer.' She put the thickest pair of socks she could find on Artie's feet and threw the blanket over him. By the time Bess returned from the kitchen Artie was asleep. Ena pulled the blanket up and tucked it around his shoulders, before leaving the room with Bess.

'I made a couple of cheese sandwiches and left them by the kettle.'

'He probably wouldn't make himself anything, but if it's there he'll eat it.'

'That's what I thought.'

Driving back to the West End, Ena and Bess discussed Artie's abduction, if that was what it was. Neither women thought the men who had kidnapped him, for want of a better word, had any intention of harming him. He had been taken for another reason. They decided it was a warning.

'Was the warning meant for Artie, or for you, Ena?'

'I'm not sure. But, until we know, we need to find out as much as we can about Artie's pal, Hugh Middleton, at GCHQ.'

'Okay, so, what do we already know about him?'

'He went to school with Artie - and that's about it.'

CHAPTER TWENTY-THREE

'I wonder why Artie's abductors chose to leave him in Jolson Street.'

Bess shrugged. 'You said you thought it was because of Brick Lane market. That there'd be a lot of people about and Artie would soon be found.'

'And I still think that's the reason, but why? I also think the hotel where they kept him would have been on that side of London. If not in the East End, somewhere nearby.'

'It would make sense. And, the man with the dog?'

'He wasn't a passer-by whose dog just happened to run into the old bottle factory and bark. He was either one of the abductors, or he works for military intelligence. He could have followed Artie home after he'd been to see his friend from GCHQ and followed him to Mayfair.'

'What? And then to the hotel where the kidnappers took him and again in the morning to Brick Lane?'

'No. It wouldn't have been possible.'

'He telephoned The Prince Albert's stage door and asked Stan to give *you* a message, which means he knows you and he knew you'd be at the theatre.'

'Artie would have told him where to find me.'

'Even so…' Bess frowned. 'Why didn't he ask to speak to you?'

'Stan said the man didn't want to speak to me. He said he only wanted to get a message to me.' Ena laughed. 'If the man with the dog knows me, I probably know him. In which case he'd be worried I'd recognise his voice.'

From the Embankment, they drove along the Strand, turned into Southampton Street and from there Maiden Lane, parking the car at The Prince Albert's stage door. 'And if I recognised his voice, I would know who he worked for.'

Bess pulled on the handbrake. 'You know what? The whole thing was a bloody set up to waste our time.'

'I agree. But why?'

Ena and Bess were met at the door of the visitor's room by Natalie. 'Margot has stayed at the rehearsal rooms with the dancers to lunch on sticks of celery, carrots and apples. Claire, as you know, was meeting a friend who she'd worked for in the war. She popped in to say they were going to Dooley's for lunch and hopes you're back in time to join them.'

'Did she say when she was coming back here?' Ena asked.

'No, just that she'll be at the restaurant.'

'I need to tell Claire what happened this morning.'

'I'll grab a sandwich from the café, do you want one?'

'No thanks, I'll get one on my way back. Phone and check on Artie, will you?'

'Of course.'

At the Coffee Bar Bess went in to get a sandwich and Ena walked on to Southampton Street where at the bottom she crossed the Strand to Dooley's Restaurant. 'I'm sorry to disturb you,' she said, as she approached the table where a tall distinguished looking man with intelligent blue eyes, a square jaw and a head of thick white hair was sitting next to Claire.

'You're not disturbing us. We haven't ordered yet. Take a seat, please.' The man handed Ena a menu.

Ena looked at the menu without reading it. 'I'm not hungry thank you, but if I may, I'd like a quick word with my sister.'

'Ena? I'd like you to meet a very good friend of mine, Colonel Smith.'

'How do you do, Colonel?' Claire had told her about Colonel Smith. He was the colonel who, as Head of the Special Operations Executive, had recruited Claire to work in France with Mitch and the resistance movement in the war.

'How do you do, Ena? Claire has told me about your husband being falsely accused of murder. A serious business, which we will get to when we've eaten.'

Ena was so tired that Colonel Smith's smooth, deep voice and warm smile could have persuaded her to do anything. She looked again at the menu and when the waiter came, said, 'Chicken with roast potatoes and vegetables.'

'I'll have venison,' the colonel said.

'And beef for me. Thank you,' Claire added, handing the menu to the waiter.

Colonel Smith ordered a red wine that Ena had never heard of and anyway declined saying she needed a clear head as she was working in the afternoon. He poured a glass for himself and one for Claire.

They ate in relative silence. No one wanted a sweet, but they all had coffee.

'So, Ena,' the colonel said, 'Claire tells me that the body of the mole at MI5, the personal assistant of your husband's late boss who your husband is accused of murdering, was found in your office?'

'It wasn't my office then. We were moved from Mercer Street some weeks previously, The Cold Cases department is part of the Home Office and Director Bentley thought it best if we were based at the HO in King Charles Street.'

'And you think your husband is being framed for

her murder?'

'I know he is.'

Colonel Smith beckoned the waiter who brought the bill on a small silver dish. Taking several notes from his wallet he put them on the tray and discreetly waved away the change. 'I think it would be prudent to adjourn to The Prince Albert theatre and discuss this matter in private.'

Claire and Ena agreed. And while Claire helped the colonel into his coat, the waiter held Ena's out for her to slip her arms into. He then did the same for Claire.

Wrapped up against a biting winter wind, Ena, Claire and Colonel Smith crossed the Strand and walked the short distance to Maiden Lane.

They were met in the visitor's room by Bess and Natalie. Once out of their outdoor clothes, Claire introduced the colonel, and Bess showed him to a seat at the conference table. When they were all seated around the table, Natalie poured coffee and the colonel took a silver case from the inside pocket of his jacket, took out a cigar and lit it.

Exhaling the sweet, woody aroma of cigar smoke, he said, 'Now, Ena, tell me why you don't believe your husband killed Helen Crowther.'

'I know my husband, and I know he couldn't kill anyone in cold blood.' The colonel acknowledged the statement with a nod. Ena sighed. She wanted to explain the situation without sounding like a wife blindly pleading for her husband. 'Henry is a clever man. If he had killed Crowther he would have had an airtight alibi. He wouldn't have left his fingerprints all over the crime scene, let alone on a bottle of whisky and two glasses that until Christmas Eve had been in the drinks cupboard in our apartment.'

The colonel made a small gesture with his hand for

Ena to stop speaking. 'Are you saying someone broke into your home and took the whisky and the glasses?'

'Yes, while we were away at Christmas.'

'Go on.'

'And, on the day Crowther was murdered, an identical car to ours was seen parked on the waste ground opposite the office at the same time that Henry was driving from Leconfield House to our home in Stockwell.' Ena fought back tears of anger. 'Why would anyone, let alone someone as experienced as Henry, do something as stupid? A newbie, an office boy, who had only worked for military intelligence for twenty weeks would know better than do that. Henry has worked for MI5 for more than twenty years. There's no way he would leave his car outside the building where he was going to kill someone. Henry was framed! Someone murdered Helen Crowther and is doing their best to get my husband sent down for it.'

'Does Henry have any enemies?'

Ena was taken aback by the question. 'Not personal enemies… Not now.'

Colonel Smith leaned back in his chair and looked questioningly at Ena. 'But he did have?'

'Yes, but both parties are dead now. After the war, Henry worked undercover. To crack a spy ring he went on the run with a German spy named Walter Voight. Walter died in prison and his sister Frieda was convinced Walter was murdered and blamed Henry. Frieda told me that Henry had promised to get Walter back to Berlin if she worked for British Intelligence. Because he broke his promise, Frieda tried to kill Henry last year, but,' Ena swallowed hard to rid herself of the memory of that night. The nightmares, after seeing Frieda fall from the roof of St. Leonard's Church, still invaded her sleep, still brought tears to her eyes and a lump to her throat. 'Frieda is also dead.'

'Then who would want to see Henry go down for Helen Crowther's murder?'

Ena blew out her cheeks. 'No one that I know of. He doesn't talk about his work at MI5, but I'm sure no one in his office... Unless someone at Five worked with her. I can't think of anyone who was close to Helen Crowther other than Mac Robinson but he's dead too.' Ena dug deep into her memory. 'No, I can't think of anyone who'd want to frame him.

'My biggest fear is that Crowther's associates will go after Henry if they believe he killed her.'

'Some are known to us, some we're investigating. I'll let you have a list, Sir,' Claire said.

The colonel tilted his head and looked over the top of his glasses. 'Off the top of your head?'

It was Ena who replied. 'I worked with Frieda Voight in the war and she told me she lived with her brother and their uncle in Northampton. The uncle's name was Villiers. When she and Walter - and the rest of the spy ring - were caught, the uncle disappeared.'

'Unless he was taking revenge for the death of his niece, I can't see the uncle reappearing after being off the radar for twenty-plus years?' The colonel shook his head. 'No. If your husband was framed, revenge could be the motive. For one person to plan a murder and execute it in such a way would take a lot of time and organising.'

'We believe a spy who has worked for MI5 and MI6 named Shaun O'Shaughnessy, aka Herr Krueger, is in some way involved in her death.' Claire looked at Ena. 'Is it alright if I show the colonel the photograph of the newspaper cutting and the translations?'

'Of course.'

While Colonel Smith read the transcript of the

Hitler Youth rallies with Crowther and O'Shaughnessy, Natalie refreshed the coffee jug and poured them each another cup. When he had finished reading he took a sip of his coffee. 'What do you know about Herr Krueger?'

'He calls himself Shaun O'Shaughnessy, though we don't think that's his real name. He says he's an actor, so it's probably his stage name. As I said, he has worked for MI5 and Six. I met him last year at Crowther's house. He's a thug and a blackmailer. He drugged a friend of mine to get information out of him and I believe he killed a colleague of mine when he was getting close to exposing Crowther as the mole at MI5.'

'What is O'Shaughnessy's connection to Helen Crowther?'

'We're not sure, but Helen Crowther...' Ena stopped speaking. She couldn't tell the colonel how she knew Helen Crowther was a lot older than her English passport and birth certificate stated, nor that she'd had a child, or she would be dropping DI Powell and Sandy Berman in it. 'We think O'Shaughnessy might be Crowther's son.'

'In which case, if he thinks Henry killed his mother, he will go after Henry.'

Ena's stomach churned and her heart began to pound. She took a steadying breath. 'He could be Crowther's son, or,' she continued, 'he could be part of the same spy ring. If O'Shaughnessy knew I'd found out Crowther was the mole at MI5 and I was going to investigate her, as I intended to do in the New Year, he may have killed her. He's ruthless. The fact that they had been close in Germany, in Brighton too, wouldn't matter to a sociopath like O'Shaughnessy.'

'He has already moved into Helen Crowther's

house, in Brighton,' Claire said.

'Have you seen him?'

Now it was Claire's turn to pause. 'Yes. And, from what we saw,' she looked at Ena, 'Mr O'Shaughnessy is living life to the full. He showed no sign of remorse, or that he was grieving.'

'He's a cold fish. He doesn't have a conscience.'

The colonel stood up. 'On that note, I had better go.' He picked up his attaché case. 'It has been a pleasure meeting you,' he said to Ena, taking in Bess and Natalie. His eyes settled on Claire. 'Stay in touch, won't you?'

'I will. Thank you, Colonel.'

Ena was first out of her seat. 'I'll see you out.'

'Claire told me Rupert Highsmith was at Frieda Voight's funeral. He isn't on your list of suspects,' the colonel said out of the blue, as they walked along the narrow passages at the back of the stage.

Ena felt her cheeks flush. 'Should he be? I did suspect Highsmith. He was in Berlin in thirty-six with my colleague, Sid; the colleague who was killed last year when we were investigating Frieda Voight and getting close to exposing the mole at MI5. Highsmith also knew Special Branch had brought Henry back to London at Christmas, among other things. He was too knowledgeable about the situation for my liking. I can't think why he'd kill Crowther and frame Henry unless he was part of the spy ring that she headed. Good God! As you know, Highsmith works for GCHQ and he has the ear of the Prime Minister. The amount of damage a man like that could do if he was a spy doesn't bear thinking about.' Ena exhaled loudly. 'Highsmith would have the wherewithal to kill Crowther and frame Henry.'

'What did your colleague, Artie Mallory, say about Highsmith after meeting with Hugh Middleton in Cheltenham yesterday?'

Ena was astounded. 'You know about that?'

'Yes. Mr Mallory was asking questions about Rupert Highsmith.'

'He was, for the reasons I told you. Artie's old school friend didn't tell him much. He said Highsmith had friends in high places, that he had been to the right school and university and he was homosexual. Artie didn't think his friend Hugh liked Highsmith very much.'

'I'm sure he doesn't,' Colonel Smith said, pushing

open the door leading to the stage-door. He held it for Ena. When they were both in the small backstage entrance lobby the colonel said, 'Highsmith is one of us. It's Mr Mallory's friend Hugh Middleton who is not who he seems.'

Ena was unable to hide her surprise. 'Good Lord. Artie didn't suspect anything. He said, he and his friend had parted on good terms and were going to meet up again. Artie went to meet my sisters...' Suddenly the metaphorical penny dropped. 'Was it you who took Artie to a hotel last night and this morning left him in the factory in Jolson Street?'

'Not me personally, but yes. I needed to be sure Mr Mallory wasn't mixed up with Hugh Middleton. We did a background check on him and, while he has done some dubious things in the past, he isn't one of Middleton's circle of friends.'

'It all makes sense now, except for one thing. Who was the man with the dog, and how did he know where to find me?'

'Ena?' Stan shouted from the door of his office. 'Sorry to interrupt, but there's a telephone call for you. Wouldn't give his name, but he said it's urgent.'

Ena looked from the stage doorman to the colonel. 'Another urgent call. It isn't the man with the dog again, is it?'

'No,' the colonel said, his face softening in a smile.

Ena walked quickly into Stan's office and took the telephone receiver from him. 'Ena Green, here.'

'Hello, Ena, it's DI Powell.' Giving Ena no time to return the greeting, he said, 'Would you come to the station right away? I have Mr Mallory here.'

'Of course. But why is Artie with you?'

'He's helping us with an enquiry.'

'Oh?' The policeman's stock answer for he's been

176

nicked, Ena thought.

'He says you'll be able to verify his whereabouts last night and this morning. I'm afraid I can't tell you any more.'

'I'll be there in ten minutes.' Ena replaced the telephone receiver and returned to Colonel Smith. 'Artie is being held at Bow Street Police Station. The DI wants me to vouch for his whereabouts last night and this morning. This morning I can vouch for, I was with him, but last night he was in a hotel somewhere in the East End of London with your people.'

The colonel opened his attaché case, took a card from it, and gave it to Ena. 'Give this to the inspector at Bow Street and tell him that you can vouch for Mr Mallory's whereabouts last night. If he needs further verification, tell him to telephone me on this number in...' Colonel Smith stretched out his arm and looked at his wristwatch, 'two hours.'

Ena took the colonel's card, looked at it for a second, memorised the number and put it in her coat pocket. 'Thank you.'

'My car is outside. I'll give you a lift.'

A large black government car, not the type of car used for surveillance but the type used to transport government officials and military top brass, was parked at the Southampton Street end of Maiden Lane. Ena and the colonel stood outside the stage door and watched the car pull out into the lane and cruise slowly towards them. The car stopped smoothly and silently and the driver jumped out. He saluted to the colonel and gave Ena a cursory nod before opening the back door of the car. The colonel gestured for Ena to get in. As she began to lower herself onto the soft cream leather seat, he walked round to the other side of the car, opened the door, and swung his tall frame into the

177

rear of the car.

'Where to, Sir,' the driver asked, pulling away from the kerb.

'Bow Street. We're dropping Mrs Green off at the police station and then it's back to Cheltenham.'

WPC Jarvis was waiting for Ena when she arrived at the station. She escorted her through the door marked 'Private' where, unless you were a witness or villain being interviewed about a crime, there was no public access. The woman police officer tapped on the inspector's door. A second later Ena heard the familiar and welcoming voice of DI Powell call, 'Come in.'

From behind his desk, DI Powell thanked WPC Jarvis and with an outstretched hand, beamed Ena a smile. 'Thank you for coming so quickly, Ena,' he said, gesturing to the chair next to Artie.

She lifted the chair from under the desk, gave Artie a reassuring smile and sat down. 'Now,' she said to her colleague, 'what have you been getting up to since Bess and I left you a couple of hours ago?'

'Nothing.' Artie rolled his eyes and looked indifferently at DI Powell.

He didn't react. 'Mr Mallory was with you until what time today, Ena?'

'It was the other way around,' she said. 'My sister Bess and I were with Artie at his flat in South London until a little after eleven o'clock this morning.'

'And last night?'

'Last night Artie went to meet my sisters, Bess and Margot, at...'

The inspector leant forwards and turned his head to the right as if to hear better what she was saying.

'The Blue Beau. It's a nightclub in Mayfair, but I think you already know that.'

The inspector's eyes glinted with amusement. He cleared his throat and feigned surprise. 'So, your sisters Bess and Margot were with Mr Mallory last night?'

'I didn't say that. I said, Artie went to meet my sisters. Unfortunately for him, he didn't make it into the club, he was abducted outside.' Out of the corner of her eye, Ena saw Artie's shoulders sag. 'However,' she continued, 'I have the authority to vouch for Artie's whereabouts last night. Whatever you think Artie did last night, he could not have done.' She took Colonel Smith's card from her pocket and passed it across the desk to the inspector. 'Artie was the unwilling guest of GCHQ last night. He was abducted outside The Blue Beau at eight o'clock and taken to a hotel in the East End of London.'

'What?'

That it was GCHQ who had abducted him was news to Artie. Ena looked at him and shook her head very slightly.

'And as soon as it was light, they took me to an old bottle factory and left me to freeze to death,' Artie added.

Ena glanced at the clock on the wall. 'Colonel Smith will be at the number on the card in an hour and forty-five minutes. He'll confirm what I've told you.'

'That won't be necessary, Ena.' The DI's forehead creased in a frown. Holding the card between his right thumb and forefinger, he tapped it against the fingers on his left. Ena saw indecision in his eyes. He scribbled down the colonel's telephone number on the top of his blotter and handed the card back to her.

'The colonel asked me to give the card to you. You keep it, Inspector.'

'I won't telephone the colonel today. I'll ring

tomorrow.'

Now it was Ena's turn to frown. She didn't understand why the inspector needed to telephone the colonel at all. 'If you believe Artie was with Colonel Smith's men last night, and with Bess and me all morning, do you mind me asking why you need to telephone the colonel?'

'Hugh Middleton has disappeared. No one has seen him since he left his office to meet Mr Mallory yesterday afternoon.'

The colour drained from Artie's face, but he didn't speak.

'I see.' Did Ena see? She fully understood why Artie, being the last person to see Middleton was of interest to the police, but why was DI Powell involved? What had a Metropolitan Police inspector in London's West End got to do with the disappearance of someone who worked for GCHQ and was last seen in Cheltenham?

DI Powell pushed back his chair and stood up. Ena and Artie did the same and followed him to the door. As he always did, the inspector opened the door and stood to one side.

Ena drew level with him. 'Inspector, I don't understand why the Met is involved in the disappearance of Hugh Middleton. Forgive me for asking, and of course you are not obliged to tell me, but why was it you who brought Artie in for questioning?'

DI Powell gave Ena a knowing smile. 'No, Ena, I am not obliged to tell you but, since I wasn't ordered not to - and I know what I tell you will not go any further.' He looked at Artie who put up his hand in acknowledgement. 'My colleague at Special Branch brought me in on this case because Hugh Middleton

180

was a known associate of the late Helen Crowther.'

'If it wasn't the middle of the afternoon, I'd suggest we go to the pub for a very large drink,' Ena said as she and Artie left Bow Street Police Station. 'Good God, this bloody Crowther case gets more complicated by the day.'

They walked on through Covent Garden without speaking. Then Artie said, 'I'd never have thought my old pal Hugh was a spy. Is his disappearance my fault, Ena?'

'No, Artie, it is not your fault. We are each responsible for the choices we make in this life. If your friend chose to throw his lot in with Helen Crowther, it's no one's fault but his own.' Artie shivered and linked his arm through Ena's. 'But we don't know he is a spy. Being an associate of a spy doesn't make him one.'

'About Crowther? Do the police still think Henry was involved in her death?'

'Killed her, you mean? DI Powell doesn't, but Special Branch are still looking at Henry for it.' Ena was suddenly overwhelmed with emotion. 'I haven't seen him for two months. He sends me postcards that say, 'having a lovely holiday, wish you were here and missing you'.'

'So you know by the postmark where he's being held?'

'I know anyway, Henry told me.' Ena caught her breath.

'What is it?'

'The cards are posted all over the place - Shrewsbury, Aberdeen. The last one he sent was posted in Lincoln.' She took Artie's arm from hers and said again, 'Lincoln.' She cast her mind back to the coded message Henry had written and laughed. 'Did you telephone the Home Office?'

'Yes.' Artie looked puzzled. 'I left a message for Director Bentley saying I wasn't well but hoped to be at work tomorrow.'

'Good.' At Southampton Street, Ena looked at her watch 'Would you go to the theatre and tell my sisters what DI Powell said?'

'Yes, but aren't you coming.'

'I've just remembered I have an errand to run. I'll see you in an hour. Tell the girls about Middleton, yes?'

'I will.'

As Artie turned onto Maiden Lane, Ena ran down to the Strand. She hailed the first taxi that approached. 'St. Paul's Cathedral, please.'

CHAPTER TWENTY-FIVE

The taxi pulled up behind a row of school buses. 'I'll have to drop you here.'

'That's fine.' Ena jumped out of the taxi, paid the driver, and looked back along Ludgate Hill. She was sure she hadn't been followed, but as a precaution she stood on the pavement and consulted her watch every few minutes as if she was waiting for someone to join her. If she had been followed by spooks in a surveillance car they would have parked so they had a clear view of the Cathedral's main entrance. She looked across the road. There were no cars parked opposite. She waited a while longer and when she was certain she hadn't been followed, she moved on.

In a relaxed manner, she looked up and down the street again, casually observing the faces of people passing by. None were familiar. Those heading towards the Cathedral were consulting leaflets and discussing what they wanted to see in Wren's magnificent building - and those leaving were discussing the wonders of what they had seen. No one showed the slightest interested in her.

If the Bletchley three-three code Henry used on the card from Lincoln meant three o'clock on the third day of the month, Ena had twenty minutes to get up to the Stone Gallery. She strolled by the third and second bus until she reached the doors of the first. Two female teachers were counting heads as children clamoured down the steps of the bus and formed two lines on the pavement. Looking up in awe of the iconic dome, Ena waited for the children to go past. The last person to vacate the bus was a man in his mid-twenties. Scuffed brown shoes, tweed overcoat with frayed cuffs, no gloves but with a college scarf wound around his neck told Ena he was a teacher who had only recently left teacher training college. She fell into step with him.

'How lucky children are these days,' she said, 'to be allowed to visit wonderful buildings like St. Paul's Cathedral.'

'I'm not sure they appreciate how lucky they are,' he said, wearily.

'They will when they're older.' Ena mounted the steps to the Cathedral at the side of the young teacher - smiling at him as if they were colleagues. To anyone watching, Ena was just another teacher taking school children on a trip to St. Paul's Cathedral. In the Nave, she held back from the group and when they were shepherded down the long central aisle leading to the dome, she walked on. She mounted the ancient steps that took her to the Whispering Gallery - and from there she went up to the Stone Gallery.

An information sheet in a glass case told her she had walked up 378 steps to reach the Stone Gallery. Her lungs were in agreement and as she stepped outside onto the walkway encircling the dome she inhaled the cold afternoon air. Her aching calf muscles were instantly forgotten when she caught sight of the view over London's rooftops. She pulled her coat tightly around herself and folded her arms across her chest. It was cold and there was a sharp wind whistling round the dome from the north side.

There were a lot of visitors on the walkway, but nowhere near as many as there had been in the Whispering Gallery, the High Altar or the Nave. Ena fell into step with the slow flow of people. A middle-aged couple stopped and looked across the city. They were within a few feet of her. She moved away from them. If Henry made it to the Stone Gallery, she wanted him to see her. People moved on. Ena stayed put.

'It's a beautiful view from where I'm standing,' a man with a deep, warm, familiar voice said as he passed behind her.

'It is?' Ena's heart was thudding in her chest.

'I can't believe how beautiful. I have missed it,' he said.

'So have I.' Ena began to tremble. 'Missed it more than I can tell you.'

Henry moved into view and held the rail by her side. 'Are you alright?'

'I am now I know you're alive,' she whispered. 'What's happening? Do the Branch still think you…?' Ena didn't say, killed Crowther, she didn't have to. Henry nodded.

He looked up at the dome. 'Goodbye, love.'

'You're not going?'

'I have to.' For the briefest moment, Henry brought his focus back to Ena. 'Enjoy the rest of St. Paul's.'

'Please don't go,' she pleaded, 'I have so much I want to tell you.'

As he turned to leave, Henry bumped into her. 'I love you.' He put his hands on her shoulders as if to steady her. 'Wait ten minutes before you leave.' He looked into her eyes and apologised for bumping into her.

Giving the clumsy man a friendly smile, Ena said, 'I love you,' and waved the apology away. 'Write soon,' she whispered.

'I already have.'

Ena turned her back on Henry and held onto the rail. She couldn't bear to watch him leave. She wanted to run after him, tell him how much she loved him but he had said she must stay where she was; that she must wait ten minutes before she left. That was Henry's way of saying she wasn't to follow him. To stop herself from crying out, Ena gripped the handrail until her knuckles felt bruised.

After the longest ten minutes of her life, Ena entered the Stone Gallery and exited with a group of Swedish tourists. She wandered around with them, looking at everything and seeing nothing until they left the Cathedral twenty minutes later.

Outside, she leant against the Cathedral wall, looked up at the sky and closed her eyes. Fine rain fell onto her face. It felt refreshing. She wanted to walk, to think about Henry and relive the few precious minutes they had spent together, but she needed to get back to the theatre. To understand about Crowther and O'Shaughnessy in 1936, she needed to read the transcripts of the newspaper cuttings that Claire had translated into English. She inhaled the cold, damp air and put up her hand. A cab pulled up immediately and she got in.

'The Prince Albert Theatre, stage door, Maiden Lane.'

Ena paid the driver and left the taxi. It had grown dark. Clouds hid the stars and threatened heavy rain. Ena pulled on the collar of her coat and dug her hands deep into her pockets. Something rustled between her gloved fingers. Sheltering in the backstage doorway, Ena took a piece of paper from her pocket and read, *Darling, stop the investigation. It's too dangerous. Leave it to the Branch.*

Ena had been longer than she told Artie she'd be and by the time she got to the visitor's room he had left. Claire was sitting at the conference table writing.

'Where's Artie?'

'He telephoned the Home Office and asked for a few days leave. They gave it to him and he went home.' Claire put down her pen and looked up at Ena. 'Satisfactory errand?'

'Yes and no.' She dropped Henry's note on the table. 'Anything we didn't know about Crowther and O'Shaughnessy in the newspaper cuttings?' she asked, while Claire read Henry's message.

'On your desk.'

Ena took off her coat, put it over the back of her chair and sat down to read the notes.

'Ena?'

She looked at Claire.

'Whatever you decide to do, I'm with you.'

Natalie arrived before Ena could reply and slumped into the chair next to Claire. Her face was pale and tears filled her eyes.

Ena crossed to the conference table and sat next to her. 'Natalie, what is it?'

Natalie looked from Ena to Claire. 'Margot's alright,' she said, 'there's nothing to worry about, but she collapsed during rehearsals. I sent for the theatre doctor and he said she was suffering from exhaustion.'

'Where is she now?'

'Bess has taken her to Hampstead. I telephoned my GP. He will be there when they arrive.'

Ena ran to her desk. 'This can wait,' she said, 'we need to go to Margot.'

Natalie crossed to Ena and helped her into her coat. 'I'm sorry I won't be able to come with you. I'll get the company manager to come in early and be home as soon as I can.' She picked up the newspaper translations. 'I'll put these in the safe,' she called after Ena as she ran out of the room.

Natalie looked at the sheets of paper and burst into tears. 'It's my fault Margot's ill. I shouldn't have let her take rehearsals. Working with young dancers is too strenuous.'

Claire put her arm around Natalie's shoulder. 'You couldn't have stopped her. No one could have. Margot was determined to work with them. She was in her element. She loved every minute of it.' Claire took the translations out of Natalie's hand. 'Ena will also blame herself for Margot being ill. I'll give her these when we get back to her place tonight, hopefully they'll take her mind off Margot. For a little while at least.'

Ena didn't ring the bell. She didn't want to disturb Margot. She led the way to the back of the house and looked through the kitchen window. Bess was on the telephone. When she finished the call and put down the receiver, Ena tapped the glass.

Bess ran to the door and opened it.

'How's Margot?'

'Asleep.'

'Has the doctor been?'

'Yes. He said she is exhausted and dehydrated. He mixed up an orange concoction; a drink that they give elderly people to help them hydrate. The good news is, she's okay to travel so I'm taking her back to the Midlands first thing in the morning.'

'Have you spoken to Bill?'

'Yes, just now. He sounded all in, poor chap. He's naturally worried to death about her. When I told him I was bringing her home tomorrow, he told me she had an appointment at the Walsgrave Hospital in Coventry the day after tomorrow.'

'What? Did Margot know?'

'Yes.'

'Why didn't she say anything?'

'Because from what Bill said, she had no intention of keeping it. She was going to stay down here to rehearse the next chorus line for the next show.'

'But she isn't strong enough. Her health is...' Ena put her hands up to her mouth for fear she'd cry out. 'It's my fault. If it hadn't been for my bloody job, Crowther wouldn't have been murdered, Henry wouldn't have been framed for it and Margot wouldn't have risked her health by coming down to London. It's been too much for her.'

'Ena, she wanted to come.'

'She wouldn't hear of us coming down without her.'

'If we'd left her behind it would have broken her heart. She needed to feel useful. Bill has everything working like clockwork at the dance school. Margot said the place runs itself.' Bess looked at Ena's tear-stained face. 'Margot wanted to help you and Henry, okay?'

'I know.' Ena sniffed and wiped her eyes. 'Can I go and see her?'

'She's on the settee in the front room.'

Ena crossed the hall and opened the door. She quietly tip-toed across the room. Margot was tucked up under a satin quilt. Her eyes were closed and her face was pale. She looked like a china doll. How unfair that someone as young as Margot should be crippled with arthritis. Ena turned to leave.

'I'm not asleep,' Margot said.

Ena looked back at her sister. 'Alright if I stay for a bit, then?'

'Of course. Did our bossy big sister, Bess, tell you she's taking me home tomorrow?'

'Yes, and it's a good job she is. You can't go missing hospital appointments.'

'Mm... I suppose you're right. But I wanted to see the murdering bugger who framed our Henry swing for killing Crowther.'

'And you will.'

'I don't know that I'll be allowed back.'

Ena's heart sank. Did her sister mean she wasn't going to be well enough to come back?

'You can stop with the miserable face, our Ena. I don't plan to get my wings any time soon. I meant Bill won't let me come back.'

'Would he be able to stop you?'

190

Margot laughed until she coughed. Ena took the glass of water from the occasional table at the side of the settee. Margot sat up, took a sip and caught her breath. 'Bill's got a lot on his plate. What with work and me not being able to pull my weight at the school, it means more of the day to day running of the place falls to him.'

'He's a good man.'

'He is. You know, in the war, when I was the leading lady at The Prince Albert Theatre, I had a thousand friends. The Talk of London they called me. Margot Dudley, Star of the West End! My fans hung around the stage door just to get a glimpse of me. Whatever the weather, newspaper men waited outside nightclubs to get a photograph of me arriving and leaving. Club owners, managers and band leaders asked me to sing with the house bands. They would lead me by the hand to the stage as if I was the Queen of Sheba. The audience would go wild. I loved the attention, the applause, and for a long time, I needed it. I didn't believe I was worthy without it. But it wasn't real. I pushed everyone who really cared for me away. I thought they were jealous of my success. I thought Bill was boring.'

'Margot!'

'I'm ashamed to admit it now, but I did. Then, when things started to go wrong, when I began drinking, couldn't sleep without sleeping tablets. When I wasn't able to perform for them, give them what they wanted, those cheering applauding people - my so-called friends - were nowhere to be seen. It was Natalie and Anton Goldman who were with me during that awful time. They got me through my drinking and addiction to pills. They saved my life. And, Bill...' Margot wiped tears from the corner of her eyes, 'my Bill still

191

loved me. He never once judged me, you know? And,' she said, laughing and crying at the same time, 'when we left London and went home to Coventry, I realised Bill wasn't boring at all. All the time I was in London, chasing my career, I was so wrapped up in myself that I hadn't noticed that my wonderful husband had become *Mr Margot Dudley*. And he never complained. My Bill was, and still is, the most clever, interesting, funny - and loving…'

Margot closed her eyes. When her sister's erratic breathing became steady and rhythmical, Ena quietly left.

'Margot's sleeping.'

'Then we'll go.' Claire got up. 'I'll poke my head around the door, but I won't wake her.'

'Is she okay?' Ena asked on Claire's return.

'Yes, still asleep.'

'She'll be fine, so don't you two worry.' Bess led the way to the front door. 'I'll get her home tomorrow and Bill will take her to the hospital appointment.'

Ena and Claire put on their coats and kissed Bess goodbye. As they drove away, Ena looked in the reverse mirror. Bess was standing in the doorway of Natalie Goldman's house waving. Ena flashed the car's lights.

'I don't think Margot will be back. I mean, not after these tests.'

'I hope she doesn't come back. Not until the doctors find out what's really going on.'

'Arthritis is one thing, but her breathing is getting worse. She needs to see a specialist.

Hopefully, by the time she's better, Henry will be home and we can come up to Foxden and go to Coventry to see her.'

'When you were with Margot, Bess said that she

and Frank had several functions booked at the hotel at the end of the month and then there's Easter. She said she may not get back to London until after the May Bank Holiday. I told her not to worry. Now the groundwork has been done, you and I can do the rest.'

'We can. We've got a lot to go on.'

'And a lot to sort out.'

'Which we'll do tomorrow. First, I need to read the transcript of the old newspaper cuttings. What's the time?'

Claire held up her left arm and squinted at her watch. 'Almost ten.'

'Good. The show will still be on. We'll swing past the theatre and pick up the cuttings.'

'No need. I put them in my bag before we left.'

Ena gave her sister a sideways smile. 'Yes, I think we can do the rest. Whatever the rest is.'

Ena brought the Sunbeam to a halt at the foot of the steps leading to the flat. She pulled on the handbrake, turned off the ignition, but made no attempt to leave the car.

'What is it, Ena?'

'I'm tired. I'm worried about Margot and I'm worried about Henry. What the hell is going on, Claire?'

'I don't know, but whatever it is we'll get to the bottom of it.'

Ena reached into the back seat and took hold of her bag by the strap. 'And the note Henry put in my pocket at St. Paul's. How did he know I'm still working on the case?'

Claire laughed. 'Because he knows you.'

'I suppose.' Ena smiled. 'I only saw him for a few seconds, but it was wonderful.'

'Come on. Let's get inside.' Claire picked up her handbag from by her feet. 'We'll light the fire and have something to eat.'

'And have a drink.'

Both women laughed. 'I could do with one,' Claire said.

'And I'll read about Crowther and O'Shaughnessy in Berlin.'

The sisters left the car, locked it and mounted the steps to the flat.

'Stop!' Ena put out her arms to prevent Claire from going further.

'There's light coming from somewhere. It's reflecting on the tiles in the entrance hall.'

Claire leaned forward until her forehead was almost touching the glass in the door. 'Maybe one of the other tenants has just got home.'

Ena was not convinced that was the reason. She unlocked the street door and gasped. Fear burned through her body from her head to her toes as the reality hit her. The light was coming from her flat.

Ena put her forefinger up to her lips. Claire nodded. Together they entered the building and moved silently across the hall to the open door. Ena pushed on it gently. It opened several inches. She strained her ears but could hear nothing. She looked at Claire and lifted her shoulders. Claire pointed to the interior of the flat. Ena nodded and opened the door wide.

The two women stood in the hall. Neither spoke. Ena's bedroom door stood ajar, as did the door to the sitting room. Claire, nearest to the bedroom, approached it and pushed it open. Ena did the same to the door of the sitting room.

'What the hell!' Drawers had been pulled out of the sideboard and thrown on the floor; their contents were strewn over the carpet. The fire; paper, wood and coal, ready to light when they got home that evening had been taken from its basket and spread along the tiled hearth. The armchair next to the fire had been slashed, the sacking fabric underneath was torn and the stuffing had been pulled out. The settee had received the same treatment. Cut to shreds, it had been tipped over. Horsehair stuffing spilt from its underbelly.

She crossed to the sideboard. The brown casing of the wireless had been smashed, the valves ripped out and discarded. 'What do these bloody people want from me?' she screamed, as Claire ran into the room. 'Look,' she said, tears falling from her eyes. 'They've trashed the place. Why? What did they want? What were they looking for?'

Claire picked up the telephone. The handset was still attached to its black Bakelite base, but the metal panel underneath had been removed and lay on the floor. The drawer at the front had been torn out and lay beside it. Claire put the telephone back together and dialled. She sighed with relief as it connected.

'My name is Claire Mitchell. Would you put me through to Detective Inspector Powell, please?' Claire handed the telephone to Ena.

'What is it, Claire?'

'Inspector, it's Ena. The flat has been broken into again.'

CHAPTER TWENTY-SEVEN

Taking care not to disturb anything, Ena and Claire went to the kitchen. 'I'm sure we can make a cup of tea,' Claire said. 'I doubt whoever broke in touched the kettle.'

Ena pulled open the door of the refrigerator using the corner of a tea towel. 'We don't have any milk.'

Claire took the empty milk bottle from the sink. It lay next to several other empty bottles and jars. 'Nor sauces or vinegar.'

Aware that the floor was slippery, Ena looked down. 'What on earth?' Her left foot was sliding about in a couple of ounces of melted butter. She took the dishcloth from the sink and wiped the sole of her shoe. 'What the hell were they hoping to find in half a pound of butter?'

Not wanting to smear grease over the sitting room carpet, she kicked off her shoes.

What were they looking for that was so small it could have been hidden in a bottle of milk or a few ounces of butter? She wondered, perching on the edge of a dining room chair and making sure she didn't touch anything. The memory of Sandy Berman, the police pathologist at St. Thomas, discovering the first clue to finding her friend, Sid's, killer came into her mind. A piece of paper, no bigger than a postage stamp, was trapped between Sid's broken teeth and jaw. The note was wrapped in a transparent cover folded like an envelope made of glassine to keep it dry. Ena felt the colour drain from her face.

Claire handed her a cup of black coffee. 'What is it, Ena?' she asked.

'I was thinking about when my colleague, Sid, was killed. Before Ena had time to tell Claire about Sid, there was a knock at the front door. Claire put down her coffee, ran into the hall and opened it. 'Come in, Inspector Powell, WPC Jarvis. Thank you for coming so quickly.'

The inspector entered the sitting room first. 'Are you alright, Ena?'

'Yes. But...' She looked around the room. She could feel tears building in her eyes and cleared her throat.

'Don't worry about this. As long as you and your sister haven't been hurt.' The inspector looked at Claire. She shook her head.

'The fingerprint officers are on their way. Before they get here, is anything missing?'

'No. They wrecked the place for nothing. We don't keep anything important here.' A thought flashed into Ena's mind. The room could be bugged - and trashing the place might be a smokescreen. She waved her hand at the inspector and pointed to the light fitting in the ceiling. 'We don't have anything of value to steal.'

He looked up. 'What about the other rooms? Would you mind having a look round to make sure?'

The inspector accompanied Ena to her bedroom. WPC Jarvis went with Claire to hers. Neither women found anything missing. Ena's bed had been upended, the wardrobe doors were open and hers and Henry's clothes, still on their hangers had been taken out and thrown on the floor. The tallboy, chest of drawers and bedside cabinets had been searched. Underwear, socks, blouses and shirts were scattered over the floor and Ena's jewellery box had been opened and its contents left on the dressing table. Her jewellery was all there.

'Nothing missing. Very strange.'

'Strange indeed.'

In the hall, Claire motioned to Ena and the inspector

to stay where they were. She shut the bedroom, kitchen and sitting room doors and then took the cuttings that she had translated that day from her shoulder bag. 'I wonder if these were what the burglar was looking for?'

'If they were, how would they know you had them?'

'They wouldn't know. I gave them to Director Bentley before Christmas. Well, most of them anyway.'

'It's possible that whoever broke in tonight thought you might have made copies, or even kept back some documents, which you did.'

'I only kept back Sid's letter to me, which was personal, and the compromising photographs. Neither have any bearing on the Crowther case. And I didn't keep them here. They were in a safe place where no one except me...' Ena stopped abruptly. She wasn't going to put Inspector Powell in the position of having to explain himself.

'And me,' the inspector said. 'Until recently I knew where they were.'

'They were safe.' Ena smiled at the only person other than her sisters she trusted. 'So,' she said, opening the sitting-room door, 'why do this?' DI Powell and Claire followed Ena into the room, WPC Jarvis stayed in the hall.

Ena looked at the slashed fabric on the settee and the stuffing around the armchair. 'What were they looking for, if not...?'

'Something else to incriminate Henry?'

'There's no telling.' DI Powell shook his head. 'No telling at all.'

WPC Jarvis poked her head around the sitting room door. 'Sir, the finger print officers are here.'

'Show them in, Jarvis. We'll get out of their way.' The inspector ushered Ena and Claire out of the sitting-room as the fingerprint men came in. 'You can't stay here tonight. Is there anywhere you can go? Could you stay with Mrs Goldman?'

'Not tonight. My sister Margot isn't well. Bess is taking her home to the Midlands tomorrow. Besides, we'd have to tell them why we can't stay here, and it would worry them.'

'We could stay with Natalie tomorrow night,' Claire said.

'But tonight it's The Hope and Anchor. It's nearby and does bed and breakfast. I stayed there last year after I'd collected Sid's case from Waterloo Station. I know the landlord, he's ex-military intelligence.'

'I know the pub, Sir.' WPC Jarvis gave the inspector the nod.

'Good. Grab enough clothes for a few days and Jarvis will drive you to the pub.'

'What about my car? I'll need it if we're going to be staying in Hampstead with Natalie.'

'I want the fingerprint boys to give that the once over, in case anyone other than you and Claire has been in it.'

Ena and Claire went to their respective bedrooms. Each packed an overnight bag and returned to the hall where they said goodnight to DI Powell before leaving for The Hope and Anchor with WPC Jarvis.

Scrutinising the photograph that Claire had taken of the original in the newspaper, Ena caught her breath. 'Look closely at this photograph of Crowther.'

'What am I looking at?'

'Crowther's eye line. Follow it. She isn't looking ahead as the others on the march are, she's looking to the left. She's looking at… Good God, Walter and Frieda Voight.'

'So she is. And, so is O'Shaughnessy.'

'Yes, he is. They must have known each other all those years ago.'

'The Voights may not have known Crowther and O'Shaughnessy, but they certainly look as if they knew the Voights. At least Crowther does.'

Ena dropped the photograph onto the table. 'Whether they knew each other or not, we're no nearing finding Crowther's killer. We know it couldn't have been Walter or Frieda Voight because they were both dead.'

'We need to find the child Crowther had before she was married.'

'You don't think it's O'Shaughnessy, do you?'

'I'd be very surprised if it was. He didn't show any signs of unhappiness at having just lost someone close. Even a cold fish like him wouldn't be living the high life so soon after his mother had been murdered. No,' Claire shook her head, 'I've got O'Shaughnessy down as Crowther's murderer, not her son.'

'Don't forget the Voights had an uncle. His name was Villiers. He was never caught.'

'He'd have hightailed it back to Berlin after the Voights were caught.'

'That leaves us with Crowther's son?'

'Or daughter.'

'If Crowther's offspring did kill her, they'll have gone back to Berlin by now.'

'That's if they came from Berlin.'

'Crowther did, Walter and Frieda Voight did.'

'It doesn't mean Crowther's child was brought up in Berlin.'

'No, it doesn't.' Ena shuddered. 'If someone else

200

killed her and her child thinks it was Henry, they might still be in London.'

'Planning their revenge?'

'It's a long shot, but why not?' Ena got up and went over to the window.

'What is it?'

'Don't ask me why, but I know Crowther's murder has something to do with the Voights.' She exhaled loudly. 'So, where do we go from here?'

'We need to find a connection between Helen Crowther and Nick Miller.'

'Miller has a top of the range car dealership in the East End of London. That could be where the Sunbeam Rapier that was seen in Mercer Street the day of Crowther's murder came from.'

'Proving it won't be easy.'

'That's where your friendly Metropolitan Police inspector comes in.'

CHAPTER TWENTY-EIGHT

'Milk, no sugar.' DI Powell handed Ena a cup of tea before pouring one for himself.

'I have the Vintage Car magazine that was in the house of the boys who found Helen Crowther's body.' The inspector took the magazine from his desk drawer and gave it to Ena.

'Have you spoken to the boys about it?'

'Not yet. They were at school when I went to the house. Mrs Hardy, their mother, said the magazine was given to them by the local newsagent.'

'That's not very likely, is it?'

'I wouldn't have thought so, but she swore that's what the boys told her. I think she knew it wasn't true. She was on the defensive as soon as she saw me so I didn't press her.' The inspector laughed. 'She was in battle mode, leaning against the door frame with her arms folded across her chest. She answered my questions in words of one syllable. I could see she wasn't going to help me the minute she opened the door.

'WPC Jarvis went to the house the following day after school hours. Mrs Hardy was less belligerent with Jarvis, invited her into the house to talk to the boys.' The DI glanced at the clock. 'Mrs Hardy agreed to bring her sons to the station but said she didn't have the bus fare. Jarvis said the boys were fascinated with cars. They never stopped talking about police cars and motorcycles. They couldn't believe that a 'girl' was allowed to drive a police car and asked her if she'd take them for a ride. Jarvis said if they agreed to come into the station and promised to tell the truth about the car they'd seen in Mercer Street…'

'The Sunbeam?'

'Yes. But Jarvis didn't say the name, the boys did. She said she'd pick them up in the police car. They agreed, and that's where Jarvis is now.'

'WPC Jarvis is a clever woman,' Ena said.

'She's a good copper,' the inspector agreed.

'Does Mrs Hardy have a husband?'

'She does, but he isn't around at the moment.'

'It must be difficult bringing up three boys without a man. Do you know where he is?'

'In the Scrubs serving time for armed robbery, among other things. She swears he's innocent. Says he was framed…'

'I sympathise with her if he was.'

'Arnold Hardy wasn't framed; he was caught red-handed. The man has convictions from here to Timbuktu. He's been in prison more years than he's been out, but Mrs Hardy won't hear a word against him.'

'That's love for you.' Ena sighed. 'It wouldn't do for me.'

'Glad to hear it, Ena,' the inspector joked.

No sooner had the DI finished speaking than the rumble of a small herd of elephants echoed along the corridor. 'What have I let myself in for?' the DI said. Getting up from his desk he went to the door and opened it.

Three little boys with muddy shoes and scrubbed faces froze when they saw the inspector. From behind them, their mother pushed the tallest of her children into the room first. Going down in size, the smallest and presumably the youngest boy, trooped in behind his older brothers. They stopped as one in front of Ena.

'Thank you for bringing the boys in, Mrs Hardy,' the inspector said. He turned to Ena. 'This is Mrs Hardy, Ena, the mother of our three young witnesses.'

'Pleased to meet you,' Ena said, gesturing to Mrs Hardy to sit in the chair next to her. Ena turned to the boys. 'I'm pleased to meet you boys, too,' she said, looking at each of them in turn.

'This is Alfred,' the inspector said. The oldest boy set his mouth in a straight tight line. He acknowledged Ena with a nod and a frown. 'Next is Gerald.' The middle boy looked down at the floor shyly. 'And, last but by no means least, the youngest member of the Hardy family is William.'

William looked indignant. 'I'm Billy,' he said, to Ena, 'everyone calls me Billy.'

'No they don't,' Gerald scoffed.

'Yes they do!'

'Well, never mind what anyone else calls you, I shall call you Billy. I'm very pleased to meet you, Billy. Pleased to meet you too, Alfred and Gerald.'

Billy beamed Ena a broad smile while the other boys fidgeted with their hands in their pockets.

'Right!' the inspector said, 'I've heard there are sweets in WPC Jarvis' office when you've told Mrs Green and myself what you saw the day you found the lady in Mercer Street.'

Their attention now was on WPC Jarvis who had driven them to the police station in the DI's black Wolseley. The subject very quickly changed. 'Will you take us 'ome in the cop car an all?' Alfred asked. Gerald and Billy called out, 'please' and 'will you' at the same time.

WPC Jarvis scrunched up her shoulders, pulled a wide-eyed excited face and nodded.

'Boys?' Ena waited for them to stop chattering and settle down. When she had regained their attention she said, 'You like cars, don't you?' Again they began to talk at the same time, none of them listening to what

204

the other was saying. 'I drive a Sunbeam Rapier,' she said, above the hullabaloo. All three boys fell silent.

Ena turned to Alfred. 'Was it you who saw a Sunbeam Rapier in Mercer Street?' Alfred didn't answer. 'You were playing on the waste ground opposite the building where you found the lady?' Ena hadn't had much experience with children and didn't know whether the solemn look on Alfred's face was one of defiance or fear. She decided it was the latter.

'There's no need to be frightened, Alfred. You won't be in trouble if you are unsure,' Ena said, 'nor will you be in trouble if you were to suddenly remember that it wasn't a Sunbeam Rapier you'd seen that day.'

The two younger boys stared up at their older sibling. Gerald nudged his big brother and Billy whispered, 'Tell the lady what 'appened, Alfred.'

'Shut up or we'll cop-it. Remember what the lady said,' Alfred hissed.

'Yes.' Billy's bottom lip began to quiver.

WPC Jarvis, sitting at the table by the window writing down what the boys said, pushed back her chair and walked over to them. Her young face softened into a warm smile as she crouched down in front of them. 'What did the lady say, Alfred?'

'She said...' Alfred sniffed. 'She said if we told anyone she'd come back as a witch and take us from our beds, then our mam'll be on 'er own.'

Billy looked up at WPC Jarvis, his eyes brimming with tears, 'I don't want to be taken from my bed by a witch.'

'No one is going to take you from your beds,' Constable Jarvis said. She stood up and turned to the DI. 'Inspector Powell wouldn't let anyone do that, would you, Inspector?'

'Not if the boys tell the truth, WPC Jarvis.' Inspector Powell looked sternly at the oldest boy. WPC Jarvis returned to her chair by the window and resumed her note-taking.

'Now, Alfred, if you tell us what happened you won't be in trouble.'

'What? Not from the rozzers for lying?'

'As the top rozzer,' the DI said, 'I promise.'

'You see, boys,' Ena added, 'this is a very important case and you are very important witnesses.' She waited for the word important to sink in. 'We need your help. We need to know if you really saw a Sunbeam Rapier that day, or if you only thought you saw it. Could it have been another make of car? One that perhaps looked like a Sunbeam?'

'Alfred?' It was the first time Mrs Hardy had spoken and she did it with authority. 'Tell Mrs Green the truth, son, or you'll get a clip round the ear.'

'The lady what gave us the car magazine made us say it. She showed us the picture of a Sunbeam and said we was to tell anybody what asked that we saw a Sunbeam when we was playing in Mercer Street the day before Christmas.'

'Were you in Mercer Street when the lady gave you the car magazine?'

'No, that time we was on the rec near our 'ouse.'

'But you'd been in Mercer Street, before,' the inspector said.

Knowing the Hardy brothers' passion for motorcars, Ena said, 'Did the lady take you in her car?'

Alfred shook his head.

'Did you jump a bus? Some of the kids run alongside the buses and when the conductors go upstairs, jump on and sit among passengers who have paid their fares. Is that what you boys did? Alfred?'

The two younger brothers giggled and nudged each other.

'Well?'

'Not that time we didn't.'

'Then how did you get to Mercer Street?'

'The lady gave us the bus fare.'

'And ten bob,' Gerald added.

'Each,' Billy said excitedly.

'She came on the bus too, but she didn't sit with us.'

'Had you ever seen the lady before that day?'

Three heads of untidy sandy curls shook as they said no.

'No,' Alfred repeated.

'Have you seen her since?'

Billy began to cry. 'I don't want to be took away in the night, Mam.'

Mrs Hardy took her youngest son by the wrist, dragged him to her and lifted him onto her knee. 'No one is going to take any of you away from me,' she said, 'now shush.' She turned to her eldest son. 'Alfred!' she ordered.

'She said she'd give us another ten shillings if we came back after Christmas.'

'But she didn't,' Billy said, his mouth downturned.

'She couldn't, you daft noggin,' Gerald chided, 'she were dead.'

'Are you sure it was the woman who had given you ten shillings that was dead?'

Alfred grimaced. 'I didn't look at her face, but she had the same coat and 'at on.'

Ena almost laughed with relief. If what Alfred said was true - and she had no reason to believe otherwise - the woman who had given the boys a car magazine and ten shillings to say they'd seen a Sunbeam Rapier like

207

Henry's in Mercer Street on Christmas Eve was Helen Crowther's killer.

Desperate to discuss the prospect, Ena glanced at the inspector. WPC Jarvis, having written down what the boys had said, had taken the notebook to him. The DI motioned that she should give it to Mrs Hardy.

'Mrs Hardy, would you read the witness statements. If you agree that what I've written is a true account of what your sons said, would you sign it here?' Jarvis pointed to the bottom of the page. She turned to the inspector. 'I'll take the boys next door.' WPC Jarvis told the boys to follow her, promising them sweets before she drove them home.

Billy scrambled down from his mother's lap and she began to read. When she had finished she wrote her name and stood up.

'I hope the boys are getting over the shock of finding a dead body,' Ena said, standing up when Mrs Hardy did.

'They'll be alright. The oldest two saw their grandfather dead so they weren't so upset. William didn't see him, he was too young. The woman in Mercer Street was his first. He's had a few nightmares but he's tough, he'll get over it,' she said. As she was leaving, Mrs Hardy turned to Ena. 'Thank you for your concern, Mrs Green. I hope my boys have helped and you find the person who killed that woman.'

Mrs Hardy closed the door and Ena beamed the inspector a smile. 'The boys certainly have helped.' Before she could elaborate, Alfred burst into the room.

'There was a man. Me and Gerald saw a man.'

Ena's heart plummeted. 'When?'

'When we was going home. Me and Gerald was at the top of the street and we noticed William weren't with us. It was when we went back to fetch him that

208

we saw a man in a doorway down the street, watching us.'

'What made you think he was watching you?'

'Nothing, then. But when we got William, I looked back and saw the man going into the building where the lady had gone.'

Lines formed on the inspector's brow. 'Are you sure, Alfred?'

'Yes, Sir.'

'Do you remember what the man looked like?'

'He was a gangster,' a little voice piped up at Alfred's side.

'What makes you think he was a gangster, Billy?' Ena asked, the surprise in her voice masking her laughter.

'His coat was long like a cape. He pulled his collar up all menacing like, and he wore one of them big flashy hats pulled down over one eye like a spiv. Same as the baddies wear in the gangster flicks.'

'How do you know,' Alfred mocked, 'you've never seen a gangster flick?'

'I ain't seen one, noooo, but I've seen pictures of gangsters on the boards outside the picture houses.' He looked at Ena. 'He gave me this.' Billy opened his grubby hand to reveal a silver sixpence. 'He was a gangster, honest.'

That the boys had seen a man go into the building on the night Crowther was killed didn't bode well for Henry. Ena had hoped their statements would clear him. Not after this revelation, they wouldn't. Henry didn't look like a gangster, Ena told herself. Not that she thought Billy had seen a gangster. Whether he had or not was of little consequence, the man he saw would have been wearing a disguise.

'Why did you go into the building?' the inspector

asked.

Alfred glared at his young brother. 'We went in to get William.'

'The lady said she'd give us another ten bob.'

'He went into the building to ask her for it.'

Tears welled up in Billy's eyes. 'But she were on the floor dead, so we ran like 'ell.'

'Straight into two rozzers,' Alfred grumbled.

The inspector glanced at the notes he'd made when Billy Hardy related the story about the gangster. 'I don't think there's anything helpful in Billy's statement. A little boy being over-imaginative after seeing a poster of Richard Attenborough in Brighton Rock.'

'Billy wasn't born when Brighton Rock was on in the cinemas. Besides, Pinkie Brown wore his trilby pushed off his face if I remember correctly.'

'It was pulled down in the film.' The inspector looked at Ena and exhaled. 'The boy remembering the man doesn't help. I'll write up his statement and give it to WPC Jarvis later.' As the inspector dropped the notes on his desk, the telephone rang. He picked it up. A second later he put his hand over the mouthpiece. 'I need to take this, Ena.'

'And I need to get back to the theatre.' Picking up her handbag, Ena took her coat from the stand and made for the door. 'Thank you,' she said. Closing the door she heard the inspector say, 'I interviewed the boys who found Crowther's body today. They said a woman gave them a car magazine with a picture of a Sunbeam Rapier in it.'

Ena stood in the corridor long enough to hear the inspector tell whoever was on the other end of the line that the boys were given ten shillings each to say they'd seen the Sunbeam on the waste ground in Mercer Street before Christmas and were promised the same amount of money on Boxing Day.

CHAPTER TWENTY-NINE

'Who is Villiers?'

'No one.'

'He must have been someone. A middle-aged man named Villiers with the initial H posed as Frieda and Walter Voight's uncle. He had a house in Northampton. The Voights called themselves Duncan when they lived with him. Walter Duncan was at Oxford University with my husband, Henry.'

'Ah, your husband the artist, at least that's what he wanted to be - and no doubt would have been if the war hadn't got in the way.'

'Mr Miller, you said you would only speak to Mrs Green, so perhaps you'd stop wasting our time and answer her questions,' DI Powell said.

Looking at Ena, Nick Miller ignored the inspector. 'Horst Villiers was also a painter. He was quite well-known in Berlin. He'd have made a name for himself as an artist if he hadn't been greedy and got caught forging masters.'

'How did he end up in Northamptonshire?'

'Like so many men and women with talent, Villiers was given a choice by Germany's military intelligence service. A *get out of jail free card* to carry on painting - in England - or go to the Eastern Front and fight.'

'Not much of a choice.'

Miller shrugged. 'Both jobs were serving the Fatherland but Villiers, being an artist, chose England. Voight couldn't paint the side of a barn so Villiers was sent to England to paint for him while Walter was studying at Baliol College, Oxford, preparing for Bletchley Park.'

'Villiers still lived in Northampton during the war when Frieda worked with me in engineering.'

'Frieda! Everything was going to plan until she turned up and put the cat among the pigeons. That's when Walter left the cottage he shared with your husband and went to live in Northampton with his uncle - and Frieda. Instead of painting for Walter, Villiers became a chaperone. His job in Northampton was to give respectability to Frieda and Walter living together.'

'I don't see why a brother and sister needed a chaperone.'

'Although they told everyone they were brother and sister - and they were by law because they had been adopted at birth by the Voights - they weren't blood-related. I believe it was when they were in their teens that they found out they were adopted. Shortly afterwards they became lovers. Frieda was obsessed with Walter. She wouldn't let a woman, or a man for that matter, get close to him.'

'I can tell by the way you say her name that you didn't like Frieda.'

'It wasn't a case of liking or disliking the woman. She was too visible. She threatened to blow their cover unless she was allowed to live with Walter - and I mean in the biblical sense.' Miller took a double tube silver cigar case and lighter from the inside pocket of his jacket. 'Alright if I smoke?'

DI Powell nodded.

Miller offered the case to the inspector. He shook his head. 'Do you mind, Ena?'

'Not at all.'

DI Powell got up and went over to the window. He took an ashtray from the ledge and returning to his chair, pushed it across the desk.

Miller smiled, took a cigar from the case and arching his back dug his hand in his jacket pocket and took out a cigar cutter. He snipped off the cap end of the cigar, dropped it into the ashtray and flicked the wheel of the lighter with his thumb. As he put the flame to the cigar Miller sucked and a puff of smoke rose into the air, dispersing above his head. He leaned back in the chair. 'Frieda was a liability. She was resourceful too. She inveigled her way into Bletchley Park.'

'Which she did by making herself indispensable to the boss of an engineering factory where I worked.'

Miller gave Ena a cynical smile. 'She became your friend and gained the trust of the boffins at Beaumanor as well as Bletchley.'

'It was at Beaumanor that she reacquainted herself with my colleague, Sidney Parfitt and began blackmailing him.'

'That was a bit of a *putsch.* Or, as you English say, an unexpected stroke of luck.'

'Not for Sid,' Ena spat.

Miller raised an eyebrow. 'Parfitt was a weak man.'

'Sid was not weak. He was a decent man. He had no choice but to do Frieda's bidding. She threatened to have his mother killed.' Ena bit her lip. She had said too much. She'd had no intention of telling the gangster and spy, Nick Miller, anything. She turned away. She couldn't bear to look at him, let alone speak to him.

'All this is very interesting, Mr Miller, but so far you haven't told us anything we didn't already know. You said you had information that you wanted to share, discuss.'

Ena spun round, unable to contain her anger. '*Mr* Miller means he'll give up the others in the spy ring if he gets a ticket to a country where there's no extradition. Isn't that right?'

'Not quite, Ena. You don't mind if I call you Ena, do you?'

'Get on with it, Miller,' Alan Richardson barked. It was the first time the Special Branch inspector had spoken. 'What do you want in return for giving up Helen Crowther's killer? And your word isn't good enough. We'll need proof.'

'Alright. I want a ticket to Vienna.'

DI Powell looked at Richardson. His eyes flickered in agreement. 'That's doable.'

'You've put a stop on my bank accounts. I'll need to access them.'

'And what do we get in return?'

'In the vault at one of my banks, there's a safe deposit box. It holds information about Sid Parfitt's killer and McKenzie Robinson's killer. And,' Miller looked at Ena, 'there's a sworn statement, witnessed by my solicitors, that proves Henry Green did not murder Helen Crowther.'

'Which bank?'

Miller threw his head back and let out a cynical laugh. 'Inspector, do you really think I'm going to tell you which bank while I'm sitting here? Dear, oh dear, I'm going to have to spell it out to you.' He gave Ena a lopsided grin. 'I shall give that information to Ena in Vienna.'

'What? Mrs Green can't travel with you to Austria, she is a civilian. It's against regulations.'

Ena opened her mouth to contradict the inspector. He didn't give her the chance.

'I will not allow Mrs Green, a member of the public, to travel on her own anywhere with you.'

Miller stubbed out his cigar. 'Then the deal is off!'

'Stop!' Ena pushed her chair back and stood up. 'You're right, Inspector Powell, I am a member of the public. I'm not a member of the police force, nor am I a member of military intelligence. I am a civilian and as such I do not need your permission, the permission of the Home Office, or,' she shot Inspector Richardson a disparaging look, 'the permission of Special Branch to travel anywhere. As a member of *the public,* I can go where I please and with whom I please.'

'You work for the Home Office, Ena. Director Bentley would never give allow you to go with Miller as insurance.'

'*Director Bentley* suspended me, if you remember. As far as I'm concerned, I no longer take orders from him. Nor do I have to comply with Home Office regulations. And if Bentley or anyone else at the Home Office says otherwise, I'll resign.' Ena looked defiantly at the man who, until now, had been her friend and ally. 'If it will save Henry from hanging for a murder he did not commit, I will accompany Mr Miller to Austria.' Ena sat down heavily.

'I understand why you want to go, Ena.' The inspector spoke in a steady calm voice, 'But I can't let you.'

'Unless you arrest me, you can't stop me.'

'That's settled then. As I was saying, Ena will accompany me to Vienna. She'll wait at the airport until I've safely arrived at my new address. When I'm sure I haven't been followed, I'll let her know the name of my solicitors. They are expecting a visit from her.' Miller turned his attention to Inspector Powell. 'Ena will then take the next available flight back to London and you,' he said to DI Powell, taking in DI Richardson, 'will have the evidence you need, not only to prove Henry Green didn't kill Helen Crowther but to prove who did.'

'How can we be sure that once you're in Austria

216

you'll give us the information?' Alan Richardson said.

Ena sighed loudly. She wished he'd kept his mouth shut. His superior attitude wouldn't suit Miller's ego.

'You could change your mind and disappear. You might never have had any intention of telling us who killed Crowther.'

Miller gave the Special Branch inspector a withering look. His eyes sparkled with contempt for the man. 'Because I give you my word!'

Ena heard the anger in Miller's voice and looked to the heavens. She was reminded of the saying, 'honour among thieves'. Being a gangster and a spy didn't mean Miller wasn't a man of his word.

Miller directed his demands to Inspector Powell. 'I clear customs without being searched. There'll be a car waiting for me. When I leave the airport I will not be followed or stopped - and there will be no staged accidents. When I arrive at my destination, if I am certain that I have not been followed, I'll let Ena know the name and address of my solicitor. They have been instructed to give Ena, and only Ena, the name and address of the bank and the key to the safe deposit box.' He glanced at Ena. 'They'll give you everything you need.'

Miller looked questioningly at DI Powell, and then at the Special Branch inspector. 'Well?'

Neither man spoke.

Miller shrugged. 'It's a one-time offer, take it or leave it.'

Inspector Richardson was waiting for Ena when she and DI Powell arrived at London Airport. 'Nick Miller is dangerous, Mrs Green,' he said, following Ena into the Europa Building. 'It isn't too late to change your mind.'

'I am not going to change my mind.' Ena looked

from Richardson to Inspector Powell.

'Then two of my men will accompany you. They won't hinder Miller, but they'll be there if you need them.'

'Is it really necessary?'

'Yes, it is!'

'If they follow Miller, he won't give me the evidence I need to prove my husband didn't kill Crowther.'

'They won't follow him, I give you my word. They are only there for your protection.'

Ena exhaled. 'Alright.'

Inspector Powell turned to her. 'Are you sure you want to do this, Ena?'

'Yes! I want this *nightmare,* which has gone on for three months to be over and I don't see there's any other way.'

A steward entered the room. 'It's time to board, ladies and gentlemen.' Ena picked up her holdall and handbag and stood up.

At the door, DI Powell put out his arm and barred Nick Miller's way. 'If you change any part of our agreement the deal is off, understand?'

Miller winked at Ena. 'Come on, Ena, I'm dying for a drink. I'm hungry too. They say the food on aeroplanes is very good these days.'

Ena's stomach took a dive. Food was the last thing on her mind. She followed the steward and Miller followed her. Once through the airport departure lounge, they were ushered past a queue of people waiting to board the plane. Ena and Miller were shown to their seats at the back of the plane. From her seat Ena watched the other passengers arrive. Men and women, young and old, chatted and discussed their seat numbers, found them and handed the stewards and stewardesses bags and other items to put on the overhead racks. Among them there were two men, both over six-feet tall, both built like the side of a barn, wearing dark grey suits - and with regulation military short-back-and-sides. Ena pretended she hadn't seen them and busied herself putting her holdall under her seat. Out of the corner of her eye, she saw Miller salute them.

When the last few passengers were seated and the exit door had closed the aeroplane's engines ignited with a roar. Ena hadn't expected the plane to set off so quickly nor the sound of the engines to be so loud. She gripped the arms of the seat and took several calming breaths.

Refusing to admit she was nervous, Ena looked out of the window. The aeroplane was taxiing slowly away from the airport. At the beginning of the runway the plane stopped, the growl of its engines grew louder and it began to move again. Slowly at first, the engines grew even louder, the plane barrelled down the runway and took off.

Having lifted off the ground the plane began to climb. Ena felt as if she was being forced back in her seat. Then, the sound of the engines changed from a roar to rushing wind which soon became dull and muffled until she couldn't hear anything at all. She swallowed, but it didn't help. She put her fingers in her ears. That was no help either. She was deaf. When she felt the plane level she swallowed again and her ears popped.

Ena wasn't sure about anything that might or might not happen in the next twenty-four hours. One thing she was sure of, she did not like flying. She closed her eyes.

CHAPTER THIRTY

'Drink, Ena?'

'Alcohol?' Ena's stomach churned at the thought and she groaned. 'No, thank you.'

'Go on, live a little. Have a glass of bubbly. It's on me.'

Despite feeling nauseous, Ena laughed. 'You really are a cocky sod, aren't you, Nick?'

'Ouch! And here's me thinking we were getting on so well.'

'A bottle of your best champagne and two glasses,' Miller said to the stewardess. 'And give the two big fellas on the other side of the aisle whatever they want.'

When the stewardess brought the champagne and glasses, she gave Miller the receipt. 'One bottle of champagne. Didn't you ask my friends what they wanted to drink?'

'Yes, Sir. They…'

Miller put up his hand cutting short the stewardess' explanation. 'I can imagine. It's the British stiff upper lip,' he said and laughed. 'They don't know what they're missing.' He raised his glass at the two Special Branch men.

'Don't rile them,' Ena said. 'They're only here as chaperones for me. They won't get in your way.'

'I know. I heard the head honcho telling you.' He poured a glass of champagne for Ena and one for himself. 'Here's to going home at last,' he said, raising his glass.

Ena felt like pouring her drink over Miller's head, but that would be a waste. She took a sip. It tasted good; slightly dry and very refreshing. 'How did you know Helen Crowther?'

If Miller was surprised by the question, he didn't show it. 'Helen and I go all the way back to Berlin. Her husband was my tutor at university.'

'Ah, through her husband.' Ena did her best not to sound surprised and took another sip of champagne. 'That would be, Herr Krueger?'

Miller turned and faced her. 'You're fishing, Ena,' he said, laughing. 'But yes, Professor Martin Krueger was my tutor. A tough high-ranking ex-military man. He was considerably older than Helen.' He laughed, again. 'She was a real looker in those days. When she disappeared, a rumour went round the university that she'd had an affair with one of Martin's students, he had found out, so she'd fled Berlin rather than face him.'

'Did you know she'd had a child?'

'No!' Miller looked genuinely shocked by the news. 'There were rumours of course, but there are always rumours when someone suspected of having an affair suddenly disappears. And she did literally disappear. We thought old Krueger had killed her, or he'd had her killed. I wouldn't have put it past him. I couldn't believe it when she got in touch with me in forty-two.' Miller drank down his champagne and laughed loudly. 'By then she was the Personal Assistant to the Director of MI5 no less.'

'Wasn't she worried that her husband would find her when she began working for an organisation like MI5? It wouldn't have been difficult.'

'Krueger was long dead by then. He died in nineteen thirty-three or four.'

Which is why she was able to go back to Berlin and why she was photographed on the Hitler Youth marches with O'Shaughnessy, Ena thought. 'Did you know Shaun O'Shaughnessy in those days?'

221

'That waste of breath. He turned up out of nowhere in thirty-six.'

'Do you think he could have been Helen Crowther's son?'

'Lord, no.' Miller looked at his hands, lifted one finger and then another, and shook his head. 'The dates don't fit. Besides, he's English. At the time he told Helen some cock and bull story about being a student of drama.'

'But you didn't believe him?'

'I didn't believe a word that came out of the liar's mouth. I still don't. He was always in The Minchin Club. He'd arrive late, often drunk, and cosy up to the theatre and film people who had come down from London. The man was a leech.'

Was? Ena took a sip of her champagne. 'What do you mean, *was* a leech?'

Out of the corner of her eye, Ena saw Miller's body stiffen. 'Was, is, who cares about O'Shaughnessy?'

Miller's friend, Hugh Middleton, obviously did. Ena had seen him with his arm linked in O'Shaughnessy's on the night she and Claire broke into Helen Crowther's house. Ena glanced at Miller. He looked rattled. She didn't want that or she wouldn't get the information out of him that she needed. In a flash of inspiration, she remembered Sid's mother had been a lecturer at the University of Berlin, which was why Sid went to school there. 'Did you know a female lecturer named Parfitt?'

'Sidney Parfitt's old lady? She was a bit before my time. She lectured in Politics and Humanities, if memory serves. I've never been interested in the philosophical garbage that goes with Humanities. I studied Politics, Modern History and Languages.'

'There must be universities with excellent

reputations in Vienna. Why did you choose to study at the University of Berlin?'

'I could say I wanted to spread my wings and see some of the world, or thousands of students study in other countries, etc., but since whatever I tell you isn't going to make a difference to my present situation, I might as well tell you the truth, Ena.'

'That would be novel.'

Miller threw his head back and laughed loudly. He then took the champagne bottle and replenished their glasses. 'My father was from Vienna, my mother from Berlin. Dad worked for a German engineering company and not long before I was born, the part of the company he worked for relocated to Berlin. My parents moved with it and I was born in Berlin. Austrian by heart, German by birth. When I was twelve my mother died and the following year my father married again.' Miller paused. 'She was a Jew.'

Ena shot him an angry look.

'Don't jump to the wrong conclusion, Ena, I was delighted for Dad. He didn't function well on his own. He needed a woman, a companion. Miriam made him happy. She was a kind person and her family welcomed us both with open arms.'

Miller paused. He looked at the champagne in his glass, swirled it around and drank it down. Ena sensed that recalling those days was emotional for him. 'Miriam didn't try to take the place of my mother, but she treated me as if I was her own son.' Miller's grey eyes were moist. He rubbed them and carried on. 'Anyway, when Hitler was appointed Chancellor of Germany in thirty-three, my father and Miriam went back to Austria and in thirty-seven they emigrated to America. There were strict emigration laws. I suspect, although I'll never know for sure, that because my

223

father was not Jewish, they allowed him and Miriam to stay.'

'And you were left in Berlin?'

'Yes, but it was my choice. I haven't seen my father more than a couple of times since. Dad was angry that I had stayed in Germany and Miriam was frightened for my safety. I messed up at university. I got into drugs. But I was lucky. I met a beautiful woman who straightened me out. Anneke was the love of my life. I have never met anyone like her since.'

'If your reputation is to be believed, there have been more than a few women in your life since,' Ena said.

'And not one of them could hold a light to Anneke.'

Ena wondered what had happened to her, but decided that if Miller wanted to talk about the woman he loved, he would.

And he did. He took a drink, and said, 'We were young and our political views opposed.' He lifted his glass. 'To Anneke,' he said with a catch in his voice. 'She wouldn't have approved of me staying in England after the war ended. She would have seen that as me abandoning Berlin, turning my back on the Fatherland. Maybe she was right.' He looked at Ena, his eyes full of tears. 'If I'd stayed with her, I could have saved her from becoming a Nazi.'

'I don't think a person can save another from anything. They can try, but I think people have to save themselves,' Ena said.

'You're probably right. That's something else I shall never know.' Miller wiped his tears.

'Why did you come to England?'

Miller lifted his glass to take a drink and stopped. Holding the stem of the champagne flute between his finger and thumb he twirled it around. 'You wouldn't believe me if I told you.'

224

'Try me.'

He inhaled and let out a long breath as if he was giving himself time to think. 'Just before the war started in thirty-nine, I decided I didn't want to fight. I'm not a pacifist, but I'd been on so many rallies where my friends - Anneke included - had been brainwashed. I watched ordinary people whipped up into a frenzy of loathing for their friends and neighbours because of their religious preferences or their lifestyles. Speakers from the Nationalist Workers Party incited hatred, encouraged disgust and suspicion, so I stopped going on rallies. My absence was noticed and I was told by a neighbour who had joined Heinrich Himmler's SS that my name was on several lists, including the most feared - the Ministry for State Security - the Stasi.

'I didn't like what the Nazi party were doing. I didn't believe in their ideology and I didn't believe Germany was going to war with the rest of Europe for the right reasons. So, because I had studied languages at university, I went to the military intelligence offices in Berlin, they interviewed me, and I became an overseas intelligence gatherer. When I had completed my training I was sent to North Africa. In September 1942, along with dozens of other undercover operatives, I was pulled out of Africa. By Christmas that year I was in England.'

'Where you met Helen Krueger again?'

'She was Helen Crowther then of course. When I first arrived in England, Helen was my controller. Because she was clean, no one suspected she was a German agent. At the time she had just started working with McKenzie Robinson as his secretary. To be the secretary of someone climbing the career ladder at MI5 was the most impressive job of all the agents.'

225

'And as Mac Robinson was promoted, so was Helen Crowther.' Ena took a drink of her champagne. Just thinking about Helen Crowther and how she had conned her into believing she was her friend when all the time she was manipulating her, wheedling information out of her about the investigations into Frieda Voight and the spy ring she was involved in, made Ena baulk. Anger rose from her stomach as bitter-tasting bile when she remembered how Crowther had befriended her at McKenzie Robinson's funeral, how she had sympathised with her when Ena told her that she and Henry were not getting on, and how she had offered to help her solve the murders of Sid Parfitt and Mac Robinson while all the time she was plotting to have Ena killed.

A cold shiver ran down Ena's back. She didn't want to talk about Helen Crowther, but she needed to tie up loose ends that were niggling her. 'My husband Henry was recently suspected of working for Helen Crowther, as a spy. Ridiculous, of course.' She paused, waiting for Miller's reaction. There was none. She needed to know for certain that Mac Robinson was not a German agent. Every fibre in her body told her he wasn't, so why did she fear Miller's answer? 'Even the late Director of MI5, McKenzie Robinson, was in the spotlight when I told my boss at the Home Office that Crowther was the mole at MI5.'

Miller turned slowly in his seat and faced Ena. 'Are you asking me if McKenzie Robinson was a spy?'

Ena hadn't expected Miller to be so blunt. 'Of course not. That would be unthinkable. Besides, Henry would have known if Mac had been.'

'No, your husband's boss was not a spy. He had an unblemished work record and was as loyal and as patriotic as Churchill himself. The only stain on the late McKenzie Robinson's character was his affair with his PA.'

'Crowther told me as much when I stayed with her in Brighton last year. So,' Ena said, relief encouraging her to be forthright, 'England has been good to you. The war was very good to you. You made a lot of money out of other people's misfortunes.'

'That's not how I see it. Factories were being bombed, goods were being damaged, and the owners were either uninsured or the insurance companies didn't pay out. So, I bought the damaged goods at a fair price and sold them on at a fair price.'

'Honestly? Fair price on the black market?'

'To most people, the price was better than fair. To those who could afford it, the price might have been a little higher. Isn't that what the Americans call a win-win deal?'

Ena laughed. 'You were a regular Robin Hood.'

'During the war I was. By the end of it, I'd made some good friends, I had a couple of *legitimate* businesses and I liked the food, so I stayed.'

'And I'm the Queen of Sheba.'

Miller chuckled and held up the empty champagne bottle to attract the attention of the stewardess. She brought a replacement bottle and took away the empty one.

'Not for me,' Ena said, as Miller began to pour her another drink. 'I've had enough.'

Miller filled his glass, stood the bottle on the table in front of them, but didn't take a drink. 'What about you, Ena? You know everything there is to know about me, but I know nothing about you. What motivates Ena Green?'

'The truth. I don't like liars or injustice. My father was a great role model, he abhorred injustice and prejudice of any kind. My father was the head groom on a country estate before the war and my mother was a housemaid until my oldest brother was born. My siblings and I came from humble beginnings, but were brought up to believe that no one was better than us - and we were better than no one.'

Ena wanted to know more about Miller and changed the subject from her family to the work she did during the war. 'In thirty-nine I went to work in an engineering factory. I made small components for machines. Ena didn't tell Miller her work was for Bletchley Park. The work done at Bletchley was still classified top secret. I won't bore you with details, but I ended up having to prove that I hadn't been party to my work being stolen by the woman I worked with, namely, Frieda Voight...' Out of the corner of her eye, she saw Miller flinch. Did he know Frieda and Walter Voight? If she played Miller's game of twenty-questions, she might find out. 'After the war, I married Henry. He went to work for MI5 where, as you know, Crowther worked, and I went to work for the Home Office in their cold case department.'

'With Sidney Parfitt?'

'Yes.' Ena wondered why Miller had mentioned Sid's name again. 'Do you know who killed, Sid?'

'Yes.'

Before she could ask Miller who had murdered her friend, he said, 'And so will you, in time.'

The conversation was cut short when the steward brought lunch. Theirs was a last-minute booking which meant cold fare. The Austrian equivalent of a ploughman's lunch; ham, cheese, hard-boiled egg and sliced tomato. The ham tasted sweeter and looked paler than the off-the-bone slices Ena bought from the Co-op, but it was fine. Bread rolls were brought round and there was salad dressing if you wanted it. Ena helped herself to two rolls and two small squares of butter. She was hungry and although her stomach churned at the prospect of being in a country where she didn't speak the language and had very little currency, she might have to wait until the return flight to England that night before she ate again.

CHAPTER THIRTY-ONE

'What's the banging noise on the side of the plane?'

'The wind.' Miller looked at his wristwatch. 'We're flying over the Alps. Mountains create strong winds.'

'What? Oh my God, I'm going deaf.'

'That's because the plane is climbing.'

'Again?' Ena looked out of the window and caught her breath. Bright spring sunshine reflected off the tops of snow-covered mountains. 'Alps!' she exclaimed. 'For as far as I can see, the Alps covered in snow.'

'Relax and enjoy the view,' Miller said, enunciating each word so what Ena couldn't hear over the noise of the wind and the aeroplane's engines she could lipread.

'How long until we land in Vienna?'

'Depends on the wind. An hour, maybe less and we'll be down.'

As Miller said the word 'down' the plane dropped like a stone, leaving Ena's stomach high in the air. At least that's what it felt like. She gripped the arms of her seat. She wasn't frightened of flying, as such, but she hadn't reckoned on it being so windy. She closed her eyes and listened to what sounded like muffled thunder and dogs growling.

Ena felt someone tap her on the shoulder. She woke with a jolt. For a moment she wondered where she was.

'We've landed, Mrs Green. If you would gather your belongings and follow the other passengers to the exit.' Ena looked around. Where was Miller? She began to panic and then spotted him several passengers ahead. She grabbed her coat from the seat and her bags from the floor and pushed forward, saying 'Excuse me' every few seconds until she caught up with him.

'Did you think I was leaving without you, Ena?' he said, grinning.

'Don't start, I'm not in the mood.'

The two Special Branch officers were still seated. Ena guessed they would vacate their seats now she had. Their job wasn't only to protect her, but to keep watch on Miller.

Ena had always hated confined spaces and was relieved to be out of the plane. Standing on top of the aircraft's metal stairway, she breathed in the fresh, cold Austrian air and immediately felt better.

The arrivals building looked more like a military aerodrome than a commercial airport, which it had once been. During the war, a German aircraft manufacturing company had designed and built bomber aircraft for the Luftwaffe. In 1945 - for the duration of the British occupation - it was RAF Schwechat. Even though the airport was now Austria's principal aerodrome, it probably hadn't changed much. Not surprising, Ena thought, it had only been thirteen years since the end of the war. She held onto the handrail and walked cautiously down the steps behind Miller.

Ena didn't have any suitcases to collect from the baggage claim hall. She had only brought an overnight bag which contained her toiletries, nightdress and dressing gown, and a change of clothes in case she had to stay overnight. Miller had assured her she wouldn't have to stay over if Special Branch kept their word. She hoped he was right. She was booked on the eight o'clock flight back to London. As soon as she had proof that Henry was innocent of Helen Crowther's murder, she'd be on her way home.

A motorised vehicle towing a trailer arrived with Miller's suitcases. The rest of the passengers followed signs for baggage claims. Ignoring security and passport control, they followed the vehicle through a wide doorway with 'Nothing To Declare' written above it to the arrivals hall.

When Miller's party walked through the door from customs into arrivals, a crowd of people standing behind a roped-off barrier surged forward. Miller tensed, as did Ena, but the crowd paid no attention to them and when no one else appeared, most of them stepped back.

Ena looked over her shoulder. The Special Branch men, their eyes usually dull with boredom, sparkled with interest as they scanned the crowd. Both agents had undone the buttons on their dark grey overcoats. Both held the side of their coats with their left hands, leaving their right hands free to reach for their guns, if needed. They looked nervous. Ena hoped they didn't overreact to someone excited to see a loved one enter the arrivals hall behind them.

An airport official approached them. He said something to the Branch officers before beckoning Ena and Miller to follow him to a blandly decorated, sparsely furnished waiting room.

When Miller sat down, Ena sat next to him. The two Special Branch officers dropped into chairs some distance away by the door.

'Not long now, Ena.'

'I hope not.' Ena sighed. 'I want the nightmare I've been living in to be over.'

Miller looked at his wristwatch. 'Be patient for a little while longer. The car picking me up will be here soon.'

Miller was right. The official who had escorted them to the private room returned. 'Your car is here,

Mr Miller.'

Miller got to his feet. 'You'll soon have the evidence you need to clear your husband of Helen's murder, Ena.'

'Thank you.'

'There's just one thing.'

Ena closed her eyes and exhaled, 'Which is?'

'If we're followed, I won't give the police or Special Branch what they want.' Ena's heart sank. 'But,' he said, 'whatever happens, I promise you that you'll have enough evidence to clear your husband.'

Emotion, like a lump in Ena's throat, threatened to stop her from replying. She whispered, 'Thank you.'

Miller shook her hand before crossing the room to his suitcases. He pushed the trolley to the door, and a second later was gone.

Less than five minutes had passed when Miller strolled back into the room.

Ena leapt out of her seat. 'What's happened?'

'Half a dozen heavyweights in plain clothes were outside waiting for me. It's not the weather for standing around smoking cigarettes.'

'Were they British?'

Miller shook his head. 'I have no idea - and I don't care.' He turned to the two Branch officers sitting by the door and shouted, 'Get rid of them or I'm not leaving. And if I don't leave, your intelligence services won't get the information they want.'

Looking non-plussed, the two agents hauled themselves out of their chairs and left.

'Come on, Ena.' Miller grabbed Ena's holdall and threw it on top of his suitcases. 'I'm trapped in here and those bastards know it. Let's go somewhere where there are a lot of people.'

*

The café area in the airport lounge was bright and cheerful, yet crowded when Ena and Miller arrived. Ena stood on tiptoe and craned her neck. She spotted a family of four vacating a table by the window. Miller was on the edge of the seating area with the trolley and suitcases. She waved at him as she weaved her way through tables and chairs, taking care not to step on handbags and other paraphernalia that threatened to trip her up. Finally, she secured the table.

'I need coffee,' Miller said, claiming the chair opposite Ena by dropping his gloves on the seat. 'Coffee or tea, Ena?'

'Coffee.' She could have done with something stronger, but coffee would do.

Miller returned with a newspaper under his arm; carrying a tray. On it was cake, a small cup of black coffee for himself and a large cup with milk for Ena. He took both from the tray and set them down on the table.

'Now this,' he said, taking a dish with a slice of iced chocolate sponge from the tray and beaming a smile at Ena, 'is called, Sachertorte.' He took a fork and sliced through the layer of dark chocolate icing to reveal soft chocolate sponge. Jam oozed from it. 'This wonder of culinary delight was invented by a man called Franz Sacher for Prince Metternich of Vienna in eighteen thirty-two. It's Vienna's most famous speciality. At least that's what it says on the advertising poster on the wall at the back of the counter.'

With a piece of cake balancing on the fork, Miller leant across the table and winked. 'Go on, Ena,' he teased, 'you know you want to.'

Unable to help herself, Ena laughed. She leant forward and took the cake from the fork. 'Mmmm... dark chocolate and apricot jam. I wouldn't have thought of putting the two ingredients together. Delicious,' she said when she'd eaten it.

'I told you you'd like it.' Miller passed the plate with the remainder of the chocolate cake across the table to her and began to eat his own portion.

'An Austrian newspaper,' Miller said when they had finished eating. 'The Krone, soon to be called The Neue Kronen Zeitung. But that's fine. Its editor-in-chief is Austrian. It's been a while since I've read a newspaper printed in Vienna. When I was last here all the papers were German publications; German editors and owners. The rights to this paper have just been bought by an Austrian.'

While Miller read his newspaper, Ena watched a plane come in. It taxied from the runway, stopping directly outside the window where she and Miller were sitting. She watched as engineers in orange overalls pushed portable steps to the plane's exit. A few seconds later the door opened and passengers began to vacate. There was a short hiatus where no one left the aircraft and then the stewards and stewardesses made their exit followed by two men in grey suits and peak caps. The pilot and co-pilot, Ena thought.

When there was nothing to see outside, she turned her attention to what was going on around her. Smartly dressed businessmen and women carrying briefcases crossed the arrivals lounge in haste. Mothers of toddlers bounced them up and down on their knees, while fathers entertained older siblings by reading to them.

Miller put down his paper. 'I'm sorry you've been delayed, Ena.'

'It isn't your fault. Special Branch is to blame for not honouring their part of the bargain.'

'Even so…' He gave Ena a sad smile.

For the first time since she had met Nick Miller, Ena could see the man beneath the swagger. He was no longer the nightclub owner, spy, or gangster, but someone who was genuinely apologetic, even though her being delayed was not his fault.

'I gave them my word they would have the information they needed and they gave me their word I wouldn't be followed.'

'Will the driver come back for you?'

'Yes. He was at the exit waiting for me, but I didn't speak to him. He saw me turn away and go back into the room. He'll have known something was wrong. He'll come back when... He'll come back for me.' Miller put his hands up to his face and rubbed his eyes. 'I'm tired, Ena. I'm tired and I want to see my father.'

Ena couldn't help herself and she reached out to him. She put her hand on his arm. 'I'll get some more coffee.' She took her purse from her handbag.

'Ena?' Nick pulled out a roll of Austrian banknotes from his jacket pocket. 'In case the car comes before you're back.'

'I can't take that, Nick.'

Miller looked up at the clock above the counter of the café. 'At this rate, you'll need to buy dinner. And, if you miss your flight back to London, there's enough here to pay for a room in a decent hotel.' Ena began to protest but Miller put up his hand. 'Take it! Please.' He looked into Ena's eyes and held her gaze. 'I won't be needing it.'

Ena understood by the way Nick said he wouldn't be needing the money that he wasn't staying in Austria. 'In that case, I'll take it.' She put the roll of notes in her handbag and pressed the clasp shut. 'Thank you.' And, what's left, I'll give to DI Powell when I get back to England, she thought. She walked over to where coffee and tea were being served and ordered two large coffees. Further along the counter, she asked for sandwiches. The young woman serving pointed to a selection in a glass cabinet. Reading the cardboard name tag in the foreground of one arrangement of sandwiches, Ena said phonetically, 'speck mit ei?'

The girl giggled and said, 'bacon with egg.'

Ena nodded and put up two fingers. 'Two, please.'

She paid with a twenty-schilling note that Special Branch had given her at London Airport and dropped the change into her purse. With two coffees and two rounds of sandwiches she returned to the table. Nick wasn't there. For a second she thought he had left or had been arrested. She began to panic. Then she saw his suitcases on the trolley against the wall and sat down.

'Cigarettes,' he said, throwing a pack of twenty into the middle of the table.

Ena took a cup of coffee from the tray and put it in front of him. She did the same with his sandwich. 'You should eat something.'

He took a sip of his coffee and turned up his nose. 'English style coffee; too little coffee and too much water.'

'Stop complaining and drink it. And eat your sandwich!' she ordered. There was something about Nick Miller she liked. Maybe 'liked' was too strong a word. What she felt was hard to fathom. Everything about him, his lifestyle, money, his overconfident personality, alienated her. She had met a lot of men like him in her line of work. She thought she knew the type, she thought she knew Nick Miller. She was wrong.

Ena ate her greasy bacon and rubbery egg sandwich

in silence. When she had finished, Miller pushed his half-eaten sandwich to one side and picked up the cigarettes. He opened the pack and offered it to Ena. She took a cigarette and waited for Miller to take one. He did, but then he put down his cigarette and lit Ena's. 'I'm going to the Gents.'

Ena watched him cross the black and grey tiled concourse. He walked with his usual swagger in his trademark overcoat that hung open from his shoulders like a cape. Ena caught her breath. The voice of a small East End boy called Billy Hardy came into her mind. *He was a gangster. He had a long coat like a cape. He wore one of them big flashy hats like the spivs wear pulled down over his face. Like what you see the baddies wear in the gangster flicks.* When his older brother contradicted him, Billy had held out his hand to reveal a silver sixpence.

'A Groschen for them.'

Ena jumped. She was deep in thought and hadn't heard Miller come back to the table. He had brought more coffee. He sat down and lit his cigarette.

'Well?'

She had given the woman at the till a twenty-schilling note and, although she hadn't counted the change, there was a couple of coins with 'groschen' written on them among it. 'They're worth a lot more than a penny.'

'I think however much they're worth, what I gave you will cover it.'

Ena shot Miller an angry look. 'Let's get something straight, Nick. I didn't want your money. I took it because if you're delayed again and I'm stuck in Vienna overnight, which, if I am will be your damn fault, I shall need to pay for a taxi and a room in a hotel.'

Miller pulled down the peak of his trilby and pretended to hide behind it. He then put up his hands. 'It's yours to do with as you wish, Mam.'

Ena stubbed out her cigarette. Was it him who the Hardy boys had seen in Mercer Street on the night Helen Crowther was murdered? The hat, the coat like a *cape*, was more than a coincidence. Ena looked at Miller for some seconds. She was angry with him. She wanted to ignore him, but there were things she needed to know. She swallowed her pride, took a cigarette from the pack and allowed Miller to light it. 'Thank you.' She sipped the coffee he had bought; it was too strong. She pushed it aside and took a drink of the English style coffee. It was cold. She drank it anyway.

'I was thinking about the day Helen Crowther's body was found by the boys who she paid to say they'd seen Henry's car in Mercer Street on Christmas Eve.'

'Who told you about the boys?'

'I met them. Three brothers.' Miller didn't look surprised. 'DI Powell invited me to sit in on their interviews at Bow Street.'

'And you want to know if I was there?'

Miller's quick reply caught Ena off guard. She took a drag of her cigarette. The few seconds inhaling and exhaling gave her time to compose herself. 'Were you there? Did you give the smallest boy a silver sixpence?'

'Yes and yes. But I didn't kill Helen. She was already dead when I got there.'

'I don't understand. Why did you go there?'

Miller finished his coffee, picked up his cigarettes and lighter and got to his feet. 'If I'm going to tell you about that night, I shall need a proper drink.' He looked over at his suitcases, 'Come on.'

'We'll have sat in every part of the airport soon.'

239

'We'll be keeping Special Branch on their toes then, won't we?'

Ena put on her coat, picked up her bags, and caught Miller up as he pushed the trolley with his cases across the concourse to an area with wooden tables and benches. A sign above the counter said, 'Gastgarten.'

'Beer or wine?'

'Whatever you're having.'

Miller left Ena with the cases, went to the bar and returned with two glasses of sparkling wine. 'Deutsche Sekt, the nearest thing they have to champagne.' He took a sip and swilled it around in his mouth before swallowing, 'It reminds me of my youth in Berlin.' He sipped the sparkling wine again and grimaced. Eventually, he said, 'Helen had a crazy idea.' He paused, lit a cigarette and took another drink. 'She knew it was only a matter of time before you exposed her as the mole at Five.'

'I'd known about her for some time, but I needed more proof.'

'She knew that too.' The colour drained from Miller's face. 'I don't know whether she did or not, but...'

'What?'

'She said she would kill herself rather than suffer the humiliation of a trial that would inevitably lead to the death penalty.'

'I don't believe you.' Miller shrugged his shoulders. 'She couldn't have killed herself. It wouldn't have been possible. I was called to the office in Mercer Street where she'd... died. She couldn't have done it on her own. She might have asked someone to kill her, but she could not have killed herself.'

'You're forgetting that Helen was highly intelligent, a master of deception. She had been a German spy for decades without anyone suspecting.'

'I suspected.'

'You did, eventually. But Helen had deceived people all her life. She was resourceful. She had a brilliant mind. She was also determined and unforgiving. You said she told you that she and McKenzie Robinson had been lovers.'

'She did. And not only by what she said but by the way she said it, it was obvious that she had been *in love* with him. In my opinion, he was the love of her life.'

'He was. But there was someone she loved more. And to keep that person safe she killed the only man she had ever loved.'

'Crowther killed Mac Robinson?' Revulsion swept over her. The nerves on the top of her stomach tightened like coiled springs. She thought she'd be sick. Then the realisation hit her. 'Oh my God.' Tears filled her eyes. 'Mac was going to help me to find… Frieda Voight.'

'And Helen couldn't allow him to do that.'

Ena looked at Nick, her eyes searching his for answers. 'Did Frieda know Crowther was a German agent, the mole at MI5?' Ena put her hand up to her mouth. 'Was Frieda working for Helen Crowther, for German intelligence as well as British and Russian intelligence?'

'No.'

'What then?' Ena was near to tears again. 'What happened that was so bad that a kind, clever, decent man like McKenzie Robinson had to die?'

'Helen knew that Mac Robinson had put two and two together and come to the conclusion that she was Frieda Voight's mother.'

Ena froze. Her head began to spin, her mouth was

dry and her hands trembled. 'Mother?' she heard a small voice that sounded like her own say.

'Mother,' Nick repeated. 'Helen Crowther; her name was Krueger at the time, was the birth mother of Frieda Voight.'

Thinking about it now, Ena's earlier conversation with Miller made sense. Miller had looked shocked when she told him that Crowther had a child. He looked shocked, not by the news of a child but because Ena knew about the child. He had joked telling Ena that Helen Crowther, who he knew in Berlin as Helen Krueger, his university tutor's wife, disappeared and his fellow students thought her husband had killed her. And all the time he knew why she had left Berlin. He knew she was pregnant. She should have known Nick knew about the baby. It was why he changed the subject to Crowther getting in touch with him when she began working for MI5.

Ena sat in silence for some time trying to digest the unbelievable information that Nick had given her. 'You said you went to the office in Mercer Street to stop Crowther killing herself and she was dead when you got there.'

'Yes.' Miller lowered his head. He spoke in short monotone bursts. 'She was still warm. I felt for a pulse. There wasn't one. She had gone.'

'So you left?'

Miller looked up at Ena, shook his head slowly as if he was ashamed, before saying, 'Yes.' There was a deep sadness in his eyes. A dark shadow, perhaps it was guilt, spread across his face like a shroud. 'As much as I wanted to, there was nothing I could do for her. So, yes, I left. And I prayed I hadn't been seen.'

'But you had. The boys said they'd seen a man, which Richardson of Special Branch assumed was my

243

husband, Henry.'

'I'm sorry, Ena. If I could go back and change what happened that night I would, but I can't. All I can hope is that what I've told you will go some way to making amends, and to clearing Henry's name. You now know what I believe happened.'

Ena shook her head in disbelief. 'But I don't! How can you be sure? Someone could have killed her and left before you got there?'

'It's possible, yes. But, even if someone did kill her, Helen planned it, set it all up. We both know your husband didn't kill her. She orchestrated her own death to frame Henry for her murder.'

'Why Henry? Exposing her as the mole at MI5 had nothing to do with him.'

'You still don't get it, do you?'

'What don't I get? Tell me, for God's sake.'

'Helen didn't care about being exposed as a spy, a mole, she didn't give a fig about herself or her own life. She didn't care whether she lived or died, she only cared about Frieda. Helen was driven by hate. She blamed Henry for Frieda's death. In her eyes, Frieda didn't commit suicide. Helen had convinced herself that Henry pushed Frieda off the roof of the church in Brixton. She believed Henry should have hanged for murdering Frieda. When he wasn't, she planned that he would hang for murdering her.'

'I see.' Did she see? 'And you're positive that you didn't see anyone when you got to Mercer Street or when you left?'

'No. There was no one around except the three boys. You said they saw me. If they'd seen anyone else they'd have told you wouldn't they?' Ena nodded. 'Helen planned her revenge on Henry meticulously.'

'And she almost pulled it off.'

'Nikolaus?'

'Yes.' Nick turned with a start. 'Is the car here?'

'Parked outside the main exit.'

'Thank you.'

As the driver of the car that was about to spirit Nick Miller away to his new life took the two largest suitcases, Nick picked up the remaining smaller case.

'How am I going to convince Special Branch that Helen Crowther killed herself?'

Miller put down the case and took Ena's hands in his. 'You won't have to, I will.' He looked into her eyes. 'I promise.'

'Thank you.'

Nick nodded, let go of her hands, picked up his case and walked away. He had only taken a dozen steps when he turned around.

Ena ran to him. 'What is it?'

'Don't trust Alan Richardson. Special Branch and MI5 are using your husband as a scapegoat. Five will do anything to keep secret the fact they've had a mole in a top job working at Leconfield House all these years. They won't want it to be known that a German agent worked with Henry, and certainly not that the agent worked closely to Director McKenzie Robinson. That kind of news would show them up for the incompetent organisation they are. They'll do their best to cover up Helen's death; pretend it never happened. If they can they'll classify it and red stamp it 'Top Secret'. But if it's too late and the mess Helen caused can't be consigned to the bowels of MI5's archive in Argyle Street, they'll have no choice but pin it on Henry. They'll leak information to the press suggesting he was having an intimate relationship with Helen.'

'What about the age difference? Would journalists

believe it?'

'They wouldn't have to believe it; they'd be reporting what they'd been told.' Nick laughed. 'From experience, the hacks in Fleet Street would print anything to sell newspapers. But it's more likely they'll say Henry was part of the spy ring and he killed his boss at MI5 because she suspected Henry.'

'But they can't do that if it's only me who knows the name and address of the bank and the number of the safe deposit box, where the evidence to solve the murders of Mac Robinson and Sid Parfitt - and proof that Helen Crowther killed herself - is kept.'

'No, they can't. When I'm safe you will have everything you need to clear Henry's name.' Nick hesitated. 'You have my word.'

'I know.'

'I'd better make a move.' Nick smiled and said, 'I've enjoyed getting to know you, Ena. Another time, another place, we might have become friends.' Leaning forward, he kissed her on both cheeks. 'Goodbye, Ena.'

Miller picked up his belongings and walked towards the main exit doors. Ena scanned the crowd, watching to see if anyone followed him. No one did. As far as anyone was concerned, Nick Miller was just another traveller leaving the airport.

It looked like the intelligence services had this time kept their word. Ena exhaled with relief and sat down. Nick had left his cigarettes and lighter on the table. She took a cigarette from the pack and lit it. Her hands were shaking. There was nothing she could do now but wait.

Ena had been sitting on the hard-wooden bench in the beer garden area of the arrivals hall for more than an hour and her backside was numb. There had to be somewhere more comfortable. She picked up her bags and wandered across the concourse of the arrivals terminal. She couldn't see a seat that looked more comfortable and turned to go back. It was then that she spotted a row of padded seats with headrests. Four square cushions to each seat faced a wall of glass. It was an area where people could sit and watch aeroplanes take off and land.

She flopped down on the nearest seat and stared into the night. The black wall of glass was a stark contrast to the bright lights of the airport's interior. Her eyes were tired. She closed them to shut out the glare of the fluorescent lights, lifted her feet and tucked them underneath her. With her arms around her holdall and handbag she leaned her head against the headrest.

'Mrs Green?'

'Yes?'

'Excuse me, I didn't mean to startle you.'

Ena opened her eyes fully and pushed herself up into a sitting position. She had fallen asleep and slipped sideways. Her neck was stiff. She rubbed it and rolled her shoulders.

'I believe you are waiting for this.' The driver of the car that had collected Nick a couple of hours earlier handed her a thick, larger than letter size brown envelope. 'From Herr Müller.'

'From?' Ena got to her feet. 'Yes, of course, Nikolaus Müller.' The driver called Nick by his real name. 'Thank you.' Relieved, she seized the envelope as if her life depended on it. Henry's life did.

Her feeling of relief was soon overshadowed by a feeling of foreboding. She looked at her wristwatch. Something was wrong. Two hours for Nick to get to his destination and his driver to come back to the airport meant he hadn't gone far. She had first thought that because Switzerland was neutral in the war - a safe haven for refugees - Nick would have gone there. It was still neutral and would have been the ideal place for him. Ena shook her head. Vienna to the Swiss border was too far away. She cast her mind back to the journey from London to Austria. The plane had flown over the Swiss Alps and it had been almost an hour before it landed in Vienna. The same journey would have taken seven or eight hours by car. Nick had not gone to Switzerland. A feeling of trepidation swept over her. Germany bordered Austria too. Vienna was nearer Germany than Switzerland, but then Nick would never risk going back to Germany. She thought about the Austrian schillings that Nick had given her. He'd said he wouldn't be needing them. She cast her mind back to what she knew about the countries in middle Europe. Austria bordered Hungary and Czechoslovakia. Hungary was too far away, but Czechoslovakia wasn't. It was perhaps an hour by car to the Czech border.

'Did Herr Müller arrive at his destination, safely?'

'He is safe.'

That wasn't what Ena had asked, but said, 'Good. It's just that you have only been gone a couple of hours. I was worried that the men who followed Herr Müller the first time you came for him had followed you again and they had stopped your car en route to…'

'The British intelligence men, your Special Branch, did follow the car. They pulled me over on the way to the Czechoslovakian border.'

Ena tensed. 'And Nick?'

'Nikolaus wasn't in the car.'

'He wasn't? Where was he?'

'He caught the last flight out of here,' the driver looked at his wristwatch, 'an hour ago.'

Ena put her hands up to her mouth and stifled a giggle. 'So, you were a decoy?'

'That's right. He didn't trust the Special Branch to keep their word, and he was right. I didn't take Nikolaus' suitcases to my car, I took them to the departure building, bought him a one-way ticket to New York and booked in his suitcases. When he got to the departure lounge, I left. By the time Nikolaus' plane took off, I was on the autobahn heading for the Czech border. When your Special Branch men stopped my car, Nikolaus would have been flying over the Swiss Alps.'

Ena laughed again, this time loudly. 'I'm glad. Special Branch may not have kept their word, but Nick kept his.' She lifted the envelope that the driver had given her. 'Thank you for this. It is very important.'

The driver bowed. 'My pleasure.'

An unsettling thought crossed Ena's mind. 'There's just one thing. You said Nick caught the last flight out of here. Did you mean the last flight to New York, or the last flight anywhere?'

'His was the last flight to leave the airport tonight. There had been several storm warnings before Nikolaus left. Bad weather is due to hit the Alps this evening. As the flight paths to New York and London are over the Alps, it will become too dangerous to fly.' The driver pointed to the window.

It was too dark to see from where Ena was standing. Fear that she would be stuck in Austria took hold of her. She ran to the window and peered out. 'Good God.' Snowflakes the size of half-crowns driven by a raging wind gusted across the window. She looked up at the sky. There were no planes landing and none were taking off.

'I didn't want to stay in Vienna overnight, but if I have to…' She let the sentence trail off. If she had to stay in a hotel at least she had the money to pay for it, thanks to Nick. She picked up her handbag.

'I will take you to a hotel.'

'Thank you, but there's no need.' Ena didn't want to offend the young man but, Nick's driver or not, she had no intention of getting into a car with a stranger. She only had his word that Nick caught a plane to New York. For all she knew he could have driven Nick somewhere and handed him over to goodness knows who.

'I'll be fine, really. Besides, I ought to go to the departure terminal to make sure there aren't any flights to London tonight. If there aren't, I need to book a seat on the first plane out tomorrow. While I'm there I'll ask the booking staff to get me a taxi.'

'Then I will escort you to the departure terminal to book your flight.' Nick's driver was speaking to her, but looking over her shoulder.

'There's really no need.' Ena lifted the envelope. 'Thanks again for this,' she said, and as she turned to leave, she caught sight of the two Special Branch officers strolling into the arrivals lounge.

'Turn! Now!' the driver ordered. 'Give me the envelope. They've searched me once. It is unlikely that they'll search me again.' Snatching the envelope from her, Nick's driver slipped it under his coat, buttoned it up to the neck, and tightened the belt before taking Ena by her upper arms and pulling her to him.

'What the hell are you doing? Let go of me. You're hurting me.'

'Shush! We must not be seen by the two men entering the airport. They are very dangerous.'

'They're Special Branch officers. They travelled here with Nick and me. They're here for my protection. They won't harm me.'

'The two men who came in after them will. They are the Stasi.'

'What? Who is the Stasi?'

'Germany's official state security service. The men following the Special Branch agents are not only German intelligence officers, they are highly feared secret police whose counterparts are the Soviet Union's KGB.'

Ena felt her knees buckle. She leant against Nick's driver, grateful that he had hold of her. Good God, what had she got herself into? The German military police surely wouldn't be interested in her. It would be Nick they'd want to talk to. But, she thought, in Nick's absence they might think she knew where he was and interrogate her. She'd rather not stick around to find out.

Nick's driver picked up her holdall and put his arm around her. As if they were a twosome they strolled along the length of the window, pausing every now and then to look at the falling snow, chatting as any normal couple would.

CHAPTER THIRTY-THREE

The freezing air took Ena's breath away. It was full of ice particles. She lowered her head as Nick's driver guided her along the slippery pavement. Snowdrifts blown across the path leading to the departure terminal made it difficult to walk. He held her tightly as she crunched through snow that came to the top of the cuffs on her ankle boots.

In the departures lounge, Ena stamped clumps of frozen snow from her feet and brushed snowflakes from her coat. She took off her hat, shook it, and pushed strands of dripping wet hair that had once been curled out of her eyes.

'Thank you for getting me out of the arrivals terminal.'

'Think nothing of it. Nikolaus was worried for your safety. It is under his instruction that I'm here. I don't know why the Stasi were following the Special Branch officers,' he said thoughtfully, 'but Nikolaus didn't trust them.'

'Nor do I. They went back on the deal they made with Nick and me.'

'The deal to let Nikolaus leave England in exchange for information your military police need?'

'Yes.' Ena was surprised that Nick had spoken about the deal to anyone, let alone a driver. 'Did Nick tell you about the arrangement?'

'He said he had evidence that would help the London police to solve two murders and that he had given you his word that he'd send it to you once he was safe. I guess somewhere over the Atlantic is safe enough.'

'I would think so. Nick also has evidence that will clear my husband of a murder he's been falsely accused of committing.' Ena shook her head in anger. 'Nick made it clear to Special Branch that if they didn't keep their part of the bargain; if they stopped him, apprehended him, hindered him in any way, he would not be obliged to keep his part of the bargain.'

'But he did.' The driver took the envelope Nick had promised her from beneath his coat and gave it to her. 'Come,' he said when Ena had secured the envelope in her handbag, 'let's book your flight to London. The sooner we get out of here the safer it will be for both of us.'

The desks of the airlines that should have been flying to a dozen destinations between 6pm that evening and 12pm the following day were manned by a handful of weary-looking ground staff. Ena approached the Austrian Airlines departure desk that had 'London' written above it. After explaining that the planes were grounded because of the extreme weather, the assistant asked Ena for her ticket.

'Will the ticket be exchanged, or do I need to buy another?'

'Exchanged at no cost,' the assistant said.

'That's good. Then could I exchange it for a ticket on the first available aeroplane to London, tomorrow?'

'Certainly, madam. That will be the twelve o'clock flight. I suggest you get here early, as the plane will be full.'

Ena's stomach did a somersault. She hadn't forgotten the inward flight, although she'd tried. 'I will. Would you get me a taxi to take me to a hotel?'

'I'm afraid there are no airport taxis available. They're all busy taking passengers whose flights were cancelled earlier to hotels.'

'What about a private taxi?'

'The private firms who are working in this storm are booked up for several hours.' The airline assistant nodded towards a queue of thirty or more people standing or sitting on their suitcases. 'You will have a long wait.'

Nick's driver touched Ena's arm. 'It's up to you, Mrs Green, but as Nick asked me to make sure you caught your plane to England, I'll be staying in a hotel tonight and coming back tomorrow at eleven. That is if there aren't more delays.'

'Are there likely to be more delays?' Ena directed the question to the airline assistant.

'Only if the weather doesn't change, but it will. Blizzards like the one we are experiencing this evening are rare. The last time we had such a fierce snowstorm that it grounded the planes was more than ten years ago. Thankfully, these storms don't last. They wear themselves out in three or four hours. In the morning the storm will be over and sun will be shining.'

'So, the plane to London should be okay to take off at midday?'

'Oh, yes. Once the runways have been cleared, it will be business as usual. By twelve o'clock it will almost certainly be good to fly.'

Ena looked again at the queue of people waiting for taxis and then at Nick's driver. 'Could I change my mind and take you up on your offer of a lift to a hotel?'

'Of course.' He exhaled loudly. 'Now I can keep my promise to Nikolaus.' He began walking towards the exit. 'The taxis will be taking people to the hotels closest to the airport. I stayed in a really nice place last year. It's a bit further away, so it's sure to have vacant rooms. It's typical Vienna style.'

'I don't care what style the hotel is as long as there's a bed and a bath, and I can have something to eat.'

'All the rooms have bathrooms.' He looked at his wristwatch. 'If we leave now the restaurant should still be open.'

'Thank you. There's just one thing.'

The driver raised his eyebrows as if to say, 'What now?'

'I don't know your name.'

He looked relieved and said, 'I am Rolf.'

'Pleased to meet you, Rolf. I'm Ena.'

The car was only a short walk away. Covered in snow, Ena had no idea of the make. It was a saloon of some kind, big, with wide tyres. Ena hoped the tyres were heavy enough to grip the road beneath the several inches of snow that made it impossible to see where the road ended and the path began.

Rolf wiped snow from the handle of the passenger door, unlocked it and took Ena's bags while she got in. He shut her door and after a few seconds had passed, the driver's door opened. He slid into the car, turned on the ignition, switched on the heater, and jumped out again shutting the door. Ena watched him scrape the snow from the car's windscreen and windows.

'Several inches of snow have fallen since I returned to the airport,' he said, getting into the car. He revved the engine several times before slowly pulling away from the kerb.

The blizzard was getting stronger and the snow more concentrated. Every few minutes the wind, more powerful than she had ever experienced, gusted, the car rocked and the windscreen wipers struggled to clear the weight of snow forced on them. Ena gripped the seat and peered through the windscreen. 'How do you know where to go?'

'I'm used to snowstorms. Not this severe, but we have strong winds and heavy snowfalls at home in the winter.'

'I can see dark shapes. Are they buildings?'

'Yes, we're on the outskirts of Vienna. It's one of the most beautiful cities in the world, and such a shame you won't have time to see it.' After slowly steering the car to the right, Rolf parked in front of Hotel Wien. 'We're here.'

Ena lifted her handbag and holdall from between her feet and opened the car door. A gust of wind swept it out of her hand and it flew back on its hinges. Rolf jumped out of the driver's door, locked it and was at Ena's side in seconds. He took her bags and helped her out of the car. Without letting go of her, he kicked the door shut and locked it. Huddled together they crunched their way through several inches of snow to the hotel.

Walking across the hotel foyer to the reception, Ena spotted a sign saying, 'Toilette'. She took half a dozen notes from the roll Nick had given her in the airport and offered them to Rolf. He looked embarrassed and put up his hand to push the money way. 'It isn't my money,' Ena said, 'Nick gave it to me before he left. He insisted I took it in case there was an emergency. Tonight, is an emergency, don't you think?' She put the money on the reception desk, asked for two rooms, and taking her handbag from under Rolf's arm, left him to pay while she went to the toilet.

Washing her hands, she caught sight of herself in the mirror above the handbasin. Her hair was wet and flat, what remained of her makeup was smeared and she had dark rings under her eyes. She took a handkerchief from her handbag and wiped smudged mascara from them. She looked tired. She was tired.

She combed her hair. She looked no better, but she felt better.

When she joined Rolf at reception, he gave her a ten-schilling note, some coins and the key to her room.

'If I may have your passport, madam?' the receptionist asked.

'Because you're a foreign visitor the hotel needs your passport. It's hotel procedure,' Rolf explained. 'You'll get it back when you leave tomorrow.'

Ena took her passport from her handbag and handed it over.

'The restaurant closes in half an hour. The receptionist said if we want dinner, we should go in now and see our rooms later.'

'Fine by me. I'm starving. Let's eat.'

The menu was in Austrian, naturally, which Rolf interpreted. They both decided on the soup to start. For her main course, Ena chose a traditional Austrian dish called Backhendl - chicken fried in breadcrumbs with lemon wedges and parslied potatoes. Rolf settled on a thick gravy goulash called Wiener Saftgulasch and asked for a bottle of wine that would complement both red and white meat. The waiter looked bemused.

'I'm not a wine drinker,' he said. 'You choose, Ena?'

Ena thought of Nick and grinned. 'A bottle of Deutsche Sekt, please.'

'Wow!' Rolf laughed. 'Do you have Deutsche Sekt in England?'

'No, but I once shared a bottle with a friend.' She didn't elaborate. The waiter returned with a bottle of Sekt and poured the sparkling wine into their glasses. Ena raised hers and said, 'To Nick.' Rolf did the same.

CHAPTER THIRTY-FOUR

'So,' Ena said, 'What do you do when you're not rescuing stranded females from airports in snowstorms, Rolf?'

'I'm at university. I also help out on my father's farm. It's predominantly a dairy farm. We have a professional cattleman look after the herd. We also grow wheat, ryegrass and alfalfa - and some fruit and vegetables. I work on the farm through the summer vacation, and again during the harvest gathering in grain crops and storing them for winter fodder. The fruit is mainly picked by students. They come from the city for a kind of paid vacation. In the autumn and winter, local women harvest the root vegetables.'

'Potatoes.' Ena screwed up her face and pretended to shiver. 'I remember having chapped hands from potato picking in the winter.'

Rolf's eyes lit up with surprise. 'You live on a farm?'

'No, I was brought up on a country estate. It was turned into arable land in the war by my eldest sister and a team of women called land girls. One of my sisters was in the WAAF and one was in London, but muggins here, who lived at home and worked locally, got roped in to help out in the potato picking season. In England, it can be a short season because we have a lot of rain.'

'Are you from what they call landed gentry?'

Ena burst into laughter. 'No. My father worked for landed gentry - a Lord. Dad was in charge of the estate's horses.' Ena took a drink of her wine. 'So, Rolf, what are you doing in Austria?'

'I came to ski. I packed my suitcase, jumped on an aeroplane and I'm having a paid vacation. When I leave university and work for my living, I'll have to find somewhere closer to home to ski. But, while I'm at university and get long holidays, it's Austria every time. I'll be going back to Innsbruck from here. I have another week as a ski instructor.'

'That's different.'

'Not if you're Austrian.'

'Are you Austrian?'

'I was born in the USA, but have Austrian blood in my veins. Austrians have been skiing for pleasure as well as necessity for almost a century. Now it's becoming a popular pastime for other Europeans. It's also a competition sport, not just a hobby for the wealthy who have been holidaying in the French and Swiss Alps since the early nineteen-thirties. The war put an end to anyone travelling overseas on holiday, but when it ended foreign travel resumed. Switzerland was then the favoured destination. Swiss shops were stocked with luxury goods, and the hotels had plenty of food when food in England was still rationed. Now Austrian skiing holidays have become popular. I love to ski. For me, working as a ski instructor is like being on holiday.'

Rolf took a drink of wine. 'Do you work?'

'Yes. Nothing so glamorous as teaching people how to ski, I'm afraid. I work in an office, in administration.' Rolf leant forward. 'I make sure the correct information is on documents. If a date or someone's age is missing, I look it up and add it before the document is filed.' Ena laughed. 'I'm a glorified clerk.'

'How do you know Nikolaus?'

Ena had just taken a drink of wine. She gasped with surprise at Rolf's question. Air and wine met, raced down her throat at the same time and she choked.

Rolf poured water from a jug on the table into a tumbler and passed it to her. She took several sips and eventually stopped coughing. 'Thank you.' She took another drink of water and having fully recovered said, 'Well, it's a long story.' She needed time to think, speared a piece of chicken with her fork and put it in her mouth. A stupid thing to do, it would more than likely make her choke again. What the hell could she tell him without making Nick look like a sleazy nightclub owner, a gangster, or worse - a lapsed spy? Perhaps Rolf knew Nick had been sent to England by German military intelligence at the beginning of the war. She looked up from her plate and smiled broadly at her dinner companion. He had finished eating and was looking at her; awaiting her reply.

When she had chewed the chicken for twice as long as was necessary, she put down the fork and wiped her mouth with a napkin. 'I work and live in London,' she said, cheerfully. 'But I often spend weekends with friends in Brighton. It's a seaside resort where Nick had a night club called The Minchin Club. It was ages ago that my friends first took me to his club. Because they knew him, I got to know him too. What about you?' Ena lifted her glass to take a drink. 'How do you know Nick?'

'He's my half-brother.'

'Nick's your half-brother?'

'Yeah. I was born in New York just after his father and my mother emigrated in nineteen thirty-seven.'

'I thought you were from the east coast of America by your accent, but even when you said Nick had gone to New York, I didn't make a connection.'

'Probably because we don't look alike. Nick features his mother who was blonde. My mom has black hair.'

'Your mother is Miriam? Nick told me how loving and kind your mother was to him.' Looking at Rolf, Ena could now see a similarity between him and Nick. They both had full lips and wide smiles. Nick had fair hair and Rolf's was dark brown, but Rolf's dark eyes sparkled when he smiled in the same way that Nick's grey eyes did.

If Nick had told her about his family, Ena wondered if Nick had told Rolf that she was responsible for him losing his business and having to leave England. Ena felt the heat of embarrassment creep up her neck to her cheeks and she drained her glass.

'So, did you ever come to England, to Brighton, to visit Nick?'

'No. When he wrote and told my parents he was leaving England I was sorry that I had never visited him there, but now I shall be able to see him often.'

'You being in Austria fitted in well with Nick's plans.'

'It couldn't have worked out better. Nikolaus telephoned my parents and told them he was coming to New York. They told him I was in Austria skiing, so he said he'd fly via Vienna. They phoned me straight away with the news and soon afterwards Nikolaus rang me and asked me to meet him at the airport.'

Ena listened to Rolf relate the story of Nick being in Austria while he was on a skiing holiday and wondered how long Nick had been planning to leave England. She finished her coffee and sat upright 'I'm ready for bed. Would you excuse me, Rolf?'

Rolf left his seat, walked briskly round the small square dining table and pulled out Ena's chair as she stood up. 'I think the two waitresses hovering by the kitchen door will be pleased to see us go.'

'I guess they can't leave until we do.'

261

*

Their rooms were on the seventh floor. They took the lift together. Before going into her room, Ena thanked Rolf for the help he'd given her and said goodnight. The light switch was on the wall just inside the door. She flicked it on. As she closed her door, she heard the door in the room next to hers click shut. She smiled. With Rolf in the room next to hers, she felt safe. After turning the key in the lock, she kicked off her shoes, dropped her handbag and holdall on the bed, crossed to the window and closed the curtains.

The room was small, but it was warm. She looked around. There was a decent sized wardrobe and chest of drawers. Neither would be needed tonight. A dressing table stood against the wall opposite. Next to it was a door. 'A bath,' Ena said aloud. She had been dreaming of a hot soak since arriving at the hotel. She walked round the bed and pushed open the door. It was a bathroom. Like the bedroom it was small but it had everything she needed - and it was clean.

Ena put the plug in the bath and turned on the hot water tap. While it ran, she returned to the bedroom. Before undressing, she jumped onto the bed, opened her handbag and tipped it upside down. Purse, comb, makeup bag, the loose change that Rolf had given her after paying for the hotel rooms fell out, followed by the money Nick gave her - and a key. She picked it up. She had never seen it before. It wasn't the key to her flat, or anything in the flat. Nor was it the key to the visitor's room at the theatre. Where…? Nick must have put it in her handbag when she went to buy coffee. She caught her breath. It was the key to Nick's safe deposit box. He obviously wanted her to keep it separate. She laid it on the bedside table and after returning the money to her handbag, she took out the envelope Rolf had given her from Nick and read:

Ena, if you are reading this letter you will soon know the name of my solicitor in Brighton. Mitford Crane, have been instructed to give you, and only you, the name and address of my bank (the key to my safe deposit box is in your handbag) and a sworn statement, signed by me and witnessed by them, that will prove your husband did not murder Helen Crowther. And, as promised, there is a letter for Inspector Powell that contains all he needs to solve the murders of Sid Parfitt and McKenzie Robinson.

The detestable Shaun O'Shaughnessy bragged to my friend, Hugh Middleton, that Helen Crowther had hidden something in her house that would save your husband from the hangman's noose. He wouldn't tell Hugh what it was, but get your tame copper at Bow Street to search her place in Brighton. Tell him to take up the floorboards.

Lastly, Ena, some time ago, Hugh found a book with the names of the people Helen worked with and those who worked for her, which I took to mean the agents in her cell, as well as those who could have been of use to her in the future. The book is in the safety deposit box at my bank. I'm telling you this because I want you to ask Powell to go easy on Hugh. He isn't a bad chap. He was brainwashed by O'Shaughnessy; flattered by him and taken in by his lies. Remind Powell that Hugh is a little fish who, by giving me Helen's book of agents, has given him the means to catch some very larger ones.

So, Ena, it's Auf Wiedersehen. I wish there had been time to get to know you better. In another life who knows? Take care and tell that husband of yours he's a lucky fella.

All the best, Nick. x

263

CHAPTER THIRTY-FIVE

The following morning, Ena took the gold chain and crucifix that she wore around her neck from the bedside table and slipped the end of the chain through the small hole in the head of Nick's key. She fastened it around her neck and gave it a gentle tug to make sure the clasp was secure. She then dressed in a clean blouse and jumper and went down to breakfast.

The breakfast room, in contrast to the dimly lit restaurant of the night before, was light and airy. A welcoming aroma of freshly made coffee met her as she entered. On the left of the room was a breakfast bar with baskets of bread and small pots of butter or margarine, Ena couldn't tell. Next to the bread were plates of sliced sausage and cheese - and behind them, bowls of boiled eggs.

Ena took two pieces of bread and a pot of spread. The sausage looked greasy and would, she thought, be too spicy for her palate. She helped herself to two slices of cheese and a boiled egg, took the food to a table by the window, and returned to the counter and poured a cup of coffee.

She wasn't hungry, but aware that it would be some time before she'd be eating again, probably on the aeroplane home, she buttered the bread and took the top off the boiled egg. It wasn't cooked. The white was still clear and ran down the side of the shell. She pushed it to one side and ate the cheese and bread. Boiled eggs are obviously not an Austrian speciality, but the nutty smoked cheese was. So was the coffee. In a relatively short amount of time, Ena had come to enjoy the strong, aromatic aroma of roasted coffee with a strong chocolatey after taste.

'Did you sleep well?' Rolf asked, striding across the

room with his breakfast and a newspaper.

'Yes, surprisingly. You?'

'Huh-huh.' He put a plate of bread and sausage, and a cup of coffee, on the table and sat down opposite her. 'I telephoned the airport. Your flight is scheduled to leave on time. More coffee? Ena?'

'Sorry? Oh, yes, please.' Ena was miles away, thinking about Nick's letter. She smiled to herself. Nick had been flirting with her. 'I was thinking that by now Nick would have arrived at his destination.'

'And in a few hours, you'll be at yours. But,' Rolf said, 'you have two hours before you need to check-in at the departures desk. How about I show you some of Vienna? It's one of the most beautiful cities in the world. It would be a shame to have come all this way only to return to England having never seen any of the city's outstanding architecture.'

'If you're sure there's time, it would be lovely. But first I must telephone someone. Excuse me.'

Ena left Rolf to finish his breakfast and went to reception. 'I'd like to make a telephone call to England.'

'Do you wish to telephone from your room, or from the foyer?'

Ena looked across the foyer to a row of telephone booths. 'A booth will be fine.'

'If you take the first one, I shall get the international operator for you.'

As she stepped into the first booth the telephone began to ring. She picked up the receiver, heard the receptionist say, 'hold the line please,' after which there was a click followed by the sound of a telephone ringing.

'Guten morgen. I understand you wish to be connected to England,' the operator said in very good

265

English.

'Yes, please.'

'One moment. I shall connect you.'

Ena waited for some minutes and then an English voice said, 'Number please?'

'Bow Street Police Station, Covent Garden, London.'

No sooner had she asked the operator to put her through to Bow Street, she heard the familiar voice of the station's desk sergeant. She told him who she was and asked to speak to DI Powell.

'Ena?'

'Hello, Inspector.'

'You've had us worried. We thought you'd be in touch before now. Are you alright?'

'Yes, I'm fine. It's a long story that all being well, I'll be able to tell you sometime this afternoon. The plane is scheduled to leave Vienna at twelve. I can't be sure it will take off then, it depends on the weather.'

'I'll be at London Airport from one o'clock.'

'In case it's delayed, you might be better to ring the airport first.'

Inspector Powell ignored her advice. 'Did everything go to plan, Ena?'

'Eventually.'

'Sounds ominous.'

'I have what I came for, but it's no thanks to DI Richardson's agents.'

'He'll be with me at London Airport.'

'Good. Then I'll be able to thank him in person.' Despite being annoyed with the Special Branch inspector, Ena laughed. Aware that Rolf was hovering outside the glass door of the booth, she said, 'My lift to the airport is here. I'll see you later, Inspector.'

'Take care, Ena.'

She put down the telephone and left the booth.

'Are you ready?'

'I'll pay for the call to England and get my other bag. See you in five minutes.'

When Ena returned, Rolf took her holdall. 'Now you will see this beautiful city.'

'If you're sure there's time.'

'The airport is twelve miles from here. We'll drive into the city, turn around, and drive back. It would be a crime not to see some of Vienna while you're here.'

When they were in the car, Ena said, 'There's just one thing, before you start the engine.' She took the money that Nick had given her from her handbag. 'Would you give what's left of Nick's money to him when you see him in New York?'

'But he gave it to you.'

'Yes, in case I needed a taxi and a hotel. I've used what I needed. I have no use for it in England.'

'Nikolaus won't have use for it in New York, either.'

Ena laughed. 'Then you have it.' Rolf gave her a quizzical look. 'Treat yourself while you're here and pay for your next skiing holiday?'

Ena could tell by the creases that appeared on the young man's forehead that he didn't feel comfortable taking his half-brother's money. She took hold of his hand and put the money in it. 'Use what you need and get the rest changed into dollars when you get to New York and give it to Nick.'

'Okay.' He put the money in the inside pocket of his overcoat and then looked sternly at Ena. 'If we leave right now, you'll see some of Vienna, if not...' He said, wagging his finger.

'I'd like that.' Ena needed a distraction to take her

mind off flying. Her stomach flipped when she remembered the turbulence crossing the Alps and hoped it wouldn't be as bad on the return flight to England.

'Vienna is a city of castles and palaces, of beautiful green parks,' Rolf said, 'when they are not hidden beneath several inches of snow, and of music and famous composers. Franz Schubert was born just outside Vienna. He is called The Waltz King because he made the waltz popular in Vienna during the nineteenth century. He wrote five hundred waltzes, can you believe that? Mozart was born in Salzburg, but he spent most of his creative years here. Beethoven, Hayden, Berg, also lived and worked in Vienna for much of their lives.'

Rolf turned the car off the main road. 'We'll cross the River Danube by the Praterbrücke.'

'A Canadian actress named Deanna Durbin recorded a song called The Blue Danube in the thirties. I remember sitting with my father and listening to her singing it when I was a child.' Ena began to hum the tune.

'Do you like music by Johan Strauss, Ena?'

'I'm afraid I don't know any. I know The Blue Danube Waltz, but that's about it. My father and husband both like classical music, but I prefer jazz.'

Five minutes after crossing the Danube they crossed back across the Reichsbrücke. Fifteen minutes after that they arrived at The Hofburg Palace.

'The Hofburg was originally a medieval fortified castle. It dates back to the thirteenth century. For more than six hundred years it was the residence of the Austrian sovereigns. Each one built a Baroque extension. There were many balls held here then,' Rolf explained. 'Music again, Ena. Vienna is famous for it.

The palace has been the political centre of the monarchy since nineteen eighteen.' He looked at his watch. 'We must go.' He started the car and pulled away from the side of the road into the traffic.

'Do you play an instrument, or sing, Rolf?'

Her young tour guide burst into laughter. 'I wish! I'm an American, a New Yorker, Ena. Vienna's my spiritual home. I feel as if I belong here, but I'm a better scholar than I am a musician.'

'And a better skier,' Ena said.

Rolf laughed again. 'You got that right.' He turned to Ena. 'Hold onto your hat, Mam, if I don't spare the horses, I can show you the Schönbrunn Palace and get you to the airport in time to catch the twelve o'clock flight.' He gave her a cheeky grin and put his foot down hard on the accelerator. Fifteen minutes later he slowed to almost a standstill.

'Made it! What do you think?'

Ena marvelled at the sight in front of her.

'It's one of the finest Rococo castles in Europe and the most important architectural building in Austria. It has something like fifteen hundred rooms. How would you not get lost?' Rolf blew out his cheeks and the sparkle in his eyes faded.

'What is it?'

He pulled a sad face. 'Now, we really have run out of time. It's back to the airport on the autobahn if you're going to catch your plane.' He turned the car around and headed back the way they came before turning onto a three laned motorway.

A hold up on the autobahn cost them twenty minutes and when Rolf brought the car to a screeching halt outside the main doors of the departure terminal, Ena had no choice but to jump out and run to the check-in desk. The rest of the passengers had boarded, so Ena was escorted out of the terminal, across the tarmac and up the portable stairs. At the top, before she stepped into the plane, she turned and searched the windows in the departure lounge. The winter sun reflecting on the glass made it impossible to distinguish one person from another. She waved anyway. If Rolf was among the small crowd that had gathered to watch the plane take off, he would know it was him she was waving to. The door closed and Ena was shown to her seat. Excited to be on her way home, she looked out of the small round window. The plane taxied along the runway and with a thrust lifted off. She watched the beautiful city of Vienna grow fainter and smaller until it disappeared completely beneath a canopy of clouds.

She had never seen buildings as beautiful as the ones in Vienna. Then she thought of St. Paul's Cathedral. She cast her mind back to the day she met Henry on the walkway outside the Stone Gallery. She remembered that the west towers and dome, like many of the buildings in Vienna, were Baroque in design.

Ena sat back in her seat and sighed. She was happy to be on her way home to London, but sorry that she hadn't had time to say goodbye to Rolf. She took Nick's letter from her handbag and read it again. He had kept his word. She leaned her head against the back of the seat and smiling, closed her eyes. When she woke her ears were popping and the plane was about to land.

CHAPTER THIRTY-SIX

Ena saw Inspector Powell first and then Claire. She had hoped more than anything that Henry would be with them, though she knew in her heart he wouldn't.

'Ena?' Claire pushed her way through a four-person deep crowd to meet Ena halfway between the door to the arrivals terminal and the barrier. 'Thank God you're here,' she exclaimed with relief, throwing her arms around her sister. 'I was worried sick when you didn't come back last night.'

'I was well looked after.'

'But…'

'I'll tell you later. Have you heard how Margot is?'

'Yes, she's fine. She needs rest, but apart from that Bess said she's her old self. She wanted to come back to London after seeing her specialist.'

'What?'

'Don't worry, Bill put his foot down. She's now making plans for Easter.'

'Inspector?'

Inspector Powell put his arms around Ena and hugged her. 'You had us worried when you didn't return last night,' he said looking over the top of Ena's head. Without giving her time to explain, he said, 'I rang the airport and they told me about the storm in Vienna. Did you have enough money for a hotel? We should have given you more. I told Richardson we hadn't given you enough money. I didn't think about planes being grounded, but then the weather in Austria…' Inspector Powell let go of Ena, took a step back and looked into her face. 'I was worried,' he said, taking a handkerchief from his pocket to wipe perspiration from his forehead.

'Thank you, but I was fine, I had plenty of money. I

stayed in a good hotel.' She looked past Inspector Powell to see DI Richardson pushing his way through the crowd. 'I have a lot to tell you.'

'Tomorrow,' the inspector said, as Richardson arrived. 'You look as if you could do with a decent night's sleep. I'll hitch a lift back to London with Alan.'

Frowning, the Special Branch detective looked from Ena to the inspector. 'What's going on?'

'WPC Jarvis is driving Ena and Claire home.'

Ena looked at Constable Jarvis, her eyes wide with surprise. 'Have the police finished in the flat?'

'Yes, and everything has been put back in its place.'

'You wouldn't know anyone had been in there,' Claire added.

Ena sighed, remembering the last time she was in the flat. 'Thank you.'

'I'll send a car for you tomorrow, Ena. Unless you'd rather drive in?'

A broad smile spread across Ena's face. 'Have you finished with the Sunbeam as well?'

Before DI Powell could reply, Richardson said, 'I need to be there. I have a meeting first thing. Shall we say, late morning?'

'That'll be fine, Alan.' The inspector turned to Ena. 'No need to get up early then. Debrief at twelve?'

The inspector raised his eyebrows questioningly to Richardson, who gave a sharp nod. He turned to Ena and winked.

In the Wolseley on the way home to Stockwell, Ena again asked Claire about Margot. 'You're not saying she's alright just to stop me from worrying, are you?'

'No. Why would I do that? She's had the tests at the hospital and she's been told to rest. The results of some of the tests haven't come back yet. Bess said her doctor didn't seem concerned.' Claire held Ena's hand. 'She'll be fine.'

'At the airport, you said something about Easter?'

'Margot wants us all to go to Foxden at Easter. She wants everyone to go to Mysterton Church on Easter Sunday as we used to do in the old days.'

'The Dudley family together would be lovely.'

'Scary,' Claire said.

'And,' Ena said, 'Henry should be back by then.'

'I don't want to rain on your parade, Ena, but Easter's only a couple of weeks away.'

'I know.' She slid down on the soft leather seat of the Wolseley and closed her eyes. She was more tired than she realised. The car's big engine purred loudly. It was comforting, she thought and drifted off.

Aware that cold air was blowing around her legs, Ena opened her eyes. She was home.

Ena took off her coat and hung it up She closed the door and noticed a new lock and beneath it a solid brass bolt. She fingered the bolt. It should have made her feel safe, but it didn't. She knew she would never again feel safe in the flat. She went into sitting room. It was clean and the furniture had been put back in place; Henry's armchair was next to the fire, the settee was under the window, dining chairs were placed neatly beneath the dining table - and a vase of daffodils stood in the middle. Apart from the flowers, the room looked the same as it had before someone broke in and ransacked it. But it wasn't the same. It would never be the same. Ena sniffed back her tears.

'Ena? Constable Jarvis is going.'

She wiped her hand across her face. 'Sorry, Constable, I was miles away.'

WPC Jarvis waved Ena's explanation away.

'There's no need to apologise. You must be tired.'

'Yes, that's probably it. Thank you for bringing us back. I'll see you tomorrow.'

'You will.' She looked from Ena to Claire. 'If a car came for you eleven-fifteen, would that be alright?'

Ena laughed. 'No need to send a car. Now fingerprints have finished with my car we can drive in.'

WPC Jarvis looked to the heavens. 'Of course. Goodnight,' she said and left.

Ena followed her out and watched her get into the Wolseley. When she had driven off, she turned the key in the lock and put on the bolt before returning to the sitting room.

'I'm parched. Want a cuppa?' Claire asked. And without waiting for a reply went into the kitchen. When she returned it was with a pot of tea, cups and saucers, and two plates of sandwiches.

'Come and sit down, Ena,' she said, placing the tray on the table. 'I'll put a match to the fire.'

'Where's my handbag and holdall?'

'I put them in your bedroom. Sort them out later or the tea will be cold.'

'I'll only be a minute.' Ena left Claire lighting the fire. Her bedroom was clean and tidy - the bed had been made - and drawers that had been pulled out of the tallboy and dressing table had been replaced. She pulled open her underwear drawer. Everything had been folded and put back neatly. She intended to wash everything before she wore it. She opened Henry's drawers. They too were neat, as were their clothes hanging in the wardrobe. Everything looked the same as it had before the burglary. Except it wasn't. She had an overwhelming feeling that nothing in her and Henry's life would ever be the same again. She slumped down on the bed unable to stop her tears.

'Ena?' Claire called from the hall. 'Hey... What's this?' Claire came into the bedroom and sat on the bed next to her. 'Don't upset yourself, sweetheart. It'll be alright, you'll see. Come on, let's go back to the sitting room, your tea's getting cold.'

Letting Claire lead her, Ena left her bedroom and returned to the sitting room. The fire, although it had only been burning for a short time, had already taken the chill off the air.

The sisters sat on either side of the table. Claire poured them each a cup of tea. 'It isn't hot now, but it'll do,' she said, taking a sip of hers. Claire offered Ena a sandwich. She shook her head, so Claire put a round of ham on a plate, cut it in half and pushed it towards her. 'You need to eat,' she said, firmly.

Ena did as her older sister said and when they had both finished eating, Claire took the teapot to the kitchen and made a fresh brew. When she returned, she refilled their cups and added milk. 'What is it, Ena? What's bothering you? I know you're tired from travelling, but look on the positive side. The flat's back to how it was, and you're right, Henry will soon be free and you're safe.'

'I am tired, but not from travelling to and from Vienna. Not even from the uncertainty of flights, hotel rooms, or even whether everything would go to plan and I'd get the evidence I need to clear Henry's name.'

'Then what is it?'

Ena blew out her cheeks. 'It's... It's all of it. It's nothing and it's everything. Since seeing Frieda Voight in Oxford Street last July, there have been murders, suicides, false accusations, people I don't trust. And the people I thought I could trust; the people Henry and I work for betrayed us, accused him of being a spy,

275

a murderer. The very people who were supposed to be on our side, who should have believed in us and supported us, who *we* trusted, betrayed us.'

Ena got up and walked around the room. 'Did you know MI5 bugged this flat? Of course, you did. It was Sid who found the bugs and got rid of them. And it was Sid who remembered something in the cold case files that would have exposed the mole at MI5. I'm sure Mac Robinson knew who the mole was. He knew Frieda was alive too. He was going to tell me what he knew, but they killed him like they did Sid. Frieda told me as much in this room before she committed suicide.' Ena fell to her knees and sobbed. 'I shouldn't have gone after her. Henry said I couldn't have seen Frieda because she was dead. But I had to prove him wrong. I had to know the bloody truth, and by finding the truth I unearthed a hornet's nest of spies and murderers.'

Ena looked into the fire. 'Henry begged me to drop the case against Frieda.'

'Why didn't you?'

'I wanted to prove I was right and he was wrong.' She leaned against the arm of the chair. 'I can't undo what has been done, but I can give Mac's wife and Sid's mother and sister some sort of closure.' Ena put her hand up to her neck. 'Nick Miller gave me a key, and the name and address of his solicitors who will give me the name of his bank. The key is to Nick's safe deposit box. He promised me I'd find evidence to prove who killed Mac and Sid and the proof that Henry didn't kill Helen Crowther.'

'That's good, isn't it?'

'Of course. But Nick also told me that the Branch, MI5 and the Home Office, will make Henry a scapegoat for her murder if news of her being the mole at Five is leaked. I need to get the information to DI Powell as soon as possible because if anything happens to Henry it'll be my fault.'

'Come on, love.' Claire left her chair and knelt beside her sister. 'None of it was your fault. They chose to work as spies; to live dangerous lives.'

'But don't you see? If I had let the Frieda Voight investigation go when Henry told me to, Sid Parfitt and Mac Robinson would still be alive, so would Frieda.'

'And Frieda would still be selling information to enemy governments and there would still be a mole at MI5 doing God knows how much damage to the country and to decent people.'

On the outside, Ena was feeling warmer, inside she felt ice cold. 'You're right. I'm sorry,' she whispered, 'I'm tired.'

'I know.' Claire put her arm around Ena. 'Why don't you have a bath and then go to bed for a couple of hours. Try and relax. If you can sleep, all the better.'

'Alright.' Ena sat back on her heels and pushed herself to her feet. 'See you later.'

'I'll telephone Natalie, let her know you're back and I'll be in the theatre tomorrow.'

'Will you give Bess a ring and ask how Margot is?' Ena said as she left the room.

CHAPTER THIRTY-SEVEN

'Are you ready?'

'Almost.'

'I'll drop you off at Bow Street, take the Sunbeam down to the theatre and leave it at the stage door.' Claire put on her coat and hat and left.

Ena drained her cup, took her purse from her handbag and dropped the key to Nick Miller's safe deposit box in it. Ena fully understood that the key was part of the investigation and in ordinary circumstances, she would have given it to the inspector at the first opportunity. But these were not ordinary circumstances. Nothing about Helen Crowther's murder was ordinary. She would tell him about the key, but not give it to him. Nick had entrusted the key to her as he had the address of his solicitor in Brighton. It was his way of ensuring Special Branch weren't able to keep her out of the investigation. She would be involved every step of the way, even being present when Nick's safety deposit box was opened. Nick was adamant that Special Branch was making a scapegoat of Henry. By making her the key holder, Nick had made sure they couldn't plant evidence to incriminate him further.

She had telephoned the solicitor's office and made an appointment for two o'clock which she hoped meant leaving London for Brighton before DI Richardson arrived at Bow Street to debrief her. She wanted Inspector Powell with her in Brighton, but not Richardson. Special Branch played by different rules to the Met - sometimes by no rules at all. She squeezed the small bow-shaped clasp on top of the purse and it clicked shut. Before closing her handbag, she checked Nick's letter was in it.

As was his custom, Inspector Powell left his seat and met Ena at the door. Welcoming her with a smile, he led her to a chair on the opposite side of his desk. 'You're three hours early for the debrief, Ena.' The DI pulled a comical face. 'What are you up to?'

'We have a meeting with Nick Miller's solicitor at two o'clock this afternoon. That is if you can make it for two. I could telephone and arrange it for another day, but I'd rather not.'

The inspector looked perplexed. 'Where is the solicitor?'

'Brighton.'

'Brighton? Two o'clock will be cutting it fine for DI Richardson.'

'I don't want DI Richardson at the meeting. Nick said the solicitors would be expecting me. It's me who wants you there. Nick made it clear that he didn't trust Inspector Richardson to keep me involved and has given me power of attorney in his absence.'

'Which makes it impossible for Richardson to exclude you.'

'It does.' Ena told the inspector everything that had happened in Austria. She told him about the money Nick had given her, and that she had given what was left after paying for the hotel and a meal, to Nick's half-brother, Rolf. She told him how when Nick left the airport the first time, Special Branch officers were waiting outside so he returned to the arrivals lounge. She also told him that Rolf had been stopped and his car had been searched because they thought Nick was in it. And she told him that Nick had asked his half-brother to look after her; make sure she was safe and she caught the plane back to England.

'And he did look after me,' Ena said. 'He looked

after me when the German military police were snooping around the airport.'

Inspector Powell took a sharp breath. 'The Stasi?'

'That's who Rolf said they were. I don't know if Special Branch knew they were being followed, but they led the Stasi to us. Rolf said they'd be looking for Nick, but in his absence, they'd interrogate him and, because I'd travelled to Vienna with Nick, they'd also interrogate me. He not only helped me escape the Stasi, but he also took me to the departure terminal, booked me on the first flight back to England the next day and drove me to a hotel in Vienna. I don't know what I'd have done without Nick's half-brother or his money.'

Inspector Powell gave Ena a disapproving look. 'What happened to Miller?'

'He got the last flight out of Vienna before the bad weather front came in. No planes landed or took off after he left.'

'He was lucky.'

'He was. So was I. At the airport there were queues of people waiting for the few taxis that were willing to drive to the city in such bad weather. Vienna is only twelve miles from the airport, but in a blizzard after a heavy snowstorm, the roads were treacherous. As I said, Rolf drove me to a hotel on the outskirts of Vienna.'

'What happened to him after he took you to the hotel?'

'Because he was staying at a ski resort in the Alps - and obviously couldn't drive there and come back for me the following morning to make sure I got the plane to London as Nick had instructed - I, with Nick's money, paid for a room for him.' Ena took what was left of the Austrian schillings she'd taken with her

280

from her handbag and gave it to the inspector.

'There's a lot of money left.'

'There is. This is the receipt for dinner and two rooms at the Hotel Wien.'

Inspector Powell looked at the receipt and whistled. 'Expensive hotel.'

'Austria's capital isn't cheap.' Ena took the key that Nick had given her from her purse and laid it on the inspector's desk.

'And this is the key to Miller's safe deposit box at his bank?'

'Which I shall hold onto.' She took the chain from around her neck and secured the key on it as she had done in Vienna. 'I don't trust Inspector Richardson. His men followed Rolf's car and pulled it over on the way to the Czech border because they thought Nick was in it. Richardson went back on his word. He almost jeopardised the operation.'

'But not the most important part. Miller did give you the information he promised?'

'Yes. Nick knew I was straight. Richardson double-crossed him - and me for that matter.' Ena took Nick's letter from her handbag and gave it to the inspector.

When he had finished reading, the DI looked downcast. He folded the letter and gave it back to her. 'He asks that I go easy on Hugh Middleton.'

'Middleton was under the spell of that devil, O'Shaughnessy. What is it with the man? It's as if he knows when people are vulnerable.' Ena returned the letter to her handbag. 'You will go easy on Middleton, won't you?'

'I'm afraid I can't.'

'Why not? From what Nick said, Hugh Middleton was as much a victim of O'Shaughnessy as Artie Mallory was last year. And look at the information he has given you.'

'I can't go easy on him, Ena, because he's dead. We found his body in the basement of Crowther's house in Brighton.' The inspector took a silver bracelet from the drawer of his desk. 'This was next to his body.'

For a moment Ena was speechless. When she found her voice she said, 'How did my bracelet end up next to the dead body of Hugh Middleton?' She closed her eyes and screwed up her face in anger. 'O'Shaughnessy!' she hissed. 'I took my gloves off and stuck them into the pocket of my coat to get a better grip on the drainpipe on Crowther's veranda when Claire and I broke into the house. I had to move quickly because O'Shaughnessy and Middleton suddenly appeared in the kitchen and the window looks out onto the veranda. I realised later that my gloves had fallen out of my pocket, but I daren't go back for them. I must have pulled the bracelet off with the gloves and O'Shaughnessy found it. Bizarre isn't it? Henry is being framed for the murder of Helen Crowther and O'Shaughnessy is trying to frame me for the murder of Hugh Middleton. If it wasn't so absurd, it would be funny. When you found Middleton's body had O'Shaughnessy skipped town?'

'No. He was at Eve Robinson's house.'

'Claire and I saw Eve Robinson and O'Shaughnessy coming out of Crowther's house on the day I lost my gloves. I knew she was a friend of Helen Crowther's, but I wouldn't have had her down as a member of O'Shaughnessy's circle.'

'She isn't. You were right when you said Helen Crowther had started writing McKenzie Robinson's memoirs and that O'Shaughnessy had taken over the job. We were only able to speak to Mrs Robinson briefly, but she told us that O'Shaughnessy had turned up at her house after Helen Crowther had been killed and offered to finish writing her husband's memoirs. After a couple of meetings, he arrived drunk and told her that Helen Crowther had been her husband's mistress and that they had been in love. He said they'd been having an affair all the time she was married to McKenzie and that they were together right up until the time he was murdered. Mrs Robinson said O'Shaughnessy took pleasure in telling her about her husband's affair with her friend.'

'The bastard.'

'And that's not all.'

'There's more?' Ena leaned back in her chair, wide-eyed.

'He told Mrs Robinson that Helen Crowther was a spy, a German agent, and when Eve said she didn't believe him, O'Shaughnessy told her everything he knew about Crowther. Apparently, she was married when she came to this country.'

'To a professor at the University of Berlin named Martin Krueger.'

Now it was Inspector Powell's turn to look surprised. 'How did you know?'

'Nick told me. So, why did O'Shaughnessy go to Eve Robinson's house? Was it for an alibi?'

'No. He went there to shut her up, to kill her. He told her she knew too much and tried to strangle her. She said she'd been terrified ever since the night he'd told her that Crowther was a spy, so yesterday, when she saw him walking up the drive to her house, she telephoned John Street Police Station. The police got to her in time.'

'Thank God they did.'

'O'Shaughnessy knocked her about badly. He tried to strangle her but she passed out, which the doctor said saved her life. She isn't out of the woods yet, but she will be. Her neck is bruised, she's hoarse, can't speak without coughing and she can't swallow, but she'll be okay. She was lucky. If the police hadn't got to her when they did... Another minute and she'd have been dead.'

'But she *will* recover?'

'Oh yes. The doctor said she should make a full physical recovery, but mentally, who knows? It isn't every day you find out someone you believed was your friend had a love affair with your husband, was a spy, and the man who told you tries to kill you.'

Inspector Powell reached for the telephone. 'Jarvis, telephone DI Richardson at Special Branch, will you? He won't be available as he's in a meeting, so leave a message. Say the Yard has asked me to go down to Brighton for a meeting with Inspector Armstrong at John Street. Tell him I'll phone him when I get back to arrange a convenient time for us to meet with Mrs Green later today, or tomorrow.'

DI Powell gave Ena a boyish grin. 'Look sharp,' he said, leaping out of his chair. 'We'd better leave straight away. If Jarvis is put through to Richardson, he'll be ringing back insisting he comes to Brighton with us.'

Ena jumped up and grabbed her coat. 'You mean you'll come with me to Nick's solicitor in Brighton?'

The inspector took his coat from the stand behind the door. 'I'll drive.'

CHAPTER THIRTY-EIGHT

The offices of Mitford Crane were in Queen's Place, off the London Road. The double-fronted two-storey building had a square step leading to a glass door with an elegant *M C* choreographed in gold letters. Above the door was a frieze, it's central character was Solon, the ancient Greek statesman, lawmaker and poet, who laid the foundations of Athenian democracy. On either side were fluted columns with plain bases and scrolled volutes on top.

'Looks very posh. Nick has friends in high places.'

'It's money that gets you these kinds of friends, Ena.'

'I expect it is. I'm glad you're with me. I'm not sure I'd have dared go in on my own.'

The inspector pressed the brass and china bell push at the side of the door. It was answered almost immediately by a slender middle-aged woman in a smart but plain dark grey suit and pale grey blouse, who Ena assumed was the woman who she had spoken to on the telephone.

'Mrs Green?'

'Yes.'

After acknowledging the inspector with a polite smile, the woman pushed open the door fully and ushered them in. The entrance was square with two doors on either side of an ornate staircase that rose in a sweeping curve to the first floor.

'Mr Crane is expecting you. If you'd like to follow me.' The woman knocked on the door of the first room on the ground floor and entered without waiting to be asked.

Dwarfed behind a huge mahogany writing desk, an elderly white-haired man wearing half-frame spectacles, lifted his head. 'Thank you, Mrs Le Flem. Horace Crane,' he said, getting to his feet and ambling over to shake first Ena's hand and then DI Powell's. 'Take a seat, I won't keep you a moment.' Returning to his chair he finished what he'd been writing. 'Well, well, well,' he said, treating Ena to a wrinkled grin, 'my old friend Nick has finally flown the coup.'

Ena opened her mouth, but was too shocked by Mr Crane's description of Nick's departure to speak.

'He was something of a Jekyll and Hyde character, you know. Much more Jekyll than Hyde, of course. Oh yes.' Looking thoughtful, the elderly solicitor rubbed his chin. 'Nick was a good man when you weigh it up. He made a great deal of money in the war; spent most of it repairing people's homes and businesses in the East End of London. That was before he came to Brighton; before he bought The Minchin Club. Got it for a song after it had been bombed and rebuilt it.'

Horace Crane left his seat and went to a large grey safe in the corner of the room. He took a key from his watch-chain, inserted it into the brass keyhole next to a handle, turned both at the same time and pulled open the door.

'Helped a lot of young people after the war. Got a youth club set up, started a boxing club; said it would get youngsters off the streets. You know the sort of thing. Paid for it all himself too. Yes,' he said again, 'Much more Jekyll than Hyde.'

As if he had just been told a very funny joke, the elderly man burst into laughter. 'Often flew by the seat of his pants, as they say. A good man all the same.' He closed the door of the safe, turned the key and handle again, this time clockwise. For a second he looked quizzically at the envelope. 'Oh yes. The address of Mr Miller's bank and his bank details are in here.' He

286

returned to his chair, slid the brown A4 envelope across the desk to Ena, but didn't let go of it. Ena's heart beat fast with anticipation. 'There is also a statement from Mr Miller, witnessed by my partner and myself.'

The solicitor took his hand off the envelope and Ena picked it up and opened it. She took out a document addressed to DI Powell and passed it to him. She then took out another document, the one Nick had promised her would prove Henry didn't murder Helen Crowther. Holding her breath, astonished by what she was reading, she decided that until she had read the document again; understood and digested the complicated lengths that Crowther had gone to in order to frame Henry for her murder, she would keep the contents of the letter to herself. Inspector Powell finished reading the document addressed to him and returned it to the A4 envelope. Ena did the same, before folding it and putting it safely in her handbag.

'Satisfactory?'

'The...? Yes, very. It's exactly what Nick promised.'

The solicitor leaned his elbows on his desk and looked into Ena's eyes. 'Anything else?'

'Er...' Ena was taken aback by the abrupt way in which the solicitor asked. 'Everything I need is in here. Thank you, Mr Crane.'

'No need to thank me, Mrs Green. Only doing my job.'

As if she had second sight and knew the meeting was over, Mrs Le Flem gave the door a sharp rap and, as she had done when she showed Ena and the inspector into her boss' office, she entered. 'Your next appointment is here, Mr Crane.' Without waiting for a reply she turned to Ena. 'If you'd like to follow me, I'll show you out.'

Ena and DI Powell got to their feet. At the door, Ena turned to thank Mr Crane again. He had already picked up his pen. His lips were moving and his eyes were darting from left to right across the page, as he read the document he'd been writing when they arrived.

'That was short and sweet,' Ena remarked, as they walked along Queen's Place to where the inspector's car was parked on London Road.

'The old boy was away with the fairies if you ask me,' the inspector replied.

'He liked Nick.'

'Made him out to be a regular Robin Hood.'

Ena laughed. 'Those are the exact words I said to Nick in Vienna. Still, if what the solicitor said was true, Nick wasn't all bad.'

'No one is all bad, Ena.'

Ena shuddered. 'Shaun O'Shaughnessy is.'

Inspector Powell brought the car to a sudden halt. 'A telephone box! I'll ring my friend, Geoff Armstrong. He's Head of the Murder Squad at John Street. If he's in the office we'll drop in; tell him about the meeting with Miller's solicitors.'

'And ask him to get a search warrant for Crowther's house.'

The inspector was back in a few minutes. 'Geoff's in his office and Alan Richardson's with him.'

Ena couldn't help but laugh. 'Oh, dear. Are we in trouble?'

Inspector Powell was looking in the rear-view mirror. When there was a gap in the traffic he put his foot down and quickly filled it. With a defiant grin on his face, he said, 'Two upstanding British police inspectors and you, Ena, against one dodgy Special Branch inspector. The poor chap doesn't stand a chance.'

Thinking about when she had first met DI Armstrong, Ena said, 'I hope the inspector has forgiven Claire and me for breaking into Crowther's house.'

'I'm sure he has.'

'Claire almost pulled the detective sergeant's arms out of its socket.'

'Geoff told me. He laughed about it. He told the young DS to get himself lessons in self-defence. The poor chap took a lot of stick from his colleagues.'

Ena bit her bottom lip. 'Claire is pretty handy in those kinds of situations. Shame about the Mickey taking.'

'He'll get over it.' Turning off the road, DI Powell steered the Wolseley into the car park at the back of John Street Police Station.

Inspector Armstrong's office was a partition made of thin wood and glass at one end of a large office that had desks and a blackboard at the other end. Half a dozen plainclothes policemen were huddled around a desk in front of the blackboard. They stopped speaking when Ena and Inspector Powell entered. Ena was aware she was being watched. Someone gave a soft wolf whistle and she felt her cheeks colour.

Inspector Armstrong stood up when they entered his office and welcomed them with a smile. Inspector Richardson remained seated and stony-faced.

'Come in. Have a seat. Good to see you again, Mrs Green. Dan?' Leaning across his desk, he shook their hands briefly. 'You know Inspector Richardson of Special Branch, of course.' Inspector Powell gave

Richardson a friendly smile, the Special Branch inspector replied with a curt nod as Ena took her seat. When DI Powell sat down, Inspector Armstrong lowered himself back into his chair.

'Congratulations, Mrs Green. I understand the mission to gain information about the Voight-Crowther investigations was successful.'

'It was, Sir.' No thanks to Richardson, Ena thought, but said nothing.

'So, what have we got?' He looked from Ena to DI Powell.

'We have information that could lead us to the members of the spy ring that Crowther ran. And, we now know the address of Nick Miller's bank.'

'Do you have the key to the safe deposit box?' Richardson asked.

Ena put her hand to her neck and cleared her throat.

'Miller gave the key to Mrs Green. She'll bring it to the bank to open Miller's safe deposit box when the time comes.'

Out of the corner of her eye, Ena saw DI Richardson's head jerk in her direction. 'It's in a safe place, I hope? We can't risk losing it or the work we've done so far on this investigation will have been for nothing.'

'That…' Ena was about to say, is rich coming from you. Instead, she said, 'I won't lose it, Inspector Richardson. I wouldn't jeopardise the investigation by doing something so stupid!'

'I assure you, Alan, it's quite safe,' Inspector Powell cut in, and without pausing said, 'When we have confirmation of the bank's address, I'll telephone and make an appointment.'

Inspector Armstrong scribbled a note on the pad in front of him. Richardson gave a reluctant half-hearted nod.

'And, Hugh Middleton, the chap we found dead in Crowther's house yesterday, told Miller that evidence relating to the murder of Helen Crowther was hidden somewhere in the house.'

'Under the floorboards,' Ena added.

'We'll search the place thoroughly, Mrs Green. If there is anything hidden in the house, we'll find it.'

'What has O'Shaughnessy said since he's been in custody?'

'Nothing that makes any sense. The first time I interviewed him he became agitated. He rocked back and forwards, made out he could hear voices. He rambled on about something, stopped mid-sentence, gazed across the room and began speaking to someone. There was no one else in the room of course.'

'What was he saying?'

Nothing at first, just a string of random words. The only thing he said that made any sense at all, although it wasn't true, was that it wasn't him trying to hurt Mrs Robinson. He said it was a wicked boy. It was an act of course. He was playing us for fools. He asked for a psychiatrist when we brought him in, not a lawyer.

Inspector Powell brought his fist down hard on DI Armstrong's desk. 'He's an actor, a fantasist. He'll put on a show of not being in his right mind and a good brief will try for diminished responsibility.'

Ena looked at Inspector Powell. 'And, if the lawyer is successful, O'Shaughnessy will get a reduced sentence; manslaughter instead of murder. Tell me that won't happen,' she pleaded. 'The murder of Sid Parfitt and Hugh Middleton - and the attempted murder of Eve Robinson - were all premeditated.'

'It'll be up to the judge,' DI Powell said. 'His defence will use The Homicide Act 1957 when they plea. He's a clever bugger. His lawyer will do what he instructs him to do…'

'He won't get off with a conviction for manslaughter,' Ena said. 'Nick Miller said he could prove O'Shaughnessy killed my colleague, Sid Parfitt, last year. If it's the last thing I do, I'll see that creature O'Shaughnessy hang for killing Sid.'

Silence followed Ena's outburst. It was Inspector Richardson who broke it. 'Then we had better get to that bank and see what Miller has given us.'

For once Ena agreed with the Special Branch officer. She opened the top button of her blouse and pulled out the gold chain to reveal the key to Nick's safe deposit box. 'When?'

'Tomorrow,' Inspector Powell said. 'I'll telephone the bank and make an appointment. This afternoon I'd like to see the house where O'Shaughnessy lived.'

'And I need to get back to the office. I'll take you back to London, Mrs Green.'

'Thank you, but I want to look for whatever it is that's hidden in the house that got Middleton killed, especially as it's evidence that will prove Henry didn't murder Crowther.'

'It's a crime scene, Ena, you can't go to the house.'

'When forensics have finished processing the scene, we'll tear the place apart,' Inspector Armstrong added. 'I promise you, if there is anything to find, Dan and I *will find it.*'

'We will,' Inspector Powell assured her. 'And Ena? I'll telephone you to let you know what time to be at the bank tomorrow.'

'Thank you.' Ena knew police procedure. Asking to go to the house was a long shot, but she had to try. If Inspector Powell was going alone, he would have let her visit the crime scene. He had done after Christmas when Crowther's dead body was found, but she understood that Inspector Armstrong had a more complex investigation on his hands. He needed to limit the number of people going in and out of the house. Too many people tramping over the crime scene could destroy vital evidence.

Inspectors Powell and Armstrong left John Street Police Station to drive two miles to the south-west suburbs of Brighton. Ena and Inspector Richardson set off in the opposite direction to drive fifty miles back to London.

CHAPTER THIRTY-NINE

There was more traffic coming into Brighton than there was going out. The change from cold to more clement weather was probably the reason, as well as parents taking advantage of their children having broken up from school for the half term.

Ena loved the sea. She was fascinated by its vastness, stretching out as far as the eye could see and beyond. Alan Richardson drove the car away from the seafront and the view of the sea was left behind.

'So, it was a successful mission,' Richardson said, out of the blue.

'It was.'

'The officers who stopped the car they thought Miller was travelling in have been reprimanded. Their job was to make sure you were safe, nothing else.'

'I did wonder. They could have wrecked the operation. They followed Nick out of the airport earlier too. Did they tell you that?'

Inspector Richardson inhaled loudly, but remained silent.

'I didn't think so. Anyway,' Ena said, 'I'm sorry that I thought you'd gone back on your word. I'm afraid I've called you a few unsavoury names. Have your ears been burning?'

'I'm used to that,' Richardson gave her a crooked smile. It was the first time Ena had seen him smile. 'We'll soon be in London. Are you going into the West End, or shall I take you home to Stockwell?'

'Neither,' Ena said, 'drop me off at an Underground station. I need to see Artie at the Home Office. Hugh Middleton was an old school friend. I'd rather Artie hear about his death from me than through the grapevine.'

'I'm going to Scotland Yard. I'll drop you off at King Charles Street.'

Maybe she had got Alan Richardson wrong. Henry used to say she was too quick to judge. Was she? She looked at the clock on the wall next to the Home Office's blue and gold emblem. The receptionist told her to take a seat as Artie was in a meeting. She didn't want to bump into Dick Bentley, so decided to leave if Artie wasn't out in five minutes, She sat down, looked out of the window and watched people as they walked along King Charles Street. It had been three months since she had been suspended. What did Dick Bentley call it? Relieved of her duty at the Home Office.

Aware that the door to the main Home Office buildings had opened, Ena looked across the foyer hoping it was Artie out of his meeting. It wasn't. Speak, or in this case, think, of the devil and he shall appear. She picked up a magazine on immigration, opened it and began to read.

'Ena?' Dick Bentley called.

Damn! She looked round to see Bentley striding across the foyer. Artie was trailing behind him pulling a face.

'Good to see you. I understand there's been a breakthrough in the Crowther case.'

Artie looked up at the ceiling as if to say, he didn't hear it from me.

'I'd like to get my hands on that damn fool, Nick Miller. Using you as insurance to escape the consequences of his treachery was wrong on all counts. I'd have put a stop to it.' He turned to Artie, who nodded quickly feigning agreement. 'I told Powell and Richardson so; said I didn't approve; that it was too dangerous for you, but they didn't inform me until you had left the country. If they had…'

'If they had,' Ena cut in, 'there wouldn't have been anything that you could have done or said to stop me accompanying Nick Miller to Vienna. It was my choice.'

Bentley blustered on for a further few seconds, then said, 'Well, yes, of course, but… Right! Better get on. I look forward to reading your report, Ena. Sooner rather than later? And, if there is anything you need in the meantime, don't hesitate to telephone.'

Ena forced herself to smile. She didn't thank him, nor did she indicate she would telephone him. Her boss of twelve years, who knew Henry almost as well as he knew her, thought Henry capable of murder. Hell would freeze over before she asked Dick Bentley for help with anything.

'I'm sorry he came out with me, Ena. He was in the cold case office when reception phoned through to say you were here.' Artie leaned forward and put his arms around her. 'It's good to see you. What's new? How's the investigation going? Did Nick Miller spill the beans?'

'Yes, he did, and yes, the investigation is going well.' Ena sat down. 'Do you have five minutes?'

'For you? Of course.'

Artie sat next to her. He frowned. 'What is it, Ena? Something's wrong, I can tell.'

'Your friend Hugh Middleton gave Nick Miller a notebook containing Helen Crowther's contacts - names and addresses of her associates, anyone that could be of use to her - blackmail possibilities, I expect. I haven't seen the book yet, it's in Nick Miller's safe deposit box at his bank. Inspector Powell is making an appointment. Anyway, O'Shaughnessy must have found out because…' Ena took Artie's hands in hers. 'He killed Hugh. I'm sorry.' Artie's eyes filled with tears. 'It's no consolation, but Nick asked DI Powell to go easy on Hugh, and Powell would have done. He knew O'Shaughnessy had manipulated him.'

'In the way he manipulated me?'

'Worse. You were lucky to get away from O'Shaughnessy when you did.'

'When did he kill Hugh?'

'The day before I went to Austria. And, he tried to frame me for it.' Artie shot Ena a worried look. 'On the evening that Claire and I looked around Crowther's house, my bracelet must have come off because the DI at John Street in Brighton found it lying next to Hugh's body. O'Shaughnessy had put it there.'

'He tried to frame you like Crowther's killer tried to frame Henry?'

'Yes.'

'Poor Hugh.' Artie wiped the tears from his eyes with the cob of his hand. 'I'm going to hunt O'Shaughnessy down and when I find him, I'll kill him.'

'I wouldn't let you. O'Shaughnessy has ruined enough lives. Anyway, you don't have to worry. He's in custody. The police caught him trying to strangle Eve Robinson.'

'Trying? I'm glad she isn't dead but…'

'What?'

'If the police can't prove O'Shaughnessy killed Hugh, he'll only be done for attempted murder.'

'He'll be tried for murder. The police know he killed Hugh and they'll prove it. And, from what I understand there are other deaths attributed to O'Shaughnessy. I don't know all the details, but rest assured, Shaun O'Shaughnessy will hang.'

297

CHAPTER FORTY

Ena picked up the telephone and listened for its buzz. She put the receiver down and it rang immediately. 'Hello?'

'This is Stan. The telephone extension in the visitor's room keeps flashing. Are you having a problem ringing out?'

'No, Stan, it's me who's the problem,' Ena said, 'I'm being impatient. I'm expecting a call and was checking the line was working.'

'I'll put the call through as soon as it comes in, Ena, don't worry.'

'I know you will. I'm sorry.'

'It's like a watched kettle,' Claire said, laughing, 'it won't ring until you stop watching it.'

As soon as Ena walked away from her desk, the telephone rang. 'Hello?'

'Detective Inspector Powell for you.'

'Ena, we have an appointment at The International Bank of Austria, London Bridge, at half-past eleven. Corner of King William Street and Clements Lane. Can you get there? I'm at the Yard with Alan Richardson, or I'd pick you up.'

'I'll be there. I'll get a taxi.'

'And, err… Afterwards, I'll give you a lift back to the theatre.'

'You found something in Crowther's house, didn't you?'

'Yes. That's right. Good. I'm seeing Sandy Berman, but not until late this afternoon, so I'll have plenty of time to drive you back to the West End. Until eleven-thirty then. Goodbye.'

Ena got out of the taxi on the opposite side of the road

to the International Bank of Austria. The grand six-storey building stood out from its neighbours in marble splendour. The main door into the bank was sheltered beneath a marble archway that rose as high as the second-floor windows. Small windows ran along the length of the upper floors, ending at each corner with a statue in an alcove. Beneath the roof, poised with her sword drawn as if going into battle, was Ena's idea of what Brunhild or some other legendary Germanic heroine would look like. The nearest statuesque figure was clad from head to foot in body armour, a shield in one hand and a sword in the other, while the female warrior on the far corner of the building wore nothing but a winged headdress, her femininity covered by long plaits.

While she was admiring the statues on top of the building, Ena felt a spot of rain on her face. She looked up at the sky. It was still bright, but there were grey clouds in the distance. The promise of a spring shower persuaded her to run across the road to the bank. She had been looking up for so long that it took a moment for her eyes to become acclimatised to the bank's dark interior. When they did, she marvelled at the circular lobby with its ornate floor and domed ceiling, and sat down on a padded chaise-style seat facing the entrance. Inspectors Powell and Richardson arrived at exactly eleven-thirty.

Inspector Powell led the way from the lobby to the main bank. Ena and DI Richardson waited inside the door while Inspector Powell went to the counter.

A second later. the inspector joined them. 'Someone is coming to take us down to the vaults.'

Ena instinctively put her hand to her neck.

'Not forgotten the key have you, Ena?' Inspector Powell said, with a grin.

'No. It's still on my chain.' The nerves in her stomach were fluttering. She took a deep breath. Foreign banks, vaults, safety deposit boxes, were new to her, but she was with two police inspectors, she had no reason to be nervous.

A tall angular man with a moustache, wearing a dark grey pinstriped suit, white shirt and highly polished black shoes appeared from an unmarked door behind them. He introduced himself as Michael Steiner, the bank's assistant manager. When he had shaken their hands, he asked them to follow him.

The vaults were below ground, accessed only by a lift. On the wall next to the lift's steel grey doors was what looked to Ena like a small set of typewriter keys. The assistant manager punched in a number, the lift doors opened, and the four of them entered. He pressed a button with an arrow pointing down and the lift began its journey to the bank's vaults.

When the lift stopped, the doors opened in a large room that was wall to wall grey metal.

'Mrs Green, I have a signed third-party mandate from Mr Miller and a letter from his solicitors, Mitford Crane, confirming your power of attorney. Do you have Mr Miller's key?'

'Yes.' Ena took the key from the chain around her neck.

'If you'd be kind enough to show me some identification. A driving licence will suffice.'

Ena produced her driving licence and passed it to Mr Steiner with shaking hands. 'Sorry, I don't know why I'm so nervous.'

'Perhaps you'd prefer it if the gentlemen weren't in the room when you open the safe deposit box?' he said, referring to, but not looking at, DI Powell and DI Richardson.

'No. I'm happy that they're here,' Ena said, relieved that both men were able to stay while she opened Nick's box.

Mr Steiner took a key from his pocket and crossed to a wall of small metal doors with keyholes. 'If you'd like to bring *your* key. We need to unlock the door to the box together.' Ena joined him and when he had turned his key in the lock on the right, she turned the key that Nick had given her in the lock on the left, and the door sprang open.

Mr Steiner pulled a long oblong box out of the wall, carried it to the table in the middle of the room and put it down. Ena's stomach turned cartwheels when he placed it in front of her. 'The contents of this box now belong to you, Mrs Green.' Without waiting for Ena's reply, Mr Steiner walked across the room. 'I shall be outside if you need me,' he said, opened the door and left. At the same time, Ena lifted the lid of the metal box.

'Shoes?' Inspector Richardson exclaimed.

'And Helen Crowther's notebook that Hugh Middleton took from her house and gave to Nick Miller. The notebook that got him killed,' Ena said to Inspector Powell. Ena crouched down until her eyes were level with the top of the box. 'The shoes have blood on them,' she said. Richardson reached over to pick them up. 'No!' Ena knocked his arm out of the way. 'I'm sorry, but that is the blood of my late colleague, Sid Parfitt. And that,' she pointed to a small oval smudge, 'is a fingerprint.' She beamed a smile at Inspector Powell. 'This is the evidence Nick promised me. The evidence that will convict Sid's killer.'

She took a clean handkerchief from her handbag. It was too small to wrap around the bloodstained shoe. She crossed the room and opened the door. 'Mr

Steiner, do you have anything I could put the contents of the deposit box in. I should like to take it with me.'

'I do,' he said, 'I won't be a moment.'

Ena returned to the table and using her handkerchief, lifted the notebook out of the box. 'The names and addresses of Crowther's associates,' she said, handing the book to DI Powell.

When the manager returned it was with a stack of brown paper bags in a variety of sizes. He put them on the table and looking at the shoes pulled two of the largest from the pile.

'Ena?' DI Powell took a pen from his pocket. 'I need to date the bags.'

'Of course.' When the inspector had finished writing, Ena used his pen. She pushed it under the tongue of Sid's shoe with the blood on it, lifted it out of the metal box and placed it in a bag. She did the same with the other shoe. 'Fingerprints will have an easy job with the first shoe,' she said, handing both bags to Inspector Powell.

'Do you have any idea whose fingerprint is on the shoe, Ena?' DI Richardson asked.

'Shaun O'Shaughnessy's.'

'Alan, I need to get these shoes to forensics. I'll drop Ena off in the West End and I'll see you later.'

'I'll make a start on the address book.' Inspector Richardson put out his hand. 'Start going through it.' The two inspectors stared at each other. Neither spoke.

Ena looked from one to the other. 'Nick Miller gave me the key to the safe deposit box and it was me who he wanted to read the notebook to help Henry.' She took the book out of DI Powell's hand. 'Why don't the three of us go to Bow Street and look through the notebook together?'

The suggestion agreed, Ena and the two detectives thanked the bank manager and left for Bow Street. When they arrived, they were met by Inspector Armstrong and the pathologist, Sandy Berman.

'Presumably, you two have already met?' Inspector Powell said to Geoff Armstrong and Sandy Berman. Both men nodded. 'Geoff, you already know Alan. Alan, you have yet to meet, Sandy. Sandy Berman, police pathologist at St. Thomas', meet Detective Inspector Alan Richardson of Special Branch.'

The two men shook hands but didn't speak. Alan crossed the room and hung up his coat and Sandy joined Ena at the table by the window. Ena saw Sandy's lip curl. 'He's alright,' she whispered.

The pathologist looked at Ena, his mouth in a downward curve. 'If you say so.' He didn't sound convinced.

Inspector Powell picked up the telephone on his desk, but before he dialled, he called over to Sandy Berman. 'Sandy, come and take a look at these shoes before I get WPC Jarvis to take them to the lab for fingerprinting.'

Ena and Inspector Richardson looked through the names in Helen Crowther's black notebook. She had separated the pages into three sections held apart by rubber bands. The first dozen or so pages were headed, 'Co-workers'. The middle section was titled 'Possible' and the last, 'Not Possible'.

Ena lifted her head and said, 'Co-workers will be spies - that's clear enough. Possible will be people she could turn or blackmail into working for her, and the not possible are the people she knew she couldn't turn.'

'What do the endless rows of numbers beneath the headings mean?' Alan Richardson asked.

'It's a code. And it's so simple I'm disappointed. Everyone goes on about how intelligent Crowther was, but a child could break this.'

Ena took a pen and a piece of paper from her handbag. She laid the paper next to the notebook and flipped over the first two sections until she came to the last. She jabbed her finger at the first line of numbers. '8 - 5 - 14 ...'

'18 - 25. And, the next four numbers spell your surname, Ena. It's clear that the first name on the 'Not Possible' list is Henry Green.'

'Yes, it is.'

Richardson grinned and said, again, 'Henry Green.'

'Thank-you-Nick-Miller!'

At that moment WPC Jarvis entered the office. Ena and Inspector Richardson lifted their heads from the notebook at the same time to see DI Powell take the paper bags containing Sid Parfitt's shoes that he had been showing Sandy Berman from his desk.

'Get these to the fingerprint boys. Tell them to stop whatever they're doing. This job takes priority.'

'Yes, Sir.' WPC Jarvis, holding the bags by the top,

one in each hand, turned to leave.

'And, Jarvis?'

She swung round. 'Sir?'

'I need the results by the end of the day.'

The young policewoman raised her eyebrows. 'Yes, Sir.'

'Tell them we believe the shoes in these bags were taken from the Waterloo Bridge murder scene last year. Oh, and I want the shoe with the blood on it processing first. I want to know if that print in the blood is Shaun O'Shaughnessy's. The other shoe needs dusting too, but the one with the blood takes priority. It's dry, so it needs careful handling.'

A nod from the WPC said she understood.

When she had left, the inspector took several documents from his desk, took them to the table where Ena and Inspector Richardson were sitting. He laid them on the table. Ena took the letter Nick had written from her handbag and placed it next to the notebook.

DI Richardson began to speak, but Inspector Powell put up his hand. 'Hang on, Alan. Are you alright for time, Sandy?'

The pathologist nodded.

'Geoff?'

'Oh, yes.'

The beginning of a smile showed as small creases in the soft flesh at the corners of Inspector Powell's eyes. 'You wouldn't have come all this way from Brighton unless you'd found something of interest in Crowther's house after I left. What is it, Geoff?'

'Poison. I don't know for sure, but I strongly suspect that this half-empty bottle found beneath the floorboards in what I assumed was Helen Crowther's bedroom, is cyanide.' He gave the small brown glass bottle in a plastic bag to Sandy Berman.

305

The pathologist held the bag up to the light. 'Potassium cyanide, I'd lay money on it.'

'And what have you got for us, Sandy?'

The pathologist took a folder from his briefcase, extracted several pages from it and passed them across the table. 'A copy of my findings. Don't bother reading it now. It'll be quicker for me to tell you what's in it.' He looked around the table. 'I found a white substance under Helen Crowther's fingernails. I can tell you without a shadow of a doubt that it was potassium cyanide. The cyanide in the whisky glass, the whisky that had been spilt on the table, and the fatal dose of cyanide ingested by Helen Crowther on December the twenty-sixth last year were all potassium cyanide.'

Ena looked at Inspector Powell. 'Nick Miller was right. Helen Crowther did kill herself.'

'The facts don't lie, Ena.'

'I've sent a copy of my findings to Director Bentley at the Home Office.'

Hearing her old boss' name made Ena prickle. 'I can't wait to hear his opinion,' she said, sarcastically. 'I'll never forgive him for standing me down. If I'd had his support and the backing of the Home Office, we'd have got to this point in the investigation months ago.'

'You didn't need him, Ena. He'd have probably dragged his governmental feet. Neither the Home Office nor military intelligence know what to do about Helen Crowther's death, but they had better decide soon because the facts speak for themselves. When what we have here comes out, and it will, neither the Home Office nor Five will be able to bury it.'

Sandy Berman brought the palm of his hand down hard on Inspector Powell's copy of the pathologist's report. He gave Alan Richardson a cold stare and added, 'Even if they wanted to, facts are facts, and what we have here proves conclusively that Helen Crowther's death was suicide.'

While the four men discussed Sandy Berman's findings in greater detail, Ena turned the pages of the notebook back to the beginning; to 'Co-workers' and deciphered the name she had hoped she wouldn't see; 18 - 9 - 3 - 8 - 1 - 18 - 4 - 2 - 5 - 14 - 20 - 12 - 5 - 25. She closed the notebook, slipped it into her jacket pocket and joined the men.

When there was nothing new to be said about Helen Crowther, the party began to disperse. Inspector Armstrong was first to leave followed by Sandy Berman.

'Will you keep Crowther's notebook in your safe, Inspector?' Ena didn't give the DI time to reply. 'Alan and I will decode the rest of the names tomorrow. Is that alright with you, Alan?' Ena hoped that by calling Inspector Richardson by his Christian name he would agree to leave the notebook at Bow Street, instead of asking her twenty questions as to why, which he usually did. It worked. Arranging to meet DI Powell the next morning, Alan Richardson left.

Inspector Powell picked up the notebook. 'What is it you want me to see that you didn't want Inspector Richardson to see, Ena?'

She handed the inspector the piece of paper. On it, under the title 'Not Possible' were the numbers and letters that spelt the name, Henry Green.

The inspector smiled. 'I'm not surprised Henry's name is listed here.'

'Now look at the first page of the notebook - at 'Co-workers'.' As the inspector turned the pages, Ena said, 'The numbers spell the name of Helen Crowther's closest associates.' As she did with Henry's name, Ena handed him a piece of paper with the decoded name of the first person on the list. She watched the colour drain from the inspector's face.

'Good God!'

Silence filled the room like stale air. With a heavy heart, Ena picked up her handbag, walked over to the coat stand and took down her coat. With it laid across her arm, she opened the door.

'Ena?'

She turned. 'Yes?'

The inspector walked over to her. 'Would you be able to decode the rest of the names tonight?'

'Of course. I'll do it as soon as I get home.'

He handed her the notebook. 'I'll call a meeting of everyone involved in this business for tomorrow morning. I'll telephone Director Bentley and arrange to hold it at the Home Office. I'll ring you later; let you know what time.'

Driving along King Charles Street, looking for somewhere to park, Ena spotted Inspector Powell's black Wolseley. Next to it was Sandy Berman's old maroon Jaguar. She had no idea what kind of car Alan Richardson drove. DI Armstrong would probably have come by train. A space suddenly became available when a couple of document couriers on motorbikes pulled out in front of her. She slipped the Sunbeam into the space they'd vacated. She grabbed her shoulder bag from the passenger seat and as she put the hand on the handle of the car door, it opened.

'Ena.'

'Rupert?' Shocked to see Rupert Highsmith standing on the pavement outside the Home Office, Ena said, 'Have you been invited to the meeting?'

'Not exactly.'

'I didn't think so.' She felt suddenly tired, deflated. She had garnered every bit of confidence she had to attend a meeting that she knew would be one of the worst of her career. The last thing she needed was Rupert Highsmith interfering.

'I am representing the accused.'

'What? Forgive me, but I don't have time for innuendo and double talk, Rupert,' she said and pushed past him. 'Henry?'

'Hello, darling.'

Ena threw her arms around her husband. 'I can't believe you're here. What…? How did you…?'

'Highsmith got me out of the safe house last night.'

'How? Did someone tell you that you were no longer accused of Helen Crowther's murder?'

'Not exactly.' Henry looked at Highsmith.

'You have your sister's old SOE boss, Colonel

Smith, to thank. Except you can't thank him because he doesn't know. Well, he knows, of course, he'd have to, wouldn't he? But he can't be seen to interfere.'

With her arms around Henry, Ena screwed up her face. 'Enough, Rupert, please. It doesn't matter. Nothing matters except Henry's here and he's free.' She looked into her husband's face. 'You are free, aren't you?'

'Yes!' Henry picked Ena up and swung her round. When he put her down, he said, 'You'd better go to the meeting, darling, or you'll be late.'

'Ena, don't tell anyone that Henry and I are here. We want to surprise everyone.'

'Alright.' Ena walked back along the street to the main entrance of the Home Office. Before going in she looked over her shoulder. Highsmith was getting into his car, Henry was standing on the pavement watching her. She wanted to run back to him, hold him, kiss him, but she knew she couldn't. She put her forefingers to her lips and blew him a kiss, then turned away. She needed to calm down. She took a couple of deep breaths and felt a little less excited. As she entered the foyer of the Home Office, Ena Green, government employee and investigator of cold cases took over.

The foyer was buzzing with military personnel from different intelligence services. She could see agents from MI5 and MI6 and the Home Office. There was no one from GCHQ. It was Rupert Highsmith who was representing the Government's communications agency and he'd make an appearance later. Looking around the assembly she caught Inspector Powell's eye. He nodded, and she smiled in acknowledgment.

Director Bentley's secretary opened the double doors leading to the conference room and everyone began to move slowly towards them. Sandy Berman and Inspector Armstrong were first through. Ena stood on tiptoe in search of Inspector Richardson but couldn't see him.

'Congratulations, Ena. I hear you've yet again solved the case.'

Too busy searching the crowd for friendly faces, Ena hadn't seen Director Bentley until he was standing next to her. 'Thank you. I do hope so.' That was a compliment weighted with sarcasm if ever there was one, Ena thought. She looked him squarely in the face. 'When the truth comes out about Helen Crowther's death, military intelligence will no longer be able to make a scapegoat of my husband.'

Director Bentley gave her a half-hearted smile. He didn't comment or make eye contact, but said, 'Excuse me. I think the meeting is about to begin.'

Ena watched him as he edged his way through the crowd to join his secretary and his closest staff, *yes-men* who agree with everything he says. Not this time, Ena thought but instead said, 'Of course, Director.'

'Ena?' Artie came dashing up to her and put his arm around her shoulders. 'I'm so glad you're here. Do you know what this meeting is about?'

Ena was saved from replying to Artie when they were ushered through the double doors into a corridor before being shown into the Home Office's conference room.

Director Bentley stood behind his chair at the head of the conference table. He looked uncomfortable as one after another high-ranking military men, police officers and civil service personnel filed into the room and found their places.

Jugs of water had been placed at intervals along the length of the table. Around it, in front of each chair,

311

was a glass, a pen and an A4 notepad. On the front of the notepads were the names of the men and women attending the meeting. Dick Bentley pulled out his chair and sat down. The other members of the meeting followed suit.

Ena couldn't take her eyes off her old boss. His colour was higher than usual and there was perspiration on his forehead and top lip. Trembling, he reached for a glass, filled it with water from the nearest jug and drank it down. He wiped his hand across his mouth and cleared his throat.

After the scraping of chairs on the parquet floor and the clinking of jugs against glasses as water was poured, the assembly quietened and the Director opened the meeting.

'Thank you for being here today, to attend this rather extraordinary meeting. I know you've had very little notice. I was only informed last night that the late Helen Crowther's death, which has posed an extremely difficult problem to all concerned, has now been solved.' He looked at Ena. Perspiration appeared on his lip, again.

'So,' he glanced at the notes in front of him, 'without further preamble from me, I'll hand you over to Detective Inspector Powell of the Metropolitan Police.'

Inspector Powell stood up. 'Each of you has a copy of my case notes.' The DI waited until everyone had taken their set of notes from beneath their notepads. 'I would prefer it if you didn't read the notes until after the meeting, as I shall tell you the relevant points of my investigation. I'll begin with the murder of a Home Office employee last year. Sidney Parfitt worked with Mrs Green in the cold case office.' The inspector looked across the table at Ena. She nodded. 'Mr Parfitt was murdered because he found information about a spy called Frieda Voight. And, in doing so, discovered there was a mole at MI5, who we now know was Helen Crowther.' Gasps of surprise rang round the table. 'McKenzie Robinson, the Director of MI5 was also murdered; killed because he had agreed to help Mrs Green with the Voight investigation.'

'Do you know who killed the Home Office investigator?' someone asked.

'I do. An associate of Helen Crowther's by the name of Shaun O'Shaughnessy.'

'What proof do you have?'

'O'Shaughnessy's fingerprint in blood on Parfitt's shoes.'

'And who killed Mac Robinson?'

'Helen Crowther killed Director Robinson.'

'I don't believe it,' someone said. 'They were good friends,' said someone else. 'They were lovers,' a woman Ena didn't know whispered, loudly.

The inspector looked at Ena again and sat down.

Ena stood up and waited until there was quiet in the room. 'Helen Crowther had a daughter.'

More gasps and more comments followed. 'She didn't have a daughter.' And 'What nonsense.'

'Helen Crowther, or Frau Helen Krueger as she was then, bore a child in Berlin in the nineteen thirties. Her daughter, Frieda Voight, had spied for Germany in the war. I exposed her and her brother Walter in nineteen forty-four. Walter Voight was sent to prison where he later died. Frieda blamed my husband, Henry.

'On the day of Walter Voight's funeral, a coffin with Frieda's name on it was also interred, giving her the perfect cover to work for British intelligence. Frieda and Walter were lovers. They were adopted at birth, found that out in their teenage years and had

313

fallen in love in adulthood. It became more and more difficult for Frieda to live without Walter, until it was impossible. She was obsessed with revenge and severely depressed. When she could go on no longer, she threw herself off the roof of the church where Walter was buried.

'Helen Crowther was unable to accept her daughter had taken her own life and convinced herself that Henry had killed her. Believing my husband had escaped the hangman's noose, Crowther broke into our home, stole a bottle of whisky and two glasses and, after setting the scene to look as though she had been murdered, killed herself. She framed Henry to ensure that he would hang - if not for her daughter Frieda's murder, for her murder.

'Helen Crowther was a German spy who killed the Director of MI5, McKenzie Robinson because he had begun to suspect her, and who killed herself out of revenge.'

As Ena sat down, Sandy Berman stood up.

'Berman, police pathologist.' He read the last paragraph of the toxicology report he'd shown Ena and DI Powell. 'Helen Crowther died on December the twenty-sixth, nineteen fifty-eight from cyanide poisoning. An autopsy showed a fatal dose of potassium cyanide had been ingested shortly before death. The same potassium cyanide was found under the deceased's fingernails.' Sandy glanced at Inspector Armstrong before sitting down.

DI Armstrong remained seated. 'A bottle containing an identical compound of potassium cyanide as the one that killed Helen Crowther was found in the house where she had lived in Brighton.' He paused. 'As far as the Sussex Constabulary are concerned, Helen Crowther died by her own hand.'

Slow hand-clapping from the door of the conference room made every head turn. 'And she almost got away with it, didn't she, Director Bentley?' Henry said.

Rupert Highsmith strolled into the room behind Henry. He handed Inspector Powell an envelope with the emblem of the Houses of Parliament stamped across the sealed flap on the back. 'From the PM. And this,' he said, setting a second letter down in front of Inspector Armstrong, 'is from the Chief Constable.'

The air sizzled with tension as the inspectors opened and read the contents of their envelopes. Returning the letters, Inspectors Powell and Armstrong left their seats and mirroring each other walked to the top of the table.

'Richard Bentley, you are under arrest for treason; for withholding vital evidence in a murder enquiry, for…'

CHAPTER FORTY-THREE

Ena had expected a reaction, but what ensued was nothing less than chaos. Bentley's staunchest supporters and friends refused to believe the facts they had been presented with and raged against military intelligence, saying Director Bentley was being made a scapegoat for the incompetence of MI5. The new Director of Five clutching the police report shouted that every branch of the intelligence service would be thoroughly investigated as he left. The Head of MI6 walked out of the meeting without making a comment. Some people sat in stunned silence too shocked to speak, while those who had worked closely with Bentley and realised that they had been made fools of, showed their contempt for the disgraced man by shouting 'traitor' and 'liar'. Several women who had followed Bentley blindly screamed abuse at the police before turning their anger on Ena.

'Ena? We need to get out of here.'

Fearing the wrath of Director Bentley's female followers, Ena ducked under the clenched fist of a high-ranking Naval officer and grabbed Henry's hand. Together they forced their way past Home Office staff standing in the doorway of the conference room and pushed against the tide of people heading down the corridor to see what the commotion was about.

Henry forced open the doors to the reception area and dragged Ena across the foyer to the main exit. Only when she was outside on the street did she feel safe.

'I've left my handbag in the conference room,' she said when she had caught her breath.

'Is there anything important in it?'

'The notes I made before I spoke, and my purse and

lipstick. The car keys are in my pocket.'

'I'll call in and get it tomorrow.'

As they walked to the car, Rupert Highsmith caught up with them. 'Well, that was fun. What shall we do for the rest of the day?' he said. 'We could go for a drink. I know a couple of good pubs round here. How about it?'

'Not on your spoiled life,' Ena said. 'I haven't seen my husband for months. I'm taking him home.'

'Can I come?' Artie called, running up to join them.

'No, you cannot! I want my husband to myself.'

Artie giggled. 'I meant to the pub, Ena.' He grinned at Highsmith. 'After all, I *might* soon have something to celebrate.'

'So much for keeping it under your hat,' Highsmith said. 'Well, go on then, tell them.'

Artie stood up straight and clasped his hand in front of him. 'Well, if you don't go back to the Home Office...' He inhaled sharply. 'You're not going back, are you?'

'Not until hell freezes over.'

'Phew!' he pretended to fan his face. 'Where was I? Oh yes. As you *won't* be going back to the Home Office, I'm handing in my notice. Rupert has offered to put a good word in for me at GCHQ.'

'Oh?' Ena felt suddenly sad. 'I'm pleased for you, Artie, if that's what you want, but I can't pretend I won't miss you.'

'But you said you weren't going back there.'

'I'm not. I don't know what I'm going to do. I just can't imagine not working with you.'

'We could set up a private investigation agency.'

'That's an idea.'

'Green and Mallory.'

Ena laughed. 'It has a nice ring to it. But,' she said,

'I'm not going to think about work until after Easter.'
She looked into Henry's eyes. 'We're going to spend
Easter at Foxden Hotel. We have some catching up to
do.'

'When you're ready to go back to work, why not
apply to GCHQ, Ena? We could do with someone with
your experience. Colonel Smith would jump at the
chance to have you on board.'

'To be honest, Rupert, I've had enough of
government and military intelligence agencies. I'm
sick of spies and spooks, but most of all I'm sick of
secrets. Henry and I have both had to keep secrets from
one another. I want to go home after a day at work and
talk to my husband about my job. And, discounting
present company - and Colonel Smith, of course - there
are too many corrupt people in the government and the
security services. There are too many people in top
jobs who are paid to look after the country and the
people in it who only look after themselves.'

'Can't argue with that,' Highsmith said. He turned
to Henry. 'What about you, old man? Fancy giving
GCHQ a try?'

'Thanks, but I have a few things to sort out at Five
before I make any career moves. And, it looks as
though I'm going away for Easter. Can I think about
it?'

'Of course.' Highsmith stretched out his arm and
consulted his wristwatch. 'But don't leave it too long.
We'll only be in The Marquis of Granby until two
o'clock.'

Artie kissed Ena goodbye, shook Henry's hand, and
Highsmith saluted.

'How did Rupert know about Dick Bentley?' Ena
asked Henry when Highsmith was out of earshot.

'Inspector Powell telephoned his boss at GCHQ, his

boss telephoned Downing Street, and the PM had search warrants and the paperwork drawn up to arrest Bentley straight away.'

'The inspector telephoned Colonel Smith? But, of course.' Ena remembered giving Inspector Powell the colonel's card the day Artie was taken in for questioning when his friend, Hugh Middleton, who worked at GCHQ went missing. The inspector had accepted Ena's word that Artie had nothing to do with Middleton's disappearance and dropped the colonel's card in his desk drawer.

'…and,' Henry continued, 'because there wasn't a lot of time before the meeting today, Highsmith went to Downing Street first thing and collected it all.'

'I got Highsmith wrong,' Ena said. 'Colonel Smith told me he was - *one of the good guys.* I don't suppose he's as superficial as he makes out and I expect his arrogance is a front.'

Henry laughed. 'I think he's both of those things. I think his personality stops people wanting to get to know him, which I suppose in his line of work is an asset.'

'He must get lonely,' Ena said.

'Not Highsmith. He has drinking pals in most of the pubs in South London.'

'Including The Marquis of Granby.' Ena watched Rupert and Artie disappear into the pub. 'That's it then!' Turning her attention to Henry, she reached up, put her arms around his neck, and he leaned forward and kissed her.

'You're not going back to MI5, are you?'

'Only to clear my desk. Come on,' he said, 'Let's go home.'

'What do you think about the name 'Dudley Green Associates?' Ena mused.

'Green & Dudley sounds better, it's sharper.'
'But Dudley is more memorable…'

THE END

ABOUT THE AUTHOR

Madalyn Morgan has been an actress for more than thirty years working in repertory theatre, the West End, film, radio and television. She is a radio presenter, writes poetry, and has written many articles for newspapers and magazines.

Madalyn was brought up in Lutterworth, at the Fox Inn. "The pub was a great place for an aspiring actress and writer to live, as there were so many different characters to study and accents to learn." At twenty-four Madalyn gave up a successful hairdressing salon and wig-hire business for a place at E15 Drama College and a career as an actress.

In 2000, with fewer parts available for older actresses, Madalyn taught herself to touch type, completed a two-year correspondence course with The Writer's Bureau, and started writing. After living in London for thirty-six years, she has returned to her home town of Lutterworth, swapping two window boxes and a mortgage for a garden and the freedom to write.

As an Indie Author, Madalyn has successfully published seven novels: Foxden Acres, Applause, China Blue, and The 9:45 To Bletchley are set during WW2 and tell the wartime stories of Bess, Margot, Claire, and Ena Dudley. Foxden Hotel and Chasing Ghosts are post war. There Is No Going Home is set in 1958.

Madalyn is a member of The Society of Authors, the Romantic Novelists Association and Equity. Her books are available on Amazon - in eBook and in paperback.

FUTURE BOOKS

My next book has the working title, Dudley Green Associates, 8 Mercer Street. Having read She Casts A Long Shadow you might think the address is bizarre. Not a good idea to work from the old Home Office Cold Cases office? Well, the building was cheap and that's all I'm saying. There are no cold cases planned in this book. There will be some old friends from Ena's past, but this book will be looking forward, not back.

I'm still gathering work and ideas to write a memoir of my working life. I have a collection of poetry, articles and biographies - with photographs - of characters I played when I was an actress that I think would make my memoir a little different and possibly quite interesting to read.

OUTLINE OF EARLIER BOOKS IN THE DUDLEY SISTERS SAGA

FOXDEN ACRES:
Foxden Acres, the first book in the saga, begins on the eve of 1939 when twenty-year-old Bess Dudley, the daughter of a Foxden groom, bumps into James Foxden the heir to Foxden Estate. Bess, a scholarship girl, lodges at Mrs McAllister's boarding house in London while studying to be a teacher.

With offers of a teaching job in London and Foxden, Bess opts for Foxden, to be near James. However, when she is told that James is betrothed to the socially acceptable Annabel Hadleigh, Bess accepts the teaching post in London.

When war breaks out and London's schoolchildren are evacuated, Bess returns to Foxden to organise a team of Land Girls and turn the Foxden Estate into arable land. James, having joined the RAF, is training to be a bomber pilot at nearby Bitteswell Aerodrome.

German bombs fall on London and Mrs McAllister's house is blitzed to rubble. South Leicestershire is scarred too when an RAF plane carrying Polish airmen crash lands in a Foxden field. Traditional social barriers come crashing down when Flying Officer James Foxden falls in love with Bess. But is it too late? During the time Bess has been back at Foxden she has grown to like and respect Annabel Hadleigh. How can Bess be with James knowing it would break her friend's heart? Besides, Bess has a shameful secret that she has vowed to keep from James at any cost.

APPLAUSE:

Applause is the second book in the saga. In the early years of World War Two, Margot (Margaret) Dudley works her way up from usherette to leading lady in a West End show. Driven by blind ambition Margot becomes immersed in the heady world of nightclubs, drink, drugs and fascist thugs – all set against a background of the London Blitz.

To achieve her dream, Margot risks losing everything she holds dear.

CHINA BLUE:

China Blue, the third book, is Claire Dudley's story. At the beginning of World War II Claire joins the WAAF. She excels in languages and is recruited by the Special Operations Executive to work in Occupied France. Against SOE rules, Claire falls in love. The affair has to be kept secret. Even after her lover falls into the hands of the Gestapo, Claire cannot tell anyone they are more than comrades.

As the war reaches its climax, Claire fears she will never again see the man she loves.

THE 9:45 TO BLETCHLEY:

The 9:45 To Bletchley is the fourth book in the Dudley Sisters Saga. In the midst of the Second World War, and charged with taking vital surveillance equipment via the 9:45 train, Ena Dudley makes regular trips to Bletchley Park, until on one occasion she is robbed. When those she cares about are accused of being involved, she investigates, not knowing whom she can trust.

While trying to clear her name, Ena falls in love.

FOXDEN HOTEL:
The war is over. It is time for new beginnings.

Celebrating the opening of Foxden Hotel, New Year's Eve 1948, and an enemy from the war years turns up. He threatens to expose a secret that will ruin Bess's happiness and the new life she has worked so hard to create. Bess's husband throws the man out. So is that the last they see of him? Or will he show up again when they least expect?

Bess had hoped fascism was a thing of the past, buried with the victims of WW2. Little does she know the trouble that lies ahead, not only for herself but also for her family.

CHASING GHOSTS:
1949. After receiving treatment for shell shock in Canada, Claire's husband disappears. Has Mitch left her for the woman he talks about in his sleep? Or is he on the run from accusations of wartime treachery? Claire goes to France in search of the truth, aided by old friends from the Resistance.

THERE IS NO GOING HOME:
London, 1958, Ena recognises a woman who she exposed as a spy in WW2. Ena's husband, Henry, an agent with MI5, argues that it cannot be the woman because they went to her funeral twelve years before.

Ena, now head of the Home Office cold case department, starts an investigation. There are no files. It is as if the woman never existed. Suddenly colleagues who are helping Ena with the case mysteriously die... and Ena herself is almost killed in a hit-and-run.

The case breaks when Ena finds important documents from 1936 Berlin that prove not only did the spy exist, but someone above suspicion who worked with her then, still works with her now.

Fearing for her life, there is only one person Ena can trust... or can she?

Printed in Poland
by Amazon Fulfillment
Poland Sp. z o.o., Wrocław

63329650R00200